WHEN I
Come Back

RIPPLE EFFECT
BOOK ONE

ALISE MONROE

Praise for *When I Come Back*

"A breathtaking debut that captures the raw, tender complexities of love, loss, and second chances. With lush, layered prose and an emotional depth rarely seen in first novels, Alise Monroe delivers a romance that lingers in your heart long after the final page. Achingly beautiful and wonderfully unforgettable."

— SHAYLIN GANDHI, author of *When We Had Forever*

"When I Come Back is a heartbreakingly real story about love and how it both grows and never fades between two people who are meant to be. I LOVED the raw, real emotions that poured off the page of this story."

— LANDYN HILL, author of *For Fillies and Monsters*

"My heart feels so full after finishing WICB. This book beautifully captures the real and complex dynamics of relationships—whether between family, friends, or partners. The emotional journey it takes you on is raw, relatable, and deeply moving. I connected with this story in ways I didn't expect and was completely consumed—I couldn't put it down."

— RITA, Goodreads reviewer

Book Cover by Melissa Doughty, @mel_d.designs

Formatting by Brittany Uller at The Author Experience

Chapter Headers, Scene Break, Artwork, and Map by Anastasia Campo

RED Logo by Hannah Pendleton

ISBN:

979-8-9919008-0-5 (Paperback)

979-8-9919008-1-2 (Ebook)

1st edition 2025

Authors' Note

The Ripple Effect series takes place in a fictional lakefront town called Indigo Hill, SC. This book contains mature content and is intended for an 18+ audience. Your mental health matters. If any of the following content warnings trigger you, please read with caution, and always put yourself and your mental health first.

Parent death (not on page)
Grief
Funeral scene
Chronic illness
Undiagnosed mental illness (ADHD and anxiety)
Alcohol use
Depictions of smoking
Explicit language
Explicit sex scenes
Light breath play
Cheating (not between MCs)

Playlist

something to remember	Matt Hansen
Spotless (feat. The Lumineers)	Zach Bryan
I Remember Everything (Feat. Kacey Musgraves)	Zach Bryan
Something in the Orange	Zach Bryan
You're Gonna Go Far	Noah Kahan
Stick Season	Noah Kahan
Half of Forever	Henrik
Break Up in a Small Town	Sam Hunt
My Home	Myles Smith
Rock and a Hard Place	Bailey Zimmerman
Religiously	Bailey Zimmerman
Last Night	Morgan Wallen
Hell or High Water	Bailey Zimmerman
I Want You	Savage Garden
Until I Found You	Stephen Sanchez
exile (Feat. Bon Iver)	Taylor Swift
Slow Dancing in a Burning Room	John Mayer
The Night We Met	Lord Huron
Die a Happy Man	Thomas Rhett
All I Want	Kodaline

Playlist

Lose Control	TEDDY SWIMS
Too Sweet	HOZIER
Tennessee Whiskey	CHRIS STAPLETON
Another Love	TOM ODELL
Where It Ends (Feat. JORDY)	AVERY LYNCH
you were good to me	JEREMY ZUCKER & CHELSEA CUTLER
I miss you, I'm sorry	GRACIE ABRAMS
Next to You	OLE 60
Miserable Man	DAVID KUSHNER
Thoughts of You	OLE 60
Chasing Shadows	ALEX WARREN

scan this in
spotify

Dedication

To all the people who have been in our corner since the very beginning, cheering us on, and giving us the support we needed to publish Thea and Carrington's story.
We love you all.

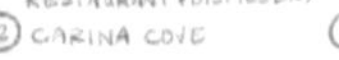

Indigo Hill
SOUTHBURY →
RED
SC
TATTOO
1 RED RESTAURANT + DISTILLERY
2 CARINA COVE
3 RIPLEY'S HOME
4 oopsie daisy FLORIST
5 BROOKS' APARTMENT
6 grayce's café
7 LOT FOR RENT
8 LOUIE'S BAR
9 PHARMACY
10 BILLY'S HARDWARE
11 MARK & MASON
12 THEA'S HOME
13 GOLDFINCH FUNERAL HOME
14 HOTEL
15 HAZEL BOWEN'S HOME

Prologue

Present

(31 Years Old)

My phone vibrates in my pocket. I ignore it since I wouldn't be able to hear anything over the raucous bar sounds anyway. Whoever is calling me at quarter to ten can go ahead and fuck off. Everyone I know is here celebrating with me.

With one hand I loosen my tie and use the other to reach around Seth and grab a fresh drink from my bartender, feeling my phone vibrate again. Whoever it is, they're persistent. I pull the device out of my pocket as I take a sip of the new top-shelf bourbon we just started carrying and almost spit it out on the back of Seth's neck when I see the caller ID.

Indigo Hill Diner.

My stomach bottoms out, and the only thing I can focus on is questioning why I still have this number programmed in my phone. It's been thirteen years since I used the number—I was certain I had lost it. Not that you can really lose something that has been burned into your memory since the day you learned how to use a phone.

It stops ringing in my hand, and I stare at the blank screen for a few more heartbeats. I faintly register Seth calling my name behind me, but my feet are already moving me around the busy tables and toward the front door when it starts to ring again. My breathing picks up as does my pace. The chilly, damp Seattle air settles on me as the door quietly closes, shutting all of the restaurant sounds behind it. I hit the green button and lift the phone to my ear, lungs full.

Silence.

"C–Cary?"

My body, my breath, my mind—all frozen. With those two syllables I'm hit with an intense wave of déjà vu of a night just like this. A phone call *just* like this. Eight years ago almost to the day. One I'll never forget regardless of how much time passes. Seconds tick by, and I still can't seem to breathe. I hear a few cars pass at my back as I stare unseeing at the restaurant window in front of me.

"Are you there?" Timid. The tinny voice breaking through the silence as I grip the phone like it's the only thing keeping me attached to this Earth is *timid*. There's something very wrong about that. She's never timid.

"Can you please say something? I–I need to know I called the right number."

My body's need for oxygen takes over, and I exhale sharply, turning around to look at the traffic. My brain's still not online with what's happening, so the best I can get out is, "This is Carrington."

There's a long pause. So long I'm almost hoping she's hung up. I watch a couple cross the street hand-in-hand.

"I'm so sorry." *What?* "I don't even know how to do this. I was hoping Brooks would..." she trails off. Her voice is so familiar yet so strange at the same time. A few more seconds pass, and I hear what I think is a heavy, resigned sigh on the other end. "I'm so sorry to be the one to do this, but I'm—I'm calling with bad news." She hiccups as if holding back a sob. "It's Owen and Hazel. There was an accident last night, it was a drunk driver, and the car..." Another long pause. A man across the street raises his hand to hail a cab. "They didn't make it, Cary. I'm so, so sorry."

There are tears in her voice. I can clearly picture her watery, chocolate-colored eyes as if she were standing right in front of me. The tear that would escape and slowly streak down her left cheek. Somehow the tears always spilled down her left cheek first. I never let them fall though. I always caught them, swiped them up with my thumb, kissed them away with my lips.

"Please say something," she whispers. The connection between my brain and my mouth has been severed. My lips can't form words of any significance.

"Thank you." It's all I can get out.

I hang up, turn around, and gaze at all of my friends through the window. Standing around, laughing, drinking, celebrating another successful year of Carina Cove. I don't hear the sounds of the street behind me anymore, just the buzzing in my ears, and all I can think is...

Why didn't I block that number years ago?

Chapter One

9 Years Ago
(22 Years Old)

"Can you just stop for one fucking second?" Cary calls at my back as I make my way toward our bedroom door.

"Why?" I breathe out with my hand on the door knob, allowing it to brace me when all I want to do is fall apart. "So you can tell me again how I'm wrong? How I just need to 'give it some time?' Or maybe you want to tell me that I should loosen up a bit again?"

I haven't turned back around to face him. I can't. All I can do is stare at the floor and hope he finally hears me this time. That maybe, just maybe, he realizes how lost I am in this city, this life. The silence drags on, and my heartbeat is the only sound echoing off the walls. It's so suffocating I contemplate turning around to finally look at him, but just as the thought crosses my mind, his even footsteps sound behind me.

His arms wrap gently around my shoulders from behind, his chest right up against my back, chin resting on the top of my head, his large frame enveloping me. I hear his breathing, the air escaping his lungs in steady breaths.

"You know I love you, right?" His words are soft, and it takes everything in me not to find them patronizing. I do know he loves me, I really have no doubt. But he doesn't realize the statement isn't the salve he hopes it is. Our issues aren't about love. We had dreams. Huge, gigantic, too-big-for-a-small-town dreams.

And he succeeded. He made it in this big, bustling city. He took his dreams, and he molded his new life around them all. He didn't let anything scare or deter him. And I am so fucking proud of him, I am.

But... I can be proud of him and disappointed for myself. My dreams are still all in my head. Nothing has worked out. No doors have opened. I've spent the last week wondering if I should just throw in the towel and face the reality that being a small fish in a big pond is making it impossible.

Seattle is full of marketing opportunities, so I thought finding something would be easy. The problem I keep running into is all the big companies want experience. They have fifty other candidates just like me who are willing to intern for free for a year. It sets them apart. It's not something I can afford to do. So I've started looking for server jobs again—anything that might pay the bills while I wait for my dream to finally become a reality the way his has.

The problem is I can't bring myself to tell him just yet. He's so excited about starting at the restaurant, and the last thing I want to do is dim his joy with my misery.

"Of course I know you love me, Cary," I reply, though my voice comes out hoarse, leaning back slightly into his embrace. This is the same fight we've had countless times over the last year. It's exhausting. I try to talk to him about how I don't think things will ever work

out for me here. I try to tell him that I don't think his friends like me much, his best friend Seth in particular. I just... try to explain how I'm feeling, and instead of listening, he tells me everything I'm feeling is all in my head. Then he tries to pacify me by suggesting we should go out and have some fun for once. Like that will somehow cure all our problems.

The truth is... I'm not made for city life. It's too loud, too crowded, too fast, too everything. There's nature, sure, but it's not the same. The people aren't nearly as friendly. I thought I could do it, I really did. I thought getting out of our small town would be freeing, and we'd live happily ever after. Turns out, circumstances make you miserable, not your zip code.

I miss my mom. I miss my friends. I miss the laid-back life of living in a small town. And that would be okay, except I know Cary doesn't miss it. He loves Seattle. He loves this new life and his new friends.

And I love him too much to ask him to give it all up.

Like clockwork, the words slip from his lips, and the hope that he will finally listen to me dies just a little more. That constantly dying hope chips away at my heart each time we have this argument. "Let's go out. We can go see that movie you were talking about the other day, maybe get dinner afterwards. It'll be fun."

I nod my head as I squeeze my eyes shut.

Don't cry. Not this time. Not again. *"Yeah, sure. Let me get changed."*

An exacerbated sigh leaves his lips as he leans down to kiss my cheek, I still don't turn around. My eyes start to burn as the tears well, and my chin trembles. I somehow convince my legs to move, out of his arms and to the en suite bathroom. Just as I start to crumble, I shut the bathroom door behind me. The tears silently fall as I lower myself to the floor with my back against the door. This is how it always goes. I need a minute. Just one singular minute where I can let myself be sad, and then I'll put on the happy mask again.

As I sit there and count to sixty, my muscles unravel, and my body relaxes, the tears dry up. I wipe the remnants from my cheeks and stand back up, ready to push forward again.

Present

(31 years old)

"Thea? Hello, Earth to Thea?" I jerk back as Ripley's snapping fingers jolt me out of my memories. The stool I'm sitting on wobbles underneath me, threatening to tip over just as I catch myself on the aspen bar counter.

"Oh my God, what?" My tone is, admittedly, snarkier than I intend, but that's what he gets for scaring the shit out of me.

"You zoned out on me. You good?" Despite my attitude, his tone is soft, and there's concern laced in his words. It's been less than twenty-four hours since I made the most difficult phone call of my life. One I never imagined I'd have to be the one to make.

I fully expected the responsibility to fall on Brooks' shoulders considering it's *his* family, *his* brother, but he's been MIA since we learned of the accident, and someone had to tell Carrington. I could have asked the sheriff to call. Then, I considered how it would feel to have the news come from someone in law enforcement and decided against it. If the roles were reversed, I'd want him to make the same decision for me.

"Yeah. Yeah, I'm fine. Just... tired," I say as I rub my forehead and pray to anyone who will listen for these memories to stay buried where they belong. It'd been years since I was throttled down memory lane, but now it's been nonstop since making that phone call.

Ripley shakes his head at me—his shaggy, dark hair catching the overhead light from the pendants accentuating his natural inky highlights. He pushes the black, square-rimmed glasses up his nose and makes a face at me like he doesn't believe the lie I threw his way. You'd think after being as close as we have been for almost a decade I'd give up attempting to lie to his face, but here we are.

"You try calling your ex after eight years of no contact and telling him his parents are dead, and see how you deal with it. I shouldn't have had to make that call. It should have been Brooks."

His face softens as he walks around the bar, pulling out the stool beside me. "Babe, I know. I mean, I don't *know*, but I can imagine how fucking hard that was. That's why I'm checking in on you. Did you even sleep last night? You were gone before I woke up."

The bags under my eyes can answer that question without me saying a word. "How was I supposed to sleep after everything?"

His hand finds mine as he shakes his head. "That's fair. Maybe you should head home? Try to nap or something." I know he means well, I do, but if sleep didn't find me last night, it sure as hell won't find me now.

I squeeze his hand then lean over to kiss his cheek. "I appreciate you looking out for me, Rip. But you and I both know that's not happening. Besides, I need to go talk to Mr. Goldfinch. Someone needs to start making arrangements for the funeral, and I don't think it's going to be either of their sons." I start to slide off the stool when Rip stops me with a hand on my arm. His mossy green eyes boring into mine.

"Thea, it's going to be okay." I silently nod, knowing I don't believe a word he's saying. How could anything be okay with Owen and Hazel now gone? They were my second family, my lifelines. Everything I knew and loved changed in the matter of a moment. Everything is gone.

Nothing about this is okay.

We decided to send the staff home. They all came in today not knowing what else to do. None of us do without Hazel and Owen steering the ship. It's all up in the air now. It seems wrong to even be open. It feels like the whole town has stopped by today, which isn't saying much since our population barely hits 1,500. They all wanted to tell us how sorry they are and how much the Grants will be missed.

Mrs. Davis only stopped crying long enough to tell us how much she'll miss Hazel's famous chocolate chip cookies. Bob couldn't stop talking about how much he'll miss his weekly bar crawl with Owen—which wasn't really a crawl because they just went to Louie's and bribed Shelley to put their favorite sports team on. Everyone is heartbroken by this tragedy.

"You sure you don't want help closing up?" Ripley asks as he closes the door behind the last employee as they leave. I'm standing behind the hostess stand, elbows planted in front of me with my chin resting in my palms, staring out the window. It's only four-thirty in the afternoon, and it feels surreal to be turning off our open sign this early. This whole day feels like one big nightmare.

"Yeah, no, I'm good. I think I need a minute alone anyway. Mr. Goldfinch told me he could meet me at his office at five." Luckily, his office is only an eight-minute drive from Ripple Effect Distillery and Restaurant, so I'll make it there just in time.

Ripley hangs his head. Like always when I'm upset, he's having an internal fight with himself about leaving me alone. After a few seconds, he finally nods, knowing I need this time alone rather than a shoulder to cry on—that will come later.

"Okay, but only if you promise to call me as soon as you're done. And you owe me a night where I actually see you. One where you don't slip out of my bed the next morning before I'm even awake."

"Okay, yeah, I promise."

"I know where you live, Thea Ashford. And I know Goldfinch's closes at six. Remember that." He points a finger at me with raised brows, but his tone is slightly teasing.

I roll my eyes at him but know he's more than serious; he cares too much to let me be sad alone. If I don't call him by six on the dot, he *will* show up at my place with ice cream and Flamin' Hot Cheetos in hand, banging on the door until I answer.

"Got it. Calling you will be the first thing I do the moment I step foot out of his office. Just know, I may be crying."

Ripley walks toward me, pulling me into him the second he gets close enough. He's almost a whole foot taller than me, so his chin sits comfortably on top of my head. The sweet, malty smell of him surrounds me. He's spent so long working in distilleries he's started to smell like them. It's something I've loved to tease him about over the last eight years, and he always takes it in stride. Hints of vanilla envelop me as I take a deep breath, the familiarity of it all comforting me for a moment.

"This sucks so fucking much," he says, his voice bringing me back to our nightmarish reality. His hands hold me up as a sob slips past my lips. I squeeze him even tighter for one more second before pushing his warm body away. Letting him hold me any longer will only end with me truly breaking down.

"Go. I'll be fine. I promise." I wipe at the lone tear that escapes down my left cheek, thankful I was able to keep it under control for the most part. I haven't let myself fall apart yet, and I don't intend to until all the hard decisions are made.

He gives me a kiss on the top of my head before backing away from me and heading toward the door. With his hand on the handle, he turns around and makes direct eye contact with me. "Six o'clock, Thea." A sad laugh tumbles from my lips as I nod my head in reply. He slips out of the door, and I bring the heels of my palms to my eyes, applying pressure to the weeping sockets willing them to stop.

I'm grateful I have Ripley. Going through this without him would have left me in a puddle of despair and no way out. He's my rock, my person. He makes me laugh when all I want to do is break down. I don't think he realizes just how special he is, and I definitely don't tell him nearly enough. Losing two people I love dearly has made me realize how precious the ones around you are. It sounds cliché, but it's made me want to not take what I have for granted.

The second he's gone, I get up to turn off the lights and shut everything down. It only takes me a few minutes since we weren't really open today anyway. I grab my purse and head toward the door, stopping at the picture of Owen and Hazel on the wall. It's from when they first took over this place when it was just Indigo Hill Diner back in the 90s. The place was small but always felt like my second home. The patio that wraps around the restaurant overlooks Indigo Lake. We kept the patio and dock during renovations. None of us could part with it, and sitting on that patio while watching the sunset is something almost everyone in this town can say they've done at least once over the years.

I press my index and middle fingers to my lips before placing them on the photo. Another photo hangs right next to it, but it's from six years back when we first started this venture together. Ripley is holding me close to him, his arm around my shoulder, mine wrapped around his waist, while Owen and Hazel are smiling some of the biggest smiles I'd ever seen on their faces. It was the start of something new, something we all believed in.

I exhale deeply before turning around to leave. With Owen and Hazel gone, I need to stay to protect what we built together. This is their legacy, and its future is uncertain.

I'm not sure what I expected when I called Carrington yesterday. I was understandably upset during the call, but I guess I expected more than a 'thank you.' I expected some kind of reaction from him despite him proving to me time and time again in the past that he doesn't talk about his emotions. He didn't have a great relationship with Owen and Hazel once we got older, but they were still his parents.

I turn the key to lock the door then spin around and try to shove the keys into my purse. They fall from my hand and hit the ground as my eyes settle on the person standing in front of the steps leading up to the door.

Carrington Grant.

Even after all these years, I could spot him anywhere. He stands tall, looking up at the sign hanging above me, with his hands in the pockets of his dark denim jeans, a light gray Henley with the sleeves pushed up his forearms. His hair is longer than I remember, pulled into a top-knot, and he's sporting neatly trimmed facial hair. It looks like he has more tattoos, specifically one climbing up his neck that disappears under his shirt, but he's still the same Carrington I left in Seattle.

His eyes drift from the sign down to me. My heart stops the second his gaze locks onto mine. His eyes have always been mesmerizing. They're a deep blue with light striations that look like lightning strikes. I haven't seen his face in eight years. He might as well be a ghost to me.

After what feels like an eternity, I scurry down the steps, breaking our eye contact, and skirt past him by cutting through the grass. I know I should talk to him. I need to explain what happened here and why this isn't the place he remembers, but I just can't. Not right now. Not without breaking down, and I promised myself I wouldn't let that happen yet. I've already got my hand on my car door handle when I hear his footsteps behind me.

"Thea. Wait," he calls.

His familiar, gruff voice stops me in my tracks. It's involuntary. Just like yesterday when I heard his deep voice, and everything around me came to a chilling halt.

A moment passes before I find my words, with my back still to him all I can say is, "I... I have to go. I'm sorry. I'm, umm... I'm meeting with Mr. Goldfinch. Unless you... I mean... you should probably be the one. I can call and let him know." I cut myself off so the rambling stops, slowly looking over my shoulder at him. He hasn't said another word. He's just staring at me, and it hits me that he probably hates me.

I'm about to start apologizing again when he finally decides to speak.

"Get in. I'll drive," he says as he turns to walk toward what I presume is his car.

"Wh-what?"

"To Goldfinch's. I'll drive us."

In all honesty, this is the last thing I expected. I expected screaming or him telling me to never step foot on his parents' property again or, better yet, telling me I have no business making funeral arrangements for them. He'd probably be right to say all of that. They aren't *my* parents.

I can't move. I think I'm in shock from everything that's happened. By the time I pull my gaze from my reflection staring back at me in my driver's side window, he's waiting at his car with the passenger door open. There's not a speck of the malice I was expecting on his face, his expression seems solemn. His eyes focus on mine, staring into my soul, and I'm lost in them, the same way I always am when his deep blues find me.

"Are you coming?"

CHAPTER TWO

Carrington

As soon as the rental car door closes, Thea starts speaking. She's nervous. She's never been good in silence. One time, what seems like a lifetime ago now, she said she had to speak because if it were up to me we'd communicate solely with eye contact and grunts. She wasn't wrong.

"...And then a few years later we decided to expand to the side lot that used to be there, you remember?" She doesn't take a breath or pause for me to answer. She also hasn't looked at me, she's been staring out the window and fidgeting with her hands in her lap. "...installed the distillery. They took such a gamble, but it's paying off—the town loves the changes. And Rip's recipes have really put RED on the map."

Rip? I vaguely remember the kid a year or two behind us in school. Quiet. She was always friendly with him. I didn't realize he was still here. I always thought he was someone who would get out of a small town if he could. Hell, everyone should get out of here.

Thea falls silent when I put the car in park in front of Goldfinch Funeral Home. I let out a sigh, finding a tiny bit of comfort that at least *something* still looks the same as I remember.

After I hung up the phone with Thea yesterday, it took me ten full minutes outside of my restaurant just breathing in and out to patch myself together enough to go in, give a quick summary of what happened to my friends, and then hurry to my apartment to pack. I was lucky enough to get the first flight out to South Carolina. I spent the two-hour drive from Myrtle Beach to Indigo Hill talking to my bar manager and best friend, Seth, figuring out how to handle everything for the next few days while I'm... here.

Seth takes everything I ask of him in stride. I met him right after arriving in Seattle, and we hit it off immediately. He reminds me a little bit of Brooks with his dry sense of humor and take-no-shit attitude. Unlike Brooks, however, the guy is as driven as they come and puts his career before almost anything else in his life. My restaurant wouldn't be what it is without him. Hell, *I* might not be here without him.

When I pulled up to where my parents' diner used to be and saw the new two-story structure with a Ripple Effect Distillery and Restaurant sign hanging proudly above the welcoming wooden double doors, I checked that the car's navigation led me to the right address. My parents' old place was the typical roadside diner with vinyl booths, Formica counters, and sticky menus that hadn't been updated since before I was born. The only appealing aspects of the diner had been the wrap-around patio and the large lot it sat on. My parents had taken over the place because they got it for a steal when the previous owners retired. They never updated it—just made as-needed repairs to keep it going.

I had begged them to let me make changes with the food, the decor, but they never wanted to hear me out. Always placating me with "maybe next summer," citing finances as the main reason. I guess I missed them coming into money.

I was only sure I was in the right place when I saw Thea step out and lock the door, her hair catching the last of the sun's rays. She was always the most beautiful during golden hour—glowing like the sun itself.

16 Years Ago

(15 years old)

I take a running leap off the wooden dock and cannonball into the cool water, hearing a high-pitched squeal right before my head goes under. Popping up, I push my wet hair from my eyes and look over to Thea, still on the dock wiping droplets off herself with her palms.

"You're going to regret that, you ass!" The huge smile she gives me as she shouts the threat tells me I don't actually have anything to worry about. Thea's been my best friend for as long as I can remember. We met in kindergarten and instantly hit it off. We don't live in the same neighborhood, and our parents were never friends, so school was the only place we got to hang out. Because the town's so small, we ended up in all the same classes for years, allowing us to grow up together.

From diapers to Depends *we always say.*

"Okay, Lem. Sure." I swim over to the edge of the dock and pull myself out of the water. As I stand, my eyes catch on her purple manicured toes and slowly rake up her tanned legs, over her purple swimsuit—a bikini her mom finally let her wear; it's been one-pieces up until this summer—all the way up to her golden, sun-drenched

the way up to her golden, sun-drenched hair. I never noticed until now just how soft her hair looks in the evening sun, wavy and wild as it swings around her shoulders.

It's the middle of August, and the sun sets late, so we often go for evening swims to unwind after a day of helping my parents at the diner—me as a busboy and Thea as hostess. We only have a few more weeks of this; school will be starting up again soon, and we'll be sophomores.

I finally meet her eyes and see she caught me looking at her—shit, was I checking her out? My face heats, and my breath catches in my throat.

"Like what you see, Dillon?" she says in a mocking tone. She knows I've been trying to get the nickname to stick all year now. Everyone easily accepted when Brooks asked to be called by his middle name but have not afforded me the same courtesy. I guess being named Hugh Grant warrants a nickname more so than Cary Grant. My parents thought they were being so cute when choosing our names—they forgot we actually have to live with them and survive high school.

Her mouth quirks in a smile, making her lips look pouty. Why am I noticing all of this? This is Thea. I know she's pretty—I do have eyes. Other guys in school have made comments; I've even heard Brooks' friends say she's gotten hot. I don't think it hit me until this moment that she might be the most beautiful girl I've ever seen.

I'm standing just a foot or two in front of her, and her eyes don't leave me. She's expecting me to say something, maybe even do something. But my mind is blank, my stomach knotting in on itself, and I panic.

She squeals again, this time with much less cheer, as I grab her shoulders and shove her into the water.

Present

(31 Years Old)

The car door closing behind Thea brings me back to the present, and I'm left alone surrounded by silence and her scent—lemons and something floral I've never been able to place. The smell tries to pull me down into another memory, but before I let it, I open my own door.

We enter the funeral home and are immediately hit with the overwhelming smell of flowers—lilies, I think—along with an undertone of stale carpet. The space is warmly lit and decorated in creams and blues, meant to be calming, but my breathing picks up anyway. I didn't really understand until this very moment, staring at a generic painting of a boat on calm water hanging opposite the door we entered through, what Thea was coming here to do. My brain can't seem to focus or process anything with her around.

Mr. Goldfinch appears in the doorway to the right of the foyer. He's a balding man in his sixties with kind eyes and a gentle voice. His presence soothes the tension building in my chest a fraction.

His face flashes with surprise when his eyes land on me, probably because my presence here not only wasn't the plan, but no one in this town has seen me in thirteen years. "Mr. Grant, Ms. Ashford. I'm so sorry for your loss. Please, follow me right this way." He motions for us to follow him into a sitting room with a prominent fireplace.

The decor matches that of the foyer, with a navy couch facing two plush, off-white chairs, a stone fireplace off to the left, and a coffee table in the middle. A grandfather clock ticks in the corner. There's a box of tissues on the coffee table, and my eyes catch on it and can't seem to let go. How many boxes does he go through in a month? Does he buy them in bulk? Are they one-ply or the soft, premium kind? He seems like he would spring for the expensive brand name.

I look over to Thea, who has taken a seat in one of the chairs, and she shoots me a quick, curious look, snapping me out of my daze. I'm doing it again. Dr. Ferris would tell me I'm dissociating. Anything to avoid thinking about why I'm here. Back in my hometown. In this room. Standing in front of the sweet man with the kind eyes who will be responsible for putting my parents six feet in the ground.

Fuck. I can't do this. The short reprieve Mr. Goldfinch's presence brought me has disappeared, and I'm now seconds away from hyperventilating. I didn't get to talk to them again. I have barely even thought about them in years after the blow up that drove us apart. Just fleeting half-thoughts, mostly in the background of memories when my mind drifted to my childhood. *To her.*

Both Thea and Mr. Goldfinch are now seated and looking at me expectantly. I've barely taken two steps into the room, and I am seriously considering turning around, running out of the building, jumping into my rental car, driving the 3,000 miles back to Seattle, and pretending this isn't happening. My lungs feel like they're seizing. I clench my fists where they hide in the pockets of my jeans. I can't do this.

"Where's Brooks?" My even tone surprises me. It doesn't betray any of what's going on in my chest. I can't take a full breath, but I sound as if I'm asking about the weather. Thea glances up at me with a look I can't decipher. Huh, I guess I've lost the ability to read her.

"I don't know. He... took off on his motorcycle shortly after we got the call. I've been trying to reach him, but he won't answer my calls or texts. That's... why I called you."

That doesn't surprise me. It's what Brooks does when shit gets hard. Rides off on his bike—motorcycle now—blows off steam God-knows-where, and reappears like nothing ever happened. He's been that way since we were kids. Not sure he'll be able to pretend this one away though. And if he's not answering Thea's calls or texts, he's certainly not going to pick up for me.

There's a long pause, and Mr. Goldfinch clears his throat. "Would you like to have a seat, Cary? You can stand if you're more comfortable, but we do have a few things to discuss." After another hesitant second, I take my hands out of my pockets, sit in the other chair, and lean forward, elbows on my knees. "I know this was very sudden," he continues. "Have you given any thought to the kind of service you'd like for them? Did your parents ever discuss their wishes in the event of their passing?"

Thea sniffles, but I don't dare look. If I see her crying I'm going to lose it, and I don't know what that would even look like. I shake my head in answer to Mr. Goldfinch's question without making eye contact with either of them. Honestly, Thea would probably know more than I do if they had any wishes in that regard. Maybe I should have just let her handle this alone.

Mr. Goldfinch nods in understanding. He pulls a brochure from a pile on the table and opens it to an array of pictures featuring different colored wood and fabric. "We have several options for caskets. Thankfully, we have your family plot reserved, they will lie with your grandparents..." His voice fades out. I'm watching his lips move, but all I hear is the same buzzing sound from last night. That and the tick-tock of the clock behind me. The seconds pass, minutes, hours maybe. I can't tell anymore.

"Can I just take this with me and look it over tonight?" I blurt out. Again, my voice is much calmer than my thoughts. I sound bored even to my own ears. The room falls silent—I guess I cut him off mid-sentence.

"Certainly." Mr. Goldfinch's tone is as kind as ever. "Let me go grab a few more from my office so you can make decisions about flowers and headstones as well. Excuse me." He stands and quietly shuffles out of the room, leaving Thea and me alone. We both stare ahead where Mr.Goldfinch sat just a moment ago.

"How's your mom?" I finally say when I don't hear the funeral director coming back anytime soon.

Thea scoffs. She shakes her head and looks down at her hands in her lap. Her fingers fidget with her many rings, a habit she's had since we were kids. Since I started finding rings left behind by tourists and giving them to her. I recognize a few, but she has several new ones. Including one on the ring finger of her left hand. I can't drag my eyes away from it. *Is she married? Engaged? She can't be. Brooks would have told me. Right?*

"Did I say something wrong?" My voice is calm despite the turmoil I feel inside. I know I sound put-together. I know this isn't how people outwardly react when someone close to them dies.

"Do you even care?" Her words are angry, and the outburst catches me off-guard. "It certainly doesn't seem like it, so why are you even here, Carrington? I'm sorry this is such a huge inconvenience to you, but I think your parents deserve a lit—" She's cut off by Mr. Goldfinch entering the room again. He looks us over and can clearly feel the tension. With a sympathetic smile, he hands over the pamphlets, then we say our thanks and make our way outside.

As soon as we're on the sidewalk, Thea pulls out her phone and starts dialing. She puts the phone to her ear and a few feet of space between us.

"Hey," she says quietly to whomever is on the other end, her back to me. "Yeah, just finished." Her tone is different to the one she used with me inside. It's full of warmth and something else I can't quite put a name to. There's a pause while she listens. "I ran into Carrington... yeah, he's here." A pause. "Mhm, he's going to take me back to RED to grab my car now... no, I'm okay. I'm going to head home. Can I see you in the morning?"

I finally identify her tone. *Tenderness.* She's speaking to someone she cares for. I can't remember the last time I heard her sound this way toward me. Long before I stopped hearing from her entirely, that's for sure.

I start walking toward the car and stop in my tracks when I hear, "Yeah, okay. Love you, babe." My heart stops mid-beat. My eyes snap to her as she turns around. I'm not sure what my face is doing, but the small smile the phone call pulled out of her quickly falls, replaced by... sadness? Anger? Worse yet, could it be indifference? She's so guarded, I can't read her anymore.

Love you, babe. Of course she has someone. They're probably engaged judging by the ring on her finger. I don't know why the thought tightens my chest. It's not like I haven't moved on. And if... *this* hadn't happened, I would probably be with my own "babe" right now.

Shit, I promised I'd call her when I got here.

We break eye contact and get in the car. The ride back to the restaurant is silent, and for once, I can't stand it.

Thankfully, it wasn't difficult to find a last minute hotel room. The town gets a huge influx of tourists and vacationers during the summer months drawn by the lake, but in the off season, it's just the locals.

Sitting on the edge of the bed, the pamphlets from the funeral home lie beside me. I tossed them there when I got back, right before I ran to the bathroom and emptied the bile from my stomach. I don't think I ate anything today. There may have been coffee at the airport before I boarded, but the memory is hazy.

My thumb trembles as it hovers over Brooks' name on my contact list. I run my other hand through my hair a few times, down my face, and over the scruff I keep trimmed short. It's been three... no, four months since we spoke. Maybe more. We dial each other a few times a year, exchange a few words, and wrap up each call in under ten minutes. I thought he was keeping me updated on what was going on here. He always told me, "Same shit, different day." And on the rare occasion when I got up the nerve to ask about Thea, he always told me she was fine. I've clearly missed so much.

Before I get a chance to click on Brooks' name, my phone rings in my hand. *That Girl From That Bar* flashes across the screen. An image of the flirty face she directed my way when she handed my phone back to me after programming her number in it six years ago flashes through my mind. I was hooked right then and there.

"What's up, Arizona? How you likin' the rain, girl?" I say automatically and cringe. I'm running on fumes and apparently just falling back on habit. It's how I've greeted her pretty much daily since our first date where we stumbled upon an outdoor showing of *Twilight* at a local park and stayed to watch as a joke. I know it's not appropriate, but my brain has completely checked out.

"Bear? Baby, how's it going out there? Are you okay?" Her concern for me is evident in her words.

"Yeah," I say with a sigh. "It's good to hear your voice. It's been a long day."

"I'm so sorry, baby. How can I help? Do you want me to come out there? I can see if I can get a flight tomorrow." As great as it is to hear her voice, I hesitate to say yes. It'd be nice to not feel so alone here, but thinking of her here doesn't sit right. She doesn't fit the life I left behind over a decade ago. I just need to wrap things up here and get back. "Bear?" I've been quiet too long.

"No. No, it's alright. I'll only be here for a few more days. I'll come back after the funeral."

"Are you sure? I'd like to be there for you."

"Yeah, I'm just going to finalize the arrangements and tie up some loose ends. I'll see you in a few days. Can I call you tomorrow?"

"Okay, of course. I love you, babe."

I hang up the phone, and *love you, babe* repeats over and over in my head, but the voice saying the words isn't that of the woman waiting for me in Seattle.

CHAPTER THREE

The funeral is beautiful. I was surprised Carrington remembered how much Hazel loved blue hydrangeas. He clearly called Mr. Goldfinch and took care of everything after our very brief, very awkward meeting at the funeral home. Snapping at him wasn't my intention, but I couldn't sit there surrounded by pamphlets about caskets and act like everything was fine anymore. Two of the people I had been closest to in this world died in the blink of an eye, and he wanted to make small talk.

Despite their fractured relationship, Hazel and Owen loved Carrington dearly. Hazel often talked about him as a little boy or wondered what he's been doing over the last few years. All they ever wanted was for him to be happy. For him to succeed. And I think they were just as heartbroken as I was when we didn't work out.

For years, everyone thought we'd end up together. We'd been so young, and he'd been my best friend for so long, I couldn't imagine it being more—until it was. By that point, I was convinced we'd get married, have kids, the whole nine yards. Life had other plans though.

The last thing his parents deserved was for their funeral arrangements to not be taken seriously, which is exactly why I'm so surprised by how perfect everything is. Right down to the casket choice—a light, aspen wood Owen would have fawned over, having been a woodworker himself. It reminds me of the bartop at RED. Carrington wouldn't know, but Owen fought tooth and nail for that exact wood to be the focal point of the bar. He'd always loved it. But I assumed Carrington wouldn't care enough to actually remember.

They are being laid to rest together, exactly how they would have wanted. I stand there staring at the flowers draped on top of the caskets as they're lowered into the ground. Everyone else has left already, the funeral having been over for a good while now. It would almost be poetic to end up standing here alone since that's how I feel with them gone—completely alone. I have Ripley and my mom, but a huge piece of my heart is being buried right before my eyes.

My mom tried to stay until the end of the service, but I saw how much the outing drained her. These days it doesn't take much. She is always so tired, so run down. It makes my heart hurt just thinking about it. Thankfully, her nurse is a saint and knows her almost as well as I do. Margot caught the haziness in my mom's eyes before I did, subtly whispering in my ear that she felt like it was time to go. I'd kissed my mom's cheek and told her I'd be by next week before watching them leave.

Raised voices catch my attention as I finally pull my eyes away from the flowers. My head turns in the direction of the noise to find Brooks and Carrington are still here and having what looks like a heated discussion.

It's been almost six days since I've seen or heard from Brooks. When the deputies came to RED and told us the news, he rushed out, jumped on his motorcycle, and rode off. I've been calling him ever since, but he never picked up. Never texted back. Nothing. All I needed to know was that he was safe. Clearly, he wasn't. He showed up right before the funeral with a black eye and a split lip. No doubt from a bar fight or something of the sort. I wonder if this will leave a mark like the other incidents that left him bloody and bruised.

I can't hear what they're saying, but it looks like Carrington is trying to comfort him. Brooks isn't having it. I watch as he shoves Carrington's hand off of his shoulder and tries to storm off. Carrington grabs him by the elbow before he can and leans in to say something low in his ear.

I wipe the tears from under my eyes before giving one more longing look at the caskets before me. "Give 'em hell up there, you two," I whisper as I run my hands down the front of my black dress then turn to walk away.

As soon as Carrington and Brooks sense me walking toward them, they both quiet down. Their gazes find mine just as I stop in front of them. The family resemblance is strong: both are tall, around six feet, have dark brown hair, blue eyes, strong, masculine jawlines, and dark brows. Where Cary's face is approachable and gentle, Brooks constantly has a sharp look about him, as if he's ready to lash out at any moment. And with the two of them in suits? They look even more alike.

"Whatever this is," I wave my hand between them, "this isn't the time or place. Either shut it down, or take it somewhere else." I don't wait for a response before I turn on my heel to walk away. I don't hear either of them following me when I throw over my shoulder, "We have a reception to get to. Please don't make me explain your absence."

As if my words released them from their stances, I faintly make out shuffling behind me as I walk to my car.

I'm overwhelmed with memories of Hazel and Owen while I drive on autopilot to RED for the reception. The staff who were up to the task have been there all morning preparing the space for us. Ripley left the funeral as soon as it ended to make sure everything was in order for guests to arrive.

This whole day feels like I'm living someone else's life. I don't know if I'm prepared to be around everyone spouting off their favorite memories. Not that it matters, this is happening regardless. All I can do is try to make it through and hope it exhausts me enough so I can finally sleep tonight.

At my request, the entire restaurant is covered in blue hydrangeas and white peonies. You'd think I planned the funeral considering the resemblance, but it was just a happy accident within a tragedy. Another reminder of how in sync Carrington and I can be.

Ripley notices my entrance the second I shut the door behind me, politely excusing himself from the people surrounding him.

"Hey, babe," he says, pulling me in for a hug I sink into as he brushes his lips against my hair in a sweet kiss. "You doing okay?"

"I'm here." It's all I can give him. He knows me well enough to understand. Over the years, we've gotten about as close as two people can. We're able to speak with just shared glances. It's one of the reasons almost everyone in this town feels the need to tell us how good we are together. They constantly ask us when we'll be getting married as a not-so-subtle nudge that they want to see us have our happily ever after.

I turn my head in Rip's arms as the door behind me opens again. Carrington and Brooks walk in looking slightly less tense than when I saw them last. Carrington's expression is unreadable while Brooks looks like he's ready for another fight. They've always been like this, Carrington hides all of his emotions, and Brooks can't contain his. They spill out of him like the blood seeping from his split lip.

As they walk past us, Ripley loosens his grip on my back, gently pulling me away from his chest. I follow his line of sight to see he's watching Carrington walk into the reception. "You ready for this?" His words are soft, and his eyes return to me shining with concern for my well-being.

I let out a small, sarcastic laugh before replying, "Never. But... I don't have much of a choice." He nods in understanding as he threads his fingers through mine and pulls me toward the crowd at the bar.

We spend the next hour or so mingling with everyone. They've all offered their condolences and shared their favorite stories of Hazel and Owen. Each time I hear a new one, it gets harder and harder to keep fresh tears from falling.

Ripley hasn't let go of me since we got here. I think he knows if he does, I may disappear. Not just physically but emotionally, mentally. He's seen me check out before. He knows the warning signs. This is the second time he's dealing with it after all. Finding out my mom's diagnosis was getting progressively worse was the first time—some of it is still blurry to this day. He'd been by my side when she'd made the decision to move into Saint Stephen's. I'd tried to argue, I told her I could handle it, but she'd been adamant about her choice.

Pulling myself back to the present, I realize we've ended up on opposite sides of the room from Carrington for almost the entire reception. He's stayed close to Brooks, but I feel his eyes on me. They've been searing into my back like a third degree burn. It's taken everything in me not to go ask him what his issue is. If we were anywhere else, in any other situation, I wouldn't hesitate.

As if focusing on it conjured him, I see him and Brooks walking over in my periphery. The couple speaking to us notices as well and excuses themselves.

No one speaks, and the awkward silence carries on for a moment too long before I'm forced to break it. "Ripley, this is Carrington Grant, Hazel and Owen's other son. Carrington, this is Ripley. I'm not sure if you remember him from school, he was two years behind us." My voice doesn't sound like my own, it's robotic and cordial.

Their eyes are locked on each other when Carrington finally says, "I remember." Nothing more. Two words. I let out a deep breath, attempting to expel the tension.

As if Ripley can't help himself, he goads Carrington back by saying, "Weird. I don't." His tone sounds casual, but I know better. I also know that's a bald-faced lie, and it makes the corner of my lips tick up, which I hide behind my palm.

"Hey, listen, can I maybe talk to you?" Brooks says after looking back and forth at all three of us and coming to the same conclusion as me: that was the end of the conversation between them.

"Yeah, of course. What's up?" My words sound casual despite the situation. I'm so used to our conversations being about work or what to get Hazel and Owen for an anniversary or birthday. The poor guy has always been horrid at gift giving.

"Cary and I were discussing RED and how I obviously have to step up now. And I..." He takes a moment to clear his throat, working up the courage to say what he needs to say. "I just wanted to ask if you'd help me? You know, teach me how to run this place and not fuck it up?" The sincerity in his eyes warms my heart, the blue a few shades lighter than his brother's but just as striking. The last thing I expected was for him to be this responsible, especially after he took off the other day.

I pull my hand from Ripley's and tug Brooks into a hug, standing on my tip-toes so I can wrap my arms around his neck. It takes him a moment to react, he's not one to show vulnerability easily. This could quite possibly be the first hug he's received since we all found out what happened. But the second his arms reach around my back, he leans into me like I'm the lifeline he needs right now. I tilt my face to his ear so he can hear me as I quietly say, "Of course. Yes. I'd love nothing more."

I can't stop the tears this time. They fall on their own accord, and I worry I won't be able to stop them. I kiss Brooks' cheek, my nose grazing the metal hoop in his own nose, before pulling back and unraveling myself from him. Ripley reaches for my hand again, lacing our fingers together, and pulling me back into his side. It's at that moment I realize Carrington hasn't spoken but those two words the entire time they've been standing here with us. I ignore the thought and turn my gaze to Brooks' black eye.

"You should really put some ice on that."

He scoffs, shaking his head, all traces of vulnerability gone. "Nah, I'm no bitch. I can handle it."

A laugh surprises me as it bubbles up from my chest, and the look on their faces at my sudden outburst only makes me laugh more. It becomes contagious as Ripley and Brooks join in. Carrington *almost* lets a smile break loose but nothing more.

I ignore his eyes on me and turn back to Brooks. "God, Owen must have ingrained that in us all. I can't tell you how many employee complaints I got about him telling someone to 'suck it up and not be a bitch about it.'"

I watch as the two brothers exchange a look, then Carrington opens his mouth to say, "We heard it a lot growing up too."

Brooks laughs some more then gives Carrington a playful shove on the arm. "What the fuck ever. More like *I* heard it a lot growing up. The only time you got told that was when you were sixteen and got grounded after you were caught sneaking back into the house at two in the morning."

The laughter continues around us, but the action in the room grinds to slow motion for me as I shift my gaze to meet Carrington's, and my smile fades. He doesn't say anything, but I know he's thinking the same thing I am. My cheeks heat as I think back on the night Brooks is referring to. His family thought he was out at some party with his friends, but really, we'd been at my house. Two teens in love, losing our virginities to each other.

My mom was on the overnight shift at work so we'd taken advantage of having the house to ourselves. We'd only been officially dating for a few months at that point, but we'd known each other almost our entire lives. It's a night I couldn't erase from my mind if I tried. It'd been awkward and painful, just like everyone's first time, but it'd also been beautiful and perfect, filled with kisses and quiet *I love yous.* Unlike most, we truly loved each other despite only being sixteen at the time.

"—right, Thea?" The sound of my name leaving Ripley's lips jolts me back. I quickly look up at him, not sure how long I'd been staring at Carrington. It felt like an eternity, but it could have been mere seconds.

I have no idea what he said, and I'm too lost in my own thoughts to even ask. "I need to use the restroom," I say before pulling away from him and walking toward the back office instead. I don't make it very far before I'm bracing myself on the wall in the hallway, hoping it can help hold me together.

The memory of that night combined with all the emotions of the last few days is just too much. I can't keep it all in any longer. I can't let Carrington being here destroy me. Tears streak down my cheeks moments before a voice behind me says, "Thea?"

I don't turn. I know who it is. His voice haunts my dreams; I could never forget its cadence. Turning around and seeing those deep blue ocean eyes won't make matters better. They can only make everything worse.

Unfortunately for me and my fragile state, not answering makes him come closer. I can feel his body heat, smell his pine tree scent—he's so close to me now that everything in me lights up like a struck match. His fingers brush my shoulder, and for a moment, I lean into it. His touch comforts me as my breathing settles. With a deep—but still shaky—breath, I step away from the fantasy of it all. If I give myself any hope where he's concerned, I won't survive any of this.

"Thea," he pleads. Our past echoes in his voice like he was stuck in the memories with me before I pulled us both out, like he'd give anything to go back.

"Just... don't, Carrington. Not right now. Please." My voice is haggard. I sound downright broken.

"I just want to... I don't know... help?" he says in that same pleading tone. I turn to look at him. Worry etches in the lines of his forehead. His eyes dart back and forth, cataloging each tear as it falls. I know he's itching to reach forward and wipe them away. Or worse, kiss them away.

"You know how you can help? Stop looking at me like that," I shoot back at him.

He shakes his head in confusion before responding, "Like what?"

"Like this hurts you as much as it hurts me. Just... stop. I don't even know why you're still here." I don't wait for him to respond before I'm walking past him. Back to the reception. Back into Ripley's arms. Back into a life Carrington Grant is no longer a part of.

CHAPTER FOUR

"**F**uck. Did they ever throw anything away?" Brooks whines as we go through the boxes from the attic at Owen and Hazel's house. He's been full of surprises in the days since the funeral with how unguarded and open he's been. I was stunned when I got his message this morning asking if I'd help at the house. He said he wants to clean it up, do some renovations, and put it up for sale. There are too many memories here to keep it. I don't blame him for making the decision to sell. It'll be sad to see someone else moving in, but it's sad just being here without Owen and Hazel anyway.

"Do you remember how much shit we had to go through before we started the work on the diner? I love your mother dearly, but the woman was a true pack-rat."

"Ain't that the fucking truth," he quips back, both of us chuckling at the memory of her reaction anytime someone mentioned throwing something "sentimental" out. It didn't matter what it was or how long it'd been since she'd seen it last, if it had any memory connected to it, she called it sentimental. As one can imagine, that meant *everything* was "sentimental" and nothing was ever thrown out. I miss them so much, but it's nice to feel something other than grief-stricken when I think about them.

"Hey, umm..." Brooks clears his throat and shuffles from foot to foot. His hand comes up and scratches the back of his neck as he says, "I'm going to do right by RED... and you, okay? I know I haven't been the most responsible—or even reliable—person in the past, but... I just promise I won't run shit into the ground. I want you to know that."

I'm stunned silent by his declaration. Clearly, he isn't ignorant to the fact that it's hard for anyone to take him seriously based on his past actions and reputation, but I guess he's going to use this tragedy as an opportunity to step up, and that means the world to me.

I meet his eyes as I say, "Thank you, I really appreciate that."

We settle into a comfortable silence, neither of us saying anything more. We continue to fill trash bags with things we can either donate or throw away. Every once in a while, we'll ask each other for an opinion on something if we aren't sure which pile to put it in. It's the calmest I've felt in days.

Going through Owen and Hazel's things, though heartbreaking, is bringing back some fond memories. I'm comforted remembering all of the moments we shared. And I'm able to turn off my brain a little with the physical labor of sorting and tossing.

I'm touched Brooks asked me to be here. Carrington is in town, but he still reached out to me for help with this. The thought forms a lump in my throat. This family means so much to me. Losing Carrington felt catastrophic, but finding the Grants and

Brooks again after the fallout felt like kismet. Now we've lost them, and everything feels bleak again.

I stretch my arms over my head to pop my back when I catch Brooks looking in my direction. "What?" I ask, confused by the musing look on his face.

"Nothing, you just... well, I'm just glad. You seem happy." His words catch me off-guard, and I make a weird choked sound before finding my words.

"I—what? I seem happy? Right now? In the wake of... everything that's happened?"

"Oh. Shit. No, sorry. I just mean with Rip. You two seem happy together." He brushes his fingers over his short hair, his nerves showing. He typically keeps his hair buzzed short, but hasn't touched it up in over a week now, so it's longer than usual.

"You do realize how fucking random that was?" I throw a wad of the newspaper we've been using to pack up the things he's keeping.

He throws his hands up in front of his face to block it from hitting him before speaking again. "Not really. I spent all day at the funeral watching him dote on you and make sure you were okay. I guess I hadn't realized before how serious you two are since you keep it professional at work."

I busy my hands by closing up the trash bag beside me, refusing to make eye contact with him. "Oh, right. Yeah, uh, I guess so," I tumble over my words as I try not to sound too awkward.

He chuckles then says, "Just makes me realize how we never would have worked out even if you had given me a chance." I look over and catch his lips quirk up teasingly.

My cheeks heat, and I cover them with my hands to make them stop. I'm still embarrassed by how I handled that whole situation. "Oh my God, stop. I've apologized so many times for that! You're basically my older brother. Besides, you never liked me like that anyway," I grumble back to him.

He brings his hand to his heart as he dramatically says, "Jilted by the one and only Thea Ashford who wouldn't even grace me with a pity kiss. I don't know how I survived."

I'm full on covering my face now as I try to keep my laughter from bubbling out. We'd gone on a whole two dates, both uncomfortable and amazingly awkward.

The people of this small town always seem to be trying their hand at matchmaking until things end disastrously. Then they all act like they never suggested the pairing in the first place.

They'd spent a whole year after I got back from Seattle asking me what happened with Carrington and if we'd reconcile. Then, suddenly, everyone moved on to shipping me with his brother and started badgering me to "give him a chance." Ms. Lucille down at the bank had even gone as far as commenting on what beautiful babies we'd make together. I shouldn't have let them talk me into something I knew wouldn't work, but I figured if I gave in and tried, showed them it was a terrible idea, they'd leave me alone. Which is exactly what happened... after I leaned away when Brooks went in for a kiss on a very public dance floor. He's never let me forget it.

I stand up and grab the two full trash bags beside me before rolling my eyes in his direction. "You managed just fine, don't pretend like you didn't. Both Nat and Tiffany have shared way too many details with me. I really wish you'd stop sleeping with the women who work at RED." I shudder and cringe at the memory of the stories I've heard about Brooks in less than appropriate situations.

The moment I turn around to leave the room with the bags, I see Carrington standing silently in the doorway. Immediately, I wonder how long he's been standing there and what he may have overheard. His face looks more like Brooks' than his own with the angry expression painted across his features giving me all the answers I need. I don't hesitate another moment before walking out of the room, pushing past him without saying a word.

Air. I need air. Every encounter with him is filled with so much tension that it steals all the oxygen from the room. The weight of his gaze is like a physical thing—it's suffocating.

I set the two bags on the sidewalk beside the mailbox for trash pickup then lift my face to the sun, letting it give me the strength to deal with whatever comes next back inside the house. My eyes are closed as I soak it in for just a moment longer before taking a deep breath, releasing all the tension in my body.

"Excuse me?" I jump at the sudden voice coming from a man I'm not familiar with standing right beside me.

When the fuck did he get here?

"Y-yes?" my voice cracks as I try to slow my heart rate.

"I'm sorry to startle you, darlin'. My name is James Elsher. I'm looking for the Grant boys and Ms. Thea Ashford. I've tried calling the number I have on file which is for a restaurant without success. This is my next attempt to contact them." His voice is warm with Southern charm, but he must notice the shock on my face because he hurries to add, "I'm the executor of Hazel and Owen Grant's will, I just—"

"Right, of course. Let me introduce you to Carrington and Brooks so you can handle that privately with them," I cut him off before he can say any more, motioning toward the house.

"Thank you, Miss..." his voice trails off, allowing me the opportunity to fill in the blank for him.

"Ashford, actually. I'm Thea." I turn and start to walk toward the front door when he stops me with a hand on my arm.

"Oh, I actually need to speak to all three of you, if that's alright," he says calmly.

The confusion must be evident in my face because he starts shuffling through his papers like he's checking to make sure he isn't mistaken in the matter. I glance over at the house to see Carrington and Brooks standing in the open doorway staring at me and the stranger with matching expressions I can't place. It looks like protectiveness, but that can't be right, not from Carrington at least. I haven't seen that look on his face in years now. Possibly since high school.

"Yes, yes, right here. Thea Carina Ashford. That is your full name, correct?"

"I—yeah, yes, it is. Let me... get them. Do we—is it done here? Now? Or..." I let my voice trail off with my uncertainty. I don't know anything about wills or how this is handled, and I'm still stunned by his sudden appearance that my thoughts aren't translating into coherent words.

"No, no, darlin'. We can handle this at my office," he says as he hands me his card. "It's in Southbury, if you don't mind making the drive. I just figure since you're all three in town currently, this may be the best time."

I can only assume I'm needed because the restaurant I consider my second home is about to switch hands just as we thought it would.

Despite asking for my help, it's possible Brooks will destroy RED if the mood strikes him. Carrington will sell it without batting an eye. I won't be able to win with the two of them. I don't think I have enough money to buy it from them. All the what-ifs spiral in my head as it finally becomes real that it's no longer something I can call mine. Mr. Elsher tilts his head down to meet my eyes, my internal struggle must be apparent from the concerned look on his face.

"Ms. Ashford? Would that be okay?" His voice is soft. This is his job, I'm sure he's had this exact conversation many times. He's probably watched countless bereaved loved ones try to make sense of the situations they're left in.

All I can do is nod my head as my fingers find my rings and start twisting them around, letting them ground me enough to take a full breath. They're all yellow-gold, my favorite. Some of them I've had for years, some are new. I never tell anyone this, but a couple of them are from Carrington. I usually don at least one on every finger, and I rotate them out so I'm able to wear them all. Or well, all but one.

There's exactly one ring I never wear anymore. It's simple, just a single band with a lemon wedge. I haven't worn it in years, but I know precisely where it is. I could save it in a fire—and I would. I just won't wear it. Not anymore.

He places his hand on top of mine causing me to meet his eyes. "I am so sorry for your loss, dear." Again, all I can bring myself to do is nod as a small sob breaks loose. The first one today. I bring my hand to my lips to keep it from turning into more as he walks away.

It's not until Carrington and Brooks are walking toward me that I start to wonder how to explain we're all needed at this meeting.

Carrington is still at least six feet away when he starts speaking to me.

"Who was that?" he says as his eyes meet mine.

I hold the card out for him to take so he can read it for himself. "Your parents had a will. That was their executor. He wants us to meet him at his office for the reading of the will."

Carrington's eyes don't leave mine as he says, "Today?"

"Yes. Now." I finally break eye contact to look over at Brooks who hasn't taken his eyes off of the car Mr. Elsher drove off in.

I don't wait for either of them to say anything else as I start toward my own car. "I'll meet you there." I ignore Carrington as he says my name, knowing there is nothing left to say. This isn't something I know how to deal with or maneuver. There's no manual for how to handle seeing your ex-boyfriend after almost a decade because his parents, who you were closer to than he was, died. So, I'm choosing not to. I'm choosing to walk away and drive to the next situation I have no fucking clue how to handle.

I walk into Mr. Elsher's office to see three chairs lined up in front of his desk. He's sorting through the piles of paperwork strewn in front of him, so it takes a moment before he realizes I'm even here. His desk is covered in documents and file folders that don't seem to be in any sort of order, and I wonder how he manages to work at a desk that's so disorganized.

"Ah, Ms. Ashford, please, take a seat. I presume the Grants are on their way?" he says as he stands up to lean over his desk and shake my hand. The folder he's holding slips from under his elbow as he extends his hand to me, the papers inside falling to his desk and the floor. He makes a grumbled sound before picking them all up and shuffling them back together.

A lump forms in my throat at the phrase *the Grants*. I'm so used to the phrase referring to Hazel and Owen that it hits me out of nowhere. He must realize I haven't answered, so he raises his gaze to find mine, and I just nod. For someone who usually can't shut up in stressful or awkward situations, I'm finding it hard to speak to the man in front of me. This is all too surreal.

I sit in the chair closest to the window, furthest from the door, setting my purse down beside me as I wait for Carrington and Brooks to arrive. My leg bounces uncontrollably. I'm already chewing on my bottom lip as Mr. Elsher greets them a few minutes later.

Carrington sits in the middle chair—right beside me, so close I can feel the heat from his arm on mine—leaving the chair closest to the door for Brooks. Not that he sits down in it. He leans up against the door frame, his hands deep in his pockets with a look on his face that says he's ready to burn the whole world down. Clearly his mood has taken a downturn since I saw him thirty minutes ago.

"I know this is a tough time for you all, but I find it's easiest to handle these things as soon as possible. So, let's get started, shall we?" Elsher's voice is still comforting, but it's imbued with an authoritative undertone like he's switched into business mode.

None of us speaks, but we all nod in agreement.

"In the interest of time, I'll skip over the legal jargon and just get to the meat and potatoes. Per the will of Owen and Hazel Grant, they left the balance of their personal bank accounts, savings, and their residential property and all personal belongings, including personal vehicles, located at 358 South Windsor Avenue, Indigo Hill, South Carolina to Hugh Brooks Grant." He raises his gaze to the three of us as his words settle in the space around us. I don't know what he's expecting. Maybe people get mad or upset once they find out what's left to whom. This isn't unexpected. There's no reason for them to leave their house to anyone other than Brooks. We already knew this would be the case.

Mr. Elsher must realize there won't be any backlash on the matter because he clears his throat, looks back down at the papers, and continues.

"Per the will of Owen and Hazel Grant, ownership and all rights to Ripple Effect Distillery and Restaurant, the land it sits on, and all business bank account balances are to be split between Carrington Dillon Grant and Thea Carina Ashford. Carrington will retain fifty-one percent of the business and all accompanying property, and Thea will own the other forty-nine percent."

The second the words leave his mouth, my whole world comes to a crashing halt. I'm not entirely sure I heard him correctly. I feel my pulse all the way in my cheeks, as the air in the entire room shifts.

Before I even have a moment to figure out why, I look over to realize Brooks must have come closer once Mr. Elsher started speaking. He's got his hands braced on the back of the empty chair. His face is flushed a violent shade of red, and he's brimming with anger like I've never seen before. Suddenly, he erupts, shoving the chair to the ground. "This is fucking bullshit," he spits out as he storms out of the office. I get up to go after him, but Carrington gently grabs my arm and pulls me back down to my seat. He doesn't say anything. He just stares right into my eyes, but I can't read his face. I have no idea what he's feeling. He must be angry too, right? He just doesn't show emotions like Brooks does.

He turns to Mr. Elsher, his searing touch still on my arm, my leg still bouncing with anxiety, as he says, "Thank you, Mr. Elsher. I apologize for my brother, this is difficult for him, but we greatly appreciate your time. Is there something we need to do now? Something we need to sign?"

Out of the corner of my eye, I see Mr. Elsher nod his head as he thumbs through his papers looking for the one he needs. "Yes. Yes, you do. I have it right here, one moment."

The room starts to spin as I wait for him to tell us what we need to do next. "Ah, here we go," he says, laying the papers in front of us. He then shuffles the stacks of paper on his desk, pulling pens from underneath with a triumphant hum. "I'll need you both to sign on the line under your names. Once this is done, I'll start the deed transfer process. It generally takes a week or two and will need another signature to finalize it before the property transfer is official."

He sounds so matter-of-fact, like this is just another day, another business transaction. He's using such clinical words like 'property' and 'process' as if the last twenty minutes didn't set my whole life ablaze.

I never thought RED would be mine. I thought losing it was inevitable. Losing what I've worked so hard for over the last three years entirely was one thing, but losing it in this way will hurt even more. Partial ownership gives me a sliver of hope for RED's future that I know I shouldn't hold on to. I may own forty-nine percent, but there's no way Carrington will carry out our plans; he'll probably sell it the moment he has the deed in hand. I won't get a say. I'll be forced to watch him do with it whatever he pleases.

The way Mr. Elsher delivered the news made it seem like this was something we expected and went into with eyes wide open. He knew Owen and Hazel—how well is unclear—but he knew them and their wishes. He doesn't know us or the complicated history we have. He doesn't realize that none of us predicted this. Mr. Elsher has no idea he just turned our lives upside down—or at least mine. Carrington doesn't seem fazed at all which shouldn't come as a surprise to me.

The moment we've both finished signing on our allocated lines, Carrington stands up and fixes the chair Brooks knocked over. He then reaches over to gently pull me up, but quickly drops my arm, turning and walking out of the room. I look down at the place his hand just held—I can still feel it like a phantom touch.

I let out a deep, shaky breath, feeling like I've been holding it in since Mr. Elsher said my name outside of the Grant house. "Thank you," I say as I reach down to grab my purse.

"Could you please ask—" he looks down at the papers on his desk, "Hugh to call the office? There are some documents for him to sign as well with regards to the house."

I nod. Everything feels like a haze as I walk toward the door that leads outside. I don't see Carrington or Brooks anywhere, so I start to panic. I take a deep breath trying to get my nerves under control, but I'm shaking from the shock. There's no way I can drive myself home, and the last thing I want right now is to be around the Grant brothers. I pull out my phone and scroll to Ripley's name, typing out a message to him.

Me: I need you, can you come pick me up?

Ripley: Yeah, of course. Where are you?

Me: Southbury. I'll explain when you get here, I'm sending you a pin.

Ripley: Okay. Be there soon.

How am I supposed to feel about this? I never expected them to leave RED to me but to leave it to us both with Carrington having the majority stake? What the fuck were they thinking? How did they think this would work? After years of fighting for what I wanted, years of waiting for my career dreams to come true, they finally did with RED.

Now, the person I broke so he could keep his dream just got handed the keys to mine on a silver fucking platter.

CHAPTER FIVE

Carrington

With my head still reeling from what transpired in the lawyer's office, I'm surprised to find Brooks leaning on the side of my rental car waiting for me. I was sure he was going to call an Uber or someone to come pick him up with the way he stormed out of the building.

We drove here together from Mom and Dad's house. Those thirty minutes were the longest time we've spent alone together in almost fifteen years. I wish I could say we took the opportunity to catch up a little, but I spent the majority of the time with my teeth clenched, white-knuckling the steering wheel, still fuming over the conversation I walked in on at the house.

"Look, I know you're pissed," he says, meeting my gaze. "I shouldn't have done that in there. I'll call him and apologize." His words catch me off-guard. I can't remember a time Brooks willingly apologized for his outbursts. He usually throws a tantrum and then disappears, popping up some time later with no word on where he's been, consequences be damned.

Mom and Dad never knew how to deal with his temper. They tried grounding him and taking away things he liked, but it never fazed him. By the time he was a teenager they'd given up and let him run off when he needed the space, hardly questioning where he was or with whom. "Can we go get a drink or something somewhere? This has turned into a shit day."

I take a long look at my brother for the first time since he arrived at the funeral looking like he got the crap beat out of him. He looks almost the same as he did before I moved away, save for a few fine lines around his eyes and the vulnerability pouring out of them. The Brooks I knew was all hard edges and cutting quips. The man before me seems beaten down and broken.

"You know what? Forget it. I'll just call a car," he says, moving to pull out his phone and step away.

"Come on. I saw a bar up the road." I don't wait for him to answer, just round the car and get in.

The bar is dimly lit with a few patrons scattered throughout, most staring at the football game streaming on the TVs above the liquor display. The floor has that permanent stickiness that doesn't seem to go away regardless of how often it gets mopped from decades of beer and food spills. A country song plays at a low volume in the background. The bartender quirks his head toward the empty booths lining the wall on the left. I take it as an invitation to seat ourselves.

I slide in, the red vinyl squeaking beneath me.

"I'm going to piss and grab us drinks," Brooks says and continues past where I'm sitting down a hall with a sign for the restroom. I pull out my phone, navigate to my recent messages, and reread the one I received earlier this morning.

That Girl From That Bar: Good morning, Care Bear. I can't wait to see your face tomorrow.

I never responded. *I'm such an asshole.*

She's been so patient with me. She's seen how I've worked to learn to communicate first-hand, and I seem to be throwing it all out the window, but I just don't know what to say.

Me: I'm canceling my flight back. I have to stay longer.

I send the message and start searching for my flight information. The reply is instant. She must have been waiting for me.

That Girl From That Bar: Everything okay?

Me: Yeah, just a complication with my parents' restaurant, just met with their lawyer.

That Girl From That Bar: Do you want me to come out there?

> **Me:** No, I'm handling it. Might be another week or so.

> **That Girl From That Bar:** Okay

Fuck. She's mad. One-word answers are a tell for her. I guess her patience does have a limit, but I can't deal with that right now. I'll just have to figure out how to fix it when I get back. Thinking that's the end of the exchange, I go back to figuring out how to reschedule the flight I had booked for first thing in the morning.

> **That Girl From That Bar:** I'm about to go meet with Sethy, I'll let him know.

> **Me:** Love you.

I watch as the message is marked read, but no response comes. Before I can give it much thought, Brooks plops two pint glasses of amber liquid on the table and slides into the booth across from me. The generous pours overflow onto the table, and he uses a couple of black bar napkins he brought with him to mop up the mess.

We sit in silence, avoiding eye contact, taking long pulls of our beers. Usually, I'm comfortable in silence. I'm not sure if it's the circumstances or the fact Brooks has changed more than I had realized, but this doesn't feel comfortable at all. It feels itchy, restless, and suffocating. He traces over one of the tattoos on his hand with his index finger, and I wonder if he's feeling the same. I bring my beer to my lips again, I could just start talking to make this feeling go away, but I honestly don't know where to start.

"You know, they laughed at me when I told them I wanted to learn how to tattoo right before I graduated," Brooks says in a low murmur looking off to the side at one of the TVs, not really watching the action though.

"Who?" I watch his profile, but it's not giving me any hint as to where he's going with this.

"Mom and Dad, who else? They actually laughed like I was standing there telling them a fucking knock-knock joke."

"Fuck." I swallow thickly a few times and shake my head. "I never knew about that, Brooks. I'm so sorry. I'm starting to think I didn't know much of anything." I look down at my beer and watch the small carbonated bubbles rise to the surface for a moment longer, thinking back to a night in early spring of my sophomore year.

15 Years Ago
(16 years old)

I lazily stroll home after spending the afternoon by the lake with Thea, my hormones still raging from our very long make-out session. We've been doing a lot of that since Christmas, when I found my balls and finally told her how I feel. As soon as I step into the house, my high disappears, and I sense the tension. It hangs thick in the air, stifling. Brooks has his music blasting in his room—something he does when he's pissed. I don't think much of it until I hear a loud crash from upstairs.

I run up the stairs, throw Brooks' door open, and stop in my tracks. His room is trashed. The dresser is pushed over, clothes spilling out of the drawers—that must have been the sound I heard. The sketches and watercolors he'd created over the years that had been hanging on every square inch of wall space now litter the floor, torn down and ripped to shreds. The wooden desk Dad built that Brooks uses as a space to sketch is nothing more than a pile of kindling in the corner. The bat he took to it—split almost in two—rests on top.

I step over to his stereo and turn down the volume. "Wh-what happened?"

"Get out." Brooks stands in front of his window with his back to me. He's breathing heavily. When I don't move, he picks up one of the books on his windowsill and chucks it in my direction. I barely manage to duck in time to avoid it hitting me in the face.

"Ugh. Fuck you!" I scream and slam his door shut behind me. That's what I get for trying to give a shit about that asshole. I make my way downstairs, figuring I'll let Mom and Dad deal with the mess he made and whatever's going on with him when they get back from the diner. His music starts back up again, the walls pulsing with the beat, making me roll my eyes.

It's not until a bit later when I'm eating the reheated diner leftovers that fill our fridge, that my anger dissipates, and I'm filled with a gnawing guilt. Brooks was crying. The quick look I got of his face when he turned with the book in his hand is burned into my mind. His face was red and splotchy, tears streaming down, eyelashes clumping together. Brooks never cries. I'm very familiar with his anger and smoldering fury but never the utter heartbreak that was etched into his features.

Present

Something about that night always felt off to me because of the way Brooks had acted; his storming rage was bigger than I'd ever seen it. It's not until this very moment I realize how catastrophic that night had been for him. That must have been the night he decided to give up on all his dreams. He wasn't a top student, and the only thing he was actually passionate about was art. His grades and attitude slipped further right around then. Our almost non-existent relationship crumbled to nothing entirely.

He had no interest in college. And despite his devil-may-care attitude, he needed his family's support. My sixteen-year old self couldn't pick up on that change in him at the time. I was too preoccupied with a new girlfriend, finishing the school year, and making summer plans. I don't think I saw Brooks ever drawing again from that day on.

"God, I wanted to get the fuck out of here so bad after high school. But I thought staying and throwing myself into the diner—and then RED—would make them *finally* take me seriously." His resigned words pull me back from my memories. "Guess the joke's on me." He huffs out a small, broken laugh then pauses, fingers absently playing with the condensation on his glass. "I know I don't have the business brain like Thea, and I would be no use in the kitchen like you. But I thought if they saw me stepping up and working hard to keep things going in the background, putting in the time helping Ripley with whatever he needs with barreling and what-not, they'd think I'm worth... something." He runs his hand down his face and then up over his short hair a few times. "I don't know. It's just a shit time."

A few beats pass as we're both lost in our own heads.

"Are you pissed they left it to Thea?" Brooks' eyes shoot to mine when I speak, and he scoffs.

"No," he says, shaking his head. "I'm pissed they left it to *you*."

After a few moments he continues, "She's worked her ass off there. She's the reason that place is anything right now. Mom and Dad struggled after you guys left. The diner never did well, and they refused to change anything. When you left it got even worse—they couldn't find reliable help. When they did finally find someone who stuck around for longer than a few weeks, we found out he had been skimming after he skipped town. I think they were ready to throw in the towel when Thea showed up on our doorstep unannounced asking for her job back. With her mom sick, Thea needed the money, and Mom and Dad didn't have the heart to tell her the job might only be there for a short time.

"I don't know if it was because they felt guilty about how things had been left with you or the things they said about Thea, but pretty much as soon as she managed to get her head out of her ass about you, she started changing things. Didn't even ask if it was okay. It was small at first, just putting together social media accounts for the diner and printing new menus that look like they came from this millennium. I think it pissed Dad off at first, but Mom didn't let him say anything for once."

Suddenly, a small smile breaks out on his face, and his eyes are unfocused on the space between us, like he's reliving a memory.

"Then one morning we got there to start opening the diner, and we found her sleeping in one of the booths with craft shit all over the place. She had stayed up half the night to put together a fucking... what do people call it? Like, a wall you take pictures in front of?" He looks at me expectantly.

"A selfie wall?" I provide.

"Yes! A fucking selfie wall. The town went crazy—fucking morons. The kids were suddenly there every day taking photos and posting on their social media, tagging the diner. She'd change the wall randomly, and they'd all flock again. The changes eventually started bringing in people from out of town. She organized live music nights and mom group meet-ups. I don't know how she got away with all of it, but Mom and Dad just let her have at it."

I smile imagining what Brooks describes. "Yeah, she has the ability to get her way and make you think it was your idea all along."

"She's a force, for sure. I don't know what you were thinking running her off." He shakes his head while taking another long pull from his glass, emptying it, and holding it up. "Another?"

I nod and drain my glass as well. Brooks stands and goes to the bar. He comes back with fresh drinks a minute later—this time instead of beer, he places two tumblers of dark brown liquor on the table.

"Indigo Hill's finest," he says. He takes a long sniff of the bourbon and follows it up with a small sip, which he rolls around in his mouth. "Fuck, that's good. Ripley's a damn genius."

"What's the story there? With Ripley, I mean. How'd he get involved... in the business?" I say as I sip my own drink. Brooks is right, the bourbon is fantastic, with deep vanilla notes and a crisp cherry finish. I swirl it around the glass, something about the flavor profile is familiar.

Brooks' lips tip up on one side, and there's a teasing glint in his eyes. "All your life you've been a man of few words, always to the point. Why don't you ask me what you really want to know?"

I imagine my face looks sheepish now that he's caught on to me. "How long has it been going on?" I know I don't have to expand on what *it* is.

"I'm not really sure exactly. They grew close quickly when she came back, but I don't think anything really happened until about a year ago. The little biddies that met every morning at the diner kept pestering her about 'getting over the Grant boy' and 'settling down,'" he says in a high-pitched, shaky voice. "She used to go on dates here and there, and then one day it was just him. I know he helped her a lot with her mom."

"How is her mom?" I saw her briefly at the funeral but didn't get a chance to talk to her. A woman, who I assume is her nurse, wheeled her away before the service even finished.

"She's at Saint Stephen's, the assisted living home here in Southbury. Thea's entire paycheck goes to cover the cost, but she's well taken care of." I guess the MS must have gotten worse if Thea put her in a facility. I can't imagine that was an easy decision for her.

"Why didn't you tell me any of this? I called you and asked about everything. About her. You told me nothing."

"What did you want me to say? Huh?" he says. "You wanted me to tell you how Mom and Dad almost lost the house... twice? How I'd hear them fight over money almost every night for years? How I considered setting that damn diner on fire just for the insurance payout?" His voice is steadily rising. "Or maybe I should have given you a play-by-play about how that fucking angel of a woman you managed to convince to love your sorry ass came back so destroyed I don't think I saw her smile for a year? How she had to work two jobs to pay for her mom's nurse?" He's breathing hard now. "You didn't want anything to do with it. You left and didn't look back. You have a whole new life, a woman you're crazy about on the other side of the country. You moved on, she moved on. Why would I bother telling you about her love life and how she's happy for the first time in years? Why are you even still here?"

With each word he says, my chest constricts a little more. *I didn't know.* I can keep repeating that to myself, and maybe I'll believe it one day. But the truth is, I didn't want to know, not really at least. I was happy living in my new life; I escaped the clutches this small town tried to get into me. I got out. Was there a trade off? As much as I'd like to deny it, I have regrets. I lost my family by chasing my dreams, and I lost my heart trying to keep them.

"I'm sorry you didn't get to have the life you wanted," I say quietly.

"Don't be sorry for me. I've made peace with my lot in life. It looks different from what I had envisioned fifteen years ago, but I'm not entirely miserable. I just thought Mom and Dad saw me as more than a disappointment they didn't trust to carry on their life's work. I just hope you figure out what you're doing fast and do right by Thea and what she built here."

Something in the way he's been talking about Thea and all she's done since I left gives me pause. I take in his sad but determined eyes.

"Are you in love with her?" I say, remembering his and Thea's conversation from this morning.

"What the *fuck* are you talking about?" he says and looks at me like that might be the last thing he expected to come out of my mouth.

"You seem... protective of her. Invested in her happiness. You were never like this before. And I heard her saying you tried to kiss her." I raise an eyebrow at him, and he rolls his eyes.

"Oh, fuck off. We went on two dates just to shut Mom and the rest of the town up. We were both miserable and now have a laugh about it every once in a while. As for my concern about her happiness—I am *deeply* invested in making sure that girl smiles as much as humanly possible. She deserves everything good for what she's done for this family, this town."

With that, all the fight leaves me, and I down what's left in my glass. Brooks follows suit and goes to settle the tab. As I wait for him, I realize why the taste of the bourbon is familiar. We just started carrying it at my restaurant, and the taste of it lingered on my tongue when I got the call that brought me out here.

The drive back is silent, but this silence is welcome. There's so much I missed, so much I didn't know about, and it's making me think back on my time here.

The more I think about everything he told me, the more the guilt and regret gnaw at me.

Chapter Six

Carrington

I was surprised how easily Thea accepted my invitation to meet for coffee this morning. My talk with Brooks yesterday answered a lot of questions I've had since coming back, but it also sprouted a million more. Paired with the meeting at the lawyer's office, I realize I missed so much in the time I stayed away. I guess a part of me foolishly expected for everything and everyone in Indigo Hill to be frozen in time. I'm hoping Thea can help fill in the remaining blanks.

I'm handing over a few bills to the young barista behind the counter to pay for my order when the bell above the door signals someone coming in. I turn and find Thea stepping inside, her blonde waves resting softly around her face. Her whiskey-colored eyes settle on me, and I see her mentally building up her walls brick by brick with every step she takes toward me.

She looks tired, bone tired. I guess yesterday's news didn't help her stress-induced insomnia. She always had trouble sleeping when dealing with big changes or challenges in her life. The lack of sleep would then put more strain on whatever situation caused the problem, and it would be a vicious cycle until something gave out—unfortunately, it was usually her tired body. She'd crash hard and sleep for days.

Barely knowing how to deal with my own emotional state, I was never good at comforting her. My tactic of ignore-the-problem-and-distract-with-food-and-fun worked somewhat. Until it didn't.

"Hey," she says to me and then turns to the woman at the register. "Can I please have—"

"A small coffee in a medium cup, four pumps of classic, and light cream to the brim," I recite.

She looks up at me, her brown eyes disbelieving. After a moment she says, "I add a sprinkle of chocolate powder on top now." We stare at each other for a moment longer until the spell is broken by the barista sliding over our drinks. I drop a couple more bills and pick up both drinks, holding one out to her. Our fingers brush as she takes it with a quiet, "Thanks."

We plant ourselves at a table in the back of the café next to a floor-to-ceiling built-in bookshelf that's bursting at the seams.

Grayce's Café has a grand total of six tables, each of them surrounded by mismatched chairs that look like they were scavenged from flea markets and yard sales. It's a tiny space located on the north side of the town's main square, squished between Oopsie Daisy, the town's sole florist, and an empty corner space that looks like it hasn't had a tenant in years, based on the yellow-tinged paper covering the windows.

The café wasn't here before I left, and everything looks fairly new. The walls are white-washed brick, and the pendant lights cast a soft glow over everything, creating an inviting atmosphere to get comfortable for a long stay devouring a coffee or tea along with one of their delicious looking pastries. It's made all the more cozy by the numerous plants hanging from every surface and the many pieces of folksy artwork adorning the walls. It makes sense why Thea chose this place. It looks like it was made for her.

"How are you feeling after yesterday?" I start.

"It was... a lot. I really didn't know what to expect when I got to the lawyer's office, but it wasn't... that." She pauses to take a sip of her coffee and closes her eyes, savoring it. "What are we going to do?"

"I've been thinking about that. I want to get to know the business. See what you built here," I say tentatively. Our interactions have been far less than friendly up until now, and I'm trying to choose my words carefully. The hard set of her jaw tells me she came here gearing up for a fight. I can only imagine what she thinks I plan to do. The truth is, I have no fucking clue what I want to do about it. The contents of the will were even more unexpected for me. I still don't understand why they left me something that clearly meant so much to not only them but both Brooks and Thea.

"You do?" She watches carefully, her gaze shifting back and forth between my eyes like she'll find the truth there.

"I can't make any decisions without knowing the full scope of things. Brooks told me a little about how it all came about, and I have to say, I'm impressed with what you've done. He told me how you helped my parents turn things around. That couldn't have been easy." I see my words are having an effect when she smiles softly, the ice in her eyes thawing a touch.

"He gives me entirely too much credit. We couldn't have done half of it without him, and none of it without Ripley." I clench my jaw at the mention of Ripley but stay quiet letting her continue. "The diner was on its last leg when... I came back. I could tell your parents were planning on closing it down, so I just put all the ideas you had for it into action and hoped for the best. Thankfully, it worked, and things started changing. But I didn't do it alone. Anyone who claims I did is lying"

"That," I lean in and point in the general direction of RED just a block away with a shake of my head, "that was not my idea." I immediately see hurt and maybe a little bit of fear flash across her face and quickly add, "I would never have thought of anything as incredible as that. Not only is it stunning, but from what I've seen, it's also had a huge impact here." Her presence seems to be doing something to me because I'm not entirely sure I'm talking about RED anymore. I clear my throat and sit back in the chair, putting some space between us.

"I first got the idea for RED shortly after I came back. Ripley came into the diner one day, and we reconnected instantly." Her face and voice soften thinking about him, while a pit opens in my stomach, a feeling I try not to examine too closely. "He had just gotten back into town himself. Right after he graduated high school, he moved to Kentucky where he got a job at a small-batch distillery working for a family friend who overlooked his age. He spent a few years there learning everything he could." She pauses to bring her coffee to her lips.

"His grandfather used to make moonshine. Ripley helped him with it when he was a kid, so the interest was always there. After his grandfather passed, I think he thought of it as a way to keep his memory alive, not realizing he'd be damn good at it. But anyway, we got drunk one night and started planning a hypothetical distillery. We laughed it off, but the idea just wouldn't let go, so I did a ton of research on what we'd need to launch it and brought a business plan to your parents. I must have caught them on a good day because they were all for it. It took some time, but we found a bank willing to give them a business loan—it helped that the land the diner stood on was worth triple the actual business. The distillery building went up first, once that was operational, we razed the diner and built the restaurant."

"Wow, that seems like... a lot of work. You're amazing, Thea." I'm so caught up in her recounting the last eight years, I don't even realize what slipped out of my mouth. She immediately flinches. *Shit*. I'm trying to get her to open up and trust me so we can work through this together, but I feel like anytime I'm finally getting somewhere with her, I say something inappropriate, and she shuts down again.

"I told you, it wasn't all me. Owen and Hazel designed a lot of the interior, and Brooks did all the branding for the distillery. He created the sign outside. I don't think I've ever seen your parents as proud as they were the day it was installed. I think they stood out there just staring up at it for an hour."

"I had no idea," I say.

"I had forgotten how talented he is." Her tone turns warm again. I'm seeing a bit of the old Thea shining through—she's always the most animated when she's talking about people she cares for. "He was so cute when he came to me with a sketch of his idea. He was so nervous he asked me not to tell your parents where it came from. Of course, they immediately loved it. I've had other business owners come to me over the years asking for the name of my designer. You've probably seen his work around town. I keep telling him he should get his name out there and start getting paid for the work, but he refuses. Maybe you can talk to him."

We both grow quiet. She knows just as well as I do I have no say in what my brother does. I barely had any influence over him before I left, and I definitely don't these days.

"What's your plan now?" I say switching the topic.

"I—I don't know. We had plans for another expansion, but now..." She pauses and takes a deep breath, and I know she's psyching herself up to say something. "Let's cut to the chase. What's *your* plan here? I can't afford to buy you out, not yet at least. I've looked into my finances, and I just can't swing it right now with everything else. I'm willing to keep things going as they have been, and maybe we can come up with some sort of payment plan so I can buy your share over time..." she trails off, a challenge in her eyes.

"I haven't made any decisions. I think I need to get a lay of the land and see how things are being run, what's working, what the plans are for the future."

Her gaze turns hard, and I know I've said something wrong again.

"So you plan on staying?" The words leave her lips, and panic fills her eyes.

"For a little bit, but I have to get back to Seattle soon. I have to go back to Car—my restaurant. My manager can only do so much without me there."

She nods in understanding before saying, "How involved are you planning on being here? The expansion we had in mind can't be put into motion 3,000 miles away if you plan on being in charge of it. And if I'm being honest, I have it handled. You can stay on as an investor or something. I don't need a partner or a boss. I don't know why they did this."

"I don't either, but I honestly don't have an answer for you right now on how it'll all work. I just need all the details before I'll feel comfortable making a decision."

The silence stretches out between us, and I shift in my seat trying to find a way back to a more comfortable topic when the bell above the door rings. Thea's eyes dart over to see who came in, and a smile breaks out on her face, the tension from a moment ago gone. I turn around and see Ripley making his way over to us.

Great.

If this wasn't the only coffee shop in town, I'd think this was planned.

"Hey, babe," he says, sitting down in an empty chair next to Thea and giving her cheek a quick kiss. He then turns to me. "Hey, Cary."

I give him a small up nod and a blank expression in greeting.

"You're here early. I can't remember the last time you rolled out of bed before eleven," Thea says with what I think is a knowing smirk.

"Well if *someone* hadn't made a racket getting dressed and out of the house this morning, I'd still be happily in bed," Ripley says, and I track his arm as it slips over the back of Thea's chair. She seems to find comfort in his grip but doesn't melt into it.

Not like she used to with me. I shove that thought aside quickly.

"I tried to be quiet, but I couldn't find my jeans." It's then I notice she's wearing the same clothes from yesterday, and the pit in my stomach from earlier opens up wider than ever.

"All good," he replies with an easy smile, settling back in his chair, his eyes on me. Ripley seems to be one of those people who's comfortable in any situation. I'm sure he can sense the tension radiating off of me, and there's a bit of a challenge in his eyes. "Whatchya guys up to?"

"We're trying to figure out what to do with RED after everything we learned yesterday." He nods at her, clearly already aware of the details of the situation.

"I'm not sure much needs to change. We all know you could run that place with your eyes closed... single-handedly," he says this to Thea with warmth, but his eyes are anything but when they cut to me.

Single-handedly—as in, without me.

Got it, Rip. You don't want me here, and Thea doesn't need me.

"Oh, stop, I know everything you do for that place in the background. Not to mention, I wouldn't even know where to start when it comes to the distillery," Thea says.

"Nothing a few hands-on demonstrations can't fix," he says salaciously. My molars grind at the insinuation, and I have to look away from the look they share.

It's then Ripley's phone chimes, and he pulls it out, quickly glancing at it.

"Oh, I have to run—Brooks says he can meet me early to transfer the mash. We're still on for tonight?"

"Tonight?" asks Thea with a questioning look on her face.

"Yeah, it's Thursday. Date night," he says, waggling his eyebrows.

I roll my eyes, but neither of them is paying any attention to me.

Thea chuckles. "Wouldn't miss it. Will you have time to take me to grab my car beforehand?"

"Of course, babe. See you, Cary." He gives her a quick kiss on the forehead, grabs a coffee at the counter, and is out the door. Thea's eyes follow him until he's out of sight.

"You seem... happy with him." My chest burns as I speak those words.

"He's... my person." Her eyes are warm with affection for the man. "He was there when I needed him, and I can't imagine what my life would look like without him." Each word feels like a papercut to my skin. I recall a time when I had been her person. I know her intention isn't to hurt me, and I honestly don't know why I'm feeling like this. She's allowed to be with whomever she wants. I'm glad to see her happy. But I can't shake this feeling that *he's* not the one who should be making her happy.

"I'm thinking we should reopen the restaurant to the public on Monday. People have been calling asking for reservations, and the staff needs to get back to work, a lot of them rely on tips," says

Thea. "We also have a big charity event this Saturday that's been booked for months that I need to finalize the prep for."

"Okay, I'll come in and help with the prep. You can show me what there is to know about RED, and I'll try to make myself useful in any way I can."

Thea nods in agreement, and we make tentative plans to meet at the restaurant mid-morning tomorrow. I sit alone at the coffee shop for a long while after she says goodbye, reflecting on everything we talked about.

I knew coming back here to deal with my parents' deaths would be difficult. I just didn't realize how excruciating it would be to have to deal with that while also seeing the woman I used to love more than the breath in my lungs love someone else.

When did I become a fucking masochist?

Chapter Seven

Should someone who's only had a handful of hours of sleep in the last week go drinking and out for date night? Probably not, but I'm not about to cancel on Ripley. Besides, I need a little bit of normal after everything that's happened. Going out with Ripley guarantees a night of laughter and getting out of my own head—which is probably why he'd been so adamant.

Louie's isn't fancy by any means, but the food is decent, and the jukebox is free. Ripley walks over to our booth from the bar with the drinks in hand.

"I got you your new favorite," he says with a smirk tilting the corner of his mouth, knowing he's the creator of my "new favorite." I'm not usually one to drink bourbon straight, but this new recipe of his goes down so smoothly that it'd be a shame to mix it with anything.

"No need to be cocky. Everyone in this town knows you make the best bourbon," I say rolling my eyes at him. He has every right to be cocky though. It's in such high demand we're getting calls from distributors all over the country wanting to sell it to their clients.

A small smile creeps up his lips. It makes me giddy that he's almost as proud of himself as I am of him.

"So…" he draws the word out as he brings his glass to his lips, the tone of his voice telling me he's about to ask me something I won't like. "Coffee with Cary, huh? Why didn't you tell me *that* was happening?"

Carrington Grant is the last thing I want to talk about on our date night. My eyes wander while I think of what to say. There are couples on the dance floor already, a few guys playing pool at the billiards tables, and more people just walking in. It's the only place in town to hang out this late—other than RED—so people are flocking to it since we're still closed.

It's not that I want to hide anything from Ripley, he knows all there is to know about my past relationship. I just can't figure out my own feelings about Carrington being back. Seeing him again has brought up all the memories I keep buried deep down. Finding out we are now business partners has left me numb.

Over the years—when we were together—I urged Cary to reconnect with his parents, but he insisted he'd closed that chapter, leaving no room for argument. I keep trying to rack my brain to figure out why Owen and Hazel did this. Why not just leave it all to Brooks? That made the most sense. But no, they left it to the son who hasn't spoken to them in over a decade and… me.

I turn my face back to Ripley. "Because there was nothing to tell. Owen and Hazel put us in a situation where I have to talk to him even if I don't want to." I heave a long, resigned sigh. "I was hoping he'd say yes to the payment plan idea, but that would have been too easy, I guess."

He reaches across the table and grabs my hand. "Maybe he still will. He's probably just in shock like the rest of us."

"That's definitely possible." I take another sip of the bourbon, keeping my other hand wrapped in Ripley's on top of the table. "I guess my issue is that his life isn't here. He can't expect me to believe he plans to stay in South Carolina for any length of time when he has a whole life in Seattle. Probably a girlfriend too." I don't like the way my voice sounds strained on that last part. The thought that's plagued me since I saw him standing in front of RED invades my mind again. I shouldn't care if he has a girlfriend. I *don't* care if he has a girlfriend. I'm just trying to make my point.

"Would it bother you... if he did?" His voice is lower than before so no one around us can hear.

"What? No. Obviously not. I'm just saying his life isn't here. Finding out RED exists shouldn't change that."

Ripley squeezes my hand, making me meet his gaze before responding, "I don't think RED is the issue."

I pull my hand from his then pour the rest of the bourbon in my glass down my throat, letting the smooth burn distract me for a moment. "Can we not? This has nothing to do with me." I stare back out to the crowd of people around the bar. Shelley, the bartender who's always here on Thursday nights, looks like she's ready to call for reinforcements. No one blames us for closing to take our time to grieve, but I feel a bit guilty as I watch her panicked eyes look over to the door as someone else enters.

Ripley pulls his hand back to his side of the table, a hint of hurt on his face evident. "Right, of course not. Sorry." He stands up, and for a moment, I think he's actually mad at me before he says,

"I'm gonna grab us another round." I nod my head in response then watch him walk toward the bar. He waves at Shelley to let her know he's there, and she holds up a finger to tell him it'll be a moment.

I run a slightly shaky hand through my blonde waves. A thought registers then: I don't know when I ate last. All I had today was the coffee with Carrington, then I went back home to look through my finances again in hopes that I missed something. Ripley and I got my car from Southbury this afternoon, but it was well after lunch.

I pull my phone out of my purse and scroll until I find Ripley's name. Who knows how long he'll be at the bar waiting, and maybe I can smooth over whatever just happened.

Me: Can you order us some food while you're up? I doubt Shelley will be able to leave the bar tonight.

I watch as he grabs his phone from his back pocket, checks the notification, and looks in my direction, sending me a wink like the absolute flirt he is.

Ripley: Of course. Usual?

> **Me:** Mhmm, but I think I want cheese fries tonight.

> **Ripley:** You got it, babe. **winky face emoji**

> **Me:** Thank you **heart emoji**

My mind settles seeing he's not upset. That would be the last thing I need to deal with right now. I'm still internally panicking over what tomorrow will bring with Carrington shadowing me at RED. I feel like I have to prove something to him. As much as I disagree with Owen and Hazel's decision to leave the business to the both of us, I also know I played a large role in making RED what it is today. I may have taken some of the ideas Carrington had before we left for Seattle, but I was still the one who put those plans into place. I was still the one here pretty much running the show all while he was living his shiny, new life.

And the responsibilities weren't just at the diner, or RED once we renovated, I've been taking care of my mom as well. He has no idea everything that I've been through or all the ways I've changed since he knew me eight years ago.

The fact he's even contemplating keeping his share of the business is infuriating when he apparently has his own restaurant in

Seattle. If I wasn't annoyed with everything, I'd probably be proud of him. I know how big of a deal owning his own restaurant is to him. And maybe I should have congratulated him earlier when he let it slip, but it wasn't the time.

On second thought, I should have been harsher when we spoke today. I should have told him he doesn't get to come back and start taking things from me when I finally found my footing.

The more I think about it, the madder I get. I never blamed him for what happened with us. I knew I was the problem, but if he takes the one thing that brings me the kind of joy I saw on his face when he got his first head chef job in Seattle, I'll never forgive him.

Pulling me out of my thoughts, the ladies a couple booths down attempt to whisper their gossip, but they've had too much to drink to realize they aren't *actually* whispering.

"Do you think she'll leave Ripley and go running back to the Grant boy?"

"If she does, I'll make sure Rip is taken care of." They both cackle at that, and I shake my head, letting out a deep sigh. I swear to God the people of this town can't ever mind their own fucking business.

Right on cue, Ripley returns with a tray of shots and lets me know the food will be out shortly. I try to put a smile back on my face, but he notices my mood has shifted.

"You up for a game of 'Redneck Wrecked?'"

I raise my eyebrows at him, my lips turning up at the corners. I swear he always knows what to say and what to do if I'm feeling down. It's some kind of weird sixth sense.

"You trying to get me drunk, Quinn Ripley?"

He shrugs his shoulders innocently. "Depends, will I get to take advantage of you later?"

I can't stop the laugh from escaping my lips as I roll my eyes. We invented the game years ago. It started at RED but really took off once we made date night at Louie's a weekly tradition. We don't always start the dates here, but we always end them here.

The game is a run-of-the-mill drinking game with an ever-growing rule list. The first rule being Ripley likes to change the rules halfway through the game once he's had a few. The drunker we get, the less we remember how to play anyway, so it works.

Since Louie's has so many regulars, it's mostly based on them. If Shelley gets hit on, I have to take a shot. If Bob plays "Should've Been a Cowboy" by Toby Keith on the jukebox, Ripley takes a shot. If Patricia, two booths down—who's already made comments tonight—hits on Ripley, we both have to take two shots. It goes on and on. Usually within thirty minutes, we're both tipsy and ready to dance.

"Maybe just a little." I smirk back at him as Shelley walks over with our food.

"Sorry for the wait, love. It's packed tonight," she says as she sets the plates on the table.

"No need to apologize, Shell. We appreciate you bringing it out to us," I offer back to her with a smile.

"You two lovebirds need anything else before I go back to drowning at the bar?" The nervous laugh accompanying the question lets me know it's better to just say no.

"If it's anything other than a drink, we'll grab it. But we won't say no to a couple more of these," Ripley says while waving his glass a little.

"Sure thing," Shelley grumbles as she walks off to the bar.

"You're brave," I say as I grab one of his tater tots and plop it into my mouth.

"What? Why?" he responds in an oblivious tone.

"If you haven't noticed, she looks one drink order away from walking out tonight."

"If I say I haven't, will that make me seem like less of an asshole?" He grimaces.

I can't help but laugh. If there's one thing Ripley isn't, it's an asshole. The man is a saint, and no one can deny that.

As soon as I open my mouth to answer, he stops me by pointing toward the bar where a dark-haired man, maybe 5'5" at the most and dressed in a suit, leans over the bar to get Shelley's attention. We both watch intently to see if he hits on her, and sure enough, the second she walks toward him, his whole demeanor changes. We can't hear what he says, but it's obvious from their body language it was something crude. We see Shelley walk away, rolling her eyes as she prepares his order.

Ripley points to my glass. "Drink up."

"We didn't even hear what he said, I don't think that should count."

"Oh, it definitely counts. Come on, Thea, down the hatch." He reaches over for one of my cheese fries before giving my drink a very pointed look.

I inhale a deep sigh then grab my shot to do as he says. "You really are trying to get me drunk."

He chuckles then says, "And it's working."

Once we're done eating, I walk over to the jukebox to line up some songs for us. Albeit, the selection isn't great, but it's free, so it's hard to complain. I find a few that strike my interest then head back to the table to wait for them to queue up. Thanks to the game, I'm feeling a little more like myself and a little less like the sad, husk version of me I've been for the last week.

As I plop back down in the booth across from Ripley, I say, "I know what you're doing."

He gives me a curious look then says, "Oh?"

I shake my head. "Mhmm. You know, most guys would get a girl drunk so she'll sleep *with* them."

He laughs then replies, "Who's to say I'm not doing just that?"

I point my finger at him and shake it menacingly. "You, Quinn Ripley, are trying to get me drunk enough so I'll sleep. Period."

"You caught me. But you can't blame me. You'd do the same for me."

I nod my head at that. "I would, you're right."

We both take another drink, a comfortable silence falling over us. The familiar tune of Savage Garden's "I Want You" starts to play, and I can't help the grin spreading across my face.

Ripley laughs then unfolds his six-foot-two frame out of the booth and steps over to my side, holding out a hand for me to take. "I guess it's time to dance."

CHAPTER EIGHT

Carrington

*W*hy am I still here?

I stopped by to pick up the late dinner I called in since this seems to be the only place still open past six o'clock, but when I saw Thea I couldn't get my feet to walk out the front door. She was looking intently at the jukebox, her brow all furrowed like it gets when she's thinking really hard. I can tell she's had few drinks by the flush in her cheeks making her freckles stand out.

It wasn't until she went back to a booth that I saw Ripley waiting for her.

Date night.

The thought churns my stomach, and the flirty look she gives him as she sits has my hands clenching tight.

After paying and thanking the frazzled looking woman behind the counter, I squeeze myself into a tiny back corner table that I can only assume isn't meant for patrons, just for the staff to roll silverware or take their breaks. It's pretty dark here, so I feel comfortable that I won't be noticed. From where I'm sitting, I have a perfect view of the entire bar, including the dance floor *and* their booth.

I can't hear what's being said over the noise of the busy bar, but I see Thea point her finger at Ripley, seeming to chastise him. The song switches over to something vaguely familiar from the late 90s, and the most breathtaking grin spreads over her face. *Fuck.* It feels like a lifetime ago that I saw her smile like that. What I wouldn't do for it to be directed at me right now.

Ripley stands and extends his hand toward Thea with a flourish. Still smiling so wide her nose crinkles, she places her hand in his, and they make their way to the center of the dance floor. He spins her slowly with one arm above her head, and they both start moving to the music, one hand held loosely between them. I watch as Thea's hips sway from side to side to the beat, her strong, tanned thighs on display in jean cutoffs.

Why is it suddenly so hot in here?

They look good together—he's got a hipster vibe about him which I'm begrudged to admit fits with her girl-next-door appearance. The ease with which they move and how in sync they are speaks volumes for how intimately they know each other. There's no hesitation in him when he runs his hands down her sides to her hips, pulling her into his body. He leans in and says something in her ear, and she shakes her head.

My eyes bounce around to every spot their bodies touch as they continue to dance—chests, thighs, arms, hips. My breathing picks up as I zero in on where his palms keep their hold when she turns around and dances with her back to his front. She turns her face, throwing him a flirty look over her shoulder, and his lips graze her temple.

Suddenly I'm transported back ten years ago to another dance floor on the other side of the country on a night similar to this.

"Let's get out of here," I say into her ear before kissing the spot right below it, making my intentions clear. Her body is hot as her ass grinds against my hard cock, and I can taste the salt from the sweat on her skin from the hours we've spent dancing. Thea pulls back, meeting my eyes over her shoulder with a heated look, and nods.

The taxi ride back to our apartment takes way too long, and the buzz from the drinks we shared is flowing freely in my bloodstream, but it's not the only thing heating me up. Thea's thigh rubs against mine as we share a deep kiss in the back of the car, my hand cupping her jaw, tongue sliding against hers.

I'm already peeling off her shirt as we step in through our apartment door, only separating from her lips long enough to pull it over her head. She's not wearing a bra, and I groan as my hands immediately find her perfect breasts. We make our way to our bedroom, slipping out of the rest of our clothes, both laughing as I stumble when my pants get caught on my foot.

She looks so fucking gorgeous lying spread out on our bed, sandy hair spread over the white pillow, pale pink nipples peaked.

"I've been thinking about your cunt all night. Is it wet for me?" I say reverently as I kiss my way down her navel, her hands in my hair, nails grazing my scalp.

The rest of the memory is a blur of her warm body moving with mine, mouths tasting each other, and filthy whispers in the dark. The image of my hand running over her soft skin transforms to that of *his* in the same position, and I shake my head to clear the thoughts of what they'll get up to later tonight. My jaw feels wired shut, and a cinder block sits on my chest. All I can do is try to draw in breath through my nose, hoping I'm getting enough oxygen so I don't pass out.

The song ends and gentle guitar strums sound, signaling the start of a song I recognize: "Until I Found You" by Stephen Sanchez. Without missing a beat, Ripley spins Thea around again and pulls her in. His hand slides in around her waist while she grips his shoulder, their other hands clasped together and drawn into their chests. They sway gently, spinning slowly, her temple resting against his chin. Thea's eyes are closed, and she looks content. I rub my sternum to help relieve some of the pressure in my chest. I still can't take a full breath.

I'm so engrossed with watching them I barely register the couple taking a seat at a table not too far from mine. From a quick glance, I recognize Mr. and Mrs. Davis. I shrink back into the corner, further into the shadow. They're in their late seventies and have been a staple in Indigo Hill since long before I was born. They never had kids of their own, which wasn't a problem for them because they became the unofficial grandparents to everyone in town. Brooks and I were often left with them when Mom and Dad couldn't find a sitter in a pinch, not that it was ever something we despised since Mrs. Davis is a fantastic cook. Her homemade chicken noodle soup is still some of the best I've ever had.

"Aw, look at that, Terry," Mrs. Davis says to her husband, tipping her chin toward the dance floor. Mr. Davis looks in the same direction. "I'm telling you: soulmates."

"You said the same thing when she was with the Grant boy," he grumbles back affectionately to his wife. I now realize they're talking about Thea and Ripley who continue to dance closely. *Soulmates.* That's exactly what they look like, and the thought fully knocks the breath from my lungs. They're looking at each other like there's no one else in the room, exchanging a few words every once in a while followed by fond smiles.

"No, I said he was her *great love*. There's a difference. That's the love you don't find twice in a lifetime. Soulmates lift you up and make you shine. Like that." She angles her head again toward the dance floor where Thea, still clinging to Ripley's shoulder, has thrown her head back laughing loudly enough at something he said that her musical laughter reaches my ears. Mr. Davis hums at her comment.

"Well, she sure does look happy now." There's a pause as they watch the couple for a while longer, then their conversation turns to the menu. The backs of my eyes prickle, and a lump forms in my throat. Between seeing them this morning and now this, everything in my head is all mixed up. I grab my to-go bag and slip around the people in the busy bar and out the door where the cool air hits my overheated skin.

Jealousy.

I can name the emotion I'm feeling. And it's because I can put a name to it that I find myself checking the time on my phone. It's only seven in Seattle. The phone is ringing in my ear before the door even closes behind me.

"It's been a while since I've heard from you. You had me worried you didn't need me anymore." Not even a hello; I love how straight forward she is.

"I'm sorry to call after hours, Dr. Ferris. Do you have a minute to talk?"

7.5 Years Ago

(24 years old)

"So what brings you in today?" Dr. Donna Ferris asks me. She's the most average- looking woman I have ever met. Average height, shoulder-length brown hair with caramel highlights, plain face. Her brown eyes aren't exactly warm, but she appears open and patiently waiting for my answer. Her unassuming appearance is comforting somehow—there's very little to draw my focus.

"My friend is worried about me," I finally say after searching for the right words for a long moment. It's vague and not a very useful place to start, but trying to put everything in my head into words makes my skin feel tight.

"Why is your friend worried about you?" she asks, tone still even.

I look down at my fingers, checking over my cuticles like I'll find the answer written there. "He said that I'm—and I'm using his words here—about to blow the biggest fucking chance of my life because I can't get over some bitch."

"And how did you feel when he said that to you?"

How did it make me feel? Is she serious? *I roll my eyes internally. I knew this was a bad idea—a shrink isn't going to help me. A cardiologist maybe. That's the doctor you call when your heart has been ripped out, right?*

"I punched him in the face." I look up at her as I say this, trying to get a reaction.

"That's what you did." She levels me with what I'm assuming is her signature unaffected look. "I asked how you felt about what he said."

Well fuck. *This is going to be harder than I thought.*

Present

"Well, it sounds to me like you know what you have to do." Dr. Ferris' monotone voice finds me on the other end of the line. I've gotten used to—and even appreciate—her detached way of evaluating the struggles I share with her. She's pushed me out of my comfort zone over the years without ever really applying any pressure.

The last ten days have been a real test for all I've learned about handling my emotions—*express, don't repress*—and I've found myself reverting to old coping mechanisms. A talk with her was overdue. She always helps me find perspective when I'm spiraling.

"Yeah, but knowing what I have to do and actually doing it are two very different things," I reply. With a sigh I add, "Thank you for taking my call so late, I know you didn't have to."

In a rare moment of sincerity she says, "I hope you know I'm really proud of you. What you're going through is not easy: grieving your parents, reconnecting with a former partner and friend, inheriting a business you knew nothing about. It would be very easy for you to shut down and internalize right now. You've come such a long way from our first meeting, and I hope you know I will always answer when you call."

I clear my throat before speaking. "Thank you, have a good night."

Dr. Ferris' words echo in my mind as I stroll back to my hotel in the cool night air. I do know what I have to do—something I should have done years ago.

Chapter Nine

I wipe my clammy hands on the front of my pants. Carrington should be here any moment now, and I can't get my nerves under control. Thankfully, I'm at least well-rested after last night's game of 'Redneck Wrecked' wrecked me. That was Ripley's goal all along. He knew a night out was the only thing that would work with how in my head I've been.

I slept a full eight hours. Ripley made sure to give me ibuprofen last night, in hopes it would keep the inevitable hangover at bay. All I woke up with was a minor headache, and thank God for that, considering tomorrow we are hosting a big charity event, A Night of Hope—a gala supporting domestic violence prevention. I need to be on my A-game. This event is one of the biggest ones that RED has on the books for this year. The entire space has been rented out along with the patio area. We're hoping the event will bring us more like it since the company hosting has a huge client list.

Now that it's just me and Brooks handling it, I'm nervous. Ripley was always going to be out of town for it, but Hazel and Owen would have been here. And once again, Carrington being in town isn't helping. If anything, it's a distraction.

I finalized the menu for the event with our head chef, Travis, earlier, and Ripley made sure we had enough liquor on hand before he left this morning. I still have to print the menus for the table settings. The to-do list is long and seems to be growing. I don't have time to deal with Carrington wanting a tour and to be shown how things work around here.

I look over at the clock by the entrance to the kitchen and see that it's ten-fifty-nine. Carrington told me he'd be here at eleven. If he's late, maybe I'll just lock the door and pretend like I forgot. He doesn't have a key yet, so it seems like a decent plan.

I roll my eyes at myself knowing I don't have it in me to be that petty. And it wouldn't matter anyway because he walks in at eleven on the dot.

"Hey," he says as he hands me a to-go cup and steps around me, farther into the restaurant. He pushes his sunglasses up onto his head, pulling my focus to his long chestnut hair tied back at the nape of his neck. I haven't gotten used to the new style just yet, but I can't deny that it looks good. Not that being handsome was ever an issue for him. The man never even had an awkward teenage phase.

"Hi," I reply before I take a tentative sip of the drink he brought me. It's my regular coffee order, exactly how I like it. He even remembered the chocolate powder. *Damn him.*

Carrington is looking around, seemingly taking it all in. It hits me then he hasn't actually been inside RED—the new restaurant or the distillery next door. It must have been odd to be handed the ownership having never seen the place.

I take a deep breath, only meaning to clear my head, but his gaze snaps back to me like it was aimed at him to get his attention.

"Sorry, I just... didn't realize how different everything would look." His voice is somber. I guess he expected the decor to be reminiscent of what he left behind and not up-scale.□

I give him a small smile before saying, "We did... a lot of remodeling. We kept the patio but otherwise, almost everything changed. It had to." Carrington knows how outdated the diner was. It shouldn't come as too much of a surprise that the place was gutted to make all of this happen. This used to be a one-story building with checkered floors all throughout—the kind that were popular in the 1950s. Now the floor is lined with wood in the dining areas and decorative tiles in the kitchen and bathrooms. We wanted it to have personality without being too loud. The second floor only goes halfway across the building, overlooking the front lobby with a vaulted ceiling and light wooden beams stretching across it.

Like I'd told him before, the patio stayed, but now there's a two-story floor-to-ceiling wall of windows that leads to it. The goal was to make sure you could see the lake even from inside and give the whole space tons of natural light. I love to sit by those windows when it rains. The raindrops rush down the window like tears cascading down a cheek. It's always calmed me for some reason.

We leaned into the natural, earth-loving look with a sage green and linen palette for the decor. There are gold accents and light fixtures throughout. The lake is our biggest draw, so we didn't want to take away from its beauty or the nature surrounding it.

He nods like he's trying to wrap his head around everything. I give him another second, knowing it'll take more than that to truly come to terms with it all. His eyes land on the two photos on the wall behind the hostess stand. One of them he's familiar with, the other is new to him and possibly the most recent photo he's seen of his parents in the thirteen years they didn't speak. His feet seem to move toward it of their own accord. I'm spellbound as I watch him stare at the photo, wondering what he could be thinking. Is he regretful they went so long without speaking? Is he wishing he'd been here to see all of this happen?

Without meaning to, I say, "That was the day before we re-opened under the new name." He looks over his shoulder at me for a moment before turning back, and some of the tension in his body disappears. "Brooks took the photo for us, insisting he didn't need to be in it. I don't think I'd ever seen your parents so happy." I pause to get up the nerve for what I want to say next. "That night," I walk toward him, stopping just a few steps behind him, "all they could talk about was how much they wished you were here with us."

Carrington's head shoots around to look at me, not realizing I'm much closer now. He closes the space between us so we're standing just inches apart. I have to tilt my head up to look him in the eyes. "Why... why would they say that?" Confusion and regret lace his words.

I shrug my shoulders, knowing it feels too nonchalant for this conversation. "Because it was true. They loved you, Carrington."

His ocean eyes scan my face, possibly looking for a tell that I'm lying to him. He's so close I can clearly see each of the striations in his eyes that I loved so much. They're more prominent in this moment; they remind me of the surf crashing into the shore then pulling back into the tide, leaving only seafoam in its wake. I'm so entranced by them, I don't realize his hand is reaching for my face until his fingers push my hair behind my ear.

"Why do you keep calling me that?" His voice is so low that even if someone were in the room with us, they wouldn't be able to catch what he said. I give him a puzzled look, and he clarifies, "Carrington. You keep calling me Carrington instead of Cary."

At that, whatever spell held me breaks, and I try to step away, but he grabs my hand. The moment I look down at our interlaced fingers, he lifts my chin up with his other hand.

"Answer me, Thea." His voice is strained. He's holding on by a thread. My heart gallops in my chest as I stare up at him through my lashes. I can't tell if my body's reaction is from the dominance in his voice or if I'm annoyed that he's demanding an answer from me.

"I—" I start to answer but someone walks into the room and clears their throat behind us. I pull back and break away from Carrington, spinning around to see Travis standing in the door to the kitchen.

"I was just about to head out to grab the few things we still need for Saturday..." he trails off, looking between the two of us suspiciously. "Unless... you need me to stay?"

"No. No, go ahead. We're fine here." I don't sound fine. I hear the panic in my own voice, but he nods his head then grabs his hat off of the coat rack in the corner. With a dip of his head in goodbye, he leaves us alone again.

I don't wait for Carrington to pull me back into whatever just happened, instead I walk toward the bar area of the restaurant. "Let's give you the tour you came in for. You still have to see the distillery and tasting room next door."

After showing Carrington everything RED has to offer and watching his impressed smile out of the corner of my eye, I grab the menu I'd left on the bartop. "This is the menu we have planned for tomorrow. I'm only showing you in case you were curious. It's already finalized and can't be changed." That's technically a lie, but I don't want to hear which parts he doesn't like.

He's silent as he looks it over, nodding his head in what I hope is approval. Without looking up, he says, "And your chef..." he looks at me expectantly.

"Travis."

"Right, Travis. He can handle all of this?" There's not an ounce of humor in his voice. He's really asking if the chef I hired and the menu I created are a good match.

I scoff. "Yes, Carrington." His eye twitches when I call him by his full name. "He can handle it. *We* can handle it. Everything is covered."

He nods his head in response, but it's obvious he wanted a different answer. I let the moment settle as he continues to stare at the menu.

"'Cary' feels too... personal. Too close," I say as I fidget with the rings on my fingers. His gaze slowly leaves the menu and finds me again. I swear he's lighting me on fire from the inside out with the way his eyes bore into mine.

"Very well," is all he says in response. He doesn't fight me. Doesn't tell me I'm ridiculous to feel that way. He just says two words that mean almost nothing.

I nod and turn away from him, speaking to him is hard enough but having to look at his handsome face while I do is even harder. Once my back is to him, I breathe a little easier. "I don't know what your plans are. And I don't understand why selling your shares to me is something you need to think about, but..." I pause and take a deep breath. "This place means *everything* to me. I know you hate me or, at least, resent me for what happened between us, but please..." Tears well behind my eyes. "Please don't take this from me."

He's so silent that I wonder if he's looking for a way to break my heart all over again and tell me that no pleading can save me or RED from what he plans to do.

"You... you think I hate you?" His voice sounds genuine but confused. I spin around out of sheer shock at his question.

"Of course I do. I left you. I broke your heart. Over the phone, no less. I hate myself for that. Why *wouldn't* you hate me?" I broke my own heart too. Not that I voice that to him, it doesn't feel appropriate to say, much less think. I learned that knowing something needs to happen doesn't always mean it won't kill you in the process.

"I could never hate you, Thea. You could stab me in the heart, and I'd still never be able to hate you. I don't have it in me. I never have, and I never will. I... miss you. I miss us."

The tears that had welled up behind my eyes are free-falling now, there is no stopping them. This is too much. I can't be here with him, I can't have this conversation right now. It's still too raw even eight years later. I never even told him why I broke up with him, and for some reason, he hasn't asked. He *should* hate me. Just as he lifts his hand to reach for my face, I step back and look toward the floor.

"You should go. I have a lot to do, and the tour is over." And with that said, I turn and walk away, wiping the tears from my face. I don't give him a chance to stop me. The past can't come back to haunt me, I won't allow it.

Chapter Ten

"No, it's okay, Travis. Take care of Melody. I'll figure something out," I say into the phone, trying my hardest not to let my voice betray my panic.

"I'm so fucking sorry, Thea. I'll come by as soon as we're done at the ER." I hear the utter disappointment in his voice. He knows how important today is for all of us, but he's a single father, and his daughter always comes first. I'd never ask him to put RED before her.

"Travis, really. I'll figure it out. Text me later, and let me know how she's doing." I hang up the call and stand there frozen for a moment. He woke up to her being violently ill, there's no way he'll make it in time. I can't dwell on it though, I have to tell his assistant chef he's been promoted to head chef for the night. If I'm being honest, I have no idea if Travis prepared him for the possibility that he'd have to take his place one day.

I've spent the last three hours rearranging every centerpiece so it's perfect, straightening out the wrinkles out of every tablecloth, and adjusting each chair at every table. I've recounted the chairs at least six times out of fear that I somehow won't have enough. The menus for the table settings just arrived from the printer, but we're waiting to put them out. I'm paranoid something will happen to them if they're laid out too early.

I haven't seen Brooks yet, and he was supposed to be here already to help with the set up. Today is quickly falling apart. I look up at the twinkling lights strung across the beams and take a deep breath. I'll figure it out. That's all there is to it. I can't call Ripley, he's in Kentucky at the bourbon conference. If he finds out I need help, he'll jump on the next flight out. I dropped him off at the airport yesterday, and the excitement was literally pouring off of him.

It just leaves Brooks. Where the fuck is he? I look over at the clock, we have two hours before the guests start to arrive, and he promised me he'd be here by now. I push a lock of hair back behind my ear and run my hands down the skirt of my black lace dress, letting my fingers trace the outline of one of the flowers. I take a deep breath and interlace my fingers, fidgeting with the rings on my left hand. My heels click as I walk toward the kitchen and find Josh already starting the prep work.

I hover in the doorway for a moment before I ruin his night. "Hey," I drag out the word. "So, bad news. And we're not going to freak out, okay?"

Josh is young, only twenty-two, but Travis says he has huge potential. I guess we're about to find out. His eyes are as big as saucers as he waits for me to continue.

"Travis isn't coming." As soon as the words leave my lips, his eyes get impossibly wider.

"Wh-what? What do you mean he isn't coming? He's the head chef. There's going to be a hundred and sixty guests, Thea." His words come out as a stutter as panic rises in his voice. We can't both be losing it. I need him to hold it together.

"I know, Josh, I do. But Melody is sick. He doesn't have anyone to take care of her. So... it's just you and me, kid. And maybe Brooks... if he ever decides to show up. *We* have to handle it." He knows what I mean by that. There are other employees. I have plenty of servers and bartenders. I even have multiple hostesses to make sure every guest is taken care of. But I can't be everywhere at once making sure there aren't fires popping up. Travis was supposed to be in charge of the kitchen. He was going to handle it all for me so I could stay up front. There are too many moving parts within the event for me not to be on the floor. Brooks was going to handle the alcohol and restock the bar as needed, maybe even serve guests if the bar got too busy.

"I'm here, I'm here." I hear Brooks' voice behind me, he sounds out of breath, but I'm so happy he's here, I look past it. For a moment, relief floods me—until I turn around.

"What the *fuck* happened to your face, Brooks?" He bats my hand away as I reach toward the gash in his cheek. A bruise forming around it already.

"I'm fine," he says as he winces.

"Right. Fine. Okay." I'm shaking my head as I say the words, trying to calm my racing heart, but I'm on the verge of blowing up. "Fuck!" I scream, my voice ricocheting off the metal pans hanging throughout the kitchen. "Now I'm down two people."

Confusion covers his face as he questions me, "Two? What do you mean?"

"Travis had to take Melody to the ER. Josh is taking his place." I don't make eye contact with Josh as I say his name. I know he's nervous, I can't let it get to my head. I'm throwing him into the deep end and praying he's able to swim. "You had one fucking job, Brooks. One! I needed you today. All I asked was that you show up and help so this doesn't blow up in my face."

He throws his hands up in response, clearly still buzzed from whatever high he gets from getting the shit beat out of him. "I'm fucking here, Thea. I'm here, just let me help."

I scoff back at him, "Help? How the fuck can you help when you look like you got jumped? I can't let you be seen like this during a fucking domestic violence prevention charity gala." He must realize that I'm right because his face softens, and regret shines bright in his crystal blue eyes.

"Fuck. I'm sorry. I'll... I don't know, I'll help in the kitchen, whatever Josh needs."

"You can't be in the kitchen when you're bleeding," I say, motioning to his face and knuckles, which are also bruised and cut up. "Just... I don't even know. I guess you get to bring the bourbon over from the distillery when I need it. You can't be on the floor. I can't have the guests seeing you."

"But—" he starts to argue, but I cut him off.

"No fucking buts, Brooks. Just go put some fucking ice on your face, and let us handle this. Keep your phone on you in case I need you." I see him walk out of the kitchen from the corner of my eye, pissed off as if he has a reason to be mad. I thought the stunt he pulled at the funeral—showing up bloody and bruised—was a turning point for him. He'd been so different afterwards, more vulnerable, seemingly *wanting* to take on responsibilities. I thought we were getting past his tantrums, but clearly, I was wrong. It's always a tornado of emotions with him. He wants to be reliable, but it's almost like he can't help but fuck it up. I storm back to my office and pull out my phone to call Margot, my mother's nurse.

The phone rings in my ear as I chant *please answer, please answer* over and over in my head. Finally on the last ring, I hear her voice.

"Thea? Is everything okay?" Today is her day off. Seeing my name pop up on her screen probably sent her into a tail-spin thinking something is wrong with my mom.

"Hey, Margot. Yeah, Mom is fine. I, umm... I need a personal favor."

"Oh. Okay. What's up?" She sounds hesitant, which is warranted. I've never asked her for anything, let alone called her personal number on her day off. Everything with us up until this point has been about my mom and her care.

"I have a friend who... well, I don't know what happened, and I'm honestly too pissed off to ask. But he might need some stitches, and I really can't afford for him to leave and go to the hospital. He has a cut on his cheek that's still bleeding pretty bad, I just need it looked at, cleaned up, and bandaged until we have time to take him to get it seen."

I'm sitting in my desk chair now, leg bouncing as I wait through the silence to see if she's willing to help. I don't really have the time to be making this phone call, let alone waiting patiently for an answer, but I can't let him walk around looking like that either.

Finally, she says, "Oh, no. I can be there in thirty minutes. I assume you're at RED?"

I shoot up out of my chair, thankful that she's willing. "Yes. Thank you, Margot. I owe you big time. His name is Brooks. He'll be in the distillery since I banished him there while our charity event is going on."

She laughs as she says, "You must be really pissed off if you banished him."

"You have *no* idea. Thank you again." We say our goodbyes, and I rush back out to the dining area—one fire down, one more to go.

We're down to forty-five minutes until guests are set to arrive, and nothing is going the way it's supposed to. A woman came in looking for Travis but wouldn't give me her name—I have to remember to tell him someone came in for him when I have a second to breathe. Josh is freaking out. Every ten minutes he comes out of the kitchen and tells me he doesn't think he can do this. I keep reminding him we don't have a choice, I have no other back-ups. I pat him on the shoulder, and he walks back to the kitchen looking defeated. I'm about ready to pull my hair out when someone spills a whole pitcher of water on one of the boxes of menus I have on the table.

Before I can truly lose my mind over it, Carrington walks in.

No. No. No. This is *not* happening.

"What are you doing here? I can't deal with whatever it is you need or want today." I don't even try to hide my annoyance at seeing his stupid, beautiful face standing in front of me with the sun reflecting off his sapphire eyes the same way it reflects off the lake. His hair is down, and it somehow accentuates his chiseled jaw covered in the perfect amount of scruff.

He looks around RED, all the servers are scurrying around, placing the final table settings and making sure everything is set up in time. "I came to help."

My eyes go wide. "You're here to help?" My tone sounds snarky and disbelieving.

He shakes his head then adds, "I was told you're down a chef and could maybe use another set of hands."

Brooks. He must have called Cary. I can't decide if I'm grateful or pissed off, and I don't have time to think about it. I also don't have time to question him or wonder what him showing up means. For RED. For us.

Not that there is an 'us.'

"Wonder who told you that. I'm not in a position to say no, but just know, I could have handled it... I'll have Josh walk you through the menu." I start to turn toward the kitchen, but his voice stops me.

"No need. I saw it yesterday, I just need to know where every-thing is located."

I want to dwell on what he's saying. I want to think it over and decipher it. Maybe even pick his brain about why he'd care enough to be here, let alone do this for me. Then I remember he owns RED. Of course he doesn't want to see it fail. Of course he's coming to rescue *his* restaurant. There's no hidden reason or bigger meaning behind it, and I'd be stupid to look for one.

I bite the inside of my cheek as I get my emotions under control. "Right, of course. Josh is in the kitchen, he can show you where everything is."

He nods and walks away. He pushes the door to the kitchen open and disappears inside. Once the door swings shut, I see him through the small window, pulling an apron off a rack and making quick work of tying it around his waist, his movements confident. He pops the buttons on his sleeves and rolls them up to the elbows, exposing sinewy muscles and tattoos. Josh looks ecstatic that help has arrived and starts talking animatedly to him. His nervousness disappearing.

Then—as if in slow motion—Carrington pulls his long hair into a bun at the back of his neck, the muscles in his forearms making my heart race and my core ache.

Fuck.

Before I can make myself look away, he glances up and catch-es me staring through the window. He smirks and winks at me right before he turns around and jumps in like he belongs in that kitchen. And despite everything, I can't help but think that he looks like he belongs too. *Fuck. Fuck. Fuck.*

Chapter Eleven

Carrington

I was already pulling on my shoes to head over to RED when I got the call from Brooks. I was going to find a way to be useful, and now hearing they are so short-handed, I'm hoping Thea won't fight me too hard on being there at least. Seeing how important tonight is for her, I want to do everything I can to help it go off without a hitch.

I park on the far side of the lot next to the distillery, leaving all the front spots open for tonight's guests. Entering through the back, I find Brooks unloading boxes of bourbon and fresh kegs from the storage area to get them ready to go out to the restaurant. It's then that I notice his face, his cheek split and swollen. He pauses his movements and hangs his head with a sigh.

"It's nothing. I'm fine," he says and begins to heave boxes again.

"You're not *fine*. You're bleeding."

"Save it, okay? Thea already ripped me a new one and exiled me here for the night. I don't need to hear it from you too. Pretty sure I heard her calling a nurse friend to come patch me up." My chest warms at the thought that despite being pissed off and over-stressed, she still cares enough about my brother to make sure he's okay.

"What happened?" I ask, my tone gentler than a moment ago.

"I fucked up." He pauses again and looks me in the eye with the most contrite expression. "She was counting on me today, and I just..." he trails off. "I needed to blow off some steam, but it got out of control. I don't know why I keep doing this. I feel like I just keep. Fucking. Up," he punctuates the last few words.

I step closer to him and am about to pull him into a hug when the back door swings open and in walks Thea's mom's nurse. I recognize her from the funeral—she's hard to forget with her wild, curly chocolate-brown hair and startling light green eyes. Her eyes land on Brooks, and the sympathy shining from them is instant.

We exchange quick hellos, and I leave her to her work and head over to the restaurant to find Thea.

As soon as I spot her, I note the worry lines on her forehead and the annoyance that flits over her face when she sees me. Her face flushes slightly, but she schools her features right before she proceeds to chew me out for coming to her rescue. I pretend I don't see the way her eyes linger on my face before she shoos me into the kitchen, or how she watches me tie up my hair. She always said she wanted to see me with long hair one day. I can't help winking at her when I catch her in the doorway—seeing how easily I can still fluster her helps calm some of the nerves I feel stepping into a foreign kitchen.

The kitchen staff at RED is great. Everyone is professional and well-trained. I'm truly impressed by their skills and ability to adapt to how I run a kitchen. Each head chef has their own style, but with their help, I find my footing quickly. And thank fuck because, although Travis built a great menu, he grossly underestimated how much extra of everything you need when serving such a large crowd.

Early in the night, I notice the hor d'oeuvres are leaving the kitchen faster than we can plate them. When I ask one of the servers about it, she tells me Thea is stressing out because there are now more people than originally expected.

I check over everyone's stations to make sure they're okay before taking off my dirty apron and stepping out on the floor to find Thea. I quickly spot her next to the bar talking to a few busboys motioning to a hallway that leads to a back storage room. As I step closer, I hear her telling them to grab the few extra tables stored there and set them up along the back wall.

"What's going on?" I ask. A piece of her hair has fallen out of her half-up style, and my fingers itch to push it behind her ear like I did the other day. Instead, I clasp my hands behind my back.

She lifts her hand as if she's going to run it over her face and then stops, probably remembering she can't smudge her makeup. A frustrated sound leaves her lips. "The company putting this whole thing together invited victims from local area women's shelters at the last minute and didn't mention it. Or they did, but I must have missed the email this week with everything else going on. So now I'm scrambling to find seating for twenty-five more people. We should be good on tables, but I need to find more chairs, and I only have enough centerpieces for the tables we planned for."

This might be her tipping point. She's run around all evening dealing with one issue after another with such grace, but I think she's finally hit a wall. Rubbing the scruff on my chin, I rack my brain for a minute.

"Okay," I say. "Prep the tables, and send a few of the servers over to the distillery. We can use the chairs from there. They won't match, but at least people won't be standing to eat their dinner. As for flowers," I turn to one of the busboys who just carried in a table, "Scott, run out to the front steps and grab a couple of the small pots of mums and bring them in here." I turn back to Thea. "Throw some votives around them and slightly dim the lights, no one will notice they don't match the rest."

Thea stares at me disbelieving. "Thank you," she clips out, and some of her worry fades. One of the guests—I'm assuming an organizer for the event—is now standing and giving a speech about the efforts of the charity they have all gathered to support.

"Nat," I quietly call out to the bartender. "Can you please give me a glass of water?" It only takes her a second to fill a pint glass for me, and I thank her. I place the glass in Thea's hand and pull out one of the stools at the bar. "Here, sit and drink. Have you eaten?"

Surprisingly, she doesn't fight me and plants herself on the stool. The hem of the black dress that reached her mid-thigh while standing rides up an inch or two with her new position, and my eyes can't help but take in her bronzed thighs.

Thea always had an athletic body. Growing up on the lake, we were active kids—in and out of the water constantly. When we were together in Seattle, she maintained herself by running every morning, and it seems like the habit has stuck because her legs are long and toned just like I remember.

"I–I think I had breakfast." Her answer snaps my attention to her face. Her blush tells me she caught me looking.

"You need to eat. I'll have a plate brought out for you," I say.

"I'm fine. I'll eat when I get home later. I really don't have time right now. I have to help with the silent auction and champagne toast. And you need to get back to the kitchen, I'm sure Josh is having a panic attack by now." She's not wrong there. He's a great kid with tons of talent, but he needs to learn to work under pressure if he wants to go far in this field.

I stay at her side until she drains the whole glass. I then reluctantly leave her to handle the front of house, while I figure out how I'm going to feed two dozen additional people. I step into the kitchen and stare at the floor unseeing for a minute, hands on my hips, while I sift through my mental catalog of recipes. There has to be something I can whip up with what we have on hand.

"Josh," I say, and his head pops up from where he's chopping.

"Yes, Chef?" Even almost a decade later, I get such a thrill having someone refer to me as 'Chef.'

"Grab the chicken from the freezer that's meant for next week. Start thawing and get a mirepoix prepped."

Sorry, Travis, you'll have to figure out a new special.

"I need you to take a bite of this." Thea has just stepped into the kitchen to check on me, and I hold out a forkful of braised chicken in a white wine mirepoix for her to taste.

"Can you stop trying to feed me? I don't have time right now. I have to check on everything on the patio," she says. At least she sounds more annoyed than frustrated, unlike before.

"Please just taste this. I can't send this out without your approval," I insist.

"What do you mean? I've already approved all the food. The menu has been set for days." She narrows her eyes at me.

"We had a bit of a hiccup with the food," I say in the most placating tone I can muster. "Everything's fine, I'm handling it. But I had to improvise a bit, and now I need you to taste this, please." I put the fork up to her face again. I know it's good enough to go out to the guests, but I also know she hasn't eaten, and this seems like the easiest way to get something in her system. She looks at my face a bit longer, undoubtedly looking for the lie I'm feeding her, but relents and eats the mouthful I've offered her. I see the moment the flavor registers because she closes her eyes and lets out a small moan that goes straight to my dick.

I swallow roughly and say, "I'll take that as approval?" I don't give her a chance to answer or say anything more by offering her a few more forkfuls of the chicken dish. She takes them greedily and then excuses herself to get back to her duties.

The night wears on, and I send a couple more small bites of anything we have extra to her, having them delivered by the servers who report back that she's begrudgingly eating them. That'll have to tide her over until the gala ends, and I can corner her into sitting down for a proper meal. I won't take no for an answer.

Tonight might have been a success despite all the complications, but she and I will be discussing her lack of self-care. I know it's what she does, she puts everyone else's needs above her own, but I won't have her running herself ragged. Not when I'm around.

Chapter Twelve

Carrington

It must be close to midnight now. I sent the kitchen staff home about an hour ago. Josh insisted on staying with me to finish the rest of the clean up, but I convinced him I had it handled and thanked him for a job well done tonight. Then I watched as Thea did the same, and the smile that took over his face at the compliment showcased how much he values her opinion.

I place the garnish on Thea's late supper and wipe the edges of the plate. Presentation matters, all of my instructors always said so. Food is eaten with our eyes as much as our mouths after all.

I come out of the kitchen, plate in hand, and find Thea behind the bar wiping down the wooden bartop, her back to me. The lights are mostly all off around the dining area, just the dim overheads in the bar illuminate the space in a warm glow. Her hair creates a halo effect around her head in the soft light. I quietly place the plate on the counter next to me, cross my arms, lean against the wall, and just watch her. She's swaying gently and quietly singing along to "Tennessee Whiskey" as she works.

She's pulled up her long hair into a messy bun at the top of her head, as always, a few wisps have escaped the tie and hang down around her face. My eyes catch on the slope of her neck, and hundreds, thousands of memories of kissing her there flit through my mind. It drove Thea crazy—she used to always let out the sweetest moan when my lips would graze the spot just behind her ear. She always smells like her flowery perfume and a lemony scent that is solely her in that spot. I have to restrain myself from going over to her and doing just that.

Suddenly she turns, and our eyes meet—her singing cutting off with her surprise. I hold my breath, waiting for her reaction.

Please don't shut me out.

Her face transforms from startled to mildly embarrassed, but her guard stays down. I push off from the wall, pick up the plate, and walk around to the other side of the bar.

"Come here," I say.

"Hold on, I still have to clean these glasses and the trash—"

"Come here, Thea," I repeat firmly. My voice brooks no argument, and before I resort to physically removing the glassware from her hand, she puts it down and makes her way around the bar. She hoists herself up on the stool next to me in front of the plate I made for her.

"You made grilled cheese," she says as she stares down at the food. Her voice is quiet—timid like the fateful phone call I hate to remember—and I can't make out what she's thinking.

"Yeah, with bacon and pesto on brioche. You used to like that, said it's how your mom used to make it. Is–is it okay?" There's a long silence while she continues to stare down at the sandwich, never once taking her eyes off of it. It's in that moment that I start to question the gesture.

When she still doesn't say anything, I make to stand up and grab the plate to take it back. "I–I can see if I can make something else. The options are pretty spar—"

"It's perfect," she says and looks up at me. It could be the lighting and the exhaustion evident on her face, but I could swear her eyes are misty. "It's just what I need after a day like today. I can't remember the last time I had one of these."

"Good. You eat, I'll clean. Then we'll drink to a successful shitshow of a night," I say with a smile. She smiles back at me and picks up the sandwich. I watch as she takes the first bite, and her eyes all but roll to the back of her head. The sound she lets out—a cross between a whimper and a sigh—is indecent, and I quickly step away and take over the cleaning tasks behind the bar.

"I hope you know that the only reason I'm letting you boss me around is because you saved my ass today," she says in between bites. "I wouldn't get used to it."

"Oh, so you're admitting you needed me?" I say, my lips curving up.

"Don't get ahead of yourself. I needed *Brooks*. You were just a pretty stand in," she says, her eyes teasing. Then she must realize what she said because her eyes get big, and her smile falls. Her focus returning back to the food.

"Second best to Brooks, story of my life," I say with mock self-pity, letting her off the hook. I'd hate to lose the comfortable, easy mood between us. I've been yearning for a moment like this since I first saw her face on the steps of RED. I pull down two tumblers and fill them with generous pours of Ripple Effect, placing the bottle on the bar next to the glasses. Pushing one over to her, I lift mine and take a sip.

"I'm sure Brooks would have something to say about that," she says when she finishes chewing her last bite. "You know he always thought your parents held you up on a pedestal."

"Pedestal? More like a cake stand. Did he somehow miss me having to move to the other side of the fucking country to feel like I could be taken seriously?"

"I love Owen and Hazel, but they didn't make it easy for you two growing up," Thea says and then covers her mouth and quickly adds, "I'm so sorry, I really shouldn't be talking about them like that."

"It's fine. I mourned my relationship with them a long time ago. Now, well, it just feels like going through the formalities." I take another sip of my bourbon. "I started going to therapy, did I mention that? I started after you—" I clear my throat and avert my eyes. "Well, it's helped. My therapist is great. You'd like her actually. She doesn't put up with my shit either."

Thea takes a long sip of the bourbon I poured for her, and I finish my glass. I pick up the bottle and pour myself another, then cork the bottle and look over the label as I make my way around the bar to sit on a stool next to her.

"You know, it's crazy. I just started carrying RED at my restaurant. I had no idea. Seth—he's my bar manager now—sourced it, and I never knew it was from here. I've been telling everyone about it, how much I love it," I say.

"Yeah, Ripley's made something amazing here. I can't believe how quickly it blew up. You hear so many stories of other distilleries and how hard it is to get off the ground, but his seemed to just take off," she says with a soft smile.

Fucking Ripley.

"I don't think it has anything to do with *him*."

"You think this is because of me?" She scoffs then adds, "I can't take credit for any of it. They're his recipes. I just made sure the world knows about them." If she was anyone else, I'd wonder if she was just being modest, but I know Thea—or I used to—and there's no doubt in my mind that she truly believes what she's saying.

"I don't think you give yourself enough credit. This," I gesture around the restaurant, "and this," I lift the bottle, "are all you. I'm so fucking impressed with what you've done here. You've put so much of yourself into this place, it's hard to see where one ends and the other begins. RED is you. *You* are RED. It's perfect."

We fall into a comfortable silence, sipping our drinks and sharing a glance every once in a while. Music has been playing softly in the background, and it isn't until this moment that I hear the song change. The first chords of Thomas Rhett's "Die a Happy Man" play out.

I take a chance and say, "Dance with me, Lem."

Chapter Thirteen

"*RED is you. You *are* RED. It's perfect.*" His words echo in my mind. The meaning behind them, and the fact that *he* said them has me paralyzed. I already wasn't sure how to feel about today. I was royally fucked before he showed up—I knew it. I didn't want to admit it, but I knew it. And in the back of my mind, I knew if I called him, he'd be here in an instant. I think part of me didn't want to admit defeat, and the other part of me didn't want to test the waters to see if I was right.

Ever since he admitted that he doesn't hate me, I've been out of sorts. I've been using this charity event to distract me and keep my thoughts at bay. Now it's over, and he's sitting right next to me. Feeding me. Complimenting me. *Looking* at me.

I spent the last eight years thinking there was no way he didn't hate me. Hearing that he doesn't feels like a piece of me—a piece I didn't even realize was broken—mended itself. I've carried around hate for myself since I made the phone call that ended our relationship.

At the time, I thought I was making the right decision. I had myself convinced love wasn't enough. It didn't matter that being away from him made me feel like I was drowning. It didn't matter that living a life without him barely felt like living at all.

He was happy in Seattle. He thrived there. As much as I loved him, I lost myself more and more everyday living there. I was breaking off pieces of myself every time I put his happiness and wants above my own. And I know he wasn't to blame. He never asked me to do that. I never told him how miserable I really was. I didn't communicate to him that I was losing myself, and the only thing keeping me stable in Seattle was him. It felt too selfish to tell him any of that knowing if I asked him to choose between me and his dream job, he'd choose me in a heartbeat. So I took the choice away. And I've hated myself every day since.

Once I arrived back home in Indigo Hill, it felt like I could take my first full breath since leaving for Seattle. The pressures of city life lifted, and that was the moment I knew I couldn't go back. I went from barely surviving to thriving professionally. And for a little while... it was enough, or maybe it *had* to be enough.

Life without Cary was dull though. Once I realized living without him hurt more than living in a city I hated, it was too late. Now, with him so close and the memories of our life together on constant replay in my head, I wonder why I ever thought a life without him could be enough. They're dangerous thoughts to have, but I can't ignore them when he's right in front of me.

I'm spiraling too much to respond to what he said. The cadence of the music playing over the restaurant speakers surrounds us, and the second the start of "Die a Happy Man" reaches my ears, I'm transported back to a night almost eleven years ago.

10.5 Years Ago
(20 years old)

I throw my head back in laughter as Cary spins me around then catches me again, pulling me back into his arms. We've been dancing for almost an hour, and I'm still not sated. I could dance with this man all night long and still want more. The glow of the neon signs hanging from the walls illuminates the dive bar we're in. We stumbled upon this place walking home from dinner. The second Cary heard the country tunes pouring from the open door as someone slipped out, his mind was made up. He pulled me into him by my hand, whispering into my ear, "Let's dance the night away, Lemon."

The bar reminds me of the one in our hometown. It's dark, stuck in the 90s, and serves greasy bar food that all smells the same. We didn't waste our time using our fake IDs to get drinks before going straight for the small dance floor. I've felt the eyes of the other patrons on us the whole time we've been dancing, but I don't have it in me to care. Every touch of our bodies burns me up, and the look in Cary's eyes tells me he's feeling the same way.

Thomas Rhett's new single, "Die a Happy Man," comes on next, and Cary pulls me even closer to him.

"Hey, baby?" he says directly into my ear with his head angled down to me.

"Hmm?" It's all I can muster with how turned on I am right now.

"Have you heard this song before?"

I pull back to look at him. "Of course I have," I say matter of factly. Anyone who listens to country music has heard this song.

"Every time I hear this song..." he starts, then pauses as his eyes find mine. "It makes me think of you. Of us. Of how happy you make me. And how nothing else matters but the love I feel for you."

His openness and rare show of emotion surprises me. Despite loving what he's saying, the words make me feel slightly uneasy because they're so uncharacteristic. I know he loves me, but he usually shows me as opposed to saying it so plainly. My cheeks blush though, his words making my heart race from more than just the dancing. We're still swaying to the slow beat of the music, but I can barely hear it. It feels like everything and everyone around us has disappeared. My eyes well up, and a tear slips past my defenses. I reach up and swipe it away before he has a chance to, then I attempt to break the tension with a small teasing smile.

"You're such a charmer. I love you so fucking much, Cary Grant."

"I love you too, Lem."

He spins me out once more, and when I'm back in his arms, I push up on my tip-toes to reach his ear. "Take me home now, please."

He wastes no time pulling me out of the bar. The walk home takes slightly longer than usual with us stopping every block to make out against the wall of a closed business, barely able to contain ourselves or wait until we get back home.

And I feel it in my bones that the song just became our song.

Present

His words bring me back to the present. It's the same song. The same man. But a very different place and situation.

"Dance with me, Lem." His hand is extended, waiting for me to take it. I stare down at it, feeling like this is a dream, and I'll wake up any moment. It's the first time I've been called Lem in so long that hearing the name out loud forms a lump in my throat.

The nickname started when we were kids. He said my hair was the color of lemons—which was wildly untrue—and that I smelled like lemons too. As a child, I laughed it off, just thankful it wasn't a name that I could be teased for. As we got older, it became endearing and proof of the love he felt for me even when he didn't say it out loud.

That's why he'd gotten me the lemon ring for my birthday one year. Though, I keep it locked in a drawer as a silent reminder of the worst decision I've ever made.

I slowly lift my eyes back up to his, looking for something in his face to tell me not to do this—not to give in. All I see shining back at me is the same love I saw in his eyes years ago with this same song playing in the background. And that... that should terrify me. That alone should send me running, but it doesn't. Somehow, it spurs me on instead. I ignore the voice in my head screaming at me that this will only lead to more heartbreak.

It's not just *my* heart at stake, but I can't find it in myself to listen.

I place my hand in his without another thought. I let him pull me up from the stool and away from the bar. We don't have a dance floor at RED, but there's a wide walkway between the bar and the tables. His hands grab mine, and he gently winds one of my arms around his neck.

As he lifts the other, his eyes snag on the tattoo at my wrist. The tattoo I got as a reminder of him, of us. Pine trees lining the lake and the reflection of it all is an almost exact image of our special spot. He looks at it for a few beats and then places my hand at the nape of his neck with a thoughtful look.

As he goes to wrap his arms around my waist, he stops mid-way. "Is this okay?" His voice is hesitant, like he's waiting for me to scream "stop" and bolt from the room.

I nod my head in response, and his arms instantly wrap around me, pulling me close. I'm enveloped in his scent, familiar yet new. He's always smelled like summer to me. The lake on a summer day, surrounded by the pine trees that line the forest. It's a scent I've spent years trying to get out of my head unsuccessfully. But there's something mixed with it now, something masculine and pleasant. I can't place what it is, but it feels like it's him still, just all grown up.

It's another moment before I find the courage to speak. "You... remember?" If I'm right, and he does, then I don't need to specify what I'm referring to. As surprised as I am that he seems to, the change in his demeanor when the song came on answers my question. I still needed to ask though. I need to hear him say the words.

"Lemon, I remember *everything*. There's not a moment of our time together that I don't remember. There's not a single thing about you that I've forgotten. I remember every. Single. Fucking. Thing." He punctuates the last few words, breaking down every wall I've spent years building up to protect my heart. It all comes crashing down around us, shattering any resolve I've had about not getting close to him again.

My hands are moving before I've fully thought it through. The second they do, his body tenses, assuming I'm about to pull away. Before I can question my own actions, I'm pushing up on my toes and crashing my lips into his. He hesitates for only a moment before his arms tighten around me, and he's kissing me back. The kiss is desperate, and there's not a hair's width of space between our bodies. His tongue runs along the seam of my lips, and I immediately let him in. The taste of bourbon lingers on his tongue, and I explore every inch of his mouth with mine.

Our kiss is like a choreographed dance that I could never forget the steps to. Touching him, moving with him is muscle memory.

His hands skate down my waist, landing just below the curve of my ass as he lifts me into his arms—never breaking our kiss. I wrap my legs around his hips.

As we move, I hear something hit the floor and shatter, but I can't find it in myself to care enough to pull away from him. When he lifted me up, my dress lifted as well, leaving nothing to shield his hands from my bare skin. Now nothing else matters but the way his touch feels on my body—his hands igniting nerve endings everywhere they land, his lips against mine. He trails his mouth down the slope of my chin and around my ear, stopping at the spot right behind it—*his spot.* "Fuck, I missed your body," he groans right before he closes the space between his mouth and that one point guaranteed to drive me insane.

The moment his lips make contact, my toes curl, and a moan escapes me. His cock tents against his dress pants at the sound and, pressed this close, I feel every inch. He chuckles seductively in my ear as he realizes that hasn't changed in the time we've been apart. He comes back to my lips, kissing me even more intensely than before.

His hands squeeze the globes of my ass before placing me down on a table top, then they come up around my waist again. So slowly that it feels like torture, he moves them up my stomach toward my breasts. The touch is feather-light, but I feel it all the way down to my soul. His touch is laced with just enough pressure that I'm being pushed down onto the table more and more until I'm lying flat on my back. My fists are bunched into his button-down shirt bringing him down with me.

As one of his hands reaches my breast, the other rests on the table beside my head as his lips move down my neck. I tighten my legs, pulling him impossibly closer. "Cary," I moan into the space between us. It's the first time I've used his nickname since he's been back in town, and I know it has an effect on him from the way his hand squeezes my breast at the same moment.

His lips land back on my own as his hand trails down to the hem of my dress, pushing it up to my waist. Neither of us says a word as his fingers trace down the top of my thigh. I keep my eyes squeezed shut, terrified that if I open them this will all stop, and reality will hit me square in the face. I can keep pretending the rest of the world doesn't exist as long as I keep them closed. Nothing and no one else matters right now. I'm willing to live in this fantasy if it means his lips stay on mine, and his fingers never stop whispering across my skin. I feel alive for the first time in God knows how long.

He leaves a burning trail as his fingers graze toward my inner thigh. Despite knowing exactly what's happening, the second his touch lands on the edge of my core, my breath hitches. He slowly runs a finger directly over my center, only my underwear between us, and my breathing stops completely.

He pushes the material aside exposing my already wet pussy. "Fuck, Thea," he groans into my mouth as he feels how ready I am for him—how much I want him. The desire for each other is so thick it's coating the air around us. "You're fucking dripping for me, baby."

He finds my clit and flicks it gently, then begins circling it with an even pressure that I love. I grow wetter with every movement of his hand. As if he can't wait any longer, he pulls away from my clit, and I let out an involuntary whine at the interruption. One finger slips inside of me, making me gasp. I bite down on my bottom lip as he starts to thrust it in and out, his mouth reclaiming the spot behind my ear at the same moment his movement quickens. My back arches as the pleasure builds within me.

He moves from my neck to take advantage of my arched body, covering my peaked and hardened nipple with his mouth over the fabric of my dress and sucking. The sounds that escape my lips ring through the empty restaurant. He slips a second finger in and changes the rhythm to a slower pace, the heel of his palm massaging my clit. His fingers curl at just the right angle, making pressure coil at my center.

I'm so heated my clothes feel restrictive. I run my hands up his neck and over his hair where it's tied back, then back down before pulling at his shirt. One of the buttons pops off as I sink my hands under the fabric, tracing the muscles of his shoulders, his skin as hot as I feel.

The walls of my pussy tighten on his fingers as my climax starts to build. He must feel it too because he puts his lips to my ear and says, "You going to come for me, Lem?"

All I can do is nod and angle his face back to mine as I pull him into another deep kiss. We're both panting and lost to this moment.

Finally, the chasm of pressure explodes, and I scream out my release into his mouth. He holds me through it, never stopping his movements until my body starts to come down from the high. I open my eyes, and the world slowly comes back into focus.

He gently pulls out of me, readjusting my underwear back into place and pulls away just enough so our lips have some space between them. He looks me in the eyes then brings his fingers covered in my release to his mouth and slips them past his lips, moaning at the taste of me on his tongue. He's still fully clothed—sans the one button—and I feel the throbbing of his dick and how hard it is against my stomach.

That realization, matched with the comedown, hits me all at once. Suddenly, my heart is racing from the anxiety and potential fallout of what we just did. The fantasy is gone, the spell is broken, and all I can do is lean into the panic.

What have I done?

He must see it on my face because he pulls his body off of me and lets me sit up from the table. He backs away, giving me room to hop down. I pull my dress down, incapable of meeting his gaze. I'm scared of the look I'll find on his face. I'm terrified he'll confirm my worst fear and tell me it was a mistake. I can't believe I let that happen.

Ironically enough, the silence must be killing him too because he's the first to speak. "Thea—" he starts.

I cut him off before he can say anything more, not knowing if I can handle what might come out of his mouth. "I... I have to go. I can't—fuck. I can't believe we just did that."

He may say something in response, but I don't hear it. Fear takes over as I rush to my office. It's the only place I can think to go right now. It's the only place I think I might be safe from the life-altering decision I just made.

I can't go home. I can't look at him. I can't do anything but walk into my make-shift refuge, slam the door, and lock it behind me. The lock clicking is the last sound I hear before I fall to the floor and break down.

Chapter Fourteen

"Let me know if you two need anything," Margot says as she leaves the room. She shuts the door lightly behind her, and I make a mental note to thank her for coming to my rescue with Brooks yesterday before I leave. I've never met a kinder soul than Margot Mason. I've never heard the girl even mutter a curse word or get snippy with someone. Mom and I call her the true saint of Saint Stephen's.

Settling into the chair by the window in my mom's room, I watch her closely as she wheels over so we can chat. Sundays have always been the day I visit her. Because the funeral was last Sunday, and I was only able to see her for a short time, today is much needed. Especially after what transpired last night between Cary and me.

Once I finally calmed down enough to drive myself home, I spent all night tossing and turning. Everytime I closed my eyes, visions of him hovering over my body and giving me the best orgasm I've had in almost a decade flooded my brain. I want to say I don't know how it happened or how we got to that point, but the truth is I've felt the connection between us re-forming since the moment we made eye contact on the steps of RED.

My mistake was thinking it was one-sided or that either of us could ignore it. Now I'm left to wonder what it all means and how much it'll hurt when he goes back to Seattle. My mother clears her throat, successfully pulling me out of my thoughts. I shake my head while biting the inside of my lip. "Sorry, Mom. I'm a little in my thoughts today."

"I can tell. I can also see the bags under your eyes. Are you still not sleeping well?" Her voice is seeping with concern as her worried eyes meet mine.

I've had stress-induced insomnia most of my life. There were more nights than I can count where my mom would make me chamomile tea sweetened with honey and run her fingers through my hair to help me try to fall asleep. If I was at the end of a string of sleepless nights, it would sometimes work. When it didn't, it would at least calm my mind and slow my racing thoughts. As I got older, others took over that role. First, it was Cary. Recently, it has been Ripley.

"It got better in the last few days until last night," I say, fidgeting with my rings.

"Hmm," she starts, "any particular reason you can think of for why it started up again?"

Her words have a small laugh escaping me. "Oh, I know exactly why."

"Well, don't keep an old lady waiting in suspense—spill." My lips tilt up in a smile. My mom and I have always been close. She was a single mother and never had any other children. My father split the moment he found out she was pregnant. He apparently wasn't keen on the whole being a dad thing. Not that she needed him. My childhood was never unfulfilling or unhappy with only one parent. We became thick as thieves as I grew up. She was the person I told everything to, the one who told me to reach for the stars and chase my dreams.

Looking back, I see now that her symptoms started before I left for Seattle. She'd waved me off anytime I brought it up, claiming she was just tired or "getting old" despite being a younger mother than most with a teenager. Once I came back home, I'd found out she'd not only been diagnosed with Multiple Sclerosis, but she'd been keeping it from me. It had progressed to a point where she could no longer hide it. And much to her dismay, she couldn't live alone anymore either.

She was the reason I came back home. And she was a big part of the reason why I never went back to Seattle. Not a day goes by that I don't remember the phone call that started it all.

8 Years Ago
(23 years old)

I look down at the time and see it's six-twelve. Cary just got back from helping with the prep for tonight. We're supposed to be at the restaurant by seven for his first night as head chef, but the drive is only about ten minutes from our apartment. It's then I realize what day it is. I've been so busy getting ready for Cary's big night, it completely slipped my mind.

Cary surprised me this morning by taking me shopping for a dress. He knows how much I dread big crowds and the anxiety that comes with them. I think he thought the dress shopping would distract me enough so I wouldn't have too much time to think about it. I've been trying to not let my anxiety cloud how proud I am of him. This restaurant is owned by a huge name in the industry, so Cary getting the head chef position is a huge deal.

When we got home, I'd surprised him with the custom knives I'd bought him as a present for landing his dream job. They're engraved with 'Chef Cary' on each of the blades. The box they came in also has a hidden 'I love you, baby' engraved on the bottom under the compartment that holds them. I wanted him to feel like he could use them at work but still think of me when he did.

Once he'd opened the gift and thoroughly thanked me, he'd left me to get myself ready for the night.

It's going on six-thirty here which means it's almost nine-thirty back home. I haven't heard from my mom all day long, and today is our weekly phone call. I'm immediately nervous that something is wrong but try not to panic without any kind of proof. Maybe she was busy and simply forgot too.

Quickly pulling up her name in my phone, I press the call button and put it on speaker so I can continue applying my make-up. It rings and rings and rings then goes to voicemail. My stomach drops. She always answers my call. It is late though. I tell myself that's all it is but call again for good measure.

Still no answer.

Opening the bathroom door, I look around the corner to see if Cary is nearby so I can ask his opinion. I don't see him, but I hear him talking to someone on the phone in the other room and decide not to interrupt him. Back in the bathroom, I place my hands on the edge of the counter and look at myself in the mirror, actively biting my lip as I try to decide what I should do. I don't technically know *if anything is even wrong. I just have this bad feeling, and she isn't answering. Despite it being late, I decide to call my mom's next door neighbor, Barbara.*

Once again, the phone rings and rings, but on the last ring, Barbara answers, "Hello?"

"Hey, Barb. It's Thea, Lydia's daughter. I'm so sorry to call so late, but my mom isn't answering, and she was supposed to call me earlier. I just have a weird feeling about it. Is there any way you can go over there and check on her?" My nerves are getting the best of me, and I have to cut myself off before I start apologizing even more for asking.

"Oh, sweetie, I'm sure she's fine. I saw her in the garden earlier today."

I nod my head to myself, but the pit in the bottom of my stomach just won't go away. My gut is telling me there's something wrong. "I know it's an inconvenience. I just... she always answers, Barb," I plead my case once more.

"Okay, okay, honey. I'll get dressed and pop over there. You'll have to give me a little bit though, I was already in bed."

I know her words aren't meant to make me feel bad, but they do anyway. I push the feeling aside. "Thank you so much, Barb. I really appreciate it."

With that, we hang up, and I go back to finishing my make-up. I have a solid five minutes to finish getting ready before Cary will throw me over his shoulder and carry me out to the car. I'm done with one minute to spare. Once we're in the car, I tell Cary about my mom, he assures me there's nothing to worry about, and it's just my nerves for tonight getting to me. He's probably right, but I need to hear it from her. I need to hear her voice, and I'll be fine.

When we're pulling into the restaurant's parking lot, my phone starts to ring. I look down to see it's Barbara calling me back and answer immediately.

"Barbara, is everything okay?" The panic in my voice is evident. And there's a small pause before she answers. It only lasts a couple seconds, but it feels like an eternity.

"Baby... I think you need to come home." Her voice cuts me like a knife. Tears fill my eyes instantly. My mind is whirring with all the worst case scenarios.

"Wh-What's wrong? What's going on?" Cary places his hand on my leg in an attempt to comfort me.

"Well, she didn't answer the door when I rang the bell, so I grabbed the extra key, you know, the one she hides in that pot in the garden." I shake my head in a silent answer, willing her to go on. "When I finally got in the door, I found her in the kitchen on the floor. She's okay right now, but I think she may have broken her ankle. She said she lost her balance and couldn't catch herself."

I finally let myself take a breath knowing she's conscious. My voice still comes out shaky, but it's better than before. "Okay. Yeah, I'll get a flight out as soon as possible. Thank you, Barbara. Thank you so much."

I hear my mom in the background telling Barbara to stop bothering me because it's Cary's big night and how she better not be telling me to come home. I smile at that, and the tightening in my chest loosens some.

"I've got an ambulance on the way, sweetie. I'll text you with the details once she's settled," she says as she ignores my mom berating her. I thank her again before disconnecting the call. As soon as I'm off the phone with Barbara, I turn to Cary.

"I've got to go home. I'm so sorry."

"Can't you fly out in the morning? Then I can come with you. There's just no way I can leave right now. Barbara said it just looked like a broken ankle," he recites back to me. Clearly he was able to hear everything she said.

"She doesn't have anyone, Cary. Barbara is in her seventies, I can't expect her to stay with her. I know you don't understand because you aren't close with your mom, but I won't leave her there alone when she's hurt," I shoot back at him, my face heating with my quick anger.

"I'm going to ignore that jab for now. This is such a big night for me, Thea. It's a big night for us."

"I know," I say but only really knowing that it's a big night for him. I feel like he's only saying 'us' to guilt trip me. "But she's hurt. I need to be there for her. I'm not going to argue with you. I am sorry though, and I'll make it up to you somehow when I come back." Before he can respond, I'm already looking up flights from Seattle to Myrtle Beach. The flight will take all night, and with the drive to Indigo Hill, I'll be lucky if I'm there before noon tomorrow. I find a redeye flight that's just over seven hours. I don't waste any time and click the purchase button.

"You're really doing this?" I don't understand why he's so upset. The tone he's using is pissing me off even more. I look at the clock on the dash to see it's now six-fifty-seven before meeting his eyes.

"You should get inside. I'll call an Uber." I unfasten my seat belt and exit the car. He acts like he might say something else, but I'm already walking away in the opposite direction of the door as I pull up the Uber app.

Present

I shake the memory away and roll my eyes at my mom. "You are not old, stop."

She laughs but gives me a 'go on' motion with her hand, the woman is unrelenting. "Well, as you know, Cary is back in town"

She nods her head as she says, "I do know that."

Wow, she is not making this easy.

"Right. So... we may have... kind of reconnected in the last week, and I don't know, I'm just confused now."

She waits for a moment to see if I'll elaborate any more, but I don't. "Do you still have feelings for him? Is that what you're confused about?" There's no judgment in her voice.

"It's been eight years, Mom. I've moved on. And we didn't work before, so there's no sense in even discussing it." My leg starts to bounce involuntarily, and my mom's eyes catch the movement.

"Moved on with whom?" The question catches me off guard, making my eyes shoot up to hers. She doesn't let me answer though. "You and I both know you aren't Ripley's... type. You may have fooled everyone else in this town with that sham, but I know better."

I don't know why I'm surprised. Of course my mother knows everything without me telling her. I can't even fake date my gay best friend without her figuring it out.

She's right though, we do have everyone else fooled. Ever since we started "dating" no one has tried to set either of us up. They all just accepted us as the perfect couple. We even started calling each other 'babe' to spice up the ruse. Now we do it as a joke regardless of who's around.

I take a deep breath, accepting my defeat. "How long have you known?"

"That you two weren't really together, or that he's into men?" she asks plainly.

"Uhh, both? Either?" I answer truthfully.

"Since the Sunday you two walked in here hand-in-hand trying to feed me that lie."

I laugh at her admission. "Why didn't you tell me sooner?" It would have saved me a lot of effort. Ripley doesn't come with me every time, but he usually tags along every other Sunday, and trying to be convincing in front of my mother has always been a concern.

"I figured you'd tell me when you wanted me to know."

I reach for her hand and lace my fingers in hers. "Sorry, Mom. I should have told you sooner."

She shakes her head, placing her other hand on top of mine. "No, baby. Don't be sorry. I know how broken your heart has been since you and Cary ended. You needed time to heal, and this Godforsaken gossip of a town just wouldn't give it to you."

I laugh and give her hand a squeeze. "You aren't wrong there." I sigh then continue, "And now he's back. It's like the cycle is starting all over."

"Or maybe, it never ended. Maybe this was just an intermission for you two." Her words hit me right in the chest. If there's one person who knew how deep my love truly was for Carrington Grant, it's my mother.

The rest of our time together is spent outside. I push her through the garden, we say hello to some of her friends, and then I cry like a baby when I have to say goodbye.

I'm dialing Ripley's number as soon as my phone connects to the car. Luckily, he answers almost immediately, "Hey, babe."

"Hey," I say back. I hope he isn't busy, this is about to be a long conversation.

"What's up?" he says. I can hear people in the background.

"Oh, just a couple of things. What do you want to hear about first? How my mom knows we aren't really dating or how Cary finger fucked me last night?" I try to say the last part as nonchalantly as possible.

He gasps so loud on the other end of the phone the people around him ask if he's okay. He ignores them and starts rapid-firing questions my way. "Fuck off, you know exactly what I want to hear about."

I laugh at his response, but before I can answer, he's already talking again. "How? Where? Oh my God, please tell me it wasn't on your couch. I love that couch. I *sleep* on that couch. Fuck. Tell me everything," he says, barely taking a breath between any of his questions.

As I answer his ever-growing list of questions, my anxiety about it all wanes, and a drive that usually feels somber is replaced with a warmth in my chest.

I didn't lie when I told Cary that Ripley is my person. I couldn't do life without him. It's the reason why our fake relationship has been so believable. No one questions it because we do love each other. I love him so much that it hurts sometimes.

142

Chapter Fifteen

Carrington

The guilt that washed over me after leaving RED last night slams back into me as soon as I open my eyes Sunday morning. I sit on the edge of the bed, elbows on my knees, head in my hands, just trying to figure out how I let it go so far yesterday.

I know the feelings between Thea and me were never resolved—hell, I've spent the last eight years discussing her in therapy almost on a bi-weekly basis. I just didn't realize how inevitable everything between us is until her lips touched mine last night. It took me a second to realize what was going on, but then it was as if no time had passed between us. She tasted the same, smelled the same, felt the same—maybe even better than I remember.

I can't help but worry about how Thea freaked out after her orgasm high ebbed. She was beautifully blissed out one second then panicking and locking herself away in the office the next. Did her thoughts stray to Ripley? Does she regret it? I wish I could say I do, but the wide array of emotions I feel about what happened does not include an ounce of regret.

And fuck Ripley.

After cleaning up the glass we knocked over in our haste to get at each other, I waited at the bar for another half hour, but she didn't come out. Knowing she needs space to deal with moments when she feels out of control, I reluctantly left. I locked the door to the restaurant behind me, and hesitated, thinking about her going back to her car alone so late. Even with the crime rate as low as it is in Indigo Hill, I couldn't help but think of the horror stories I've read about women going home late alone in Seattle.

I sat in my car and waited for her to leave about twenty minutes later. Even in the dim lighting of the parking lot, I could tell she had been crying, and it gutted me. I hate being the one to cause her any pain. She got in her car, and I followed her home at a distance to make sure she got there okay. Once I was sure she was inside her house, safe, I drove back to my hotel.

Everything about what happened felt right, until I remembered I have someone waiting for me in Seattle. Someone who has been patient, understanding, and invaluable in keeping my life going there while I'm here picking up the pieces after my parents' death.

"Fuck," I say to my empty hotel room and run a hand down my face before standing up and going into the bathroom to piss and brush my teeth. I splash my face with some cold water and take a long look at my reflection in the mirror. *Who even are you?* Avoidance is second nature to me, but it's usually out of self-preservation. I feel pathetic.

"Goddamn coward," I say to my reflection.

Stepping out of the bathroom, I grab my phone off the nightstand and check the time. It's eleven in the morning, eight in Seattle. I know what I have to do. I've been putting this off for almost a week. Though, if I'm being honest, I've been dragging my feet for years.

On paper, she's a great match for me: brutally honest, fiercely kind, funny as all hell, so smart, and independent enough to tolerate me when I retreat into my head. The only problem is that she's just not... *Thea.*

Knowing she's been up for hours already, I hit dial on *That Girl From That Bar* and sit on the edge of the bed.

"Care Bear. How did it go last night? I was hoping you'd call and tell me all about it when you got back," she says, her voice holding just a tinge of hurt. I've noticed she's been gradually getting more and more annoyed with me and my lack of communication. We've exchanged calls here and there as well as a few texts, but I know my silence must be killing her. She's a fixer by nature, and I know she's just itching to patch my life back together.

"Uh, yeah. Sorry about that. We finished up a lot later than I thought, and I just crashed when I got back." There's a long pause; she's waiting for me to continue, but words escape me.

"What's going on? I've been trying really hard to be supportive, but you have to give me a little more. I'm getting the feeling you're not telling me something. Did something happen with your brother?" she asks, her tone taking on an edge.

"Brooks is just... Brooks," I say with a scoff. "Listen, Arizona... there's just been some stuff going on here and... I–I don't think I'm making the right choices. Or maybe I'm *finally* making the right choice?" The last bit comes out as a question, and I'm not entirely sure what I'm talking about anymore. I stand and start pacing from one end of the room to the other, feeling restless

"I'm sorry, Care. I'm not following. Are you talking about your parents' restaurant? Are you planning on selling it to the manager you mentioned? What was her name? Thelma?"

"Thea," I rasp out and stop in my tracks. Her name feels like poison on my lips. How do I fucking unravel this mess? I have somehow managed to avoid all talk of Thea in the six years we've been together. I managed to skip over her when we recounted our dating histories to each other. And after I gave Seth a black eye for his comments, he hasn't dared speak of her. This is going to blindside her. We're committed—we're supposed to be happy. I can't do this to her over the phone. "I'm still not sure what I'm going to do. I don't think I'm ready to let everything here go," I say while rubbing the bridge of my nose.

"Okaaayy... so what do you need to make a decision? Do you want to get the business appraised? Have an accountant look at the books?"

"I honestly don't know," I say, running my fingers over my forehead and through my hair, tugging just to feel the burn in my scalp.

"When are you coming back?" It's the first time she's asked me this point blank, and by her cool tone, I know her patience is at an end. She's been letting me lead in terms of the time I need, but I know she wants me back on the west coast. Back to our life.

"I have my flight booked for the day after Thanksgiving. A few people at RED want to have a memorial for my parents *on* Thanksgiving, so I have to stay for that," I say.

"Of course. That sounds important," she agrees, her tone softer than before. And then after another silence, "I hope the answers come to you soon."

With a sigh and quick goodbye, I hang up. I don't stick around for the now obligatory *I love yous*. My skin itches from the lies of omission, but she deserves more than to have our relationship end over the phone.

Feeling on-edge and as though I might crawl out of my skin, I throw on some sneakers, gray joggers, and a t-shirt and head out the door. I don't have a destination in mind when I exit the hotel, all I know is I have to work some of this restlessness off. I take a right and head toward the center of town at a fast walk. Waving and nodding to some of the familiar faces, but I don't stop to chat.

Even after over a week here, everything still seems just shy of being recognizable. Some of the same businesses are still operational, but they've had facelifts. Alongside them stand several new spots, like the café I met Thea at a few days ago and a home goods store specializing in lakefront-themed decor.

From what I've heard around town, most of the town's revitalization has happened over the last few years. With RED quickly becoming one of the most sought-after small-batch bourbons on the market, it has drawn a lot of new tourists—spirits aficionados, collectors, and influencers who just come to take photos for the likes. The influx of tourists outside of the traditional summer lake season has brought much-needed new income. Indigo Hill is becoming a destination spot all year round, and the town is growing and updating to keep up with demand.

As I leave the town square, the asphalt road slowly transitions to gravel the closer I get to the water. I decide to head out to the walking trails that span much of the lake's coastline. As kids, Thea and I would spend hours every day exploring and playing along the trails, sometimes veering off and finding spots that lead down to the water that haven't been touched by tourists.

At the trailhead, I catch sight of a familiar silhouette bending over to stretch. It seems I've caught Thea at the start of her run. My eyes can't help but linger on the curve of her ass covered in fitted, blue running shorts. She's wearing only a black sports bra on top, and my mouth waters as I picture her last night, splayed out for me on the table. I can almost hear the small sounds she let escape when I sucked on her nipple through her dress. My cock twitches in my pants, and I remember I didn't get a chance to take care of myself with the stress from the last twelve hours.

"Hey," I say, walking up to her. She jumps at my words and spins around with a hand to her chest.

"Holy fuck, Grant! You can't sneak up on a woman like that," she says, chest heaving from the scare.

"Sorry, I thought you heard me coming. Going for a run?" Her brown eyes quickly look me up and down, and she nods. "Can I join you?"

When her eyes meet mine she blushes, and I imagine she's thinking about what we did last night. Suddenly her face shifts, and a smirk tilts the corner of her mouth. "Are you stalking me now?" My mood lightens seeing as she hasn't slammed her walls up again. Flirty Thea has come out to play.

"Can it really be called stalking if the town is so small there is literally nothing else to do on a Sunday afternoon?"

She rolls her eyes but smiles warmly. "Stretch. Last thing you need is a pulled muscle."

We stretch in silence, our eyes meeting every once in a while and quickly glancing away. My stomach flutters, and I feel like a teenager with a massive crush again. I catch her gaze raking over me out of the corner of my eye as I fold over to stretch my hamstrings, and it lights every nerve ending in my body.

We start running at a quick speed, keeping stride with one another. We don't speak, and the only sounds I hear are our breaths, our feet hitting the ground rhythmically, and birds in the trees. The day is unseasonably warm, and I'm thankful for the shade.

After a while, I find my mind wandering again to last night. Seeing Thea's breasts bounce as she runs does not help keep the memories at bay. *Fuck*. Running with a hard on is not a good look, and I can't exactly hide it in these pants.

Suddenly, I recognize this part of the trail and gently grab Thea's forearm to slow her down.

"What's going on?" She looks around to see what made me stop.

"I have an idea, follow me," I say with a smile as I veer off the trail to the left, toward where I know the water is. The footpath is overgrown and clearly hasn't been used in a long time, but it's just as I remember when we first discovered it as kids. We walk single file, Thea following close behind me.

"Do you remember where this leads?" I ask, turning back to look at her. She looks around confused for just a second, and then her face lights up when it clicks.

"This leads down to our cove, right?" she asks. I smile at the word "our" while continuing to walk the path, not answering her question. After a few minutes, the path opens up to a small clearing that goes straight to the water. It's just as I remember.

"Carina Cove," I say quietly.

She rolls her eyes at me again. "I still think that's a corny name." The nostalgic smile on her face tells me she's remembering all of our times here. We discovered this little private cove the summer before senior year, and it quickly turned into the place we'd come to do what all teens do when they get a bit of privacy: push boundaries and explore each other's bodies.

"Remember when you made me try smoking a cigarette with you here?" I say with a laugh, nodding at the tree stump we had sat on.

"Made you?! You stole the pack from Brooks and practically begged me to do it with you. Then we spent the rest of the night coughing our lungs up," she says, exasperated.

"That's not how I remember it. Between the two of us, you were definitely the bad influence," I say and shoot her a wink. She scoffs but laughs all the same.

We fall into a comfortable silence just watching the water lap at the bank. The trees surrounding the lake are an array of oranges and reds with the changing season. The image of them reflects back in the lake making the moment feel just as serene as I remember.

Being here brings back so many memories of the time right before we left South Carolina. Both good and bad.

13 Years Ago
(18 years old)

"Oh my God," I whisper as my eyes scan the paper. "Holy shit."

"Hey, language," Mom says, not looking up from where she's washing the dishes.

I read through the letter again. And once more for good measure to make sure I read it correctly.

"I got it," I say incredulously, a big smile spreading over my face. "I got the scholarship."

My mom pauses scrubbing and looks over at me. Dad also looks up from the paper he's reading at the kitchen table. It's a rare night in our house that all of us are home.

The diner is closed while a repair guy fixes the griddle that stopped working suddenly last night. We use it to cook pretty much everything, so it didn't make sense to stay open to only serve coffee. Thankfully, he said it wouldn't take longer than a day, and we can be operational again tomorrow. I know closing for even one day is stressful for my parents.

No one says anything for a long while when Brooks shuffles in and rifles through the fridge, pulling out a bottle of water. He drains it and only then notices the tension in the room.

He pulls the bottle from his lips, looking around the three of us and says, "What's going on?"

"I got the scholarship," I repeat.

There's a pause and then a wide smile overtakes his usually sullen features. He pulls me in for a hug. "Fuck yeah. Congrats!"

I've been waiting for this letter for two months now. This was the last thing standing in my way of setting off for Seattle. Thea and I had been planning on leaving Indigo Hill for years, but when we actually sat down to plan how we're going to do this, we quickly realized we didn't have enough money. Seattle is expensive, as is tuition for culinary school.

Thea, with her straight A's and ridiculous exam scores, had no trouble getting financial aid at the University of Washington. She received her early acceptance letter back in December.

I was planning on following her to Seattle whether or not my scholarship came through. I was going to find a job and work to pay for school, even if it meant taking only one or two courses at a time. But now that's not an issue. I have enough to cover tuition and housing.

My mind is spinning with all the possibilities. I have to call Thea. I turn to run up to my room when my dad slams the newspaper down on the table.

"Well that's just fucking great," he says with none of the same excitement Brooks' words held.

"Owen—" my mom starts.

"No," he cuts her off. "We've sat back and entertained this idiotic idea long enough. I think it's time he joins us in the real world."

"Let's not do this again, Dad," I say. "I've told you already, Thea and I have this planned out. We're going to Seattle regardless of how you feel about it. I'm going to be a chef. She's going to head up some big marketing firm. We're getting out of here."

"Oh, be serious for a minute. This is all just going to be a waste of money. That girl is going nowhere, just like her mother. Don't think we haven't seen her sneaking out of your room at all hours of the night. We're lucky she hasn't gotten knocked up y—"

"What the fuck?" says Brooks. He and I may not see eye to eye on many things, but he's always been there for Thea. This isn't the first time he's stood up to Dad for the things he says about Thea and her mom.

Dad's looked down on Lydia Ashford my entire life for choosing to be an unmarried single mother at such a young age, for not finishing high school, for taking whatever jobs pay the bills at the seasonal resorts in the area. He's even bought into the baseless rumors around town that she got pregnant on purpose to lock down some older rich tourist.

My father's words make my blood boil. How dare he talk about Thea or her mom that way?

"Are you kidding me?" My voice is rising with each word. "That's your big hang up? Not that I'm leaving and moving to the other side of the country, but that I'm doing it with Thea?"

"You wouldn't be leaving if it weren't for that girl. If she had gotten into school anywhere else, you wouldn't be set on Washington. You could stay in Indigo Hill, be a chef here. We won't be working at the diner forever. You should be making plans to take over."

"I don't want your fucking diner!" I'm screaming at him now. "I've tried—I've tried so fucking hard to get you to make changes to that shithole, but you don't want to hear it. You're running it into the ground, and you want me to take over? Fuck that."

My words reverberate around the tiny kitchen, sucking all the air out of the room. Mom—the dishes abandoned—stands with her back to the sink, arms wrapped around her middle, tears trailing down her cheeks. My dad's face is bright red with anger as he stews, still seated. Brooks is leaning against the fridge, shoulders tense.

"She's going to ruin your life. She's trash, just like her mom. At least her dad had the sense to get away from that slut when he had a chance." Before I know what I'm doing, I lunge across the kitchen. Brooks grabs me just before my hands reach my dad. He shoots up from his seat, fists balled. The chair tips back and clamors on the floor behind him.

"Owen! Cary! Please!" my mom screams.

With Brooks' arms locked around me and holding me back, I spit out, "Fuck you! I'm done with this shit. Done with you." Throwing my hands up to signal I'm no longer a threat, I say, "Let go of me."

As soon as Brooks relaxes his hold, I storm out, slamming the door behind me.

I end up staying at Thea's every night after that, only coming back when I know my parents are at the diner to pack up my room. A few days later, Thea and I take off with no intention of coming back.

Present

I shake off the memory of the fight—the details of which I never told Thea about. She thinks we had a falling out because I wanted to move so far away. It would break her heart to know the things my dad said about her, especially now knowing what their relationship grew into.

"Do you remember the last time we were here?" Thea asks, almost as if she's talking to herself. "It was right after graduation. We were so fucking excited. We had all of our big plans of driving cross-country. We were talking about all the places we wanted to stop—do you remember Carhenge?"

The look on her face is wistful as she reminisces on our cross-country trip, and she looks so pretty with her golden hair up in a ponytail, cheeks still slightly flushed from our short run.

I can't keep my hands off her anymore.

I step closer to her, crowding her against a nearby tree, making her angle her face up toward me. "Can't say I remember much about what we talked about that night, no. I do, however..." I push a wayward strand of hair behind her ear, letting my hand trail down and then gently close my fingers around the front of her neck. My eyes track the movement before shifting back to hers, "Remember what we did." The flutter of her pulse picks up under my fingers, and her throat moves as she swallows under my palm.

"Wh–what did we do?" she asks breathily. Her pupils dilate as she takes in my face, the black almost overtaking the warm brown.

"This," I say a moment before I plaster my whole body to hers and slam my mouth to hers heatedly. She meets me with force, and our tongues clash, battling it out. It's messy and wild and exactly like that night, the only difference being I'm not shitting my pants about what I'm going to do next.

I crowd her further into the tree, and she moans when my hard length presses against her stomach, our skin separated by only a few thin layers of fabric. She spreads her legs, and I press my thigh into her center. She rewards me with another moan that I greedily swallow down as we continue to kiss. Her hands trail up and down my back as if she's mapping my body with her fingers.

With my hand still on her neck, I pull my face away and look at her. Her cheeks are rosy, and her lips are swollen and a little raw from my scruff. Her eyes flutter open, and there's a question in them, like she's wondering why I stopped. I don't think she notices she's still rubbing herself on my thigh.

I gently kiss her lips again then angle her face away with the hand on her neck exposing the full length of it. I kiss, suck, and lick my way to the spot behind her ear, and she whines beautifully, all want and neediness. The satisfaction I feel from still knowing all the spots to touch that make her sound like that is primal.

"I want to taste you again. Can I taste that pretty cunt of yours?" I rasp into her ear.

"Yes. Fuck, yes." I smirk even though she can't see it and slowly kiss and suck my way down her body, hand still on her neck. I nuzzle against her breasts, feeling her drawn nipples behind the sports bra and then continue down, dragging my tongue down her belly, lower and lower until my knees hit the soft earth, and I'm kneeling in front of her, her hands on my shoulders. With my free hand I reach to peel her running shorts off her hips and meet her eyes, checking for any reservation. Her eyes are filled with need and desperation as she removes one of her hands from my shoulder and pushes her shorts and underwear down with me, allowing my other hand to stay securely around her throat.

I take a moment to admire her bare pussy. It's been so long since I've seen it, and she's a fucking work of art. She keeps the hair trimmed, just a small triangle at the top of her pubic bone that serves as an arrow pointing straight to paradise. I rub my face against it, and her scent hits my nose. It's intoxicating, making my cock impossibly harder. Running on instinct alone, I kiss and suck her milky thigh, leaving a small mark.

I part her legs some more and lick the length of her pussy, from her opening to her clit. She lets out a cry that has my cock weeping in my pants. With my free hand, I throw her left leg over my shoulder, opening her up more and keeping her in place. At the same time, her hands leave my shoulders—one coming up to grip the wrist of the hand at her throat and the other grabbing my hair.

I lick, suck, and circle my tongue around her clit until her thighs tremble and tense. Then I back off and swirl my tongue at her entrance, drinking in her sweet, tart taste. Sweat trickles down my back.

"You want me to make this little pussy come?" I say as I pull back and look at her. She doesn't say anything, just wrenches my hair to guide my face back to her dripping core. She's soaking my face, her hips thrusting against me when I return to her clit and flatten my tongue against it with even pressure.

She's close. Her breathing has picked up, her hand in my hair is gripping almost to the point of pain, and her thighs are locked around my head. I maintain the pressure and tempo of my movements until her body shudders and a loud moan—reverberating in my palm as it travels all the way up her throat—escapes her mouth.

I ease my efforts as her orgasm fades and pepper a few gentle kisses on her pussy and inner thighs. Releasing her neck, I remove her thigh from my shoulder and help her back into her underwear and shorts. I then slowly stand and take in her flushed chest and cheeks. Her heavy breaths.

When our eyes meet, she stretches up and kisses me deeply, no doubt tasting herself on my lips. That was always a big turn on for her, confirmed by the groan she lets out when her tongue sweeps my mouth.

My cock still aches, and I reach down to adjust myself. She looks at me and then down at the bulge I can't hide, apprehension crossing her face. I don't expect anything from her and to accentuate the point, I intertwine our fingers and slowly lead her back up the path we came down after another quick kiss. We walk in silence until we reach the trail.

"I, umm... I need a favor," she finally says, breaking the silence.

"That wasn't enough?" I return with a smirk, and she shoves my shoulder with a shy smile.

"Oh my God, stop," she says through a laugh. "I need help at the restaurant." My eyebrows shoot up because I was sure it would be a cold day in hell before Thea Carina Ashford would ever ask for my help at RED.

"What do you need?"

"Travis can't come in before the dinner shift tomorrow. He's still dealing with his daughter. I was wondering if you could help cover breakfast and lunch?" Her eyes are uneasy as if she's expecting me to say no.

"Of course. I'll be there." We share a smile and continue back to the trailhead in silence.

Once there, the air between us is awkward; we're both unsure of how to leave things. She's fidgeting with her rings, eyes darting around. I can't get a read of what's going through her head. To put an end to this before it can venture into uncomfortable territory I take her face in one hand and pull her in for a long, deep kiss then pull away.

"See you tomorrow, Lemon." I turn and walk toward my hotel, the sweet, dazed look on her face after I pulled away front and center in my mind the whole way back.

Chapter Sixteen

Mind-blowing. It's the only word I can think of to describe what happened between Cary and me at Carina Cove. And I have been thinking about it a lot since it happened—basically nonstop. I feel like a teenager high on hormones for the first time. I should be thinking about all the reasons this is a terrible idea. There are so many other things to consider, I just can't pull myself out of the best-orgasms-of-my-life haze to care.

I've gone as far as making up a fake reason for him to be at RED today. Josh could have handled the breakfast and lunch shifts on a Monday by himself. Even if it is our first day open since Hazel and Owen passed, he could have handled it alone. He's done it before.

Travis' absence wasn't so much a problem as it was an excuse. In forty-eight hours, I'd managed to fall so deep into the Carrington Grant hole that I am already shifting my life around looking for ways to see him again.

This. Is. Bad.

Running—almost literally—into him yesterday was a shock. I'd never expected him, or anyone else for that matter, to be on that trail. It's not somewhere locals or tourists usually venture out to during the fall and winter months. During the summer, sure.

Maybe even spring. But usually, I'm able to be out there by myself and get carried away with my thoughts. Running has always been the best thing to clear my head and after everything that happened after the charity event and then my conversation with my mom, I'd needed some clearing.

Now, I'm even more confused. Not that anyone could tell by the way I'm practically drooling while watching him cook right now.

How could I not though?

Even if he wasn't hot as hell, he also went out of his way during the lunch rush to have food sent to me in my office. Making sure I'm fed with some of the best food I've ever tasted only makes him more attractive.

I need to stop before someone sees me ogling him. The rest of the town still thinks Ripley and I are madly in love. Our fake dating stunt was never an issue before, but now it feels dirty. I'm scared someone is going to see the way I'm looking at Cary and think I'm stepping out on Rip. This town is entirely too small for me to get labeled as a hussy, even if it is a misunderstanding.

Fortunately—or maybe unfortunately, it's hard to say—the booth I'm sitting in rolling silverware gives me the perfect view of the kitchen. I know it makes me look suspicious. Monday is my inventory day, so I should be in the back counting and placing my order for anything we're low on. Two of my servers have already asked me why I'm out here and not doing just that. And as if my sins aren't grandiose enough, I lied. I told them I did it throughout the week since we were closed. I one-hundred percent did not do that. It'll bite me in the ass come Friday if I don't find time to do it at some point.

Cary's making me irresponsible.

The look on his face as he concentrates on plating the dish he's about to serve shouldn't be a turn on. He's so serious with his furrowed brow and his sharp eyes; his concentration is solely focused on the dish in front of him. The way he delicately sprinkles the garnish from up above, his fingers rubbing against each other as it falls—the muscles in those damn forearms rippling with the movement—shouldn't make me wish his fingers were on me. His hair is pulled back in his usual top knot, and God, I'm desperate to see it loose and around his face again so I can run my hands through it. Nothing about watching him work should make me wish I was on my knees in front of him returning the favor from yesterday. And yet...

I'm startled by a voice, pulling me from my inappropriate thoughts. "Thea." The voice belongs to Travis who wasn't supposed to be here for another two hours, or so I thought.

"Travis." I turn my phone over to see the time. "I thought you couldn't come in until three?"

He's already pulling his apron from his bag, wrapping it around his waist, and tying it in place as he speaks, "The sitter was able to come early. I felt terrible leaving you hanging again, so I rushed here."

I set down the silverware I'm in the middle of wrapping as I shake my head. "You didn't have to do that. I had Cary come in to help Josh in case we got busy since we were closed all last week." I pause as an idea starts to form in my mind. "However, this is great.

I have some paperwork and business things he and I need to go over today, so this works perfectly."

Travis nods then walks toward the kitchen; he isn't a man of many words unless the topic is his daughter, Melody.

"Travis, wait!" I say to stop him. "How's Melody doing?"

The smile that lights his face at the mention of his daughter warms my heart every single time. I swear she's the light of his life, no one could convince me otherwise. "She's much better. The doctors kept her Saturday night, as you know, and gave her some IV fluids. By yesterday morning, she was a lot better, so they discharged her. Then she woke up this morning back to normal, acting like nothing happened." He laughs as he says this.

"Kids are resilient that way. I'm really glad she's feeling better though. I was worried about you two," I reply with a small smile. I start to clean the mess I've made and gather the silverware I've wrapped into the bin we keep it in for the servers. As I slide out of the booth, Travis walks the couple of steps over to me and places a hand on my shoulder.

"Thank you, Thea. I appreciate how much you care. It really means a lot." Then he stalks off toward the kitchen.

I take a deep breath to get my emotions under control. The employees here are like family. That's the atmosphere we wanted to cultivate when we reopened as RED. We never wanted anyone to feel like we didn't care or that they were just here for a paycheck. Every time I'm reminded that we accomplished creating that kind of culture, it makes me so fucking proud.

I stand up from the booth and hand the bin to our server, Tiffany, as she walks by. The idea I have is... more than a little inappropriate and never something I thought I'd do at my place of work, but here we are. If I think much more about it, I'll change my mind, so I hurry and make my way back to the kitchen to find Cary. I push through the swinging door, letting my eyes wander until they land on the man who's been invading every one of my thoughts since yesterday. The second I see him in full chef mode, my resolve sets in.

I walk toward him just as he's garnishing another plate, doing the thing with his fingers again, instantly making me wet. Those fucking forearms are going to be the death of me.

Thankfully, Travis is already talking to Josh, so I don't need to explain to Cary that he's no longer needed in the kitchen. I place my hand on his arm once I'm close enough, then stand up on my toes until my mouth is close to his ear. I whisper low enough so only he can hear me, "Meet me in my office in three minutes."

I look back over my shoulder as I walk away, and he's already removing his apron with a smirk on his face.

Knock, knock, knock.

I jump up out of my chair and open the door as quickly as I can. I poke my head out and look around, making sure no one else is paying attention. Then I reach out my hand, grasp the shirt at his chest in my fist, and pull him into the office, quickly closing the door behind him.

"Thea, what the—" Cary starts, but I don't let him speak. If we talk, I might change my mind, and I really, *really* don't want to change my mind. I slam my lips against his. This isn't a sweet or seductive kiss. It's messy and hungry. It takes no time at all for him to catch on, and his hands are instantly wrapping around me and pulling me closer.

After a few seconds, and knowing I may lose my nerve if I don't escalate this quickly, I pull away from him. "As much as I'd love to keep kissing you, I have a favor to return." My voice is filled with lust, and the moment the words leave my lips, his eyes darken a shade. They remind me of a stormy night over the ocean, bolts of lightning striking down from the sky.

"Fuck, baby," he breathes out as I unbutton his dress pants. I hold his gaze, my bottom lip caught between my teeth, as I slowly pull the zipper down, reaching in to feel him already erect through his boxer briefs. The moan that escapes his lips as I wrap my hand around his base sends a chill down my spine. I give it a small squeeze, feeling it harden more in my grasp then pull away.

Bringing both my hands to his chest, I push him roughly against the door. The movement elicits a playful laugh from Cary. "Where is *this* coming from, Lemon?"

My lips pull into a smirk as my hands slowly drag down his body, feeling the outline of his abs through his shirt. When I land on his hips, I shimmy his pants down, my body moving toward the ground with them. With my knees planted on the floor, I look up at him through my lashes and put my hands back on his waist-band. He brings his hand to my mouth, running a thumb along my bottom lip while his fingers curl under my chin. He applies just a hint of pressure, pushing my head back so my chin is tilted up toward him.

"Open up, baby." His voice has a husky edge to it now. I do as he says, opening my mouth for him, and he pushes his thumb in, pressing down on my tongue. "Now suck." The command would bring me to my knees if I wasn't already on them.

I hollow my cheeks around his thumb, my eyes closing shut with the sensation. He groans as I suck and run my tongue over it. His other hand finds its way into my hair, wrapping my ponytail around his fist and pulling at my scalp. The burn brings a moan out of me.

He jerks his thumb out and pulls my head back to look up at him. "Pull out my cock, Lem."

I waste no time pushing his boxer briefs down his thighs and freeing his cock. It's the first time I've seen it in eight years. People can say what they will about dicks, Cary's is goddamn beautiful. He's not massive in terms of length, a solid seven inches. But those seven inches are gloriously girthy and veiny with a glistening pink tip. Seeing him again brings back all the pleasurable memories of our past together.

I stroke my hand over it from root to tip, giving another small squeeze when I get to the head. As I run my finger over his slit, I lick my lips thinking about what I'm going to do. I lean in toward him, his fist still wrapped around my ponytail, and run my tongue up the underside of his cock. There's a *thump* that fills the room as he leans his head back, eyes closed, hitting the door.

"Goddamn, I missed your pretty fucking mouth." His voice is so raspy now it almost doesn't sound like him. I bring my lips to the head of his cock, wrapping them around him and running my tongue over the tip to taste his pre-cum. His moan is verging on too loud, so I squeeze his outer thigh before popping off of him.

"If you can't be quiet, I'll have to stop," I warn. He shakes his head in response as I wrap my lips back around him. I hollow out my cheeks as I suck, getting a rhythm going. His moans have quieted some, but the closer I get to deep throating him, the more frequent they become. Drool slips from the sides of my mouth and lands on my legs. Cary always loved it messy.

He pulls on my ponytail again, eliciting a burn in my scalp that makes me groan just as he's hitting the back of my throat. "Fuck, fuck, *fuck*, baby. Keep going just like that." His words are making me soaking wet. I can't stand the ache in my core any longer, so I pull my hand from his thigh and reach under my skirt that's already hiked up my legs from sitting this way. I push my lace underwear to the side and start circling my clit to try to relieve the building pressure. This was supposed to be about him, but I'm burning up from how turned on I am.

Watching me, he says, "Fuck, yes, baby, get yourself off with me." The sight turns him on even more because he takes over and starts thrusting into my mouth harder. He knows how much his dirty talk and possessiveness turns me on. I squeeze harder at his base with my hand as he pushes in and out of my mouth at the same time that I apply a bit more pressure to myself.

I gag as he hits the back of my throat and holds himself there for a few seconds. The sounds filling the room are obscene, but that just makes me more desperate for release. Cary's getting rougher as the seconds go by, signaling he's close. All I can think about is how turned on I'll be tomorrow knowing my throat is sore from taking his cock so deep. The thought sends me over the edge, my orgasm hitting me hard. I moan around his dick again, and that must be the last straw for him.

"I'm about to come, Lem. Shake your head yes or no if you want it." Of course I shake my head yes. I've never once pulled my mouth away when he came before. I pull my hand from under my skirt and place it back on his thigh so I'm ready for it. "That's my good fucking girl."

Fuck. He knows how much I love praise. I swear to God, you'd think nothing had changed between us. Spurts of hot cum hit the back of my throat. I swallow him down greedily, not wanting one drop to escape my mouth. He pulls out, giving me a moment to catch my breath. His breathing is so heavy I don't think he's come down just yet. I take the moment to run my tongue over his shaft, cleaning the remnants of his release.

Once I'm done, he's pulling me up to my feet and crashing his lips onto mine. While he's still kissing me, he takes my hand and pushes it under the hem of my skirt. His lips pull away from mine just far enough to speak. "I want to taste you again, Lemon. I want you to go back to work with both of us on your tongue."

The mouth on this fucking man.

I push my lips back onto his as I do as he says, gathering my release on my fingers and bringing it back up to him. He grabs my hand in his and places my finger in his mouth then licks it clean. Once he's deemed it spotless, he places my hand on his shoulder and goes in for another deep kiss.

The kiss continues, tasting ourselves, our tongues dancing their familiar dance. I don't know how long it's been, and I honestly don't care. I'd stay in this small office the rest of the day if it meant I was with him like this.

The knock on the door makes me jump, and I clasp my hand over my mouth to keep from screaming which only makes Cary silently laugh, his broad shoulders bouncing. I bat his arm as I say, "Who is it?"

The voice from the other side is my server, Tiffany. "Sorry to bother you, Thea. A man named James Elsher is here to see you and uh... Cary too, if he's still in there—I mean here! He said he needs you guys to sign something." The deed. We knew this was the week it was supposed to go through, but we assumed we'd need to go back to Southbury to handle it.

"Yes. Yes, of course. Let me umm... find out where Cary is, and I'll be right out. Thank you, Tiff." I'm already straightening my skirt while Cary pulls his boxer briefs and pants back up.

"I'll let Mr. Elsher know," she says back before we hear her walking back down the hall. Once she's far enough away, I feel like I can breathe again. The possibility of getting caught shouldn't thrill me the way it does. I'll dissect *that* another day.

"That was..." Cary starts.

"Irresponsible?" I attempt to finish for him.

"Hot as fuck," he corrects me.

I roll my eyes as I laugh at him. Thankfully, I keep a small mirror in my desk drawer. I'm sure my hair needs readjusting since he had it wrapped around his fist for the last fifteen minutes. After a quick glance, I realize I need more help than this tiny mirror can offer.

"I'm going to run to the restroom and... clean myself up," I say. He chuckles at that, and I shoot him a glare.

"I'm perfectly capable of cleaning you up if you need assistance." His charming smirk reappears. *Jesus*. I'm not sure how I'll survive this man.

"Nope. No. We have someone waiting on us." The look he gives me is downright adorable like he's actually upset that I said no. "Don't look at me like that."

He gestures to the door, waiting for me to exit. I reach up and give him one more kiss before slowly opening the door to make sure no one is in the hallway. I slip out and head for the bathroom to clean up the mess he caused.

I catch my reflection in the mirror as I'm washing my hands, noting how rosy my cheeks are. Shit. I look freshly fucked. How am I going to seem casual in front of everyone? I dry my hands off and exit the bathroom. As I get closer to the dining room, I hear Cary and Mr. Elsher speaking to each other, though I can't quite make out the words.

As I round the corner, Cary says, "Ah, there she is! Thea, Mr. Elsher is here with the paperwork for us to sign and to congratulate us on our new partnership."

Reality hits me in the face as I remember that Cary now owns fifty-one percent of RED, and he'll be going back to Seattle soon.

I plaster a smile on my face so he doesn't see the dread welling in my stomach.

"Oh, thank you, Mr. Elsher. Can we show you around? If you're a bourbon man, I'd love to introduce you to our house bourbon called RED. It's distilled right here on-site."

He nods his head enthusiastically. "I would love that, darlin'."

Chapter Seventeen

Carrington

The mood shifted quickly yesterday once Elsher came to see us at RED. Thea was cordial and engaged, but the uninhibited, wild version that hauled me into the office was gone. In her place was the detached Thea that's kept me at arm's length up until a few days ago.

I'm not sure if it's because of what happened between us—although she initiated it and took charge of the whole experience—or if it was because the lawyer's visit served as a bucket of ice water, reminding her of her grief and her new position.

There's also the chance that once the lust haze cleared, her guilt about what her actions mean for her relationship with Ripley hit her. It's obvious he cares for her and maybe he's been good for her, but there's too much between us to just ignore it and move on. We tried that. For eight years, we "moved on." Less than two weeks and we're right back to where we were before it all went to shit. That *has* to mean something.

If I'm getting a second chance with Thea, I'm snatching it up with both hands and holding on for dear life. I'm not letting her go a second time. Fuck everyone and everything else. I know it makes me the biggest asshole—both because of the people my actions will hurt here, but also because of the beautiful heart it'll crush in Seattle. Despite guilt being a constant companion at this point, I can't make myself pause. Everything in me is screaming to forge full-steam ahead with Thea if she'll have me.

With Travis in the kitchen, I don't have a reason to go back to the restaurant today. Whether my name is on the ownership paperwork or not, the place belongs to Thea, and I'm not sure she wants to see me there this morning. We left things on a tense note after Elsher left.

Instead, I decide to go to the farmer's market.

The farmer's market has been taking place in the town square every Tuesday since before I was born. Although I went practically every week growing up, it appears to have turned into an all out event in the time I've been gone. It's easily doubled in size with vendors coming from surrounding towns and some even further. The market I knew had a small list of participants, just the few local farmers and bakers. Now, the farmers and bakers are mixed in among booths of local artisans, offering handmade soaps, art, jewelry, and the like. The place is busy with everyone picking up produce and last minute items for Thanksgiving in a few days. It's a chef's wet dream.

As I browse a produce stand, taking a whiff of an especially beautiful tomato the size of my fist, my mind starts whirring with all the possibilities of what I can do with it. The aromatic scent of the bunches of basil lying on the table mixes with that of the tomato, and I'm imagining a beautiful, crisp bruschetta topped with a drizzle of balsamic glaze. I can almost taste the bite of garlic on my tongue.

I put the tomato back and keep moving down the table looking at what else is on offer. On the other side of the booth, there sit a few boxes of gorgeous homemade pumpkin pies. It's when I'm looking at the box of pie that I notice the label: Abel's Farm and Produce.

Old Man Abel was a grouchy bastard. I wonder if he's still around or if his family runs the farm now. His farm is located on the edge of town, and he seems to grow everything: strawberries in the summer, pumpkins in the fall, Christmas trees you can cut yourself in the winter.

When we were about eleven or twelve, Thea and I got the brilliant idea to take our bikes out to his farm and help ourselves to some of his strawberry harvest. Everyone knew Old Man Abel grew the best strawberries, and since they were Thea's favorite, I thought it was a great idea at the time.

We did this a few times with no repercussions, having the time of our lives. With the town being as small as it is, news of the "crime spree" made it to the next town council meeting. Crime wasn't exactly something we had in Indigo Hill, so despite being no big deal to most, it was the news of the year for our town. Everyone was up in arms and concerned their farm would be next. Abel deemed us the Berry Bandit and put up such an upheaval, Sheriff Colson agreed to look into it.

The next time we went out for our berry shenanigans a few days later, the Sheriff caught us—quite literally—red handed. He had been sitting at the edge of the road leading to the farm and watched us bike all the way to the fields. Thankfully, he let us off with a warning, and we never went back. The mystery of the Berry

Bandit was still alive and well when I left for Seattle, you'd think we'd been serial killers who were never caught.

I chuckle to myself as I reminisce, and an idea strikes me. Pulling out my phone, I shoot off a text to my former partner in crime.

Me: What time are you leaving the restaurant tonight?

Surprisingly, it only takes a second for Thea to text back.

Thea: 6

Not the warmest response, but I'll take it.

Me: I'll be at your house at 6:30. Be hungry.

When she doesn't respond to fight me on the plans, I count it as a win. Before exiting the messaging app, I see another unread text waiting for me.

That Girl From That Bar.

After staring at the notification for a few moments, I lock the screen without opening the message and slip my phone back into my pocket.

I go back around to the produce and make my selections, picking up a few tomatoes and the fragrant basil. I'm waiting around for my turn to pay when I hear a gruff voice call out, "You plan on paying for that this time?" I look around and see Old Man Abel smirking at me. He's sitting toward the back of the booth, hidden behind the crates of produce on the table. Rubbing the back of my neck, I feel sheepish meeting his eyes.

"Meg," he says, speaking to the young woman manning the register who must be his granddaughter. "Throw in a pie for our Berry Bandit."

"Thank you, you really don't have to," I say. "You knew?"

"Figured it out about the time you started avoiding my booth here the week after the Sheriff came and told me the problem had been taken care of," he says with a laugh.

My face warms. "Sorry about that. We were just kids, you know?"

"Pretty girls will make you do all sorts of stupid shit," he says, voice much warmer than I remember.

I thank him again, as well as Meg, and go pick up a few other items from other booths. Then I make my way over to Grayce's Café to kill some time before I head to that same pretty girl's house to do some more stupid shit.

The door opens a few moments after my knock, and Thea's uncertain eyes meet mine. Her hair is down around her shoulders in soft waves. She's wearing black jeans that seem to be painted on, making my mouth water at the sight. She's paired them with a plain but fitted light green t-shirt.

"Hi," I say with a small smile, lifting the totes of produce I'm carrying. She moves aside to let me in, her expression still wary. I make my way to the kitchen to put the bags on the counter, and she follows.

"I figured you probably didn't eat much today," I say, unloading the produce.

"You figured right. It was busy. I almost stayed to help close up, but Tiffany kicked me out when I mentioned I had plans."

"We should probably give her a raise," I say with a chuckle. My joke, however, does not have the desired effect, and her face grows more serious—if that's even possible. I'm unsure how I've put myself in this situation. I'm glimpsing back to all those years ago when I was walking on eggshells around Thea, feeling like I couldn't say or do anything right. I knew she had been unhappy, but I wasn't able to pinpoint why or how to fix it.

I shake my head to clear it and face her head-on. Thanks to Dr. Ferris, I'm much better equipped to decipher another person's emotional state as well as how to regulate my own without shutting down. I worked hard to not be like my father in that regard.

Express, don't repress.

"What's going on?" I ask as I push a lock of hair behind her ear.

She grabs my wrist and pulls it away from her face. "We need to talk about RED. I need to know what you're planning for it. I can't make any plans for its future if I don't know what you're doing. Our expansion plans are already—" I put my finger to her lips to cut off her rambling.

"Let's table that for tonight." She goes to say something else, already looking annoyed, but I speak again before she gets a word out. "I promise we'll talk about it. I just need more time to wrap my head around everything. Trust me when I say I want nothing more than for RED to continue to succeed and grow. I know how much it means to you, how much it meant to my parents. All I'm asking for is some trust and a little bit of time. Can you give me that?" She stares at me for a moment like she's waging a war in her mind to determine if she's willing to lose this battle and then slowly nods.

"Good. Now," I say, turning back to the ingredients littering the counter. "Will you be my sous chef?"

She rolls her eyes, but I finally get a smile. "I'm at your service, Chef," she says with a small bow. The smile turns into a smirk, and I know she knows exactly how that sounds and what those words do to my cock. She grabs a portable speaker from the living room and places it on the counter in the kitchen.

"Here, dice the tomatoes for the bruschetta. I'll get started on the chicken." I set the oven to preheat, open the bottle of red wine I picked up before getting here, pour us each a glass, and leave the bottle to breathe. Thea grabs the fresh veggies and rinses them in the sink before beginning to chop and dice.

I sift through her spice cabinet for the basics: salt, pepper, garlic powder, and onion powder. Everything in the kitchen is exactly where her mom kept it when she lived here. It's comforting and brings me back to the many afternoons I spent here whipping up snacks for us after school. I feel more connected to her now than I have since coming back simply because of where we are and what we're doing.

We work in silence with only the slow melodic beats of Zach Bryan playing softly from the speaker Thea turned on. We move around each other in the cozy kitchen like we've been doing this exact thing for years. I catch her watching me as I season the whole chicken I got at the butcher's booth today. Her eyes are a little glazed, and her pouty mouth is slightly open.

I motion toward my mouth and say, "Is that drool for dinner or for me?" As soon as the question leaves my lips, I know she's going to give me one of her snarky answers, and the anticipation has me thrumming. This feels like before, like when I could read her every thought just by being in the same room as her.

She immediately snaps out of her daze, and sucks her lips in between her teeth, while her cheeks turn that pretty pink color I love.

"Don't be getting cocky now. I'm just hungry." She isn't fooling either of us, but I let the lie slide. Her eyes go back to the task in front of her as she drizzles the balsamic glaze over the bruschetta she's putting together. When she looks back up, she catches me staring this time, and her lips tilt up in a smirk. We continue in silence that I wish felt more comfortable. There's a layer of tension coating the air, and I'm not sure how to diffuse it.

"Bruschetta's ready," she says, wiping her hands on a kitchen towel. After a beat, she adds, "I'm sorry, but I really have to know. Are you going back to Seattle?" I should have known she wouldn't leave the difficult conversations for another day. Thea was always able to flirt one second then turn serious the next. I'm not sure how much longer I can keep sidestepping her questions, but I wanted tonight to be about us and nothing else.

"Let's not think about that tonight. Tonight is about good food." I cut off a piece of the bruschetta and hold it up to her mouth. She takes the bite and lets out a moan that almost brings me to my knees. "Delicious wine." I grab her glass then step in close to her front, backing her to the island, and lift the wineglass to her lips. She grabs it from me and takes a sip. "And mouthwatering company." I wait until she swallows her wine, and then I lean down and kiss her. I glide my tongue against the seam of her lips, gently asking for entrance. She opens, and I taste the tang of the tomato, tannins of the wine, and sweetness of the balsamic glaze on her tongue. I could spend all night kissing her plump lips, but I slowly make my way down her chin to her neck with kisses and small nips.

I take the wine glass from her hand and place it on the island next to us. Her hands come up to my face and then into my hair. I feel her tugging out the tie holding my hair back.

"Fuck. It's better than I imagined," she says looking at where my hair falls around my face as I pull back.

"You've been thinking about my hair?" I say with a small laugh.

"Among other things." She rakes her hands through it, seemingly enjoying the feeling.

"Hmmm," I hum while going back to kissing her neck. She leans her head back giving me more access and closes her eyes. "I've been thinking too."

"Oh yeah?" Her voice is breathless. Hearing her give in to what she's feeling hardens my cock behind my fly. But her vulnerability also makes me pause.

I have to try to make this work with her. I feel it with everything in my body, my soul. I can guess where tonight is leading, and I need to talk to her, tell her about my life in Seattle before we take this next step. I owe that to her and to myself. I've dug a deep hole by keeping things from her, maybe too deep. But I have to explain and try to make her understand that despite how much of a dick I've been, I can't lose her. I'll beg for her forgiveness if I have to for as long as I have to.

"There's something I have to tell you first," I say, pulling back and putting some distance between us. She opens her eyes at the change in my tone. We stare at each other for a while, tension building, and I know I have to use this moment to tell her everything. "Listen." I pause and swallow over the lump in my throat. "I know you have Ripley, and I have—"

"I think I'm still in love with you," she blurts out, cutting me off and surprising herself as if she didn't mean for it to come out.

When her words finally register, my movements are no longer my own. I grab her face and slam my mouth to hers. Her hands grab my shoulders. We kiss as though our lives depend on it. I inhale her intoxicating lemony scent and her soft moans as I desperately fuck her mouth with my tongue.

Confessions be damned.

CHAPTER EIGHTEEN

Cary's hands grip my waist to lift me into his arms. I wrap my legs around his hips instinctively, my lips never leaving his. The moment he said Ripley's name, I should have come clean about our fake relationship, but those aren't the words that slipped from my lips. No, I told my ex-boyfriend—who thinks I'm cheating on my current "boyfriend"—that I might, maybe, possibly still be in love with him. I'm lucky he didn't tell me I'm crazy and walk out the door. Instead, he pulled me into a searing kiss like he'd been waiting for me to say those exact words.

It was the best possible reaction and definitely gave me the confidence to be more vulnerable with him. I need to tell him that Ripley and I aren't actually together though. I'm such a shit human being for letting him think I'm cheating.

Before my mind can spiral too much, he lays me down on the kitchen island. The cold granite brings a chill to my skin through my shirt as my back makes contact with it. Cary leans over me and angles his head to reach my ear. "I've been waiting eight fucking years to hear those words again, *fuck*."

His lips reach the spot behind my ear, and, mixed with his words, it sends a shiver down my spine that has nothing to do with the cold counter under my overheated skin. He kisses his way back to my lips, leaving a hot trail from my ear to my chin. This kiss is different from the others. It's desperate and hungry, but there's a layer to it that's more than just desire. It's sensual in a way I haven't felt since long before I even left Seattle. His tongue has barely breached the seam of my lips when he pulls away, and I whine at the separation.

"Thea..." he starts, his breathing already heavy. "I need to be inside you. I need to feel you wrapped around me again." This is his way of asking permission, so I nod my head yes. I'm so far gone for this man I can't form words right now. He gives me a soft kiss then pulls away once more to say, "I want to taste you again first. I want to feel your thighs tremble and clench around my head as you come. And I want your cum on my tongue while I fuck you senseless with my cock." He smirks against my lips as he says his filthy words, knowing it'll turn me on.

His lips travel down my neck and his hands push my shirt up and over my head to expose my chest. He kisses the swell of my breasts, making me arch my back then he reaches around to unclasp my bra. My nipples are hardened peaks seeking his attention as he throws the material to the floor to join my discarded shirt. He wastes no time bringing his lips to the buds, sucking gently, my moan filling the room.

"Fuck, baby, your body is so fucking perfect." I reach down where his head is covering my breast and run my hands through the strands of his gorgeous hair. While he works one with his mouth, his fingers find the other, pinching my nipple to pleasurable pain that shoots straight to my clit. The sensation causes me to push his head away, further down, toward where I need him most.

He laughs and looks up at me, his chin resting on my navel. "Does my greedy girl want my mouth on her perfect cunt? Are you dying for me to fuck that beautiful pussy with my tongue?" I let out a moan in response, but he isn't satisfied with that. He pulls one of my hands from his hair and brings my wrist to his lips, pressing a small kiss on the underside of it right where my Carina Cove tattoo is.

"I need your words, Lem. I need you to tell me you really want this because once I start this time, I won't be able to stop until I'm coming inside you." We've been toeing this line since the night of the charity event. We both knew it would come to this. We've always been ravenous for each other, pulled together like magnets. Even when we'd fight, we couldn't keep our hands off of each other. This is different though. This is our first time after years apart. We aren't the same people even though it seems the same love exists between us, a love that was never going to disappear.

"I want everything with you, Cary." My voice comes out breathy, and my other hand pulls at his hair as I say it. I've never meant six words more. I don't want to do this halfway. I don't want to only have these few moments with him. I want everything. I've been too scared to admit that to myself or to him. This life with him, owning RED together, being wrapped in his arms again, it all feels so fucking *right*.

There's a moment after my words hit the air between us where he's just staring into my eyes, searching for something, but I don't know what it is. Before I can attempt to question it, he's placing my hand back in his hair with the other and focusing his attention on the fabric keeping him from my flesh. I wore jeans today. They're one of my favorite pairs—black skinny jeans that hug my ass just right. He kisses my stomach before slowly undoing the button. The sound of my zipper being pulled down barely reaches my ears over the sound of "Next To You" by Ole 60 playing in the background.

I push myself up on my elbows as he pulls my jeans down my legs, leaving only my lace thong as a barrier between us. His predatory eyes meet mine as he loops his fingers into the thin material.

"Last chance to stop me." *God*, I fucking love the husky tone his voice gets when he's high on lust.

"Fuck me, Cary." Those words undo him, all of his patience and uncertainty disappearing. My thong is suddenly on the floor, and he's throwing one of my legs over his shoulder to spread me wider for him. It's such a powerful feeling to see a man on his knees for you. My eyes roll into my head, and I lie flat on my back as his lips touch my pussy. I can't help the unintelligible words and sounds that slip out of my mouth.

He circles my clit with his thumb as his tongue travels all the way down my slit, sucking as he goes. My thighs clench around his head, and the movement draws a moan from his lips that reverberates over my opening. He always got off on making me feel good. It makes me shudder.

"Goddamn, I love how you taste, baby. I'll never get enough of you." He continues licking me, circling my opening before he pushes his tongue into me, exactly the way I like it.

He thrusts in and out, groaning against me, still circling my clit with his thumb using an even pressure but faster now. "I want you to come on my tongue, Lemon. Then I'm going to fuck you so hard you come again on my cock."

As he speaks, he reaches up with his free hand and pinches one of my nipples. My back arches again as he rolls the bud between his fingers a couple of times before grasping my breast in his palm and squeezing. I push his head further into me as my orgasm starts to crest. That's one thing that hasn't changed; Cary has always been able to bring me to climax with just his mouth.

I'm squirming with the impending pleasure. He's pushing my thighs up now, his tongue pulsing deeper into me. It takes one more circle of my clit before I'm falling over the edge and screaming his name. Cary flattens his tongue against me as he captures my release in his mouth.

As I'm coming down, he stands up and pulls me off the counter. I slide down his body to plant my jelly-like legs back on the ground, and I'm reminded that he's still fully clothed.

His lips find mine and, just like he promised, I can taste myself on his tongue. He's always said I have a sweet, tangy flavor like a lemon tart. I can't say I agree, but knowing he loves it so much always gave me a confidence about being eaten out that not all women seem to have.

My hands leave his shoulders to find the button on his pants so I can get us on a more even playing field. Cary laughs into my mouth as I struggle to unfasten his pants. "Need some help with that?" His voice is playful now, the tone more flirty than mocking, but it makes me roll my eyes anyway.

"Have I ever needed help before?" I shoot back at him, finally feeling the button loosen. I give him an I-told-you-so smile that he quickly captures with his lips. I push his pants down enough to release his cock. It quivers as I wrap my hand around it, running my thumb along his slit, feeling the pre-cum beading there, and causing him to moan low in his throat.

His hands glide down to my ass again, lifting me back onto the counter, my grip on him slipping as he does. A chill runs through me at the contact. He pushes his pants down the rest of the way and steps out of them, kicking them off to the side. His shirt comes off just as quickly, his lust-filled eyes never leaving mine. Our discarded clothes are scattered through the kitchen now.

"Lean back a little for me, baby." I do as he says, leaning back on my elbows again. He strokes himself and smears the pre-cum all over the head of his dick. One of his hands comes up to my hip, squeezing gently. He lines himself up with my center, still holding his base, then slides inside me in one smooth motion. I'm wet enough from my orgasm that there's no resistance.

We both groan as we get used to the feeling of being connected like this again. He hasn't moved yet, but I feel his cock throb in anticipation.

"This perfect pussy was made for my cock. You fit me like a fucking glove, Lem." Our bodies have always felt this way, like they were made for one another. Our hands fit together perfectly, we meld together so well that when we're connected, it's hard to tell where one begins and the other ends. I'm just the right height to fold into his body seamlessly. We feel like each other's missing piece in every way. I've never met another person who fits me like I'm the lock, and he's the key.

He pushes both his hands under my ass and lifts me off of the counter. My arms wind around his neck, and we both curse at the pleasure the movement sparks through us. His mouth is on my neck, biting then licking to take away the pain he caused. Cary walks us to the hallway leading to my room but turns to press my back against the wall instead of carrying me to the bed.

With his hips keeping me pinned to the wall—and his dick still inside me—he pulls my arms from his neck then pushes them up against the wall over my head. Our eyes meet for a moment, then he slides one hand back down my arm, the other one holding my wrists in place on the wall. I see the glint of darkness in his eyes telling me his next move.

He reaches my shoulder and gently grazes his fingers over my neck before closing his hand around it. My pussy clenches around him as his hand tightens just a bit.

"You still like being choked with a cock deep in your cunt?"

I can't answer, so I nod my head yes as much as I can manage. His hand loosens again as he starts to thrust in and out of me. He feels so fucking perfect. I don't know how I survived the last eight years wasting my time on bodies that weren't his.

He slams his mouth against mine, tugging my bottom lip with his teeth, and sucking on it—hard. The sound of our bodies slapping together drowns out the music playing from the speaker. His forearm rests between my breasts, and every time they bounce from his thrusts, the hair from his arm brushes against me, peppering my skin in goosebumps.

Suddenly, both of his hands release me and are back on my ass, moving us toward the bedroom again. My arms wrap back around his neck as I try to grind down on his dick, seeking the friction.

This is the same house I grew up in, so he knows it as well as I do. Brooks was, surprisingly, kind enough to fix a lot of the outdated and broken things for me, but for the most part, everything is the same. The biggest difference, which I'm sure is the reason why he stops and looks at me with an unspoken question, is I'm no longer in the room he remembers. I moved into the primary bedroom about six months after I put my mom in Saint Stephen's. It got real old not having an en suite bathroom.

"The one on the right," I try to say nodding to the door, but it comes out as more of a whisper. Luckily, he hears me anyway. Once we're at the threshold, he kicks the door open allowing us room to pass through. He clicks on the light, and I'm laid down on the bed. Cary pulls out of me, and I whimper in response. He looks down with a smile.

"Don't worry, greedy girl. I'm not done with you. I just want to be able to run my hands all over your body while I get you ready to come on my cock." More wetness pools at my core. I love it when he calls me his greedy girl.

He steps back, and I take in his beautiful body. I haven't seen him fully naked in so long that the sight takes my breath away. He's all hard muscle and tattoos, and I have to keep myself from drooling. The way his eyes feast on me, appreciating my body in return has me on fire for him.

I can see his tattoos now, specifically the one that travels up his neck and peeks through the collar of his shirts. The second I work out what it is, my breath hitches, and I sit up on my knees with my feet underneath me.

"Turn around," I say, my eyes never leaving the spot that clearly connects to more on his back. Out of the corner of my eye, his face bunches up in confusion like he doesn't understand the reason for my request. My eyes trail the space between the edge of his tattoo and his eyes, meeting his stare. He realizes then I'm seeking a memory inked in his skin.

He opens his mouth to speak, closes it, then opens it again. "Thea—"

"Please..." I cut him off, a hint of desperation I'm not proud of tinging my voice.

He turns slowly, and when the image comes together, my hand flies to my mouth. There's a massive tree tattooed on his skin, the branches crawling up the length of his neck. My eyes frantically search for the tattoo I hope is connected and not covered up by the image that extends over the expanse of his back. I find it moments later, my hand tracing the shape of the lemon delicately hanging from one of the branches. Knowing he didn't cover it up after all this time has my eyes welling. He turns around to face me, my hand falling down to the bed and his hand finding my left cheek to swipe away the tear as it falls.

I look back up at his face. "When I saw... I thought... I thought—fuck, I thought you covered it up. I thought you'd gotten rid of it—of me..." Another tear falls, another swipe of his thumb to catch it.

"Every memory I have of you is etched in my soul, Thea. There is no getting rid of you."

I push up onto my knees so I can reach him, place my hands on each of his cheeks, and stare into the depths of his stormy ocean eyes before pressing my lips to his. His tongue seeks mine out, and we hungrily kiss for a long moment. His hands run up my sides, pebbling goosebumps in their wake. They stop right below my shoulders before he gives them a squeeze and gently pulls away.

"Lie flat on the bed, legs spread wide." His voice is dripping with authority that makes me quiver.

"Yes, sir," I say in a teasing tone, but he likes it. He likes it a lot. I know because his cock jumps making him wrap his hand around it, stroking up and down lazily. Watching him intently, I get into the position he demanded, pulling a pillow behind my head.

He crawls onto the bed, sitting on his knees in front of me and staring down at my pussy. "You're glistening for me, baby," he says appreciatively. The praise goes straight to my core, making my clit throb with need. He grabs right above my left ankle and jerks me closer to him. I yelp in surprise as my head slips from the pillow. He hooks my leg over his hip and thrusts into me all in the same movement, making my head spin. My body is pushed back with the force, my heavy breasts bouncing, and my hands brace behind me on the headboard.

His other hand pushes down some on my lower stomach as he thrusts harder into me, making me feel even fuller. The pressure is tantalizing, already building to another peak. As his hand moves further up my ribcage to my breast, he lowers his body to catch my lips with his. The kiss is deep and vulnerable. The tone of our night has changed from needing to fuck out of desperation to making love.

His kisses trail down from the side of my mouth, all the way down to my neck and reaching the swell of my breast. He kisses, and kisses, and kisses, then suddenly bites down on the tender flesh making me scream. My hands come down to his head, threading their way into his hair. He rolls my nipple in his fingers as he licks the spot he just hurt. Just when I think he's done torturing me, his fingers are pinching my nipple again, making my whole body shiver.

Cary uses his body to push my thigh almost all the way to my stomach and swirls his other finger around my clit. I throw my head back with a moan as he grunts into my neck, his thrusts never losing their rhythm.

My climax builds with every circle he makes. I slide my hands down his back, scraping against his skin with my nails every time he thrusts into me. His hot skin welts under my grip, leaving my own marks on him.

His face is still tucked into my neck as he says, "You ready for me to fill you up with my cum, you greedy fucking girl?"

I let out a breathy, "Yes, fucking please," while nodding my head.

He moans again then asks, "How close are you?" Cary has never been a selfish lover. He's always more concerned about my pleasure, but when we've fucked, he always loved it when we came together. It was like stepping off the edge of a cliff and falling into the abyss hand-in-hand.

"I—*fuck*. Yes." That's all I can get out for him. Words always elude me when I'm in the midst of pleasure.

Cary lifts up, freeing my leg from my chest, then starts pounding into me relentlessly. His chest and abs are glistening with sweat, and seeing his muscles move gets me impossibly wetter. Within a few thrusts, my walls clench around him. His cock jerks inside of me letting me know we're both standing on the edge.

His lips crash into mine like a wave cascading against the shore as we both jump off the cliff.

We're sated, lying in bed side by side, panting in time together. Our hands have been intertwined since we both climaxed. The only sounds filling the room are our heavy breaths and the music still playing in the kitchen.

Or at least, those were the only sounds before my stomach growls, making us both burst into laughter.

"I suppose that's fair considering we skipped dinner," Cary laughs.

He brings our intertwined hands to his lips and places a small kiss on my knuckles. "The chicken's probably ruined by now, but we still have pie," he says with a hint of mischief on his face I can't fully decipher.

I shake my head as I say, "You're not eating pie off of me." His shoulders bounce with his laugh, the sound bringing a smile to my face.

"That's not what I was suggesting, but now that you've brought it up, I'm not against the idea." He smirks down at me then kisses the corner of my mouth gently. As he pulls away, I glare at him, making him throw his free hand up in the air. "Fine, fine. We'll eat the pie from plates like boring people."

I try not to laugh at him—unsuccessfully. He bends down once more, kissing my cheek this time then gets off the bed. I watch as his gloriously naked body marked by my hands moves to the bathroom. I hear water running and then he's back with a warm washcloth. With the utmost care, he spreads my legs and wipes up our combined release.

Tossing the washcloth back in the bathroom, he exits the room to grab our pie.

That ass.

It's scary to be this happy. I have this dread in the pit of my stomach telling me it's too good to be true. I keep pushing it down, but I know the second he leaves, it'll hit me like a freight train. Pulling my bottom lip between my teeth, I bite down to distract myself from the impending doom I feel.

Luckily, Cary is walking back into the room with two pieces of pumpkin pie on paper plates in his hands, effectively stopping my errant thoughts. My mouth waters at the sight of it. And him. He's still nude, and I can't take my eyes off of his body. As he gets to the bed, he hands one of the plates to me, placing a fork beside the pie.

I dig in, bringing the bite to my mouth and moaning the moment the flavors hit my tongue. Out of the corner of my eye, I see Cary staring at me. "What?" I mumbled around the pie still in my mouth.

"Should I be concerned that Old Man Abel's pie is making you moan louder than my dick did?" He laughs, and my face turns to shock at his words as I swallow down the bite of pie.

"Old Man Abel? When did you see Old Man Abel?"

"The one and only. I ran into him at the farmer's market. But that's not even the best part." He pauses, and I stare at him patiently waiting for him to continue. "He knew it was us," he says nonchalantly as he lifts a bite of pie to his own lips.

"What was us…? Wait—how? He would have killed us if he knew. He literally told the whole town he'd put a bullet in the Berry Bandit when he found out who it was."

Cary laughs, remembering the same thing. "Pretty sure that was before he found out it was just two kids in love."

My cheeks heat, and I turn my gaze back to my pie. "You weren't in love with me then. We were just kids."

"Pretty sure I've been in love with you since the moment I met you, Thea."

I'm not sure how to respond, and I'm scared if I try, it may involve tears so I shift us back to Old Man Abel. "So… what else did he say about it?"

He goes on to recount his run-in with the poor farmer we stole from as children as we eat our pie. Turns out, it's the best fucking pumpkin pie I've ever tasted. It shouldn't surprise me though, he always grew the best strawberries too.

CHAPTER NINETEEN

Carrington

My ringing phone pulls me out of my dream. The warm body lying halfway on top of me brings me to full consciousness. Thea's lemony scent mingles with the heavy smell of sex lingering in the air. I snuggle in closer to her, just breathing her in. I don't know how I've survived without waking up next to her all this time. My phone rings again, and I gently move to reach over to the nightstand for it.

Seth.

I check the time and see it's a little past ten. I'm typically an early riser, but we didn't get to sleep until just before dawn after getting reacquainted with each other's bodies and talking. The phone keeps ringing in my hand. I know I need to talk to him—he wouldn't call if it wasn't important.

Seth has been a lifesaver for me. Not just in the time I've been here, but pretty much since I met him. He's the one who picked up my pieces when Thea left me. He's the reason I started meeting with Dr. Ferris. He's an integral part of my success; I wouldn't be anywhere if I didn't have his keen business mind on my side to help with starting my own restaurant. I've told him time and again that he could do so much better than hitching himself to my fledgling business, but he says he wouldn't want to be anywhere else.

While I've been in Indigo Hill, he's managed to keep everything running as though nothing has changed. I have curated a great kitchen staff at Carina Cove, and they run like a well-oiled machine. I can trust that the culinary experience isn't suffering without me there, but I am also the face of the restaurant. People come to have me cook for them specifically. I have already missed a few important private events hosted at the restaurant. Thankfully, Seth was able to handle it with his usual grace, but it's time to go back.

I have to figure out a plan. I can't be in two places at once, but my heart is very clear about where it belongs. I have to figure out how to leave behind everything I've worked toward for almost half my life. No big deal.

And *her*.

My guilt gnaws at me. The ever-present pit in my stomach—which eases some when I'm in Thea's company—is growing deeper every day. She doesn't deserve this, and I'm sure there's a special place reserved in hell for me for what I've done to her and what I'll put her through when I get back to Seattle in a few days.

But it'll all be worth it. I ache to tell Thea I love her, but I need to do it with a clear conscience and with no attachments.

I hit the answer button and whisper, "Hold on, man. Just give me a second."

I kiss the top of Thea's head where it's lying on my chest and slowly disentangle myself from her limbs. She's a snuggler; she has always needed to have a body part touching me while sleeping. On cold nights especially, she had a way of wrapping herself around my body where I thought I'd have to wear her like a backpack if I got up to use the bathroom in the middle of the night.

Before I step out of the room, I watch Thea for just a second, enjoying her in her most relaxed state. Her face is soft, her lips slightly parted.

She's so fucking beautiful.

It's hard to walk away. I picture her underneath me last night, writhing and trembling, my rough hands on her smooth skin, the sinful sounds she made. I almost slip back into bed and wake her up with my mouth on her sweet pussy. The phone in my hand serves as a reminder that I need to leave the room, but it takes some serious effort to make my feet move. I gently close the door behind me and make my way across the kitchen while picking up my shirt and pants from the floor and slipping into them.

"Just one more second," I say quietly into the phone. I then step out onto the patio right outside the kitchen. The morning is chilly, the weather is finally getting the message that it's late November. It helps wake me up fully before I face what I know will be a difficult conversation.

"Hey," I say.

"Carrington." Seth's no-nonsense tone greets me. It took me a while to get used to his all-business-all-the-time attitude. "What is going on?"

"Seth, my man. It's good to hear from you." Even to my own ears, my attempt at a light tone sounds like complete bullshit.

He sighs. It's weighted and tinged with disappointment. He's one of the few people in Seattle who know or remember Thea.

For reasons still unknown to me, he never warmed up to her and seemed almost relieved when she left. Based on me being basically MIA over the last week and how I picked up the phone just now, I'm pretty sure he knows what I've been doing. The silence following his sigh is almost unbearable.

"Did you need something specific?" I ask.

"That's what you're going to say?" He waits for a response. When he doesn't get one from me, he continues, "I'm going to assume you just pulled yourself out of *her* bed, so I'll keep this brief." I imagine him shaking his head, and the thought makes me bristle.

"Hey, don't give me that. You know what this all means to me. I don't have to explain myself to you." I'm being a dick, and he doesn't deserve it. Between the guilt of lying to Thea while also stepping out on a six-year relationship, and the sheer joy I felt this morning waking up with Thea wrapped around me, my head is all mixed up. I know I've fucked up epically, but I don't know how to fix it. It has left me paralyzed. I have no right moves to make. Every single one ends up with someone hurt.

"No, I'm definitely not the one you have to explain yourself to." *Fuck.* I hate that he knows exactly what to say to cut me down at the knees. At that, I sink down onto one of the chairs on the patio, and my hand immediately finds my forehead. I look out over Thea's modest backyard, memories of us as kids seeping in.

"I fucked up, Seth," I pause, "I fucked up eight years ago, and I haven't stopped since."

There's a long silence and then another heavy sigh from him.

"We're going to figure this out. You know I'm always here for you." His tone is softer than before. He disapproves, but he's being a friend first and foremost.

"Thanks, I appreciate it more than you know."

"And you guys will figure it out. You'll work through it. She'd be crazy not to find a way to forgive you."

"Thanks, man," I say. "It's still early there, what's up?"

There's a long pause, and then he says, "I wanted to give you a heads up, but I decided it's not as important as I thought it was. We can talk when you get back in a few days. It can wait."

"Are you sure?"

"Yeah, Happy Thanksgiving. See you this weekend."

"Yeah, see you," I say.

I hang up and sit looking out over the yard without really seeing it for a while longer. As I replay the conversation with Seth back in my mind, I can't help but wonder which *she* he was referring to.

I feel wrung out with guilt about what I've done, and I'm dreading the fallout from my conversations with both of them. But there is only one woman's forgiveness I can't live without.

Slowly, I stand and stretch. Pulling the sliding door open, I walk inside and creep over to Thea's bedroom. I crack the door and see she's still asleep. Not wanting to wake her, I walk back into the kitchen. Rummaging in drawers until I find a pen and a notepad, I quickly scrawl out a note to her and leave it on the kitchen counter.

Eight years ago my life derailed when Thea left me and moved back to our hometown. Today, I have to start getting it back on track, and the first step is to go back to my hotel and get a plan together. I have to find a way to leave Seattle in my past.

Chapter Twenty

"So, wait, you fucked... all over your house basically, ate pumpkin pie naked in bed, talked until five in the morning, and then he left you... a note?" Ripley's voice booms through the speakers of my car, sounding more skeptical with each word.

"Okay, you make it sound like the note part is bad. Is a note bad? Was it weird to leave a note?" My heart starts to race as I enter my second bout of panic over this today.

"Deep breath, babe." He gives me a second, listening to make sure I'm doing exactly what he told me to. "A note isn't necessarily *bad*. But he's a chef. Who promised you dinner. And then fucked you instead... so I guess I expected him to wake up and cook you breakfast, not leave you a note."

I nod along as he speaks; he isn't wrong. I would have loved a morning-after breakfast. Or even just to wake up next to him, wrapped in his arms. I got neither of those. And for that reason alone, I'm spiraling. Again.

"Tell me again what the note said."

I reach over for it while at the stoplight right before Grayce's Café. Once I have it in my hand, the light turns green, and I push on the gas before reading the note to him. I have it clutched in my

"

hand on the steering wheel, turning my head slightly to make sure I read it to him exactly as it was written.

"It says, and I quote, 'Lemon—last night was amazing, leaving early so I can start tying up some loose ends in Seattle. See you later tonight,'" I recite to him, pulling into the parking lot of Grayce's.

"Hmm... okay..." he muses back to me.

"No. No. You cannot say 'hmm... okay...' and expect me to not panic. What does that even mean?"

"It means... I don't know. It sounds kind of promising? But also confusing. What would he need to leave early to tie up? Seattle is three hours behind us. It just seems like an odd thing to say."

I've got the car parked in front of the café now with my arms crossed over each other on top of the steering wheel, my chin perched on them as I chew my bottom lip to shreds. "Yeah..." is my only reply, not really knowing what else to say at this point.

Last night *was* amazing, but I can't pretend like I wasn't waiting for the other shoe to drop. Everything felt *too* good, *too* right. The note seems harmless enough. There's nothing specifically concerning about it, but matched with the internal dread I've felt since Mr. Elsher reminded me of our situation, it feels like an omen. And not one of the good ones.

Does it mean he's going back to Seattle soon?

And if he is, will he come back to me?

Is this me losing him again?

I pause my downward spiral as I grab my purse from the passenger seat and disconnect my phone, bringing it to my ear as I push open my car door.

"I'm sure it's fine, Thea."

"Yeah, probably…" I let my voice trail off, shutting the door with a thud. I push a loose strand of hair behind my ear before the wind can whip it into my face. "Anyway, tell me about your trip. Did you get to see the elusive *West* while you were there?" He can't see, but my brows waggle as I say this.

The National Whiskey Convention is an annual event taking place in Kentucky, close to where Ripley worked for a bit when he was younger. Three years ago, he met someone at the hotel bar while he was there. They hooked up, and it became their own annual event. He knows close to nothing about him, just what gets him off and his phone number. West probably isn't even his real name. To be honest, I think Rip gets just as excited to see this guy as he does to go to the convention at all.

"Nah, he couldn't make it this year, something about work." There's a hint of disappointment in his voice, but I don't push him for more.

I pull the café door open, holding the phone to my ear with my shoulder. "Dang. Well, there's always next year," I say enthusiastically. He makes some kind of *mhmm* noise but doesn't reply. "I'm getting you your usual, right?" I ask him as I enter the line. There's one person in front of me checking out.

"Actually, get me an Americano. Extra large."

I mock surprise by bringing my hand to my chest. "Wow, Kentucky changed you." I laugh as I tease him. He isn't one to switch it up, but with the cooler weather starting, I don't blame him for needing something warm instead of his usual iced coffee.

"Okay, one second. I'm up," I say to him as I move closer to the counter.

"Hey, Thea," Grayce says with a warm smile on her face. "You want your usual, sweetie?"

"Yes, ma'am. I also need a hot Americano—"

I'm cut off by Ripley's voice in my ear, "Extra large!"

I roll my eyes before cupping my hand over my mouth so I can scold him quietly, "I know! I was getting to it, my God!" I look back up at Grayce and give her a small smile that I hope translates to 'sorry my best friend is annoying and demanding.' "Extra large on that Americano, please."

Grayce nods her head in amusement and takes my payment. I thank her then step away from the counter so the couple behind me can place their order. Grayce's is tiny, and there are more people than usual—probably because more people are in town visiting family for Thanksgiving tomorrow—so it feels extra cramped today. I slide down to the pick-up counter and patiently wait for my order. Ripley is telling me about all the new things he learned from the convention, and I smile at how passionate he gets when talking about bourbon.

The barista puts my order on the pick-up station then quickly darts away to start on the next one in line. I wave goodbye to her and Grayce as I clutch the phone between my ear and shoulder to pick up the two drinks. As I spin around, I see a woman out of my periphery a half a second too late to stop from running into her. The coffee and my phone go flying and crash to the floor.

"Fuck!" I scream, much louder than what's considered acceptable for public settings. I stand there in shock as I watch the woman look down at her very expensive, very ruined pantsuit and heels. Thankfully, most of the hot coffee landed on me, but some splattered onto her. I hear Ripley from the ground screaming, "What happened?!" through the phone. I bend down to pick it up, quickly put it to my ear, stand up, and say, "Gonna have to call you back, I just scalded myself and a stranger," and hang up.

The woman still hasn't said anything, so I take the opportunity to start profusely apologizing. "I am so sorry. Oh my God. Shit, I just—"

She reaches over and puts her hand on my forearm in a placating gesture. "It's okay, really."

I'm aggressively shaking my head, fully aware that I probably look insane. "No, it's really not. I am so all over the place. I wasn't paying attention. I'm just in my head, you know? No. You probably don't know because you're probably a normal person who didn't just sleep with her ex and are now wondering if it was a mistake despite it feeling so fucking right. You know?" I throw my hand over my mouth. "Oh, wow. Fuck. You did not need to know all of that. I don't know why I said that. Or why I'm saying fuck so much, shit. I ramble when I'm nervous, and—well, surprise—throwing hot coffee on someone makes me super nervous apparently."

I pause. Not because I'm done embarrassing myself but because she's... laughing?

"Really, I promise, it's okay. I understand how a man can make a woman crazy. Been there, done that, currently writing the book." She lets out another small laugh, and I feel like I can breathe again, knowing she isn't immediately calling her lawyer to sue my ass. "You want my advice?"

I nod because, honestly, I'd take any advice at this point.

"If it feels right, it probably is. If it makes you happy, listen to the part of you that's saying it's right. I think we sometimes talk ourselves out of the good after dealing with the bad. A man who makes you feel whole and complete is worth keeping around. Just... watch out for STIs if it's new," she says with a wink. *A wink.*

Who is this woman, and why did I not run into her sooner? She's like a fairy godmother who stepped straight out of Vogue with slicked back red hair, and a good six inches taller than me.

I give her a sheepish smile at the last bit because we one-hundred-dred percent did not use a condom. It never crossed my mind. Not that I think I need to worry, I trust Cary, but... yeah, it wasn't my best moment. I'm usually much more responsible.

She must catch my drift by the look on my face and adds, "Next time then."

No one in the history of Thea Carina Ashford has ever been able to calm me down that quickly without some kind of physical intervention. Props to her.

"Let me buy your coffee. I need to get mine remade anyway," I say as I pick up the cups from the floor and quickly toss them into a trashcan, then I grab some napkins for us both. At the counter, I look over to Grayce. "Whatever she wants, I've got it along with ours remade, please. And I'll clean up the mess I made, just point me to the mop."

Grayce, of course, tells me absolutely not and sends her son out to clean up the mess. I mouth 'I'm sorry' to him as he mops it up. He's only twelve but one of the sweetest kids I've ever met.

Once the coffees are remade, I apologize to the kind woman again and thank her for her advice. The ring on her left ring finger catches the light as she wraps her hand around the coffee I just handed her.

"Holy shit, that's gorgeous!" I say with my eyes laser-focused on the ring. She moves her coffee to her right hand, freeing her left so she can hold it out for me to see.

The ring is an oval yellow champagne diamond surrounded by a starburst halo of white diamonds set in a simple yellow-gold band.

The woman smiles as she stares down at the ring on her finger, probably thinking of the man who gave it to her. "It is very... pretty. Probably not what I would have chosen for myself, but that's what happens when a man picks out the ring," she says laughing.

"Really? I think I'd die if someone gave me that. It's exactly what I've always imagined for myself," I reply as I bring my eyes away from the ring and back to her face. "Sorry, I didn't catch your name?"

She puts her left hand back around her coffee so it's braced between both hands now. "Iris."

"Thea. Nice to meet you, Iris. I'm so sorry it happened in the way it did. But thank you for the advice. I really appreciate it." I pull my purse strap back up my shoulder after it slid some during my perusal of her ring and turn around to wave goodbye to Grayce. I slip her son a ten-dollar bill on the way out while putting my pointer finger to my lips and whispering, "Shh," so he knows not to tell his mom.

Now that I've had a full-blown meltdown in the middle of the café, threw coffee on a stranger, *and* told everyone there I slept with my ex, I can only hope this caffeine gets me through my inventory counts.

Chapter Twenty-One

Carrington

I've spent most of the morning since leaving Thea's switching between reaching out to my contacts in Seattle, staring at my phone, and pacing the length of the hotel room. My head is a mess. Last night was perfect, so much better than what I remember. Watching her let go with me, come with me. It was everything. Everything I've been missing the last eight years. Everything I haven't been able to find in someone else and thought I could live without.

There's a knock at my hotel door in the late afternoon, and I don't think too much about it before I sling the door open. My stomach bottoms out when I see the woman standing on the other side.

"Hi, Care Bear!" she says with an easy smile.

"Wh–what are you doing here?" My tone is tight, and my throat suddenly feels raw. I immediately see her face fall, replaced by hurt.

"Excuse me? I thought I'd at least get a hello after not seeing you for two weeks."

"I—Hi! I'm—I'm sorry, I'm just a bit thrown. Why didn't you tell me you were coming?"

"I guess that answers my question of if you were reading my texts…" she says, pushing past me into the room, wheeling a small suitcase behind her. "I tried calling you a few times yesterday. I sent you my flight information. This wasn't a surprise trip, I just wasn't giving you the option to say no anymore."

Fuck.

I try to calm my heart. It's galloping like a fucking racehorse, and my mind spins. She turns, looking at me with an expression that's equal measure expectant and pissed off.

"I'm sorry," I say again with a sigh and pull her in for a hug. "I just wasn't expecting you, and it surprised me. I'm… glad you're here." She slowly melts into me and buries her face into my neck.

The hug is nice and familiar, but her smell is all wrong—the expensive Tom Ford perfume she asks me to get her for Christmas every year—and she doesn't fit into my body perfectly—just a few inches too tall. I'm suddenly hit with a huge wave of guilt. Guilt for what I've done to her, and the lies I've told Thea.

Thea.

On the heels of the guilt is sheer panic. *Fuck.* What do I do? I was hoping to go to Seattle on Friday and end this. I knew I'd have to talk to Thea about it eventually, but I was hoping to have things settled there first. Who am I kidding? I was hoping I'd magically figure a way out of this with minimal hurt feelings and fallout.

Fuck. Fuck. Fuck. My heart still feels like it's beating out of my chest, and I taste bile climbing up the back of my throat.

"I have to go," I say suddenly, pulling away. Her eyes are bewildered, the confusion is clear on her face. I don't blame her. I'm acting crazy.

"Wh—where are you going?"

"Uhh, I have to go to the restaurant. I have to prepare some stuff for tomorrow's memorial-slash-Thanksgiving dinner."

"Oh, can I come with you? I'd love to see it and grab a bite to eat."

"That's not a good idea," I say quickly. Too quickly. "I have a lot to do, and I won't be able to give you a tour. You'll be bored. I'll show you around tomorrow." The stress in my voice is evident, and I'm at such a loss for what to do. All I know is I have to get out of here, find Thea, and try to explain... somehow. Any way I think about approaching this, it doesn't end well, but I have to try. "Just relax here for a bit. Rest. I'll come back later, and we can talk."

I leave her still looking perplexed at my behavior and step outside of the hotel room. I lean back against the wall next to the door and run my hands back and forth through my hair, feeling my nails on my scalp.

I feel like I might be sick. I pull in a few deep breaths and take off down the hall, out the front door of the hotel, and to my car.

When I don't find Thea at home, I race across town over to RED. One of the servers directs me to the distillery, where I find her alone, taking stock of inventory in the back room. As soon as I see her, my panic ebbs a bit. She's the calm to the storm raging inside me. Although being in her presence calms me, it still feels as if there is a fist clenching around my heart.

"Thea," I say, my voice tight. She snaps her head up and gives me the biggest smile. My heart squeezes tighter, and air seems hard to come by.

"Hi, baby," she says. I haven't heard the endearment from her in over eight years, and it actually makes my knees weak. She makes her way over to me, into my arms. Stepping up on her tiptoes, she kisses me gently, and for a moment everything feels right. "I missed you this morning. I was hoping to wake up with you."

"I know, I'm sorry. I had some stuff to take care of." I take a deep breath. "I'm leaving for Seattle on Friday."

"Friday?" Her eyebrows shoot up, and her voice is a whisper. "Are you—" she clears her throat, stepping away from me, "are you coming back?" I instantly feel the loss of her body heat. Her eyes have hardened, guard up.

"Yes. Yes, definitely. I just... I have a lot to do there," I stutter out. "Listen, we have to talk—" Before I even finish my sentence, she's turning away and grabbing the papers she was working on before.

"If you want to talk, you'll have to walk and talk. I have a lot to get done," Thea clips out, already making her way out the door. I hurry to follow after her. Clearly, I've said something wrong, but I don't have the ability to figure it out right now. I just need to tell her... something. I need to get ahead of everything, so when it undoubtedly blows up in my face, I can find a way to salvage this.

Her pace has picked up, and she's speed-walking away from me toward the main restaurant. I rush to her side and catch up as she's walking through the doors.

"Please, just slow down. I need to—" I freeze just as we get to the bar. Thea notices my sudden stop and turns to look at me and then follows my line of sight to the woman sitting on one of the stools, drink in hand.

All the ways I could have prevented this moment flash through my mind, none of them are helpful in kick-starting my heart or brain. I'm frozen in place and at a complete loss at what to do.

"There you are," she says from where she's seated, her smile as warm as ever.

"Here I am," says Thea, confused.

Oh fuck, oh fuck, oh fuck. I still can't get myself to do any-thing. This must be a lucid nightmare.

"Wait, oh my God. You're the girl from the coffee shop." Thea's confusion has turned to delight, which in turn makes me scrunch my brow.

"Iris," says Iris, now approaching. When she reaches us, it's as if time slows down and everything around the three of us fades away. In exquisitely painful clarity, I watch as Iris slides her arm around my waist, fitting herself into my side with a sweet smile on her face. My shoulders are bunched, but out of pure habit, my arm comes up and encircles her shoulder, holding her to me. My eyes make their way to Thea's face, her eyebrows are at her hairline in confusion and disbelief.

"Oh," Thea breathes out. It's more a sigh than a word. "You—you're—*Cary's* your fiancé?" Now it's my turn to be confused. How does she know that?

"You know?" I say to Thea. She holds my eyes for a long moment. She's pulled her lips between her teeth. Her face is blank, but I see the hurt in her eyes. I see her chest moving rapidly with her breaths. She's almost vibrating with emotion.

She clears her throat and forces a smile, shifting to look at Iris. "Yeah, I met your *fiancée* this afternoon. I ran into her at the coffee shop. She didn't catch me at the best moment, I must say." Her tone kills me. Iris isn't catching the tension in her voice because Thea is an expert in hiding her hurt, but I know she's dying a little inside.

"I had no idea you were Cary's manager, Thea," says Iris in her usual gregarious way. "He's told me about how well you've been running things here. The restaurant is beautiful." I wince.

"Manager... right." The tone in her voice drives a stake into my heart. I silently will her to look at me, but she's avoiding my eyes.

Ripley chooses this moment to stroll in from the back. He sizes up Iris cuddled into me, and as soon as his eyes shift to Thea, he's at her side. The way she molds herself to him has me clenching my fists and my teeth. I know I have no leg to stand on, but it's taking everything in me not to rip her out of his arms. He turns and whispers directly into Thea's ear, and she nods as he continues to speak to her.

I turn to Iris and quietly say, "What are you doing here? I asked you to wait for me."

"I just wanted to grab a bite to eat. I drove straight here from the airport. I promise I won't be in your way," she says sweetly, but her face is tinged with hurt and confusion because of my cold reception.

"And who do we have here?" Ripley says in his usual easy tone. His mossy eyes shift from Iris to me and harden.

"I'm Iris," she says, holding out her hand for him to shake. "Cary's fiancée." Her words take him by surprise based on the flash of emotion on his face, but he quickly schools himself and takes her hand for a firm shake.

"Quinn Ripley. But everyone calls me Rip. Thea, here, is my girl," Rip says, squeezing Thea even closer to him.

"Oh, you must be the one I heard all about," she says looking over to Thea, who gives her a half-hearted smile.

Once they let go of the handshake, a silence falls among us while the restaurant continues to bustle. Thea still won't meet my gaze, but her face is ashen, and her brown eyes are dull with hurt and disbelief. Rip's mouth quirks up on one side, and I can't tell if it's because he doesn't notice the tension or because he revels in it.

"Well, this is fun," he says with an instigating tone. "This is a great surprise, Iris. I don't think we were expecting you." The way he's looking at me tells me he knows something is going on, and he's about to make my life worse. Much worse. "I'm sure I can speak for both Thea and myself when I say that we'd *love* to get to know the woman that's swept good ol' Cary-boy off his feet." At that, Thea's head snaps to him, and she tries to quietly get him to stop whatever he's about to do.

He looks at her with a wide smile, turns back to us, and hammers the last nail in my coffin. "You should join us for our traditional night-before-Thanksgiving dinner. Brooks should be along shortly... probably."

"I don't know if that's a good idea. I wouldn't want us to impo—" I begin to say.

"Oh, that sounds great," says Iris. "I'd love to get to know all of you. Did you guys grow up with Care?" At Iris' words, Thea sinks more into herself, and her eyes start to well.

"Thea," I say, my voice tight.

"I'm sorry," she says quietly as she slips out of Ripley's hold. "I have to finish the inventory. Travis should have dinner ready for us in about an hour." She swallows thickly and motions with her chin to the back corner by the wall of windows. "I have the back table reserved... I'll ask Tiff to put out another setting."

"Thea, you don't have to do that," I say.

"Yes," she says and finally looks me in the eye. "As the *manager*, it's the least I can do." She finally lets the anger and pain shine through in her gaze before she turns and walks out. Ripley excuses himself with that damn smirk in my direction, which seems more like a challenge than anything friendly, before following Thea.

Fuck. Me.

By quarter after seven, we're seated in the back corner with the gorgeous view of the lake spread out beyond the wide expanse of windows. My gaze is zeroed in on Thea's, sitting across the table from me. Her face is blank, but her eyes are simmering in rage. I was hoping the hour she spent in the back with Ripley doing inventory—or whatever she ran off for—would have calmed her down a little, but all it seems to have done is transform her hurt into utter fury.

I spent the time before dinner at the bar with Iris, drinking more than I should to try to tamp down my panic for what's to come. Iris hadn't caught on to the tension between Thea and me. She gave me a rundown of her life over the last two weeks and complimented RED as well as what she's seen of the town. I guess I nodded and hummed in all the right places because she still seems content and even excited to spend time with "my staff."

I wish I could just melt into the floor and disappear. Everything that's happened over the last few hours is definitely the worst case scenario that I could have imagined. Probably even worse. My mind keeps going back to the look on Thea's face when Iris asked if she grew up with me. She was gutted. I deserve nothing less than the shitstorm this dinner is bound to turn into.

The table has been filled with various small plates meant for sharing that smell delicious but seem to do nothing but nauseate me. The servers have been keeping our drinks fresh—thank God. Votive candles cast a warm glow over the table. It would be lovely if I didn't want to claw my skin off.

Ripley and Iris are carrying the conversation for the table, discussing everything from the whiskey conference Ripley just returned from to Iris' sister's upcoming baby shower. Brooks, of course, is a no-show. Even Iris didn't seem surprised by his absence. I guess I've done a good job setting her expectations when it comes to him.

Besides perfunctory answers to questions sent in her direction, Thea has remained silent. Silent and stewing.

I tried to plead with her when we first sat down to step away and talk to me under the guise of something to do with the restaurant needing attention. She shot me down quickly with a clipped, "It can wait. Wouldn't want to be rude to your fiancée."

With a resigned sigh, I sat down across from her and maintained her angry stare for the last half hour.

I don't know what Thea told him, but Ripley seems to have shaken the tension from earlier and is acting as if nothing is amiss. He's cracking jokes and engaging Iris in easy conversation. That doesn't surprise me though. Iris is easy to like and get along with. She's one of those people who makes friends wherever she goes. She draws people in because she is just so effortlessly cool. I wish I could produce a laundry list of her flaws after six years together—it might make this a tiny bit easier—but the only one I can find is that she's not Thea.

"So, Iris," Ripley says conspiratorially in between bites. "Cary has been very hush-hush about you. Why don't you tell us how you guys met?" Ripley's eyes flash to mine, and I know his untroubled demeanor is all a lie. The *fucker*. He knows exactly what he's doing. But he's just as big of an asshole as I am; he must know that stirring this boiling pot of shit that is tonight is going to hurt Thea just as much as it'll hurt me.

Iris turns to me with a giggle. Her cheeks are flushed after the two glasses of wine she's already had. I give her a half-hearted smile before I bring my eyes back to Thea, hoping she can read my apology in them.

"Oh, he's never been great at talking about that kind of stuff. He's so private, I think he'd keep me a secret if I'd let him," says Iris, giggling again.

Thea scoffs in the middle of a sip of her wine, choking on the liquid. Ripley gently slaps her back as she coughs.

"That definitely sounds like our Cary here," says Thea, finally breaking her silence. I run my hand down my face as my stomach rolls around the many drinks I've already put back.

Iris shoots her a bemused look. "I'm the food distributor for Cary's restaurant. We met on the job years ago. He was this new hotshot chef making some sort of award-winning custard dish during one of the country's biggest egg shortages, and I just so happened to personally know a few chicken farmers who weren't affected. I hooked him up... and then we hooked up," she says cheekily and leans a shoulder into me affectionately.

I swig back the rest of my drink.

Suddenly Brooks appears beside the table. "Well, look at this. I show up a little late and you give away my seat," he says too loudly for the inside of a restaurant.

He's swaying slightly where he stands. And he looks like shit. He has a fresh black eye marring the same side of his face where his cheek was split a few days ago. Although I don't see any fresh cuts, he has a few drops of blood on his open and wrinkled button-down shirt that he probably pulled out of a drawer somewhere in the back.

"Are you drunk?" I say between my teeth as I stand up to his level.

"Ah, Cary. No need to worry about that, baby brother. I'm here now. Let's get this shit started." He claps me on the shoulder before stepping around me and planting himself in the seat at the end of the table between Ripley and Iris. He turns to Ripley, but points to Iris on his left with his thumb. "You brought me a date? Who's she?"

"I'm Iris. Cary's fiancée. It's so great to finally meet you," says Iris, radiating that damn perfection. Brooks glances around, and his eyes land on me. He shoots me the biggest shit-eating grin as I lower myself back into my chair.

I don't know who I'm going to punch first tonight, Ripley for all his fucking smirking or Brooks for what he's no doubt going to say as the night wears on.

"No shit?" He's still smiling at me, but it has an edge to it, and I know I'm going to hate the next words out of his mouth. "Ex-girlfriend and fiancée at the same table. This is your worst nightmare, huh?" I fix him with a dead stare as my stomach lurches, and I seriously consider making a run for the bathroom to vomit.

"What?" says Iris, her smile slowly fading and her eyes darting around the table. I'm saved from trying to salvage the moment by Tiffany, who appears as if by magic at our table.

"Hey, Brooks," she says to my brother with a salacious smile, and then to the table, "How's everything? Anyone need any-thing?"

"Can you bring me a double of... anything?" says Thea, rub-bing her thumb and index finger on her forehead as though mas-saging a headache. Then she adds, "I'm going to need more than wine to get through this fucking night," so quietly I don't think anyone else but me heard it. Brooks orders a drink as well, and Tiffany slips away.

An uncomfortable silence falls around the table. Thea won't meet my eyes, Ripley's smiling and sipping his drink, and Brooks busies himself with clumsily buttoning up his shirt—the bomb he dropped seemingly forgotten.

I feel Iris' stare on the side of my face. I can't bring myself to look at her though. I'm not ready to deal with whatever she has to say right now. I wish the ground would open up and swallow me whole, and I could just stop existing.

Minutes tick by at our silent table. Ripley and Brooks are the only ones eating the many appetizers spread before us, and still no one says a word.

"Care," says Iris after Tiffany drops off the drinks we ordered. "I think I need you to explain."

Before I even open my mouth, Brooks pipes up again, "Oh, he didn't tell you? He and Thea go way back. High school sweethearts and all that."

"I... don't understand," says Iris, looking around the table, and then her gaze lands on me. I can't bring myself to meet her eyes, so I just keep staring at the drink in my hand. I use my fingers to turn the tumbler round and round, watching the whiskey leave legs on the side of the glass. "Why didn't you tell me?"

"Oh, it's probably 'cause it's a sore subject for him. She left him in Seattle right as he was about—"

"Brooks!" I cut him off before whatever else he was going to say falls out of his dumb fucking mouth. I glare daggers at him, but he just smiles at me. There's no humor or warmth in that smile. Brooks is looking for a fight tonight. "Just ignore him. He's still pissed that our parents didn't leave RED to him. He needs to move the fuck on and stop moping about it," I say, speaking to Iris but continuing to look at Brooks.

Brooks laughs humorlessly. "*I* need to move on?" He pauses and just stares at me. "Tell me, brother, should I move on like *you* did?" When I don't answer, he continues. "Why don't you tell Thea the name of your restaurant," he says.

"You don't know what you're talking about." I sweep my eyes from him to Ripley on his right. His eyes ping-pong around the table from one face to another. He seems to be enjoying this, you'd think he's watching his favorite sport. All he needs is a bowl of fucking popcorn.

"Oh, but I do," says Brooks. "I looked you up, baby brother. Tell her."

"What did you call it?" asks Thea quietly, finally looking at me. The silence at the table stretches on for an impossibly long time.

"It's called Carina Cove," supplies Brooks, his smile is all teeth.

"What... what does that mean?" Thea questions.

I can't find words. Or air. I keep my eyes on Brooks, slowly shaking my head from side to side in disbelief. I thought we had gotten to—not exactly a good place, but at least somewhere we could start rebuilding our relationship. In ten minutes' time, he's ruined any chance of that, and I just watched my entire life implode around me.

I finally chance a glance at Iris, and she looks devastated. She studies Thea for a moment and says, "He's the ex, isn't he?"

Thea averts her eyes and sucks her lips between her teeth. I guess that's answer enough for Iris because she slowly nods without a word, picks up her purse, and gracefully makes her way out of the restaurant.

After another minute, Thea stands up and walks away too.

"Who needs reality TV when you have small-town livin'?" says Ripley with a smile. He and Brooks clink glasses. I swallow the rest of my drink and lift my fingers to signal Tiffany to bring me another.

Chapter Twenty-Two

I never got my answer before I got up from the table to leave. I'd asked him what it meant, but in all honesty, I know. There's only one thing it *can* mean. I just don't understand why. And it's the least of my concerns at the moment because he's fucking engaged. He got down on one knee and asked another woman to spend the rest of her life with him.

Then he came here and fucked me.

Iris... God, of course he's engaged to her. She's perfect, I've known her for all of six hours, and I get it. Why wouldn't he ask her to be his wife? The look on her face when she asked if he was the ex I'd told her about will haunt me for the rest of my life. I knew someone would get hurt. I assumed it would be me. Maybe Cary. But never did I think it would be his tall, model-gorgeous, nice-as-hell fiancée he conveniently forgot to mention over the last two and a half weeks.

I'm grateful no one has followed me, I just need some air and to not be in the same room as Cary right now. Ripley is probably distracting both Grant brothers at the moment. He'd promised me before dinner that he'd not only have my back but also make the dinner hell for Cary. Brooks came prepared without me even having to ask.

I push through the double wooden doors that lead out into the crisp November night. The instant the chill hits my face, my heart starts to calm. I'm pacing the front patio with my hand on my forehead squeezing at my temples as the events of the last few hours rush through my mind again.

"Fuck!" I scream, thinking I'm alone out here to drown in my sorrows.

"That about sums it up," a voice says from the end of the patio. Iris is leaning over the railing on her elbows, covered in darkness.

I clutch a hand to my heart as I jump out of my skin from the surprise. "Shit. I didn't realize you were out here. I'm sorry. I—I can go back inside." I turn to grab the handle of the door, but she stops me.

"Oh, you don't have to do that. You're part of the Carrington Grant Broken Hearts Club too. Welcome—hope you brought the wine." A sarcastic scoff slips out at her own joke.

I take a couple of steps toward her, not wanting to commiserate but also not wanting to have to shout to be heard. "I... I didn't know, Iris." I've got my hands in front of me, fidgeting with my rings as my anxiety over the situation flares through me.

She looks up at me with a small resigned smile then says, "That much was obvious."

I don't know what else to say, if there's even anything else to be said, so I just nod back.

She turns so she's leaning her hip against the railing now, her eyes set on me. The silence drags on for some time which only makes me more anxious. I don't know this woman. I have no idea what she could be thinking right now. What I do know is that she's just as heartbroken as me, it's written all over her face.

"Could you do me a favor?" she finally says.

"Of course," I reply with no hesitation at all. Too quickly probably.

"Can you make sure he stays here for a bit longer? I need to get my things from his room and find somewhere else to stay. Maybe I'll drive back to Myrtle Beach and find a hotel there."

I'm not sure what the etiquette is for this type of situation, but I start speaking before I can second guess my own decision. "I... can probably make that happen. And I can make a call to a friend about a hotel room. It's in Southbury—about thirty minutes east."

Her eyes widen for half a second, I think she's taken aback by my offer—which is fair, considering. "Oh. No. You don't have to do that. Really." Her voice is tight, and I'm not sure what to make of it.

"It's really no big deal, if you need a place to stay. I know I'm probably the last person you want anything from—"

She cuts me off, "No, Carrington is the last person I want anything from. I'll find a place. I appreciate your offer though. I just need to not be in this town anymore."

I nod my head in understanding, seeing the headlights from a car in the parking lot gleam off of her engagement ring as I do. The sight of it makes me nauseous now knowing who gave it to her and knowing I'm part of the reason she'll probably hate the sight of it.

Without another word, she walks toward the stairs to the sidewalk, and I stand frozen in place. I never expected today to end this way, especially with the way it began. I watch as she walks to her car, gets in, and drives away. I stare off into the distance long after her taillights disappear.

It's not until I start to shiver from the chill in the air that I remember Iris' request. I pull my phone from my pocket, feeling the pit in my stomach widen as I scroll past Cary's name to get to Ripley's.

Me: Do me a favor and keep Cary occupied for at least another hour?

Ripley: Sure thing. You okay? Do I need to be concerned?

Me: Okay? No. Iris needs time to get her things, and I told her I'd make it happen.

Ripley: Gotcha. You didn't answer the other question.

Me: Because I don't have an answer…

Ripley: I'm sorry, babe…

Me: Me too. I'm heading home. Love you, thank you for tonight.

Ripley: Yeah, of course. Love you too.

I'm familiar with the five stages of grief having gone through them a couple times in my life. This time, as I mourn my second chance at a future with Cary, I skipped right over denial since reality was staring me in the face and was really fucking hard to deny. Depression hit first. I'd spent the full hour after seeing Iris at the bar in the distillery with Ripley crying a goddamn river over it all.

I never thought Cary was capable of hurting me in this way. I didn't think he was capable of being so cruel. It made me wonder if this was karma for breaking his heart eight years ago. If it is—congratulations. It got me fucking good. Ripley had disagreed though. He'd told me since I came home to help with my mom's care, I was given a free pass. He said it as if he personally knew how these decisions are made, like he has an in with karma herself. The thought made me laugh at the time.

Had it not been for Ripley, there was no way I could have attended that horrid dinner. He'd given me the option to bail. He told me he'd cover for me and say I was sick. He'd even offered to tell everyone his own secret, so I didn't have to go out there and pretend I wasn't upset because why would I be when I'm with

Ripley? I never would have let him do that though. And it was better with him by my side. I could lean on him, and no one would question it.

Ripley wasn't one to let anyone get away with hurting some-one he loves though. He'd made it his mission to make sure Cary was uncomfortable. By that point, I'd entered into the anger stage of my grief, so I was more than happy to play along. I didn't hold back my glares, and I didn't pretend everything was fine. I made sure he felt my wrath from across the table. He'd played me so fucking well. I'm still mad at myself for falling for it.

I turn to leave the patio, but my eyes snag on Iris' ring sitting on the railing. Picking it up, the facets glimmer, catching the light from the parking lot. I stare at it for a minute before I pocket it and climb down the steps.

The drive home is silent. I don't put on music, I don't call my mom or Rip, I just drive with only my thoughts to keep me company. I let them fuel my rage for Carrington Grant. I want to hold onto my anger until I slip into acceptance. Bargaining won't be a part of my grief for him or the relationship I thought we were re-establishing.

I pull into my driveway, turn off the car, and sit there for a moment. When I left my house this morning, I was excited about my future. I was nervous and anxious, too, but I attributed that to my own issues. Maybe, subconsciously, I knew something was off. I'd tried to convince myself Ripley was wrong, thinking Cary's note seemed odd. I knew it had seemed too good to be true. That's why I'd been on edge to begin with. So why was I so surprised when it blew up in my face?

The lights inside my car dim, illuminating the clock on the dash telling me it's almost ten. I take a deep breath, finally reach over the middle console to grab my purse from the passenger seat, and go inside.

I need acceptance to hurry the fuck up.

Once inside the house, I lock the door behind me and beeline for my bedroom to change into pajamas. As I walk into the kitchen, I remember the ice cream in the freezer. I need some sugar to drown my sorrows in.

As I reach for the cutlery drawer, I spot the leftover pumpkin pie from last night. My heart constricts with the memory of how fucking *happy* I felt yesterday, how everything felt like it was finally falling back into place.

Without wasting any more thought on what could have been, I shove the pie to the end of the counter and into the trash can.

I grab a spoon, forgoing a bowl because no one is here to judge me—and even if they were, I wouldn't give a fuck—and grab the cookies and cream from the freezer.

I've already determined that sleeping in my bed tonight isn't an option since it'll just serve as a reminder. The sheets still smelled of him when I got up this morning. I relished it when I woke up, now I'm seriously considering taking them outside and lighting them on fire. I could watch them burn to ash like our relationship just did.

My favorite blanket waits for me on the couch as I slouch down into it. I turn on *New Girl*—my all-time-favorite comfort show—and proceed to eat my weight in ice cream.

Around the fourth episode, I must have fallen asleep because I'm awoken by my phone ringing on the end table. I swipe at my eyes and sit up but realize a second too late that the ice cream container was still in my lap. It starts to tumble onto the floor, but I catch it at the last second, just barely avoiding a huge melted ice cream mess that really would have been the cherry on top of my shit sundae of a night.

On the fifth ring, I grab my phone and bring it to my ear without seeing who it is first.

"Hello?" my voice cracks at the end.

"Hey, Thea... uhh, it's Nat." My bartender's voice wakes me up more, I pull the phone away from my ear to see it's a few minutes after midnight. My heartbeat picks up with panic at hearing the uncertainty in her voice.

"Nat, what is it? Is everything okay?" I'm already getting up from the couch, turning off the TV, and walking toward my room to find some clothes.

"Oh, umm... kind of? I just—I didn't know who to call..." she trails off at the end which makes me even more nervous.

"You're scaring me, did something happen at the restaurant? Are you okay?" My mind is going a mile a minute as I hold the phone to my ear with my shoulder, freeing my hands to slip on my jeans.

"I'm fine! The restaurant is fine. But... Mr. Grant has been drinking for the last few hours, and when I asked him who I could call, he asked for you..." she pauses for a moment before quickly adding, "I know it's late, and I'm so sorry for that. I just didn't know what else to do."

I take the phone away from my ear to put it on speaker while I finish getting dressed, sliding an old band tee over my head. "No, no, don't be sorry. Which... Mr. Grant are we talking about?" I ask, knowing with my luck, she doesn't mean Brooks.

"Oh, right. Cary, not Brooks."

Fuck. I roll my eyes and take a deep breath.

"You did the right thing. Can he at least walk?" At this point, I don't know what I did to piss off the universe, but clearly, I did something terrible in a previous life. I don't let Nat hear the frustration in my voice though, it isn't her fault that this is happening.

"I think so, yeah," she replies.

"Alright, good. Just don't serve him anymore, I'll be there in a few minutes." I'm fully dressed now, grabbing my keys from the counter and pulling my purse onto my shoulder as I walk out of my house.

"I've been giving him watered down soda for the last thirty minutes because he kept asking for more," she admits.

"Good, good. Thank you, Nat. See you soon." I hang up the phone as I'm getting into my car. Lucky for me, I'm still in my anger stage hours later.

I slam the door of my car more forcibly than necessary, pissed off I had to drive here past midnight to pick up a drunk Cary. I weighed all my options on the way back to RED. Do I call him an Uber? Do I take him to his hotel? What if Iris is there waiting for him? Maybe she changed her mind. Me showing up with a drunk Cary wouldn't look good. Then I'd reminded myself I don't have to walk him to his room, he can find his way his-damn-self. I'll just drop him at the door. At least then I won't have to worry about whether he got to his hotel safely. Problem solved.

I stomp up the steps to the front door, fumbling with my keys to unlock it since we closed about half an hour ago. I hear the music playing as I walk into the lobby, locking the door back up behind me.

Cary isn't one to drink like Brooks, but when he does drink, he gets pretty flirty. I expect to walk in on him flirting with Nat, but instead, I hear him talking about me.

"—really fucked up, Nat. And Thea's just—she's just so pretty. Right? You've seen her. You know," he muses, slurring some of his words, as he holds his glass in the air, his elbow on the bar. My cheeks heat, and Nat giggles behind the counter as her eyes find me. He follows her gaze, his eyes lighting up when he sees me.

"There's my Lemon!" his voice booms through the empty room, excitement evident on his face. Excitement that is not reciprocated on my own, and he must catch on to my mood because his smile quickly falls. "Oh... you're a mad Lemon..."

I'm glad to see he's not so drunk he can't tell I'm pissed. He starts to get up from his seat but stumbles. I pick up my pace to put an arm around him before he falls on his face, looking at Nat as I do. "Thank you, Nat. I appreciate you looking out for him and calling me. Please take anything he said with a grain of salt."

He turns his head to me then quickly turns back to Nat. "No. No. Everything I said is true. Take it as the fucking truth."

I roll my eyes and sling his arm over my shoulder to brace him as he walks. "Right. Let's go," I say, turning to leave and dragging him with me.

"Where are we going, Lem?" he asks, sounding truly curious like he has no idea where I could be taking him.

I wince as we walk since almost all his weight is leaning on me. "I'm driving you back to your hotel," I say matter-of-factly, leaving no room for argument and never meeting his eyes.

He shakes his head as he says, "I don't have my room key. Or my wallet."

I stop us and finally look up at him. "What do you mean you don't have your wallet? Where's your wallet?"

He just shrugs and responds, "I ran out to find you and just... forgot, I guess."

I take a deep breath, going through my options in my head—again. In the off-season, the hotels in town don't have after-hours services. I'd have to call someone to come in and reprint his key.

"Fuck," I mutter under my breath. I start walking toward the door again, pulling his arm down my shoulder a little more to make it slightly more comfortable. "I guess we're going back to my house then."

He doesn't respond immediately, and I assume it's just because he's drunk. Once we're outside, and we've made it down the patio steps, he finally speaks again. "You're mad at me," he says quietly, and it comes out more of a statement than a question. I realize then his silence was more introspective than a reflection of how wasted he is.

"I'm more than mad at you, Cary." I don't elaborate—I don't need to. He knows what he did and who he hurt. We walk a bit more, almost to the parking lot before he stops me. He pulls away from my arms and stands in front of me.

"What can I do?" he asks, his voice sounds so sincere it almost breaks my heart all over again. Guilt etched deep in his drunken eyes and defeat written all over his slumped shoulders.

I throw my hands in the air at him. "There's nothing you can do. You have a fiancée. A very beautiful, very kind fiancée. You put a perfect fucking ring on another woman's finger, Cary. Why are you even here with me? You should be chasing her down before she leaves." My voice is louder now, my anger bubbling to the surface again.

He looks over at me then scoffs right before he says, "I don't want her. That ring isn't hers. It was always supposed to be yours."

His words knock the breath out of me, and I feel like the ground beneath me might cave in and swallow me whole. I almost wish it would. "Wh—what?" I stutter out, his gaze still locked on me. "Mine?"

He nods his head, not giving me anymore of an explanation.

"I don't—how? I don't understand how a ring you bought for me ended up on another woman's finger, Carrington." Even drunk, he winces at my use of his full name.

Once he recovers, he clumsily shrugs his shoulders in response and turns his eyes to the ground instead of mine. "She just... found it. What was I supposed to do?" He looks so defeated and tired.

"So you've just been living one giant lie all this time?" I ask knowing this conversation should wait until he's sober, but I'm not able to hold back the question.

"Yes. Maybe? All I know is I've been living for you my whole life. Even when you left me. God—I went as far as to grow my hair out—and don't worry, you were right, I think it looks better this way too." He drunkenly laughs at himself, but I don't have it in me to find anything funny right now.

Instead of responding, I start walking to the car. I shouldn't be having this conversation with him right now, maybe not ever. Nothing he's saying is making any sense. When I left, we were in a terrible place. We'd been fighting constantly. I was so unhappy, and neither of us were discussing it. I'm not going down the rabbit hole of possibilities when he's too drunk to explain further.

Once I'm at the car, I look up to see he's still standing there, just watching me. I open my door to get in, standing there for a moment before saying, "Get in before I leave you here, Cary."

It takes him a couple minutes, but he stumbles to the car on his own. He fumbles to fasten his seatbelt, but finally secures it. The car ride home is virtually silent aside from the music I put on. Cary is almost asleep by the time I'm pulling back into my driveway. I give his shoulder a shake to let him know we're here. He's able to unbuckle and shuffle out of the seat without my help.

Getting him inside is much harder than getting him out of RED was. The liquor seems to really be hitting him. I still don't want to sleep in my bed that smells like him, and I don't want to risk my couch having his scent all over it either. I help him walk to my room and dump him on the bed. He can sleep in his clothes, I'm not undressing him or giving him anymore of my energy tonight. I do grab the small trash can from my bathroom and sit it beside the bed in case he wakes up sick, but that's more for my own benefit than his.

I close the door behind me, hearing him groan from the other side as he shifts around on the bed. Grabbing my blanket, I situate myself back on my couch and lay there staring at the ceiling for another hour before sleep finally finds me.

CHAPTER TWENTY-THREE

Carrington

8 Years Ago

(23 Years Old)

"Are you sure you want to do this?" Seth asks me. "I thought you guys haven't been in a good place."

"She just had a rough night. She finally heard from that job she had her heart set on, but they went with someone else," I say, my eyes fixed on the display cabinet.

"I don't mean just yesterday. Though, that was hard to watch. I didn't know a girl her size could put back so much liquor."

"Yeah." I run my fingers through my short hair and over the back of my neck. "She took it a lot harder than I thought she would. And she's definitely paying for it this morning." I had left Thea in bed with the curtains drawn and some ibuprofen and water on our bedside table. I have a feeling she's going to nurse that hangover at least until late afternoon.

"But what about what you told me about the fights you've been having? Are you sure this is the best time for," he motions down with an open palm, "this?"

I look down at the rings behind the glass, sparkling like the sun off the water at the lake. Like Thea's eyes when she turned her un-

239

abashed smile at me when we first moved into our shitty apartment. Like the way her hair shines that lemony color when the sun hits it just right.

"Yes, this was always the plan," I say with a small smile. My mind is still flooded with memories spinning on an ongoing reel—running around and exploring the lake as kids, finding the first ring on the bank of the lake that I knew I had to give to Thea, our first kiss, laying on the hood of the car somewhere in the middle of the desert on our road trip to Seattle, cooking dinner together on a random weeknight.

Unfortunately, those happy memories are soon replaced by the last few months of silent evenings spent on opposite sides of the couch, watching Thea leave the bathroom and pretending I didn't hear her crying, then me shutting down because I don't know how to help her.

I shake my head to clear the thoughts. It's just a bump in the road. Every couple has them. As soon as she lands a job at one of the big marketing firms, things will get back to normal. We're happy. We have big plans. I got my dream job as head chef in one of Seattle's most popular upscale restaurants starting in a few weeks, and I know it's just a stepping stone to me owning my own restaurant. I have a five-year plan, and Thea's at the center of it. I can't do this life without her. And buying the perfect ring is the first step in showing her that.

"Can I help you, gentlemen?" An older man steps to face us on the other side of the glass display, pulling me out of my thoughts. "Are we shopping for anything in particular today?"

"Yes," I say and produce a print out of the ring I found on the store's website. I've been browsing online for the perfect ring

for a while now. I've been saving for it for even longer. When I came across Romero Jewelers' website, I knew I'd find what I'm searching for here. They specialize in antique and estate jewelry, which means most of the pieces are one-of-a-kind and not necessarily "mainstream." Just like Thea. After scouring dozens of pages of rings on the site, one jumped out at me, and I knew it was the one. "I was hoping to see this one." I hand over the paper.

"Oh, that's a lovely piece. Let me grab it for you." The man steps away, walks behind the counter, and makes his way to the other side of the store. He zeroes in on the right display cabinet and busies himself with unlocking it and getting the ring out.

I turn back to Seth with a smile. It's been a while since I've felt so excited about something. Even getting my new position doesn't match the anticipation I feel about my future with Thea. He doesn't appear to match my enthusiasm. His lips are pulled into a tight line, and his eyes look... sad?

"Just say whatever it is you're thinking," I say.

"Look, it's nothing. You seem like you've already made up your mind," he says.

"Fuck, Seth, just spit it out."

Seth sighs, squares his shoulders, and, looking me directly in the eye, says, "I think you're making a mistake." His words instantly douse the flames of my excitement. "I just... I don't think this is the right time." He looks down at our feet for a beat and then back up at me. "I'm not sure she's the right person for you."

My heart sinks at his words. I knew he didn't like Thea. I'm not sure of the exact reason why, but they never clicked. She thinks he's too bristly with his always-serious demeanor, and he sees her as aimless and unmotivated because she hasn't been able to secure a position in her field. I've been the buffer between the two of them, and it's worked until now. His words are a step too far. My temper flares.

"Not the right person for me?" I hiss through my teeth so we're not overheard by the other customers in the shop. "She's the only *person for me. Has been pretty much since the day I met her. She's forever, Seth. This," I tap a finger on the display case, "is just a fucking formality."*

I have never spoken to him like this in the five years we've known each other. His posture deflates, and his face transforms to one of hurt and resignation. He gives me a small nod.

We're spared any more awkward silence when the jeweler comes back and places a black velvet display tray in front of me. He then places the ring from the paper I handed him in the center. I pick it up to inspect it closer. It's perfect. It looks like a small sun with a bright yellow diamond in the center. The color reminds me of Thea's hair at the end of the summer when it catches the midday light.

I can't help the smile that spreads across my face as I look at it. I glance up from the ring in my hand to the man behind the counter, "I'll take it."

I've spent most of the day preparing for tonight. After taking Thea to get a dress under the guise that it's my first night at the new job, I rushed over to the restaurant to prep for the dinner service and set up the proposal. In reality, I'm starting tomorrow, and my boss, Michael, has been helping me plan and execute this proposal for weeks. Now, I'm waiting anxiously for her to finish getting ready so we can head out. The blue velvet box is burning a hole in my suit jacket pocket. I feel restless and jittery and excited. I shake out my hands trying to expel the excess energy.

My phone rings with Michael's name on the display.

"Hello?"

"Hey," he says. "Just wanted to let you know everything's set. We have the front room closed up for you until seven-thirty. I'll have your guests in the back room waiting to congratulate you. You ready for this?"

"Yeah, I am," I say with a smile. "Thank you again for doing all of this."

"Oh, no sweat. I'm excited for you, man. Just remember, I have to open up the front at seven-thirty, we have reservations," says Michael.

"Got it. See you soon," I reply and hang up.

Just as I'm slipping the phone into my pocket, Thea walks out, and all breath leaves me. She looks stunning. The dress she picked out accentuates all of her lines and curves, and the burnt orange color gives her skin a warm summery glow. It has long flowy sleeves, a plunging neckline, and a side slit that comes all the way up to her hip, all of which combine and leave my mouth dry. She's wearing her hair down, and my fingers itch to run through the strands.

Fuck. *If I didn't have twenty-five of our closest friends waiting, I'd propose right here and now, then take her to bed until the early hours of the morning.*

Somehow I manage to pick my chin and tongue off the floor and clear my voice before saying, "Wow." That's it. That's the best I've got.

She gives me a coy smile, kisses my cheek as she steps around me and throws over her shoulder, "Chop, chop, Chef. We're going to be late for your big night."

Once we're in the car, Thea turns to me and says, "I'm worried about my mom. She didn't call me today, and I haven't been able to reach her. I asked Barbara to pop over to her house to check on her."

"Oh, Lem, I'm sure she's fine. She knows how big tonight is, she's probably just giving you space to enjoy yourself, especially since you've been so nervous going into this," I say.

I had invited Lydia to join us tonight when I called to ask for her blessing. She was excited for us but said she wouldn't be able to make it due to work.

"Yeah, you're probably right." She nods, but I can tell she's in her head as she bites at her thumbnail, staring out the car's window.

The car ride is short, and as soon as we're pulling into the restaurant's parking lot Thea's phone rings. Her hands shake as she answers. I listen to Thea's side of the conversation, hearing only snippets of what Barbara is telling her: come home, broken ankle.

"Okay. Yeah, I'll get a flight out as soon as possible. Thank you, Barbara. Thank you so much," Thea says and then hangs up. We sit in silence for a few moments. I know what she's going to say next, and my stomach is in knots.

Thea turns to me. "I've got to go home. I'm so sorry." I try to talk her out of it, trying to salvage the night, citing that her mom's injury isn't serious, and it can wait til morning, she's in good hands.

She's leaving. I'm about to propose, and she's leaving.

For some reason this moment feels big. I can't pinpoint exactly why, it's not like she's turning me down, rejecting me. But it feels like the tectonic plates of our relationship are shifting, and I'm at their mercy, just along for the ride.

We exchange a few more passive aggressive snipes at each other, not outwardly fighting. She's already almost crossed a line by bringing my own mother into it, and I know if we both stay in this car much longer, it will devolve into another blow-up. She's not even looking at me, instead her eyes are trained on her phone, looking up last minute flights. She's not seeing my eyes well. I usually have a better grip on my emotions.

"You're really doing this?" I rasp out. She checks the time and then meets my eyes.

"You should get inside. I'll call an Uber." I open my mouth to say... something. Maybe it was going to be "I'll come with you" or "just give me twenty minutes" or "why does it feel like I won't see you again?"

But before anything can get past the boulder in my throat, she's gone.

Walking into the restaurant—lit candles, peonies strewn on every flat surface, and our song playing over the speakers—I should have been filled with joy and anticipation. Instead, I stood in the middle of the room with my hands in my pants' pockets, feeling like I just walked into my own funeral. My dread was flowing off me in waves. The box in my pocket now felt like a leaden weight.

Was I being selfish? Her mom was hurt. I knew she needed to be there.

Should I have gone with her? My head may have been mixed up, but one thought rang out clearly: she didn't ask me to go with her. She knew I would have. I would have dropped everything. She knows she always comes first for me. She knows her mom is important to me as well. Why didn't she ask me?

Having to then face our friends, all dressed up and ready to celebrate with us, felt like my own personal hell.

"She's... not coming," I said, looking around the room, from one pitying set of eyes to another. The room was silent, and I felt about two inches tall.

A week, three clipped phone calls, and very little sleep later, and I'm not feeling any better than I was that night. I feel abandoned, but I also feel like I'm being unfair. She's dealing with a lot with her mom's new diagnosis. She's busy looking at treatment options and nursing care, but if I could just get more than a few sentences out of Thea on the phone, I'd feel better. There's a deep, dark chasm between us, and I can't find a way to scale it.

It's Monday afternoon when I hear from her next. The restaurant is closed, and I'm attempting to use my day off to catch up on sleep, not that it's working. I'm lying on the couch when my phone rings, and as soon as I see it's Thea calling, I'm scrambling to pick it up.

"C–Cary?" Her voice is soft.

"Hi, Lemon. I've missed you," I say. She is a balm to the nerves that have been wreaking havoc inside me since she left. "How's your mom doing?"

"Listen, I umm... I don't really know how to say this." She lets out a long breath. "I—I think I have to stay."

"Okay, I get it," I say, nodding my head even though she can't see me.

"It's worse than I thought. My mom needs more help than I realized. She needs me here."

"Of course. Do you think you'll be another week? Do you want me to fly out there and help too? I'm sure I could get Mike to—"

"No, Cary," she cuts me off, an edge to her tone. "I... I have to stay. Indefinitely."

It takes some time for my mind to catch up to what she's saying. I look around our apartment, at the furniture we've acquired from friends and yard sales. The pictures Thea's put up on the walls of us smiling, happy.

"Say something, please," she says.

"I don't know what you want me to say, Thea," I reply. I'm fighting the emotions bubbling up inside me, trying to keep my voice even. "It kind of sounds like you're moving back to South Carolina."

There's another long silence, and I think I hear a quiet sob, but she seems to have covered the phone to muffle the sound.

"What are you saying right now? What does this mean?" I ask.

"*I think it'll be easier this way. You have your hands full with your new job. You won't have to worry about me anymore. We both know I wasn't going anywhere in Seattle,*" she rambles. I try to cut in, but her words don't stop. "*I've been stuck in the same serving job for almost a year now, and the marketing jobs I've interviewed for haven't gone my way.*" I call her name a few times, but she doesn't take a breath and doesn't seem to hear me.

"Thea," I say louder. She stops talking, and there's a beat of silence. Two. Three. Then I whisper, "Are we over?"

"*I think we both know we've been over for a while.*"

My eyes catch on the blue velvet box I placed on the bookshelf holding all of our favorite paperbacks. The ones with the broken spines that we've read over and over again.

I wish I could say I remember the rest of the conversation, but for all I know I stopped talking and she hung up on me after calling my name a few times or maybe I begged for her to explain.

We've been over for a while. *I think that statement broke something in me. Why do I feel so blindsided by this? If we both knew we were over, shouldn't this be less of a shock?*

Chapter Twenty-Four

I wake to the smell of bacon filling my living room and a sore neck from sleeping on the couch. I haven't opened my eyes yet, allowing my ears to assess whatever is happening before I do. All the events from last night come crashing back to me full force. I'm not as angry though, I mostly feel numb now. I wonder how much he remembers since he's apparently cooking himself a goddamn meal in my kitchen.

I let my eyes slowly blink open, squinting as the bright morning light shines in on my face through the windows. He hasn't noticed I'm awake yet which is perfectly fine with me, it gives me an extra moment to decide how to handle things. Last night would have been the more opportune time to come up with the morning-after plan, but it was late, and I was done thinking about it for the night. Pressing firmly into the bridge of my nose with my thumb and forefinger, I decide maybe it's for the best that we talk before I kick him out.

I take another second before bringing attention to myself. My eyes drag down his body, annoyed that he's dressed in his pants from last night but seems to have forgotten his shirt in my bedroom.

I sit up, allowing the blanket to fall from my chest and swing my legs onto the floor. The instant I do, he turns to face me. There are dark circles under his eyes like he didn't sleep well.

Serves him right.

I yawn and stretch when he says, "Hey... I, uhh, I made you breakfast."

I've turned my gaze to my phone on the end table, checking for notifications before responding to him. Brooks and Ripley have texted, checking in on me. I leave them unanswered for now. "I can see that. Shirtless too, how bold of you." My voice is cold and sounds bored despite my heart still actively breaking in my chest.

"I just—"

"We should talk," I cut him off, not wanting to hear whatever excuse he's about to use to try and douse the fire he created. I can tell by the look on his face that he remembers enough about last night to know exactly what I'm talking about. "About more than just last night," I add, making his brows crease.

"Okay... yeah, that's fair, we probably should." He turns off the stove, then he's walking toward me, the breakfast he was making forgotten. He sits down on the other end of the couch, leaning forward, his elbows resting on his thighs. Neither of us speaks, we just sit in silence, letting it coat the room in more tension than I knew was possible.

"You cheated on your fiancée, Cary..." I keep my gaze aimed at my hands in my lap, twisting the lemon ring he gave me when we were kids. The one I just put back on my finger a few days ago after years of avoiding it like the plague.

Internally, I'm attempting to find the good in our relationship again, the memories of the Cary I knew when I was a kid, the Cary who would never betray me—or anyone else—like this. This stupid lemon ring is the only thing keeping me from screaming at him. I know who he is. Or, at least, who he used to be. That's the man I love, not the one in front of me who cheats on women and breaks hearts like there are no consequences.

"And you cheated on Ripley, how is that any different, Thea?" he shoots back, venom filling his voice with his accusation.

Thea. Not Lemon. Why does that hurt so much?

I shake my head, still twisting the ring around and around. "It's not the same. You know it's not the same."

He's getting heated now, standing up from the couch, and throwing his arms in the air as he says incredulously, "Not the same? *Not* the fucking same?"

I don't answer him, I don't look at him, I just sit there. The ring spinning, spinning, spinning.

"Thea, look at me," he demands, his eyes boring a hole into my skin like he can see all the way into my soul. I look up to him wordlessly, refusing to give him more. My silence only makes him madder. Anger sparks in his beautiful cerulean eyes. "How the *fuck* is it not the same?" he asks again.

"It's just... not," I say simply with a shrug of my shoulders, averting my eyes away from him again to a random spot on the wall.

His voice is louder now, booming through the living room as he throws another insult my way. "So you're really going to pretend that you fucking me while dating Ripley isn't just as bad as what I did? You're going to sit there and fucking pretend you didn't cheat too? Really?" I've never heard him speak so harshly toward me. Even during our worst fights, he's never been this mean.

The tears come quickly as his words settle in the air around us. I can't keep them from falling, and I wouldn't even if I could. He can witness the hurt he brought on. He can watch the tears falling from my eyes, and I hope it brings him as much pain as he's causing me. I let my own anger bubble back up; I let it take over so the sadness doesn't drag me down.

"I wasn't dating *anyone* while *fucking* you, so you can take your callous fucking words and shove them up your ass, Carrington," I spit back at him, staring right into his eyes as I spill the truth.

His body jumps back like he's been shot right in the chest as he stutters out, "Wh—what? No. I know what I saw and what I heard."

I scoff and shake my head in disbelief. "You saw and heard what you wanted. I never once called him my boyfriend, and he never called me his girlfriend. He has never been anything but my friend."

Cary is shaking his head in denial now, still not believing what I'm telling him. "No, there's no fucking way he'd be stupid enough to only be casual or whatever with you. There's no way. I don't believe it."

I jump up from the couch so I'm standing right in front of him now. Not entirely sure how someone so smart can be so dense. "Oh my God, Cary, he's gay! Okay?" Immediately my hand flies to my mouth, and my eyes go wide. "Fuck. Fuck, Fuck, Fuck! I wasn't supposed to tell you that."

I can't believe I just outed Ripley.

Cary's face falls as he watches me start to panic. I can see he's trying to make sense of what I've told him, and the silence lingers between us.

"Hey, hey, it's fine. Okay? I won't tell anyone. His secret is safe with me, I promise," he assures me as he places his hands on each of my shoulders, looking down and forcing my eyes to find his own. His tone much calmer than a few moments ago.

He pulls me into a hug as I nod my head to him. I'm still in shock that I let it slip, he'd just made me so mad, and he wasn't understanding. His hand is rubbing circles on my back as I snap out of it and realize I can't allow him to comfort me anymore. I pull myself out of his arms and sit back down on the couch with my head in my hands.

He's standing in the middle of the living room now, staring at me like he isn't sure where to go from here. Finally, he says, "What about your date nights? And him calling you babe? Why do all of that in the first place?"

Taking a deep breath, I try to calm myself down before answering him. "The babe thing is just a joke. It all started as us hanging out so we didn't die of boredom here. After seeing us out a couple of times, people started talking, wondering if we were dating. Everyone at Louie's would be like 'this must be date night,' so we just... went along with it. Of course, it spread like wildfire, and suddenly, the whole town knew about us. And it kind of worked out great because Shelley stopped trying to set me up with her cousin's best friend, and Mrs. Davis left me alone about all her great-nephews she wanted to introduce me to." My eyes finally move back to him like a magnet. The couch dips a little as he sits back down at the other end.

"And Ripley..." he starts, keeping his eyes on the floor.

"Ripley stopped getting badgered about why he never dated. He isn't ready to come out, at least... not here..." I don't tell him exactly what I mean by that and, thankfully, he doesn't ask.

"So you... never cheated on him."

"I never cheated on anyone... just... became the other woman in your relationship." I sigh, still not sure how I managed to get myself mixed up in this kind of drama. "Do you understand the position you put me in? How it feels to be this person? To know I helped you hurt another woman?"

"You could never be 'the other woman' for me, Thea." The words come out sounding so certain, like there's no doubt in his mind. He must know it makes him seem like a terrible person even if the words he's saying are sweet. I'm not sure how I'm supposed to feel about it all to be honest. How can I love someone who slept with me while engaged to another woman? A man who didn't even tell me he was with someone. The whole thing is making my head spin.

I decide to push him on his statement because, regardless of our relationship, he asked another woman to marry him. He took that leap with someone else. "But I am, Cary. You moved on, you asked someone else to marry you. How does that not make me the other woman in your life?"

He runs his hand down his face like he's preparing himself for what he's about to say. "Do you seriously think it's possible for me to move on from you? I know it may look like I did. I didn't realize until I came back and saw you that I've been waiting for you for eight fucking years, Thea. There's no moving on from you. From the moment I met you, I was fucking doomed to love you for the rest of my life. *You* left *me*, remember?"

Those last words have my heart in a chokehold, squeezing the remaining life out of it. "Why—why didn't you come for me then? You let me go so fucking easily... I thought—I thought you didn't want me anymore..."

The noise that leaves his mouth sounds like someone knocked the breath out of him. "Didn't—what? You thought I didn't want you? Thea, I was planning to propose to you the night you left. All of our friends were waiting inside of that restaurant. Instead, I had to tell them you'd left, and I didn't know when or if you were coming back." He pauses, but I can't make words come out in response, all I can do is stare down at my hands again as I try to sort through what he's saying. As I try to not break from his words right here on this couch. I had no idea he'd planned on proposing, no inkling that dinner was anything more than just the first night in his new position like I was told.

"You were miserable when we lived here. Then when we moved to Seattle, you eventually became miserable there too. I don't know what I was supposed to think when I was the only common denominator between the two. And with the way you left... you made it look so easy, Thea. So I assumed you were the one who didn't want this relationship anymore. And it wasn't like

I ever got the chance to ask you. You ended us with one fucking phone call. Going after you felt selfish at that point, when it was so clear you didn't want this anymore."

My eyes shoot up to find his face. I never knew he felt that way. I've never heard him discuss his feelings like this. I never knew he understood how unhappy I was. It was never about him though. He was the only thing holding me together. "You... knew...?"

A sarcastic laugh escapes him. "Yeah, I fucking knew. I was constantly walking on eggshells around you. I didn't feel like I could do or say anything right. Everything I said and did just seemed to make it worse. And I didn't know what was wrong or how to even tr—"

"Your dreams came true, Cary! You got everything you wanted," I'm screaming now, letting my voice rise with the emotions thrumming through me. "And it all just fell into your lap. You made connections with your instructors, who then gave you these amazing opportunities. I was drowning. Constantly floundering through life there. Nothing was working out. It felt like I was fighting a never-ending uphill battle." I pause, taking one full second to inhale a deep breath before I continue with the truth I'm finally ready to say. "All I fucking wanted was to succeed, but being in Seattle, constantly being told I wasn't a good enough option for people... it's the worst I've ever felt about myself." My voice sounds breathless as my past insecurities creep into my present.

"Why didn't you tell me any of this before? I was there, Thea. I was right fucking there waiting for you to talk to me instead of crying in the bathroom. The first time, I expected you to come out and talk to me about it, to let me in. You never did. Every fucking time, you came out and acted like nothing happened. Like you didn't just spend ten solid minutes bawling on the bathroom floor. What was I supposed to do with that? I didn't even know how to talk about my own emotions without someone else bringing them up, so I wasn't capable of pushing you to talk about yours."

A tear falls down my cheek at his words. I never realized that me hurting was hurting him, but I see it now. I feel it in my soul. I'd never meant to cause him any pain. I'd tried to keep it close enough to my chest that it didn't burden him too. I'd just kept hoping it would go away. "I don't know, but I never meant to hurt you..."

Once again, he scoffs. "You leaving is what hurt me, Thea. It fucking gutted me."

Another tear falls. "Cary, I—I didn't want to leave *you*. The last thing I wanted was to leave you. But I also didn't want to hold you back. I knew you'd choose me over your dream if I asked you to come with me, and I couldn't let you do that."

He jumps up from the couch again, pacing the room in front of me a couple of times before he finally stops. "No, you don't get to do that. My *dream* meant nothing—fucking nothing—without you, Thea. I was a husk of a man after you left. Nothing felt right, nothing made me feel alive anymore. Fuck. The most alive I've felt in the last eight years has been the moments I was in *your* kitchen. At *your* restaurant. With *your* staff and *you* there. Don't you get it? You took my choice away. You made all the choices for the both of us, and I got no fucking say in it. Do you realize how fucked up that is?"

I just stare at him, breathing in and out, as I let my anger come back up to the surface. I'm aware of how much work he must have done to be able to be so emotionally open with me, but I can't see past my anger right now.

I know I've made mistakes. I didn't handle things as well as I could have, but I was young. I was a fish out of water in Seattle. Then my mom got sick, and I didn't know how to deal with it all. I made decisions in the heat of the moment, thinking it was what was best for us both. And yes, I'd hurt us both in the process. What I didn't do was replace him with someone new. I didn't cheat on my fucking partner with him. He doesn't get to act like our mistakes are equal because they aren't.

"Not as fucked up as cheating on the person you planned to marry," I grit out before standing up from the couch and making my way to my bedroom. I grab his shirt from my floor and stomp out to the living room. Tossing the shirt at Cary, I turn back to my bedroom, shooting over my shoulder, "Get out of my fucking house."

I slam the door behind me then slide down it with my hands over my face to cover the noise of my impending breakdown. Just a few seconds later, I hear the front door slam shut in retaliation, and the sound allows the dam inside my heart to break free. The storm that had been brewing in my chest is released and ready to tear me apart until there is nothing left.

Chapter Twenty-Five

I fasten the last button on my brown, long sleeve, corduroy button-up dress. It feels fitting for Thanksgiving, and it's still warm enough that I won't be cold despite the dress only going down to mid-thigh. It is, however, too chilly out to pair it with the heels I was originally planning to wear. I'm already running late—thanks to the fight with Cary this morning—but decide I need to change them out for my white pointed-toe knee-high boots.

As I'm slipping them on, my eyes catch on my rings. Just seeing the ones Cary has given me over the years makes my blood boil. I quickly change those out too before finally grabbing my keys and purse to leave.

I haven't told anyone about our blowup this morning, and honestly, I won't be surprised if Cary doesn't show up. I wish I didn't have to go. If it wasn't our annual Thanksgiving lunch at RED, I probably wouldn't. But Travis and Melody are coming, along with Tiffany and her current boyfriend. The rest have families they spend the holiday with but will still pop by for a drink.

It's been a tradition since Hazel and Owen took over Indigo Hill Diner. When we renovated and reopened as Ripple Effect

Distillery and Restaurant, the tradition was one of the very few things that remained the same. It's our first one without them, so using it as a memorial feels right. We'll spend it giving thanks we got to know such wonderful people and for the amazing loved ones we still have.

I miss them so much it hurts sometimes. I feel their loss every day. It comes in waves now, and today is already a shitty one.

As I pull into the parking lot, I see Cary's rental parked in our employee area. My eyes instantly roll, and I wonder how important it is that I'm here. Technically, he's the majority share owner. I'm just... the manager—I may own forty-nine percent, sure, but what does that matter if he has the final say? I park my car a few spaces down from his and throw my head back into the headrest.

One more day.

As I'm exiting my car, a woman's voice calls my name from a few spaces down. I look over to see Tiffany walking my way. "Oh, good, I thought I'd be the only one running late," she says, followed by a small, nervous-sounding laugh.

"Outfit dilemma," I respond, looking down at my boots and shrugging my shoulders.

We walk toward the front door together, her boyfriend trailing behind. "Oh, you don't have to explain it to me, I changed five different times before we left the house, and it wasn't even because of the weather." She smirks as she turns around to walk backward so she's face to face with her boyfriend. "Isn't that right, baby?"

Her boyfriend—I think his name is Jameson, but honestly, I could be wrong—laughs and says, "Pretty sure it was seven times, but yeah, that's right."

"It's not everyday I get to come here dressed up, I wanted to take advantage," Tiffany retorts. I smile politely, welcoming the distraction the two provide.

By the time we reach the door, Tiffany has fallen back behind me, hand in hand with her boyfriend now. They're cute together. I think—if I remember correctly—they've only been dating for a few months, but she seems happy. They both do from the few encounters I've had with them together. I just hope it lasts. If they break up, and I have to hear about her fucking Brooks in the parking lot behind the distillery again, I will lose it.

I open the front door, and the aroma of Thanksgiving dinner overtakes my senses. Greeting the staff I pass by, I make my way toward my office to put down my purse and compose myself before I see Cary. I didn't see Ripley's or Brooks' cars in the parking lot. Brooks showing up would probably be a miracle at this point, and Ripley is usually late to the party unless I tell him I need him sooner.

I decide to text him and see when he'll be here so I can use him as a buffer.

Me: Hey, you gonna be here soon?

Ripley: I am… leaving my house **grimacing smiley emoji**

So it'll be another twenty minutes before he's here. Fuck.

Ripley: Why? Are you okay?

Me: I'm fine. Just trying to avoid Cary. I was hoping he wouldn't show.

Ripley: He came?! After last night? Shit. That takes balls.

Me: Does it? He's the owner, he kind of has to be here.

Ripley: I'm sure he could have let you handle it. I certainly wouldn't show my face if I'd been busted for cheating.

Me: That's because you're sane.

Ripley: Eh, debatable **shrug emoji**

Me: Feel free to turn the snark up to 100 tonight. Seeing that vein in his forehead bulge will bring me joy.

Ripley: You got it, babe **winky face emoji**

I sink back into my desk chair as I put my phone back in my purse. If I stay in here too long, someone will come looking for me. I'll just have to make sure I stay surrounded by people so he can't talk to me.

As I walk into the kitchen, the smell of the food Travis has prepared for us is making me realize how hungry I am. Speaking as I round the corner, "My God, Travis. That smells so fucking goo—" Before I can finish, I realize it's not Travis but Cary who's in the kitchen. He looks up to me and gives me a thin-lipped smile, as if that would win him some kind of points. I'm frozen in place, staring at him wearing that stupid fucking apron I love so much on him.

"Don't worry," he starts, "I only made a couple of the sides, so you don't have to boycott Thanksgiving entirely."

It's an unnecessary comment. As if I'd not eat just because he made it. I roll my eyes and turn to walk away. Surprisingly, he doesn't stop me. I guess I'm not the only one still pissed off.

I see Travis on my way out of the kitchen, and he waves me down.

"Thea, hey! Happy Thanksgiving."

"Happy Thanksgiving, Travis," I say as I look him over. He's jittery and seems out of sorts which isn't normal for him. I place my hand on his forearm before asking, "Hey, you okay? What's up?"

His shoulders sag. "You know the woman who stopped by the other day for me?"

"Yeah. Did you figure out who it was?" I ask, still concerned about the way he's acting.

"It was my ex-wife. Melody's mom. The second you said she was brunette, I had a feeling, but I wanted to make sure before I said anything. Turns out, she tried to get in contact with her parents too. I didn't even know she was back in town." He's told me very little about his ex. I never pushed because it seemed like a touchy subject.

"Okay... what does that mean? You seem off," I ask as he shoves his hands into his pockets.

"I'm not sure yet. She's never done this before. I just wanted to let you know in case she came by again. She doesn't get to know anything about Melody."

I nod my head in response. "Of course. Where is Melody now?"

He points his chin toward the dining room where all the tables have been pushed together to make one large table for the holiday feast. "She's out there with my parents."

I look over my shoulder to see her giggling in Travis' mom's lap. "Good. If you need anything, let me know."

"Yeah, I will. Thanks, Thea." He heads back to the kitchen as I walk over to the bar to get a much needed drink.

We ended up eating around one-thirty so the people who have family obligations could still make it to their Thanksgiving dinners. The lunch was mostly uneventful. We all shared stories of Hazel and Owen, laughter filling the room as stories of Owen being a hard-ass came up. I watched Cary out of the corner of my eye for the whole meal as he sat quietly on the other side of the table but a few seats down from me. Only speaking when someone complimented his mac and cheese or the "fucking orgasmic" mashed potatoes—as Ripley so eloquently put it—he'd made. I'd kicked Ripley in the shin for that one. He was supposed to be pissing Cary off, not complimenting the man.

Once we had finished eating and the chatter died down, Mr. Ashton had suggested Cary make a speech. The moment he'd said it, Cary turned ghostly white, but everyone at the table was encouraging him to speak.

In all my years of knowing Carrington Grant, I'd never seen him this nervous. He's been standing up from his chair for a solid ten seconds, looking around the room and the faces around the table, no words coming out. Finally, he clears his throat.

"Wow. Uhh, I didn't expect to make a speech. This was usually my dad's thing. I should have come more prepared." He laughs nervously. "I, umm, I don't really know what to say. I've been sitting here listening to you all talk about my parents, sharing all your memories of them, and I won't lie, I'm a little jealous. I missed this part of their lives." He pauses. "As most of you know, before they died, I hadn't spoken to my parents in thirteen years. I didn't get to know them as an adult. The reason for our fallout doesn't seem so irreparable now. But I guess that's regret for you." He clears his throat again, looking slightly less uncomfortable but still unsure of himself. He hasn't made eye contact with me this entire time.

"I look around and see this community they built... with Thea's help." At that exact moment, his gaze turns to mine and sets my skin ablaze. "Truth be told, I wish I'd been here for it all. I wish I'd been the bigger person and just... called them. I wish I'd done a lot of things differently. Hindsight and all, right?" Another nervous laugh escapes him, and I break away from his stare, turning my eyes down to my lap.

"But, uhh, if there is someone here who can give a proper speech about them, it's the woman who helped them bring this place to life. She probably knew them better than I ever did, honestly. Thea?"

My eyes widen and shoot up to him as he looks at me with sincerity. Public speaking is my worst nightmare. Standing up in front of everyone—despite considering these people family—and being the only one speaking makes my heart stutter and the back of my neck prickle with sweat.

"Stand up," Tiffany whispers over to me, gesturing with her hands for me to get up out of my seat. The idea of standing is already making my head spin, but I do it anyway. I've got my hands on the table as I push myself up which means everyone can see me shaking. I quickly pull them back behind me. Cary is still standing, his eyes locked on mine. Tiffany looks over at him and gestures for him to sit down. "You had your turn, sit!" she says through gritted teeth. Her scolding him—something she'd never dare do if she were on the clock—is amusing and makes me smile.

"I, umm, I'll try to do this without crying," I say with a laugh, my eyes already tearing up. They all know I won't succeed. I take a deep breath before continuing, "Hazel and Owen were... well, they kind of saved me, in a sense. When I moved back, I was so lost. I wasn't the determined, strong-willed girl they'd known before. But they—they loved me anyway. They took me under their wing, and they—" I pinch the bridge of my nose to try and stop the tears from falling. "Sorry. Whew, this is hard. Umm, they essentially handed me my dream without me realizing it. I think—maybe—they somehow knew? Or, at least, Hazel did. She was always so intuitive." The tears fall, cascading down my face like a dam was opened. "Fuck." My hand flies to my mouth, remembering there are children here. "Sorry!" I look over at Travis who's chuckling from his seat. He waves me off.

"She's heard worse, don't worry," he assures me.

"I'm not sure I'm the best person to make a speech, guys. This is going so terribly."

Ripley grabs my hand from my other side. "Keep going, it's okay. You're doing great, babe." Cary's fist clenches on the table at the nickname he now knows is just for show.

"Okay. Yeah. So some of you might not know this, but I went to school for marketing. I wanted to be the next big thing in the marketing world," I laugh. "Or so I thought. I think what I actually wanted was to create something special and watch it grow and become special for other people. When I brought the idea of renovating to Hazel and Owen, I thought they'd laugh at me. We all know Owen was stuck in his ways. The diner wasn't doing great at the time, but I still believed in it. And they kind of... just handed me the reins, which really could have ended poorly." Laughter comes from all around the table. "The point is, they helped me find myself again through this place," I gesture to RED, "and the love they gave me. Owen—after years of him seeming to only tolerate me—became the father I never had, and Hazel was like my second mother. And I miss them... so much."

Ripley squeezes my hand, his touch comforting me. "They're woven into these walls though. It's one of the reasons I love being here. They allowed me to make a home for myself here, and I don't think I ever expressed just how thankful I am for that. So hopefully, they're looking down on us and watching this. I think they'd be so happy to see us all continuing their Thanksgiving tradition." I pause to wipe the tears away from my eyes. "Anyway, thank you all for being here and loving this place as much as I do. I appreciate you all so much. Now, I'm going to sit down before I start rambling on again."

The whole table is misty-eyed but laughing. As I sit down, Ripley's hand goes to my knee, giving me a light squeeze as he kisses me on my cheek.

The rest of the day is filled with touching stories of the two people missing from this holiday. People filter in and out, wishing us a Happy Thanksgiving then leaving to be with their families. I'm busy clearing off some of the dishes left on the table when someone touches my elbow.

"Hey, can I talk to you for a minute?" Cary says as I look over my shoulder at him.

"Umm, sure... let me just put these glasses in the kitchen," I say, gathering a few in my hands. The last thing I want to do is fight with him again, but knowing he's leaving tomorrow and after everything he said at lunch, I feel like I should hear him out. "I'll meet you on the back patio."

As he walks away, heading outside, I take a deep breath before going to the kitchen and placing the glasses in the sink.

"Hey, I was looking for you," Ripley's voice comes from behind me.

"I was just cleaning up, but Cary wants to talk to me."

His eyebrows rise as he says, "Do you want to talk to him? Things still seem pretty tense between you two after last night."

I haven't told him about this morning yet. If I did, he'd have words with Cary, and I don't want to ruin Thanksgiving. "He's leaving tomorrow. He probably just wants to say goodbye," I say with a shrug.

"Yeah, okay. Let me know if you need anything."

As he's turning away I stop him. "Actually, could you keep everyone away from the patio? Just so we can have some privacy."

He nods. "Yeah, of course."

I thank him with a kiss on the cheek. My hands are getting clammy as I walk out to the back patio. The sun is setting now, and the way it reflects off the lake, framing Cary in a glowing halo, is breathtaking. He's standing with his hands in his pockets looking out over the water. I take a moment to just stare at his back, relishing in his beauty but knowing he's about to tell me goodbye. The pang in my chest is so painful, it takes my breath away.

Before I fully make the decision that I'm ready to walk over to him, he turns around, spotting me. A smile lights up his face which only confuses me.

"I was starting to wonder if you'd told me to come out here so you could make a run for it." He laughs, trying to play it off, but I can tell he's at least half-serious.

"No, I just ran into Ripley. I asked him to keep everyone away from the patio while we talk."

"Smart," he responds.

"Yeah... so, I—I guess this is goodbye, right? That's why you brought me out here?" I say, a few steps separating us. As soon as he registers my words, he comes toward me, closing the distance.

"What? No. I mean, yes. But only for a week or so."

I scoff. "Cary, please don't feed me anymore lies. I'm really not in the mood. And I'm not falling for any of them." Looking back, I realize I'd been the only one to say I love you. He'd talked about the past and how much he'd missed me, but he'd never outright told me how he felt now. I should have questioned it, but I was blinded by my own love for him.

"I'm not lying. I'm coming back. I want—I fucking *need* to make this work with you. I can't go on the way I was before. I see now what was missing," he says as he reaches for my hand, but I pull it back.

"I appreciate you expressing your wants and needs. It seems like talking about emotions is easier for you now, but I just... don't believe you. You love Seattle and your life there. I'd never ask you to give it up for me. Even if you are telling the truth and you do leave it all for me without me asking, you'll just end up resenting me." That is what scares me the most. Him choosing me then deciding it isn't the right choice.

"You don't have to believe me. But I am coming back, and when I come back, fighting for you and for us, it's all I'll do. I've just got some loose ends to tie up," he pushes, saying the same thing his note said. The words sound menacing now when before, they seemed innocent.

"Loose ends, right. Like a *fiancée*."

"I'm going to make this right, Thea. I won't lose you a second time," he pleads.

"This hurts too much, Cary. Just... go back to Seattle. Talk to your soon-to-be wife. I'm sure she'll take you back." I pull out the ring Iris left behind and drop it into his hand before I start to turn away. He grabs the back of my arm.

"Fuck, Thea. Would you just listen to me?" he grits into my ear. "I will be back. It may take me a week or two, but I am not giving up on us."

I turn around in his arms, placing mine around his neck as I push up on my toes to reach his ear. "Goodbye, Carrington."

I break away from the hug as quickly as I pulled him in. I just needed to feel his arms wrapped around me once more before I let go forever. I don't let him stop me this time as I walk back into RED, immediately finding Ripley and telling him everything.

Chapter Twenty-Six

Carrington

It's about fifteen degrees cooler in Seattle when I land, and I wish I had thought to bring a jacket. It was just another thing I seemed to have forgotten when I boarded the plane to South Carolina three weeks ago.

I'm torn when I step outside of the airport terminal and wait in line for an Uber. Everything here feels like home. The damp, chilly air, Mt. Rainier in the distance. It's the home I've built for myself over the last thirteen years, putting my blood, sweat, and tears into making something of myself here. And although everything seems familiar and welcoming, inside I'm restless, like a string pulled too tight, ready to snap. I feel like I've forgotten something important back in South Carolina. It's taking all of my effort not to turn around and go back into the airport to find the next flight back.

I texted Iris before take off, letting her know my plans to come back have not changed. I told her I don't want to make her uncomfortable, but I do have to stop by the apartment to pick up some things. Thankfully, Seth has agreed to let me stay in his spare room while I'm here. He refrained from outright chewing me out again over the phone, but I'm sure I can look forward to it when I see him later today.

As I ride in silence in my Uber through the city to my apartment, I'm taken back to the memories I've created here. Somehow the only ones I can recall all center around Thea. Nights out eating dinner, dancing in random bars until closing time, finding all the best dessert spots, quiet rainy days spent on the couch. I somehow managed to ruin everything. Even still, I'm determined to find a way to get her to forgive me. It's a tall order, but knowing she still loves me—and I refuse to entertain the idea that she changed her mind—I can't just go back to my life here.

I have no life here if she's not in it.

By the time the car pulls up to my building, it's drizzling. I thank the driver, make sure to tip him well for the long trip, and hurry into the lobby and elevator. When I unlock the door to the apartment, I see Iris sitting on the couch under a blanket, TV off, takeout cartons on the coffee table in front of her. She looks up at me, and even with her splotchy face and eyes swollen from tears, she's poised and beautiful. It's something that initially drew my attraction to her. She always seemed effortless and in command of any situation. Having her attention made me feel special, as if I could say, *hey, she chose me.*

I hate myself for what I've done to her. Despite her posh exterior, she's the kindest person I know. Her innate goodness just amplifies the disgust I feel with myself for hurting her.

I awkwardly wave and make my way to the bedroom we shared without a word. I want to get out of here as quickly as possible. Give her some semblance of peace.

I collect more clothes, packing a suitcase, so I have more than just the duffle I traveled to Indigo Hill with. I'll have to set up movers to pack up and move my things into storage until I figure out how I can either get rid of them or ship them to the other side of the country. Most of the furniture belonged to Iris before we moved in together, and I'm happy to leave anything we bought together here. It's all her style anyway.

I pause when I get to the bathroom. Leaning my hands on the counter, I look at myself in the mirror. I feel a headache coming on—the result of the lack of sleep over the last few days and the uncertainty of the next few weeks. I stare for a few more minutes, taking some deep breaths. Then I grab the last of my toiletries, go back out to the bedroom, and drop them into the open suitcase.

Looking around the room, I realize, besides some seasonal clothes in the closet and a handful of books out in the living room, my belongings have fit into this bag. I get the sinking feeling that I've been on my way out since the day I moved in. With a sigh, I zip up the luggage.

When I make my way back to the front door, I look to the living room and see Iris hasn't moved, but she seems more put-together now. I take a few steps into the room.

"I'm sorry," I rasp out. "I'm so sorry about how this all turned out. I need you to know I never had any idea that... that would happen when I went there. I didn't even think about it." My words are met by a quiet scoff from her, and she brings her eyes to the ceiling.

"I should have known something was wrong when you were barely talking to me. I just thought you were grieving and needed space," she says. Her eyes come back to me.

"I'm so sorry," I say again. I don't have the words to express how much I regret the way I handled the situation. "There's just… so much history."

"I can see that now. I just don't know how I didn't see it in the six years we've been together. How could you not tell me about her? In the back of my mind I knew there was always something off. You never really let me in fully. I should have listened to my gut when you kept putting off setting a date." She pauses. "Tell me, Cary. Why did you even propose?"

There's a long silence as her resentful question hangs in the air between us. I take a deep breath and answer, "I didn't."

3 Years Ago
(28 years old)

I have the restaurant's monthlies spread out on the coffee table in front of me and on the couch next to me, trying to make sense of the reports Seth sent me. The man loves a good spreadsheet and seems to keep track of everything in his life on Excel. I've been staring at the numbers for over an hour, and I'm no closer to figuring out what he thinks I need to see here. I run my hand through my long hair and stretch out my neck.

It's Monday afternoon, my day off since Carina Cove is closed. Iris has also organized her schedule so she has Mondays free. We typically spend the day running errands or just being lazy at home. Today, she insisted on spring cleaning, so she's in our bedroom, rummaging through the walk-in closet tossing clothes out into several piles. She says she has a system—I just know I have to make myself scarce.

"Care Bear," Iris says, and I hear her padding down the hall to me. She stops in front of me, the coffee table between us.

"Hmm?" I say, eyes still on the papers in front of me.

"I'm sorry," she says. At that, I look up and am greeted by a sheepish and worried look on her face.

"What's going on? Why do you look like that?" She's holding her hands behind her back.

"I'm so sorry. I was cleaning out the closet, and I found it. I know it was all the way in the back of the closet with your things, but I just wanted to shift some stuff over, and it fell off the shelf. And then I couldn't help but look, and it's beautiful." She's rambling, which is very much out of character for her. I would find it cute, but I still have no idea what she's talking about, and my face must say as much because she continues, "I don't know what you had planned, but I'm really so happy, so just know, my answer is yes."

"Arizona, what are you talking about?" I ask.

She pulls her hands from behind her back and holds a small blue box in her palm. I instantly recognize it for what it is, and my heart stutters. Memories of what seems like another life fill my head: wavy blonde hair, warm brown eyes, standing alone in a room full of lit candles and peonies.

Iris' smile is wide and tears are welling in her blue eyes. It's exactly the expression I was hoping for when I presented the ring, unfortunately it's the wrong girl's face shining all that love at me. I can't force any words out, and Iris takes that as shock at her finding the ring. The ring she probably hates. It's not her style at all. She hasn't gone so far as to send me pictures of the types of rings she wants, *but I just know after being with her for three years, living together for two of them.*

She rushes to me around the coffee table and hugs me tightly, repeating yes *and* I love you *over and over. I still haven't said a word.*

Present

"What do you mean you didn't?" she asks, tears welling.

"Iris." I pause, not knowing how to continue. "You found the ring. You... assumed. After all the time we'd been together, I didn't know how to tell you the truth. I didn't know how to tell you that I was still heartbroken five years after the woman I bought that ring for left me without looking back." My voice falters, but I continue, "I didn't know how to tell you that I carried that ring with me for a year after she left, and it wasn't until I had been seeing my therapist for months that I felt ready to leave it behind every day. I still couldn't get rid of it though. And then you found it. And you were so happy. So I figured I could find a way to be happy too."

"Oh my God." She devolves into sobs.

"I'm so, so fucking sorry." I have no other words, so I just step close to her and envelope her in a hug, trying to help comfort her the best I can. I kiss her head and whisper I'm sorry again, before pulling away.

I gather my bags from where I left them by the door and quietly leave. I thought my biggest regret in life was not following Thea when she left. Now I know it's lying to the amazing woman I left crying on the couch. She deserves so much better than I gave her, and I'll live with the guilt of the hurt I've caused her forever.

I steel myself before knocking on Seth's door. He and Iris have grown close over the years, so I've put him in a difficult position. When I called to ask if I could stay with him for the next week or so, I could tell he knew what happened before I even started speaking. Thankfully, his loyalty to me won out over his sympathy for Iris.

Seth opens the door and doesn't say anything. He just turns and walks into his kitchen. I take my time removing my shoes and coat then move my suitcase and duffle down the hall toward the bedrooms before I meet him in the kitchen.

The disappointment rolling off him is palpable as he stands with his hip propped against the counter. My actions are hitting too close to home for him. Seth's father's cheating while married to his mother resulted in a messy divorce. His mother was torn up about it, and he was left to help pick up her pieces even though he was barely twelve at the time.

I put my hands in my pants' pockets and lean on the doorframe. I'm sure he's dying to say something, but, like me, he doesn't know where to start.

Suddenly, he pushes off and makes his way to the fridge, pulling out two beers. He pops them both open and hands one over to me. I nod in thanks and take a long pull of the bottle.

"I know I fucked up," I finally say. "Can we just skip the part where you lay into me? Trust me, I'm feeling bad enough about what I did."

"No, I don't think you are," Seth says and takes a sip. "What the fuck were you thinking?"

"I wasn't thinking, alright?"

"No, *not* alright. Not fucking alright. You can't keep it in your pants for three weeks?" His voice is rising, frustration and anger on Iris' behalf clear.

"Fuck you, man," I throw back, my own anger rising. I know what I did was wrong. I know, and I feel like shit about it. I came here hoping for a friend, not a lecture. "You of all people know that isn't how it went down. I didn't go to South Carolina intending for any of this to happen. My parents fucking *died*. And Thea... fuck, she's been perfect throughout this whole thing. You know she's it for me. She always has been."

"You made a commitment to Iris. *She* was supposed to be it for you. You promised her forever, and then five minutes with Thea, and Iris doesn't even exist to you." A flash of hurt crosses his features, and I'm not sure why. I understand sympathizing with Iris, they're close. But this feels more personal. Though as quick as the emotion flits over his face, it's quickly replaced with that same disappointment from before.

"You know I'd never hurt Iris if I could avoid it." I pause and sigh. I'm not here to fight with another person I consider important in my life. "I know what I did was fucked up, I know. And Iris deserves so much better than that. The woman is a saint. But you also know I never promised her forever. That ring wasn't for her."

My words are met with silence, and I imagine he's thinking back to that day at the jeweler's. He drops his eyes to the floor, and I continue, "I had no idea Thea still cared for me. Hell, I didn't even let myself hope that she thought of me on occasion. Everything I shoved down deep—that I tried to get rid of with therapy and work and... Iris—it all came back as soon as I saw her. It felt right—inevitable. The only thing separating us was—is—miles. Everything we had, all the feelings, they're all still there. Maybe even stronger now because neither of us is afraid to speak the truth or hurt each other's feelings anymore."

Another silence stretches between us. Seth takes another pull from his bottle and places it on the kitchen island in front of him. After a few moments, he nods slowly and looks up at me.

"What are you going to do?" he asks.

"I'm leaving. I know that puts a lot on you, and I know you had to miss your trip already, but I just... I have to figure out a way to step back from Carina Cove. I love the restaurant, but I belong wherever Thea is," I say.

He huffs. "You're just going to give it up to go back to your small town to... what? Run a restaurant in a seasonal tourist town? You could be huge here. You're so close," he pleads with me.

"I know you don't understand this, but I can't find happiness in numbers on a spreadsheet. Success here means nothing to me if she's not part of my life."

"I think you're making a mistake," Seth says, resigned.

"I think this is the first right thing I've done in a really long time," I say with a smile before finishing the rest of my beer.

Chapter Twenty-Seven

11/30 2:22 a.m.

Cary: Fuck, I miss you so much already… I ended things with Iris. I'll spare you the details, but just know, I'm still coming back. I love you.

Read 2:24 a.m.

11/30 10:03 a.m.

Cary: Good morning. I'm going to figure out how to step away from Carina Cove today. Maybe investors? I'm not sure yet. I love you, Lemon. Please wait for me.

Read 10:04 a.m.

12/1 2:24 p.m.

Cary: If you think not answering will deter me, you're wrong. I'm not giving up on us, not this time. I'm counting the days until I can fly back to you. 12/15, let the count-down begin: 14 days

Read 2:36 p.m.

12/2 4:51 p.m.

Cary: It's raining for the first time since I got back. The rain never used to bother me, but now I'm starting to really not like it. Although, rain in SC sounds nice. So maybe it isn't the rain and it's just… Seattle. **heart emoji** 13 days

Read 4:59 p.m.

12/3 11:34 a.m.

Cary: Have I said how much I miss you yet? I'm still looking into finding investors. Seth has been less than helpful since he doesn't want me to leave. I told him there's nothing to keep me here anymore. He believed me about as much as you did, but I'm serious. I'll prove you both wrong. I promise. Love you. 12 days

Read 12:17 p.m.

12/4 9:08 p.m.

Cary: I heard our song on the radio today. I used to hate hearing it because of all the memories, but now it just makes me smile and think of you. I love you so much, Lem. 11 days

Read 10:56 p.m.

12/5 9:22 a.m.

Cary: I hate the rain now… and Seattle. Vehemently. 10 days

Read 9:23 a.m.

12/6 5:44 p.m.

Cary: Got a shipment of RED in today. I don't think I ever really told you how proud I am of you for making it this big of a deal. I know you'll tell me it was Ripley, but I don't think it would be nearly as big without you. You're incredible. When I come back, I'll make sure to remind you every damn day. 9 days

Read 6:36 p.m.

12/7 1:01 p.m.

Cary: Fuck I wish you'd respond. Today was rough. Bad news, the first investor I talked to probably isn't going to work out. Good news, I'm not going to let it stop me, I'm still looking. I love you more than anything, Thea. I really hope I can get you to believe me. 8 days

Read 1:07 p.m.

12/8 3:04 a.m.

Cary: Today was insane. I don't think I sat down or stopped moving for 14 hours straight. Now I'm home, in bed, and instead of sleeping, all I can think about is how much I wish I was there with you. 7 days

Read 3:25 a.m.

12/9 11:02 a.m.

Cary: I'm finally getting a day off since I've been back. I don't know what to do with my time since you're not here. You won't believe this, but I decided to start looking at houses in Indigo Hill. I forgot how much cheaper SC is than Seattle. Do you think

> a one-story or two-story would be better? What about land? 6 days

Read 11:11 a.m.

12/10 10:49 a.m.

> **Cary:** Damn. I really thought the questions might get you to answer. It's okay though, I'll just show you the options once I'm back. 5 days

Read 11:39 a.m.

"Yeah, okay. Thank you," I say into the phone as I hang up the call. Ripley walks over to me, a glass of wine in his hand. He slides it over as he sits down on the stool next to me.

"Who was that?" he asks, sipping his glass of bourbon.

"The Planning and Zoning Committee." My voice is void of any life. The same way it's been for the last two weeks. I don't try to hide it, especially not in front of Ripley. He turns to face me, his questioning expression telling me he needs more information. "They approved the permits for the expansion. Not that it matters, pretty sure they're invalid now since we changed ownership." My gaze is locked onto the glass in front of me.

"Okay, so we just re-apply. I don't see the issue." His voice is filled with hope. A kind of hope I can't even try to muster.

"The issue is Carrington."

"I'm sure he won't stop you from expanding, Thea," he assures me.

"Maybe not. But then I'd have to speak to him." I put the glass to my lips, the tannic merlot flowing over my taste buds.

"I take it he's still texting you, and you're still not replying..." He trails off at the end, almost like he isn't sure if it's a statement or a question.

"Every. Single. Day," I respond, allowing each word their own space as I enunciate them. He laughs, but it isn't humorous. It's a laugh of disbelief, one that makes me look over at him so I can figure out where it's coming from.

"What?" I ask.

"You know what I would give for someone to love me that much?"

"I—" He cuts me off before I even get a second word out.

"Listen, I know he fucked up. Believe me. But I've also seen the way he looks at you. I've seen the way you two ignite a room when you're both in it. I also know you *still* love him. So why not just hear him out? Or at least give him the chance to make it right. Why are you fighting this so hard? I hate seeing you like this, Thea. If forgiving him will make you happy, maybe you should consider it."

I'm shocked this is coming from Ripley of all people. "Forgive him? For making me fall back in love with him? For sleeping with me when he was *engaged* to someone else? I'm fresh out of forgiveness, Rip. I can't trust him to not break me." Pausing, I take a deep breath. "I can't believe anything he says. Every time he texts me something sweet or that he's looking at houses here, all I can think is—*is he lying to me again?* He did that. He broke my trust, possibly irreparably. It sure as hell isn't fixable from thousands of miles away."

Ripley stares at me, at a loss for what to say.

"I appreciate you wanting me to be happy, and I know you're worried. I just... need to work through this," I say.

He taps the table a couple of times with his fingers before he finally says, "That's fair. And I can respect that. However, I know you aren't sleeping again, and that's a problem for me."

I don't respond. I'm not sure how. So we sit, sipping on the drinks in front of us.

After a few minutes, I break the silence lingering between us. "I think I'm going to go see my mom. Can you close up for me?"

"Yeah, of course. Just let me know you get there and back okay since I know you'll refuse my offer to drive you." That brings a small smile to my face, knowing he knows me well enough to not even ask.

"I will," I say as I hop off the stool, grabbing his shoulder to pull him down so I can kiss his cheek. "Love you."

"Love you, too," he says as I walk away.

"Thea?" Margot calls from down the hall as I'm walking to my mom's room. I stop and turn around as she makes her way to me.

"Hey, Margot," I pause. "Sorry, I didn't call ahead."

She shakes her head as she speaks, "No, no, it's okay. I just wanted to make sure everything was alright."

"Oh, yeah, just needed to see my mom." I smile to bury any upset that may show on my face.

"She'll be thrilled. She told me you seemed really sad on Sunday, so she's been worried about you," she states, gesturing for me to follow her to the side of the hall so we aren't blocking the path.

"It's just been a rough week," I assure her, hoping she'll believe the half-lie.

"I get it. Hey, umm, while you're here, can I ask you something, uhh, more personal?"

I tilt my head in curiosity, Margot usually keeps things between us professional. Though, me calling her to patch up Brooks probably warrants some kind of explanation. "If this is about me calling you to help out Brooks—"

She cuts me off, "Oh, no. Well, maybe kind of? Not exactly. I—sorry. No, not specifically about that. But about him, yes. Is he... okay?"

My brows furrow at her question. "What do you mean?"

I can tell she's uncomfortable bringing this up.

"I—well, he wasn't at the memorial. I assumed he would be, considering. And I tried texting him yesterday—just to check on his wounds!" she quickly adds, like I would assume differently. "I wanted to make sure he's all right," she finishes, the look on her face showing the same concern I've seen her have for a patient, but her cheeks have turned rosy.

"He does this. And I know you said it wasn't about me calling you, but I am sorry I pulled you into that. I shouldn't have breached that line between us. I'll go check on him though. I need to speak to him anyway."

That seems to settle something in her. "Okay. Good. I'm sure he's fine. Like I said, I just wanted to check in. And really, don't worry about the whole calling me thing. If I wasn't comfortable with it, I would have told you," she insists. "Let me know if you and Lydia need anything while you're here."

I nod my head in thanks. "Yeah, for sure. And I'll let you know what I find out about Brooks."

With a nod, she walks away, and I make my way toward my mom's room, preparing myself for the conversation we're about to have.

"You know, I told Margot something was up," my mom says after I finish telling her everything that's transpired between me and Cary since I saw her last. It's later than I usually come by, almost seven now. She's already in bed and was watching 'Days of Our Lives' reruns when I walked in. The woman thrives on soap opera dramas, which is good considering the show is on season fifty-nine, so it's unlikely she'll ever have to be without it. "And the second you walked in here wearing different rings confirmed it before you even opened your mouth."

I look down at my fingers, the missing ones are glaringly obvious to me, but I didn't think anyone else would notice. "I just... needed some distance," I say from the chair next to her bed. I'm sitting so close my knees are pressed up against the mattress.

She laughs in response, making my eyes shoot up to her. "What's so funny?" I ask.

"Baby, if you think taking off those rings is going to magically make your love for him disappear, you're sorely mistaken," she says, her voice softening as her laughter dissipates.

"So what do I do then?"

She tilts her head before asking, "What do you want?"

"It doesn't matter what I want," I say as I pull my lip into my mouth, biting on the edge.

"First off, it always matters what you want. Second, you've known that boy a long time, and he never once cheated on you or gave you the impression he ever would," she says in his defense. And she's right, but that was before.

"So it shouldn't bother me that he cheated on someone else? Or that he lied to me?" I retort.

"You should absolutely give him hell for lying to you. But you also need to remember that you lied by omission. For some unknown reason, you had him and everyone else convinced you and Ripley were together." She pauses for a moment, sipping from the glass of water beside her. "And as for him cheating, he cheated on someone else *with* you. I am not condoning it, but I think it's worth noting that his love for you meant more to him than a relationship that came after you."

"So you're saying I should forgive him?" I ask incredulously.

"I'm saying," she starts, grabbing my chin so I can't look away, "don't waste time being mad that someone loves you enough to throw everything else in their life away. It may not be the grand gesture you expected, but it's grand nonetheless. Unconventional. Possibly scandalous. But still grand. Life is too short to waste more time being upset about it all. You two have already spent so much time apart. Don't waste a second chance on something as trivial as a mistake." She lets go of my chin, cupping my cheek instead.

"I just don't know how to trust him again," I say as tears start to form. It's the real issue with forgiving him. I can see past what he did. She's right, it should mean something, and it does. My problem is the lying. I might not have corrected him when I knew he thought I was with Ripley, but at least he knew Ripley existed. I didn't even know about Iris. He had the opportunity to ask if I was in a relationship, I didn't.

I can't trust he means what he says. I believed every word he told me, then I found out he was with someone else. That revelation made all his words feel watered down. Moments with him that felt like we were mending what was broken between us are shadowed in doubt now.

"It'll come with time, love. He has to get a chance to earn your trust back first. And it may happen quicker than you think," she tries to assure me. She's holding my hand now, the smallest tremor moving through her hand to mine.

"What if he ends up resenting me?" My voice is almost a whisper.

"Why would he ever resent you, Thea?" The confused look on her face tells me she seriously doesn't see a way that he could. It's the fear I've always had though. It's the reason I never asked him to come back with me—to choose me. I didn't ever want to be a burden to him or feel like a consolation prize while he missed out on his dreams.

"Because he hates Indigo Hill..." I trail off, not needing to elaborate. Even my mom knows how much he wanted to leave this town when we were kids. It was all he ever talked about. I don't think anyone was surprised when he left, they were just surprised he never came back, not even to visit.

"Didn't you say he sent you a message saying he hates Seattle now too?" I roll my eyes thinking back to the texts he's sent throughout the week. I'll never admit it, but the admission that he is starting to hate it there did make me smile, just a little.

"I mean... yeah... but I feel like he's just saying that to win me over," I muse. Another feeling I've had that I haven't said out loud until now.

She shifts on her bed so she isn't having to turn her neck as much. "Darling, people don't uproot their entire lives for someone they don't love deeply. You're focusing too much on the what-ifs and everything that can go wrong."

"Because it already went wrong once," I remind her.

"No. You came home because of me," she says, stopping for a moment to let it sink in. Again. We've had this discussion plenty of times over the years. "We don't know that things wouldn't have worked out between you two if you hadn't come back here after my accident. He was about to propose. You could have been married with little ones by now."

"I don't know..."

"I do," she responds with all the confidence she can muster. "Everyone hits rough patches, love. Not all rough patches end relationships. It's clear neither of you truly moved on, so maybe you owe it to you both to try again. Those what-ifs in your head are going to haunt you if you don't. We both know that." She's right. God, is she right. They've already haunted me for the last eight years. I'm not sure I can do a whole lifetime of what-ifs when it comes to him.

"Yeah... okay, Mama," I finally concede. This is why I come to her. She's always given me the best advice without sugar-coating it. She's never once told me to take the easy way out. She always pushes me to do what's going to make me happy, regardless of how hard the trek will be to get there.

"Okay. Now get out of here. It's getting late. You better come see me on Sunday still." I look over to the clock sitting on her bedside table and see it's been almost an hour now. I push my chair back away from the mattress, lean down to grab my purse, then stand.

"I will, I promise. I love you, Mama," I say as I lean over to kiss her cheek.

"I love you too, Thea Bean."

I exit the room, shutting the door softly behind me, already hearing she's turned her show back on. I can't help the small laugh that escapes my lips at hearing the familiar voices I grew up with. I walk down the hall and say a quick goodbye to Margot, hug her, and assure her I'll have Brooks reach out.

By the time I get to my car, it's a minute past eight. I start the car then reach over to pull my phone from my purse to text Ripley when I see a new text from Cary.

12/11 7:56 p.m.

> **Cary:** You think Ripley will show me the ropes at the distillery when I get back? I've never had so many people compliment a bourbon we carry. Also I hope you know how hard it is to text you only once a day… I love you, Thea. 4 days

Read 8:02 p.m.

The message makes me laugh. The 'I love you' brings a smile to my face for the first time since he left. I still don't text him back. I don't want to distract him while he's working, and I need to go check on Brooks anyway. But I tell myself I'll respond to the next text he sends. Doesn't matter if it's one of his daily thoughts he wants to share or him telling me he misses me, I'll answer either way.

Knowing I've made this decision settles something in my chest as I pull away from Saint Stephen's. It isn't huge, it's only a text message, but it's the first step in letting him back into my heart.

I pull into the driveway of Hazel and Owen's home after going past Brooks' apartment and not finding him there. There are lights on in the house, so the fear that he's gone completely AWOL again eases. I'm still hesitant about what I might find inside, but at least I'm not going to be worrying all night about *where* he is.

Brooks has always been a wildcard, but recently, it's gotten a bit out of hand. He isn't talking to any of us, and he keeps disappearing then reappearing with fresh cuts and bruises. Before Hazel and Owen died, he'd do this every once in a while, sans the cuts and bruises, but he'd always turn up a couple days later and apologize for the disappearing act. We don't seem to be getting apologies now.

I knock on the door, waiting impatiently for him to answer. After ten seconds of silence, I knock again. This time, he comes barreling to the door so quickly, I hear his heavy footsteps from outside. The door flies open, and he looks like he is about to yell, but his face drops when he sees me.

I put my hands up in surrender. "It's just me. Jesus," I say pushing past him and into the house.

He shuts the door behind me then runs a hand over his buzzed hair. "Sorry, Thea. Some guy pushing solar shit came by earlier, and I just assumed it was him again."

"No worries," I say, looking around the living room noting all the empty beer bottles. "So, this is what you've been doing?"

He huffs and makes his way to the couch before dropping down onto it, pulling out a pack of cigarettes from his hoodie pocket. "Did you come here to lecture me, Thea?"

I put my purse down on the bar then look back at him. "Would that help? Because you missed the memorial. You've got Margot asking questions. You didn't even say goodbye to Cary before he left. And now I find you... surrounded by beer bottles with more bruises on your face than the last time I saw you."

He pulls the cigarette he was about to light away from his face, his brows scrunching as he says, "Margot is asking questions about me? Why?"

Men truly are oblivious.

I walk into the living room, sitting down on the couch opposite him. "Oh, I don't know, maybe because she had to bandage up wounds that you refuse to talk about, and then you apparently neglected to answer her texts? She said she was trying to check on you and make sure your face was healing okay."

He shakes his head, bringing the cigarette back to his lips and lighting it.

"You know your mom hated that you smoke, and now you're doing it in her house?"

He takes a deep inhale before looking over at me. He exhales the smoke then says, "Not like she can stop me now that she's dead." His words are harsh, bringing tension to the room. Along with the fear that this is worse than I thought.

"Cool. Good talk, Brooks." I stand from my seat and start to leave the living room but stop short to say one last thing. "Listen, either tell us what's going on with you, or figure out how to get your shit together on your own. You're like a fucking bomb ready to go off, and I can't deal with another explosion in my life."

He doesn't respond, not that I'm surprised. As I'm grabbing my purse from the kitchen bar, I see a stack of papers sitting on the end of the counter. They're similar to some of the documents Mr. Elsher gave me and Cary when we got the new ownership paperwork for RED.

"What are these?" I ask, shuffling through the documents as I wait for his answer.

"I don't know. A bunch of shit Elsher gave to me when I signed whatever bullshit that got me the golden key to this humble abode," he says, never looking my way, focused on trying to blow smoke rings and probably wishing I'd just leave.

I move a couple more papers to the side when something catches my eye. It's an envelope with mine and Cary's name on it, another with Brooks' name right underneath it.

"Brooks..." I start, shock creeping into my veins as I realize what I'm looking at.

"What?"

"There are letters here," I state, all the emotion gone from my voice.

"What?" he asks again, but this time he's less annoyed and more curious. He raises his head from the back of the couch. A split second later, he's jumping up and coming toward me. "What the... I swear, Thea, I didn't know these were here. I fucking swear."

I nod my head, my eyes never leaving the envelope with Hazel's handwriting staring back at me. After a moment of silence, he grabs the one with his name and disappears into whatever room he's staying in, the door closing behind him.

I slowly reach for the envelope, wondering if this is going to break me further. Once it's in my grasp, I decide I need to be alone to open it, much like Brooks. I quickly walk to my car, my purse getting stuck in the door as I try to close it hastily. I push it back open, pull my purse all the way in and throw it into the passenger seat before pulling the door shut again.

My fingers tremble as the sound of the breaking seal fills the car. Tears well in my eyes as I unfold it and see it's a letter to Cary and me in Hazel's handwriting. A letter we should have gotten at the reading of the will. A letter that was left for our eyes only.

My loves,

If you're reading this, it means we didn't get a chance to talk to you both in the same room before we passed. I'm sorry if that means this came as a shock to either of you. We always expected to have this conversation in person, but we needed to have a failsafe in case that didn't happen.

Carrington — I am so sorry for any pain your father and I caused you. I am sorry we let our pride get the best of us. I say 'we' because your father and I are truly partners in this life. We should have reached out with more than just a yearly card. I should have called you and talked some sense into your father. You getting this letter means that never happened. I hope you never questioned how proud we are of you. Despite the distance, your father and I made sure to always read any article about you and your success. Our relationship being what it was is my life's biggest regret.

Thea — I know I am not your mother, but I hope you know that I saw you as the daughter I never got to have. I don't think you realize just how much light you brought back into our lives when you showed up on our doorstep all those years ago. You, my dear, pulled us from the wreckage and helped us become whole again. I hope our appreciation for everything you did was clear. I know how heartbroken you were, and I hope time has healed that wound. If it hasn't, this probably feels cruel to you. I assure you our intention with this decision was to show our gratitude for everything you did. If we're gone, you deserve to have a piece of what comes next. Owen was always very adamant about this business staying in the family when we were gone and this way, it will. I know you'll do right by it. I know you love it as much as we do and won't let any harm come to it. And as for sharing it with Cary... well, I knew you'd need some backup. And you two were too close to never speak again.

We love you both so very much. I hope you'll lean on each other in our absence.

Please don't make the same mistakes we did by never making things right with each other.

—Mom

Tears cloud my vision as I read it a second time, not quite believing my eyes. This existed all this time, and we had no idea. This is the answer to the question I kept asking myself. This was—shit. *Cary.* I need to send this to Cary. He needs to know how much they loved him and how proud they were of him.

My hands are so shaky I have to take the picture a few times before I capture one that isn't blurry. I wipe the tears from my eyes as I attach the picture to the email. The subject just says 'Read this...' As I press the send button, I realize knowing their intent, knowing why they did it the way they did, makes RED feel more like mine. I assumed they only left me part of it as a way to pay me back for all the work I put in. I didn't realize they split ownership strictly so it stayed in the family.

I just... didn't think it was something as simple as that. It'd felt like a slap in the face knowing they'd trusted Cary with it more than me, but that wasn't the case at all. That thought alone makes me feel like a terrible person though. Cary had proved he could run a restaurant and was more than trustworthy. I was just too close—too close to it *all* to see reason.

I put the car into reverse, eager to get home. I plan on spending the night letting myself cry and miss them. I'll probably read the letter a hundred more times. And once Cary messages me or calls me after reading my email, I'll tell him everything I've been holding back.

CHAPTER TWENTY-EIGHT

Carrington

I typed out my daily text to Thea, sent it off, and tossed my phone on top of the sea of paperwork on the desk in front of me almost an hour ago. Even after two weeks of radio silence, I still hope one of these days the "read" notification will be followed up by a bubble indicating she's responding. It hasn't happened yet, but it doesn't stop me from checking every chance I get.

I've commandeered Seth's office at the back of Carina Cove to sort through all the restaurant's finances, compiling reports for prospective investors and organizing the documents to help make the transition as smooth as possible.

I've been at this every day since getting back from South Carolina, and I'm *so* close to having everything finalized. I reached out to Michael, my old boss, who put me in contact with an investment group that specializes in restaurants and the hospitality sector. After Seth and I met with them last week, they've shown interest and—pending the financial reports I'm working on now—will move forward with taking over majority ownership, giving me an opportunity to step back and be solely a silent partner.

A big selling point for the investment group was that Dan, my sous chef, agreed to take over the executive chef position. I wouldn't trust anyone else to head my kitchen. Dan has been with me since day one, helped me develop the menu, and was integral when we hired almost every other kitchen staff member.

As for Seth, he will be moving up to a general manager position, and the investors agreed that nothing will change without Seth's input and final sign off. He himself is investing as well and will hold a share of ownership. It's something I should have offered him a long time ago—he's definitely earned a right to call Carina Cove his own.

Seth and I reached an unspoken truce after our fight my first night here. After a few tense days around the apartment, he tabled his animosity toward me so we could prepare for the meetings with the investors. I know he's still unhappy with my decision to leave Seattle, but I can live with that. I hope he'll learn there are more important things in life than work one day.

With any luck, this time next week, I'll be back in Indigo Hill with Thea ignoring me to my face instead of over text. One issue at a time.

I put down the printed profit and loss statement I've been poring over and rub the heels of my palms into my eyes, trying to stave off the headache I feel coming on. After another minute, I heave a heavy sigh and reach to pick up the papers again when my phone pings with an email notification at the same time as a knock sounds at the door.

"Come in," I call out, turning to the door, leaving the phone on the desk, email unread.

The door opens, and Dan pops his head in. "Have a second, Chef?"

"Of course, come in," I say and drop the papers again. I motion for him to have a seat in the chair on the other side of the desk from me. As soon as he steps fully into the small office, I know I'm not going to like what he has to say. His body language is speaking volumes before he even makes it the couple of steps to the chair. His hands are fidgeting, and his brow is dewy with sweat. As he sits, his eyes refuse to meet mine. "What's up, Dan?"

His eyes continue to ping around the small space, looking at anything but me. After a beat, I finally see resolve settle across his features, and he slides his eyes to me. "I've accepted an offer at Exodus. I'm here to give my notice."

"I don't understand," I say, trying to keep my voice level to hide my panic. My mind is whirring with how this could possibly be happening. All of my plans to move back to South Carolina slowly start circling the drain.

"Someone must have talked about all the changes going on here, and they reached out to me. They're offering me the head chef position but also ownership shares when their new restaurant opens in a few months. It's a significant offer."

I school my face so he can't see just how much this is affecting me. My stomach has bottomed out, and I'm fighting down the anger that was first to rise within me. Dan is pivotal to the deal to sell to the investors. Without him, the deal will fall apart.

Finding a new chef with the experience needed to run our kitchen is not an easy task. Besides the necessary skills, whoever will replace me needs to be able to seamlessly fit in from day one. It's not a small ask. Transitions in kitchen leadership make or break restaurants. I can't leave my life's work to just anyone, and I don't have the months it would take to find someone else.

I run my hand over my scruff a few times before speaking, trying to collect myself. "Well, I can't say I'm not disappointed. You're leaving us in a tight spot."

"I know, and I'm so sorry. I wouldn't even consider it if it weren't everything I've been dreaming of. I'll pretty much be doing what you did six years ago—not only head chef, but owner. You know I wouldn't leave for anything less." Dan's a great man and a hard worker. He deserves this, and his sincerity douses some of the anger inside me.

"How much time can you give us before you move on?" I ask.

"I asked them for four weeks. I want to give you some time to find someone else or get Eliza up to speed." Eliza is one of our chefs de partie, and although she's talented, she's fresh out of school and not ready to step into the executive chef position. I was hoping Dan would promote her to sous chef after my departure.

I stand to signal the end of the impromptu meeting and hold my hand out to Dan. He quickly stands and grips my palm. "I'm really sorry to see you go, but I get it. I wouldn't be able to pass it up either."

Dan nods, and the relief in his eyes is evident. He quietly makes his way out. I stand for a minute or two with hands on my hips and head hanging, trying to think of my next steps.

"Fuck!" I scream and swipe everything off the top of the desk in front of me. Papers, pens, and my cell all clatter to the floor. Dropping back into the chair, my head lands in my hands as I lean forward with elbows on the desk. I dig my nails into my scalp.

I was *so* close. With each breath I take, my hopes of seeing Thea anytime soon seem to move further and further away. There's no way I can find a new chef to replace me in just a few weeks. Without an executive chef to carry on the restaurant's standards, the investors will pull out. Without the investors, my only choices are to stay on personally or close up shop and say goodbye to everything I have worked toward my entire adult life.

How do I go back to South Carolina knowing that closing Carina Cove will put twenty-seven people out of work?

It's after one-thirty in the morning when I finally get back to Seth's. After my conversation with Dan, I threw myself into the dinner service, only coming up for air long after the last customer left, and I'd let the kitchen staff go. I had stayed and deep cleaned the walk-in freezer. I needed something to keep my hands busy while my mind worked to come up with a solution.

Three hours later, the freezer is spotless, but I'm no closer to finding a way back to Thea without throwing away everything I've created here.

After hanging my coat up in the hall closet and tossing my keys in Seth's key dish, I beeline directly for the fridge to grab a cold beer. As soon as my hand makes contact with the fridge's door handle, I throw my head back with a long sigh. I turn around and go back to the door to make sure my boots are on the shoe tray. Seth is rigid about his apartment, and the last thing I want to wake up to is another one of his speeches about how everything has its place.

Fuck. I have to get out of here.

After grabbing a can of beer and popping it open, I finally drop onto one of the stools at the island. I take a few pulls of the crisp IPA and enjoy the silence for a few beats. Seth is more than likely asleep in his room since he's an early riser, usually getting to the gym by five. He hardly ever goes out unless it's work related, or I force him out with our friends. I can't remember the last time he had a date. He'll become a complete workaholic if I leave.

When. When I leave. There can't be a choice here.

I pull out my phone to text Thea. I have to tell her what's going on. She needs to know that this will take a lot longer than I was hoping. I promised to be an open book with her. My fingers hover over the screen. I can't make myself tell her I'm not coming.

Closing out of the message app, I switch over to my email, hoping for something from the investors. An email from Thea catches my eye. *Read this...* I immediately click on it and try to make sense of the picture. As soon as I recognize my mother's handwriting, I know what it is.

I read through the letter once and then twice more to make sure I didn't miss anything. Answers. Acknowledgement. *Valida-tion.* It's all I've wanted from my parents for the last thirteen years. Of course it comes too late.

"Fuck!" I scream and toss the half empty can across the kitchen and into the sink. Beer splashes on the counter and tile backsplash. Apparently, emotional outbursts are all I can do today. I drop my face into my hands as I hear Seth run out of his room and into the kitchen.

"Wha—what's going on?" His voice is raspy from sleep, but his eyes dart around looking from me to the mess on the other side of the kitchen and back.

"Sorry, man. I didn't mean to wake you. I'll—I'll clean that up." I stand and start making my way over to grab some paper towels, but Seth's hand lands on my forearm before I can get around him.

"No, stop. What happened?" He shoves me back down on the stool and goes around the island to clean it up himself.

"Did Dan tell you he's leaving?"

"What?" Seth's head snaps to me. "No. What do you mean? Leaving where?"

"He got an offer from Exodus. Executive chef and part-ner-owner."

"Fuck." He sighs and turns back to wiping the counter.

"Oh, and Thea found a letter from my parents," I say.

"A letter?"

"Yeah, an in-case-of letter. They apologized for everything, explained their reasons for leaving RED to me and Thea. I don't know how to deal with all of this. We were so close with those investors. How am I going to find another chef, let alone get them up and running in the time frame we discussed?"

Seth tosses the paper towel in the trash under the sink and reaches up to another cabinet to bring down a couple of tumblers. "I think you need something a little stronger than beer right now." He pulls down a now-familiar looking bottle of whiskey and pours us each two fingers.

I nod my head in thanks and take a long sip.

"So," he says, taking a sip himself. "Should I start updating my resume?" he asks with a wry smile, but I see a hint of apprehension in his eyes.

I drain my glass and say, "I don't fucking know." Running my fingers through my hair, I then add, "I don't fucking know anything."

"Your parents are only human. We often idolize our parents and place them on a pedestal. We think because they've been around longer, they have all the answers and know the difference between right and wrong. Your parents were only a few years older than you are now when you left. Do you think you'll have all the answers in six or seven years?"

There's a long pause. Dr. Ferris agreed to see me at seven thirty this morning after I texted her in the middle of the night once Seth and I finally said goodnight following two more refills.

"Okay, let's reframe this," she says. "What's your greatest regret?"

I look up at her and say without missing a beat, "Letting Thea go."

"Okay. And how long would you have stayed away from her if your parents hadn't passed and you didn't have to go back to South Carolina?"

"Fine, I get it. We're a family of cowards."

"I don't think cowardice has anything to do with it. I think when emotions are high, it's easier for people to create distance as a means of self-preservation. Once enough time goes by, we convince ourselves that it's easier to continue on maintaining this distance than to face the emotions again to try to fix what's broken. Let's call it emotional inertia."

"So you're saying I can't be angry with my parents because it's human nature that kept them from reaching out?"

"Now you know I would never tell you *not* to feel something. Points for being able to name the emotion you're feeling, by the way. For the longest time, you would come in here and talk to me about what happened with you and your family, but when I asked you how you felt about it, you'd say 'I don't know,'" she drops her voice to imitate me on the last words. I give her a flat look and she continues, "Eighteen months."

"What's eighteen months?" I ask.

"Eighteen months is how long it took for you to be able to label what you felt toward your parents, your brother. Not until you told me about that last fight with your parents. That was the first time you said, and I quote, 'I have never been more angry.' Talking about that particular incident opened the floodgates." She pauses and looks at me with her usual pointed gaze. "But going back to your question; you are free to feel toward your parents however is appropriate for you. But do you think it's also appropriate to grant them the same grace you've allowed yourself for staying away from Thea for so long?"

I lean forward, elbows on my knees, hands clasped in front of me. My eyes are cast down on the carpet, tracing the swirls in the pattern.

Seeing she's not going to draw an answer out of me, Dr. Ferris says, "There is no right or wrong answer here. Your parents are no longer here to help you find closure. It is entirely up to you how you choose to move forward."

"But none of this helps me figure out what my next step is right now. Do I abandon the career—the name I've created for myself—here or do I spend the next six months to a year finding and training someone to replace me? Because, realistically, that's how long it will take. I don't think Thea will wait for me. I'm already on shaky ground with her after everything I've put her through the last month. This may very well be the last thing she needs to close the door on me—on us—forever."

"What do you want?" she asks flatly.

"I want Thea. More than anything. Full stop. But I also want my career. Right or wrong, it's part of my identity." I pause then add, "Is it selfish to want to have my cake and eat it too?"

Dr. Ferris narrows her eyes at me, and we sit in silence for a minute. She glances at her watch. "Looks like the hour's up. But before you go, let me just say this: you're a chef; seems like you have the skillset to bake another cake at any time. But this *piece* of cake that you've been pretending doesn't exist for the last eight years will not be around for you to eat forever."

"That's not your best metaphor, Dr. Ferris," I say with a smile, standing up and making my way to the door.

"It's the best I've got before my second cup of coffee, but I think you get the idea."

I thank Dr. Ferris again for meeting me so early and head out. I glance at the time and see it's only eight-thirty, but suddenly I really want a piece of cake.

Chapter Twenty-Nine

I look down at my phone for what feels like the seven-hundred-and-sixty-fifth time today; Cary hasn't texted me in over twenty-four hours now. It shouldn't bother me. He texted me daily for almost two weeks straight, and I never once answered. Him going radio silent for one day should be no problem. Especially after the email I sent him. He probably needs some time to process the letter just like Brooks and I did.

Or at least, I assume that's what Brooks is doing, I haven't heard from him since we found the letters. I texted him this morning to check in, but he didn't reply. I shouldn't be surprised. I'm more than used to his disappearing act. I decided I'll just let Cary handle it once he's back in town. Which is supposedly happening in three days.

He promised he'd be back on Sunday, the fifteenth. I don't one-hundred percent believe him, but part of me turning over a new leaf with him is believing he was—and still is—telling me the truth. So, he'll be here. He's probably just packing and settling things in Seattle.

I huff as I chuck my phone on the counter, frustration coursing through me.

Ripley rifles around behind the bar, and I suddenly hear "Hate To Say I Told You So" by The Hives start playing throughout RED's empty dining room.

He stands up sporting a Cheshire Cat smile. "Hardy har har," I deadpan with an eye roll. He flicks his eyebrows up with that usual smug face I'd like to slap off him one day. In a loving way, of course.

"I know, okay? I know I shouldn't have frozen him out like that," I whine. "But what do I do now? Do you think he's pissed? And if you think he's pissed, do you think he's pissed at me? Or just because of the letter in general? If you think he's pissed at me, do you think it's because I haven't answered him? Do you think he might have gone back to Iris? What kind of fucking name is Care Bear anyway? Fuck, I should have listened to you and answered him. Should I call him now? I should ca—"

"Okay, first—stop talking," Ripley cuts me off. "Second, Care Bear is a stupid fucking name, and I will be calling him that every chance I get. Third, drink this." He slides a shot glass filled to the brim with clear liquid toward me.

"Is that tequila or vodka?" I ask.

"It's a surprise," he says, his lips quirked in a smirk.

"No, a surprise is finding a five-dollar bill on the sidewalk. This is a fifty-fifty chance we'll be picked up by the sheriff's deputy skinny dipping off the dock."

"That happened once! And I still think someone slipped something into our margaritas that night," Ripley replies, affronted.

"Yeah, tequila..." I say with an eye roll.

"Regardless, old Brucey's probably really bored this time of year, it'll make his night," he says as he walks around the bar until he's beside me. He grabs my hands which have made their way to my lap, spinning the rings on my fingers without me even realizing.

"Listen, you know I'm just giving you a hard time. It's my love language, babe. It's entirely possible Cary's just busy. It's only been a day, let's table this for tonight, and if he hasn't reached out by morning, I give you full reign to freak the fuck out," he says as he pulls me into a hug. I nod into his chest, not knowing what else I could say. "Let's get drunk on this here tequila."

I take a deep breath just as Ripley's suggestion reaches my ears causing a strangled sounding laugh to escape me. "That seems like a terrible idea," I say as I pull away from him.

He shrugs. "I didn't say it was a *good* idea. But it'll at least distract you for a bit." His smile isn't one that reaches his eyes. That realization makes me want to ask why, but he's already pulling away to grab the drinks from the bar. Before I know it, there's a shot in one of my hands and a lime wedge in the other. "Drink up, babe. And then we dance."

The last few days have been a blur. I've tried to keep busy and not think about why Cary isn't reaching out to me. Part of me is screaming 'I told you so' to myself while the other part is begging for me to give him more time to prove me wrong. The problem is, I know how it feels to be loved by Carrington Grant. I know what the sliver of hope feels like thinking he could be mine. And I know he wanted me enough once to buy a ring, I just didn't stay long enough for it to land on my finger.

I'm reminded of the first time he ever told me he wanted to marry me. It was such a mundane moment, one where things felt more up in the air than settled. We'd just moved into our first apartment together.

13 Years Ago
(18 years old)

I'm watching him from the kitchen bar where I'm standing, not sitting on a barstool, since the consignment store we planned on going to was unexpectedly closed today. Because of that, we are now living in an empty place until Monday.

Weekends usually go by fast, but I have a feeling this one won't. I've been bummed and so stressed about moving into an empty space that Cary decided a gourmet meal was in order. It's his fix to every problem in life. Sad? Eat some amazing food. Mad? Let this French inspired dish settle your anger. I can't even fault him for it since it usually works.

The thought brings a smile to my face at the same moment he decides to turn around, his eyes coming off of the dish in front of him for the first time since he started cooking.

"Oh, she's smiling now! I told you this would help," he mocks.

I put the glass of water in front of me, letting it rest on my bottom lip for a fraction of a second before tilting it into my mouth. As I set the glass back down, I swipe my tongue across my bottom lip into my mouth to catch the residual liquid away, never letting my gaze waver from him. "Or is it the view?" I joke, a smile pulling at the sides of my mouth as my gaze flits to his ass.

"Oh, I'm sure getting to stare at my ass uninterrupted... helps some. I won't deny that. But the food is going to make you forget all about your worries," he promises with a wink.

"I should probably go find the plates before I get too carried away with my thoughts of said ass."

He points the spoon he's been using to stir the sauce at me. "Yes! Good idea." Sauce drips from the spoon, and his eyes jerk down to the floor. "Shit. I'll clean that up, go, go," he says, shooing me away in the direction of the boxes.

I take one more sip of my water as I laugh, before I start toward the boxes that line our otherwise empty living room. We have two unopened boxes labeled 'kitchen' that could contain the plates. We'd opened the other two to find the pans and cooking utensils he needed to start dinner. I open the first one and shuffle through it quickly but come up empty handed. After having the same luck with the second box, I huff a breath in exasperation. Once I check the others we'd already been through to make sure they weren't missed, I decide today just isn't my day.

I pad back over to the kitchen, my annoyance obvious on my face.

"What?" Cary questions.

"Can't find the plates," I state plainly.

"What do you mean?"

"I mean... I looked through both remaining boxes and no plates. Not a plate in sight."

His face scrunches into confusion. "But those are the only two kitchen boxes left."

I nod. "Mhm, they are."

He squints his eyes at me. "You're being way too calm about this."

"Oh, I'm freaking out, I'm just trying to keep it in so I don't scream." That makes him laugh. "Nothing about this is funny, Cary," I say with a pout.

He turns off the burners then steps toward me. "You're cute when you're frustrated," he says as he wraps his arms around me.

"Why is nothing going right?" I whine into his neck, my voice slightly muffled. "This was supposed to be our perfect new start."

"Because life is like that sometimes, but it's okay. Want to know why?" I nod my head in response. "Because we have each other, and that's all I really need to be okay."

I chuckle then pull away from him to look him in the eyes. "'All you really need?'" I parrot back at him.

"Well, yeah. You and delicious food. My two favorite things," he says resolutely.

"Even if there are no plates to eat the delicious food off of?"

He shrugs. "Eh. We have paper plates, it's fine."

I move my hands up to his neck, cupping his nape as I play with the hair there. "So we're going to eat the gourmet meal you just cooked on paper plates with our hands while... sitting on the floor?"

He leans in but stops as his lips hover right over mine. "Will it make you feel better if I eat my dessert splayed out on the living room floor as well?"

My cheeks heat at the insinuation as he closes the small distance between us, his tongue immediately dancing with my own. The kiss ends as quickly as it began, but he presses a peck to my nose before pulling away completely, his arms still wrapped tight around me. "I want to do everything with you in this apartment, Thea. All the big things and all the small things. I want to fuck you in every single room. I want to put a ring on your finger one day. I want to drink coffee with you on Sunday mornings in front of that window. I want to watch you grow our children in that beautiful body of yours. I want to do all the mundane things in between. I want everything. Plates and furniture mean nothing as long as I have you and this life we're building."

The tears welling behind my eyes threaten to fall at his words. He always knows what to say to calm me down or put things into perspective. "You want to marry me?" My voice comes out as almost a whisper.

"Does that surprise you?"

I shrug and turn my face away, but he grabs my chin and pulls my gaze back to his own.

"Everything, Thea. I want everything with you. Please don't ever forget that."

Present

I had forgotten. I'd let that moment slip from me, and I'd gotten too caught up in all of life's problems. I don't want to make the same mistake twice, but I'm scared I've missed my second chance. I pull my phone from my pocket, deciding to text him. If I open the line of communication, he'll know I'm not giving up on us. As I find his name in my messaging app, Travis knocks on my open office door.

"Hey, sorry to interrupt," he says.

"No, no, it's fine. Come in," I reply as I place my phone screen down on my desk in front of me. My office is small, but there's one chair on the opposite side. It's mainly used for Ripley to annoy me while I'm supposed to be working or for interview purposes. Travis sits down, and I can already tell he's nervous, maybe even shaken, which in turn makes me nervous. "What's up? You seem... not yourself."

A half-huff, half-chuckle escapes him. "Yeah, I... uh, well, I need to talk to you."

The tone in his voice makes my back stiffen, alarms going off in my head. "Okay..."

It takes him another moment to start speaking again, his eyes avert to his hands, and every second only heightens my onset of panic.

"I think I have to leave Indigo Hill." He finally looks up and meets my gaze. I can't help whatever shocked expression is surely written all over my face. I'm not sure what I expected him to say, but it wasn't that.

"Wh—what? Why?" The questions leave my mouth before I even really process what's happening.

He shakes his head then looks back down to his hands in his lap. "I... fuck. I didn't expect this to be so hard." He opens his phone and scrolls through until he finds what he's looking for then sets it in front of me. It's a picture of a car parked across a residential street. "This is a picture one of my sitters took. They said the car sat there all day, and they felt like they were being watched, so they took a picture of it." He pulls the phone back, closing out of the photo. "Turns out, it was Maureen." An audible gasp slips through my lips.

Travis has only told me minimal details about his ex, Maureen. I know she had issues with drug use, and they divorced soon after Melody was born. She signed away her parental rights shortly after. That was eight years ago now. I never asked too many questions for fear of being too nosy.

He's still pacing the small room as I'm piecing it all together. "Wait. Why does this mean you have to move? Just get a restraining order."

He sits back down in the seat, placing his elbow on the desk and his head in his hand. "She was basically in my yard today. Talking to Melody."

"What? How?" My questions come out harsher than I intend from sheer shock.

"I stepped inside to grab us some drinks and a snack. The fence is locked and it's not like there are strangers in this town. But when I came back outside, I heard Melody talking to someone. I assumed it was a toy, but when I came around the corner, she was saying 'bye, Mommy,' and I saw Maureen walking to her car. The same car the sitter saw."

My hand flies to my mouth, but I don't know what to say. I can't imagine how scary that must have been for Travis to walk in on.

"I rushed Melody to my parents, dropped her off, and came straight here to talk to you. I can't... fuck, Thea. I can't have her coming around Melody like that. I don't even want to be in this town anymore if she's back. Maureen is volatile and unpredictable, and if she's using again, I'm afraid of what she'll do."

I instinctively bite the inside of my cheek, not knowing what to say or how to make this better. I'm not sure there's anything I can say, so I nod my head in understanding. He's scared, his distress stifling the air around us.

"I'm going to stay with my parents for the next few weeks while I try to find somewhere else to go. I'll help you find someone, train them, do whatever it is you need me to do, but... I can't stay. I'm so fucking sorry," he pleads. His voice is dripping with sorrow. I know he doesn't want to leave, but Melody comes before anything else, just as she should. I reach over and place my hand on his arm, urging him to look at me.

"It's okay, Travis. I—I understand. I'm sad, obviously, but I understand, okay? Just... do what's best for your family."

His eyes linger on my hand on his arm for a moment longer before he looks back up at me, placing his other hand on top of mine. "Thank you, Thea. Thank you so much for understanding. I'll never find another boss as great as you."

An awkward laugh fills the air around us as I try to bypass the compliment. "And I'll never find a chef as great as you. But we'll both be okay."

I hope we will at least. Once again, my plans are crumbling around me.

Chapter Thirty

Carrington

I haven't slept in days, and my stomach is in knots as I push the door open. As soon as the air conditioning hits my face, and the familiar sounds of a busy restaurant envelop me, I raise my eyes and immediately connect with hazelnut brown ones across the large space. The warm eyes make me feel like I'm home. The angry face they're attached to tells me I have my work cut out for me. I take in a large breath and let it out slowly, not even trying to fight the smile spreading across my face.

I feel like it's been years instead of just under a month since I left. I also feel like I've been through war just in the last week with the meetings and constant phone calls, all of which amounted to me making the decision to say *fuck it all* and hop on a plane to be here.

I couldn't stay away any longer. Leaving Carina Cove without an executive chef is a shitty thing to do, but I promised Seth I'd continue to interview candidates remotely. Thankfully, the investors didn't pull out of the deal when we told them about Dan. They're giving us six weeks to find a replacement. I have called in every favor I can think of, and I'm hoping we'll find someone soon.

I should have been back last Sunday, and I've been MIA for even longer, so Thea has every right to be angry with me. But right now, I can't find it in me to care. I cross the room in a few long strides, and before I get within spitting distance, I see she's gearing up for a fight.

"Don't, Lemon," I cut her off before she gets started. "I'm so tired. But I'm here. I know you're pissed. And go ahead and be mad—just... just do it tomorrow." I step closer to her and hesitantly wrap her in my arms as though she's a wild animal that may lash out, taking the hug I desperately need. "Fuck, this is nice." I pull her in closer and shut my eyes, getting lost in her citrus smell.

I don't know how much time passes, but her arms eventually wrap around me too. I can finally breathe when she presses closer.

"Cary," she speaks quietly right into my ear. "I'm... I'm about to start an interview."

I pull away and suddenly notice the woman standing next to us looking rather uncomfortable.

"Interview?" I ask.

Thea runs a hand through her hair and nods. "Yes, for the head chef position. Can we talk about this after?" Her widened eyes tell me I'm intruding.

"Wait, what about Travis?"

"Travis has given his notice, so we're looking to fill the position," she says in a professional tone. She gives the mousy-looking woman a reassuring smile, clearly trying to apologize for my behavior.

I turn to the woman and say, "I'm so sorry to interrupt. I'm Cary Grant, one of the owners here. Could you please give us a few minutes?" Thea releases a frustrated huff, but before she can say anything, I wrap my fingers around her wrist and pull her with me, making my way to the back office.

"Cary, I don't have time for this... whatever this is. I can't have Rachel leave, she's actually qualified," Thea says as soon as we're behind the office door.

"What's going on?" I ask.

"Cary." My name on her lips comes off frustrated, entirely wrong.

"Thea, just... please tell me what's happening."

"Travis put in his notice last week. He's having issues with his ex-wife and needs to move. He didn't give an exact end date, but I know he wants to get Melody away from here as soon as possible." She looks so defeated. "Please, let me get back to Rachel. She's the first half-decent candidate I've managed to agree to interview. We can't afford for her to leave."

"Where is Travis going?"

"I don't think he has that figured out yet. As far away from here as possible, I'm sure."

There's a long pause between us as I take it all in, and she's looking at me like I've lost my mind. Granted, I am smiling wide at what should be horrible news, so I don't blame her for thinking I've lost it.

"Okay, I don't understand what's going on here, but I don't have ti—" Thea starts to push past me to the door before I cut her off.

"Here," I say as I hand her a large envelope. After a beat, I hold out my other hand as well, pushing the bouquet of peonies

I've been holding toward her. "These are also for you." Thea looks between the envelope, flowers, and my face, clearly puzzled. She slowly reaches out and takes both, bringing the flowers to her face quickly, taking in their aroma, her eyes fluttering shut at the scent, and a miniscule smile ticks at her lips. When she opens her eyes, her face hardens again in annoyance.

"Okay, yeah," I say, rubbing my hand over my scruff. "I'd like to interview."

Her milk chocolate gaze snaps to me, questioning.

"I want to interview for the head chef position," I clarify.

As soon as the words leave my mouth, Thea huffs out an exasperated sigh. "Okay, Cary. I really can't deal with this right now. Please, just let me get back to my meeting."

"No, listen. I want to work here. I want to be considered. I'm sure I have the experience you're looking for." When her expression doesn't change, I continue, "I'm sorry, I'm running on no sleep. Please open the envelope. It'll make more sense then."

Thea narrows her eyes at me and after a few moments shoves the flowers at me, freeing her hand to open the envelope and pull the contents out.

"What is this?" she asks as her eyes slide over the papers.

"It's all yours. RED, the land, all of it," I say. "You just have to sign at the tabs."

"I—I don't understand."

"This," I say pointing at the papers, "is RED. I told you before: RED is you. You are RED. And it's perfect the way it is. You don't need me to run it. I had Elsher put everything in your name. You just have to sign."

I watch her face. At first, all I see is confusion. But it slowly morphs into disbelief and cycles through a dozen other emotions I can't quite decipher. She ends on anger.

Not exactly what I was aiming for.

"Are you—so you're just going to wash your hands clean of this place? Go back to Seattle? *That's* your plan?" It hits me then that this isn't simply anger, she's furious. "This was your big plan? Drop off the face of the Earth for almost a week and then just sign everything over and go back? Cut all ties? I should have known. It's wha—" I gently put my hand to her mouth, cutting off her rant.

"Let me stop you right there," I say calmly. "RED doesn't belong to me, or at least it shouldn't. You deserve this place. You deserve to run it, own it... grow it." I pause and watch her, still skeptical of me. "But I want to be here to see what you do with it. If you'll let me. Once you sign those papers, I have nothing tying me here to Indigo Hill. Nothing but *you*. And I choose you, Thea. I don't want to be where you aren't."

"But what about Seattle? What about your restaurant? Opening your own was your dream come true..." she says, eyes tearing up.

"No. You, Thea. You're my dream come true. Not some restaurant in Seattle. Not a diner here in South Carolina. You're *it*. And as for my apartment, I put it on the market, and I'm a silent, minority partner in the restaurant. Seth has more of a voice in what happens there than I do now." I step closer to her, taking her face in my hands. Using my thumb, I brush the tears that have escaped onto her left cheek. "So, Lemon, for all intents and purposes, I'm unemployed. Can I please interview for the chef position?"

And before she can protest, I add, "I also think there might be a great opportunity for Travis in Seattle, if he wants it."

"Thank you so much for coming in," Thea says as she and Rachel stroll past me to the front door of RED. The restaurant is mostly empty now, just a few tables filled with the late lunch stragglers. It won't pick up again for a few hours when dinner service starts.

Nat refills my water glass as I follow Thea's movements across the restaurant with my eyes. They stop by the door and continue to chat, Thea smiling and nodding at something the other woman said. Despite offering myself for the position, Thea insisted on taking the interview with Rachel. They had been holed up in the office for over an hour.

When she first brought Rachel to the back, I assumed it was perfunctory, out of obligation, since she took the time to come out here. I took an empty seat at the bar to wait for her. After about fifteen minutes, the door to the office remained closed. After thirty, sweat started to prickle the back of my neck. Intrusive thoughts telling me maybe she didn't want me here at all started up in full force.

At the forty-five minute mark, Nat dropped a Mediterranean salad topped with salmon in front of me. "Eat," was all she said before stepping away to make drinks for other patrons. I savored the sweet tomatoes and tangy artichoke, imagining how the dish could be elevated with a simple dill vinaigrette.

With my stomach full from lunch, and my mind full of doubt, overwhelming exhaustion hit me like a train. I was in the middle of a yawn when the office door finally opened.

With a wave goodbye, Thea turns and heads straight for me. Her eyes take in my face, and she must see the fatigue in my features because with a quick, "Let's go," and a grab of my hand, she's pulling me off my stool and out the door. We're at her house in about fifteen minutes. She'd filled the car ride with music, silently telling me talking was off the table for now.

"You go take a nap, I'm going to read through these," she says, lifting up the envelope I gave her earlier, after we walk inside. "Then, we'll talk."

"Thea—"

"Cary, go. Now." Her tone leaves no room for argument, so I make my way down the hall to the bedrooms. I pause before opening the door on the right. She might have meant for me to use the guest room, but I opt for her bedroom instead.

Undressing to my briefs, I slide under the comforter. I'm swathed in a sense of calm, surrounded by her mouthwatering scent that clings to the pillows. I replay the one night we spent here together before a deep, dreamless sleep takes me.

It's dark when I wake, and I don't immediately recognize where I am. I do recognize Thea's lemony, floral scent all around me, so I'm instantly put at ease. I check my phone and see it's just a few minutes after eight. Rubbing the sleep from my face, I stand and find my clothes. As I open the door of the bedroom, I hear music playing softly somewhere in the house.

Thea's in the living room, curled up on the couch with a blanket on her lap, a mug of tea in one hand, resting on her knee, and her phone in the other. She's wearing a threadbare t-shirt multiple sizes too big for her, the neck hole so big it hangs over one shoulder. The envelope and papers are spread out on the coffee table in front of her next to a portable speaker and a vase holding the peonies I brought her. She's lit a fire in the fireplace, and besides the soft harmonies of John Mayer's "Slow Dancing in a Burning Room," the crackling is the only other sound in the house.

Her head tilts up from her phone when she senses me watching her. She looks me up and down, her gaze landing on my face. I hold my breath, waiting to see what type of reception I'm walking into. I know there's a lot we have to talk about, but I'm aching for a smile from her. Her face is mostly in shadow, the fire providing the only light in the room, but I can see the side of her mouth tick up.

"Your hair is doing all sorts of things." Her tone is warm and quiet, like the flames from across the room. It unwinds something inside me, and I smile at her.

I run my hand through the strands trying to tame the bed-head but give up as I sit on the couch, leaving a cushion between us.

"I'm sorry, I didn't mean to sleep so long."

"It's fine, you seemed like you needed it. Would you like some tea?"

"No, thanks," I say. Why does this feel so stilted? There are so many things we need to discuss, but the words just won't come. We sit in silence for a while. The flames flicker, the logs spark.

"I take it you looked over the papers?" I finally say.

"Yes," Thea replies and then with a sigh adds, "But I can't sign them. Your parents left RED to you. They want it to stay in the family."

"You are my family, Thea," I say with no hesitation. Her eyes snap to my face, and her brows draw in.

"Cary, that's not what they mean—"

"And I can promise one day there will be a ring on your finger making it official," I cut her off.

"You are getting way ahead of yourself," she huffs out as the hand not holding her mug covers the other, and she starts fiddling with her rings.

"Thea, I'm jobless. I have nothing but time. And if you think I'm going to waste a second of it not trying to win you back, you're in for a big surprise. I was serious when I said I choose you. I made the biggest mistake of my life letting you walk away from me. I will not do that again. I. Choose. You. And I will continue to choose you everyday. So, please, sign the damn papers."

"I don't think I can do this alone," she whispers.

"Baby, you won't be doing this alone. Ever." I lean in close and clasp one of her hands in mine. "Can't say I'll be much help, though." I chuckle. "The last few weeks have taught me I'm hopeless with the operational side of running a restaurant. Seth's the only reason Carina Cove exists. I didn't realize how much he did until I had to meet with investors, and I felt like I had no idea what I was talking about. I'm a chef. That's what I'm good at. That's all I want to do anyway."

"Are you sure this is what you want? What about Brooks? I haven't seen him in over a week now. Do you think he wants a say in what happens at RED?"

"This is exactly what I want. I want to cook, and I want to come home to you every night." I kiss the knuckles on the hand of hers I'm holding. "As for Brooks, I think my parents made the right decision not tying him to RED. He needs to figure out what he wants from his life, and I can assure you, it won't be the restaurant."

We fall into silence again. A new song starts playing from the speaker, something mournful by Zach Bryan. Thea pulls her hand from my hold and leans over to put her mug on the coffee table. When she sits back, her hands land in her lap, and she twists a ring I remember giving her when we were seventeen. The gold band and tiny lemon wedge catch the light from the fireplace.

I can't see it from where I'm sitting, but I know the ring has the tiniest diamond embedded in the design. I saved for a year to get that ring. It was a promise from a lovesick teenage boy to the prettiest girl he'd ever seen. A promise of a future I still plan to give her.

"I'm sorry," her whisper is barely loud enough to be heard over the faint music.

I'm sorry?

My heart clenches. I knew there was a chance she didn't want the same thing as I do, but I didn't think she had completely closed the door on this—us.

She must see my emotions on my face because she quickly says, "Oh, no. That's not—I mean I'm sorry for how I handled everything eight years ago. I was... overwhelmed. I was heartbroken about my mom's diagnosis, and I felt so cornered. I felt like I couldn't leave her alone, and I really couldn't go back to Seattle. That last year had broken something in me, and I knew I had been slowly breaking us. It seemed like it would be easiest if I just didn't go back. But I should have fought for us. Fought for you."

"Thea, I—I'm so desperately in love with you. I don't think I ever really stopped, if I'm being honest. You've had my heart since we were kids, and I don't want it back. I never have. It's made a home with you."

Her eyes well as she says, "I don't think I ever stopped loving you either. I love you so fucking much."

CHAPTER THIRTY-ONE

Carrington

I lean in and kiss the tear that's slowly tracking down Thea's cheek. The left one. Just like always. The familiarity of that alone ignites a pang in my chest. The salt of the tear awakens my taste buds. Thea's lemon scent mingles with the jasmine tea she's drinking and makes my mouth water. I wish I could bottle this smell. I trail small kisses lower down her face and across her jaw. My eyes catch the goosebumps erupting all over her skin.

I pull back just an inch and allow my eyes to focus on hers. Heat has replaced the sadness from a moment ago. Thea's eyes flick down to my lips, and that's all the permission I need. I slant my lips across hers, and she immediately opens for me. Our tongues sweep against each other, and we move together. My hands find themselves entangled in her waves, and she's pushing me back into the couch. Her thighs straddle mine, and the most delicious whimper escapes her.

I pull her to me, but I'm desperate to get closer. Her hands find the hem of my shirt, and she moves back to make room to pull it over my head. She rakes her palms and lust-filled eyes over my torso. In the dim light, I can just make out her brown eyes tracing the tattoos across my chest and down my arms.

"Fuck. How is it possible you got hotter?" she whispers, mostly to herself, I think. I chuckle and pull her back to me, capturing her lips once again. I can't get enough of her mouth, the feel of her tongue gliding against mine, her taste, the small involuntary whimpers she breathes out. My hands trail down her back to her ass. I grip it and slowly guide her hips to move against my already hard cock. We're separated by just a few layers of clothing, and I can't wait to have nothing between us. Feel her wet pussy on my skin. Just the mental image has a groan climbing up my throat.

As soon as she catches on to my intentions, she grinds her core down on my cock, and I let out another groan at the added pressure.

As she continues to rub herself against me, I trail kisses down her jaw to her neck, gently nipping at the sensitive skin, drawing out a small gasp from her.

"Goddamn, those sounds drive me wild, Lemon." Her pulse hammers under my tongue as I continue my assault on her neck. I know I'm leaving marks, but I don't care. I want her skin to be covered in me—my bites, my smell, my cum. The thought sends a shiver down my spine that settles low in my groin.

My words spur her on, and she bucks harder against me. My hands knead into her ass, guiding her to help find her pleasure. Thea's head is thrown back, hair hanging loose behind her, eyes closed. She's panting heavily. *Fuck.* I want to be inside her, worshiping her, filling her up. The oversized t-shirt has ridden down, exposing one of her shoulders and a large portion of her chest, her skin is golden in the warm light of the fire. I lick and suck there too.

I can't get enough. I want to taste every inch of her. Reacquaint myself with every birthmark, every freckle.

"Are you going to come for me, baby?" I ask. "Are you going to rub that cunt on me until you fall apart? I bet you're so fucking wet." She moans at my words, and her body tightens in my hands. Her muscles clenching, winding up. Her movements and breathing become scattered.

Suddenly, she brings her head forward, leaning her forehead against mine. "Fuck, fuck, fuck, Cary. Please," she begs. She's close, so fucking close. I want to help tip her over the edge.

"What do you need, baby? Take it. Use me."

"Just... more." She's whining now. I grip her hips tighter, pulling her impossibly closer. My fingers will leave bruises, and my dick gets harder at the thought.

The extra pressure must be exactly what she was looking for because for just a second she stills, her heavy breaths cease as the orgasm washes over her. She trembles in my arms and rasps out a deep moan that has me almost coming in my pants like a fucking teenager. I love watching this woman fall apart for me.

Thea's eyes open and find mine. She sucks in a ragged breath and kisses me deeply, biting on my bottom lip when she pulls back. There's a huge smile on her face. "We haven't done that in a long time," she says, and I chuckle.

"I hope you know I'm not done with you yet," I say, kissing her again, my tongue mapping out the inside of her mouth. I could spend hours, days just kissing her. But just as I think I'm about to flip us so I can get a taste of her pussy, she slides down my body, her knees hitting the floor in front of the couch.

□She drags her hands down my chest and abs to my pants, quickly undoing the button and zipper. Before she can reach in and wrap those warm fingers around my cock, I gently grip her hands.

"I have a better idea," I say. She looks up at me, her dark eyes huge and questioning. I see the shadow of her tongue dart out and lick across her lips.

I stand up, and she pulls back to sit on her feet. *Fuck.* She looks so gorgeous. From this angle, I see what my hands have done as they gripped her hair, some of the faint bite marks already marring her perfect neck. Her lips are swollen and glistening from our kisses. She looks fucking debauched, and I can't wait to wreck her further.

She sits there, her legs under her. The oversized shirt hanging off her frame. Eyes wide and full of the same lust coursing through my veins. She looks like such a good fucking girl.

She looks like *mine*.

I grip my cock through my pants to help relieve some of the ache as I take in the sight of her for a moment.

Grabbing the blanket she had draped over herself before I came in, I lay it down on the soft rug in front of the fire. Then turn to Thea and hold out my hand for her. She grips it, stands, and makes her way around the coffee table to the edge of the blanket. I grab the hem of her shirt and slowly slide it up over her head. Thea raises her arms to help me. When it drops to the floor, she's left in nothing but a yellow pair of lacy panties. Saliva pools in my mouth, and I swallow heavily as I take her in. Shadows dance across her skin, highlighting the curve of her hips and the swell of her breasts.

I step closer to her and run a hand down her arm, mesmerized as goosebumps pebble in the wake of my touch. A small shudder courses through her. Everything in me screams to rip that tiny piece of fabric she calls underwear off her and plunge into her, fuck her without abandon, leave her boneless. But I want to take my time. I want us both to remember every fucking second of tonight. Because this is the start of the rest of our lives. No matter what happens with RED or my job or my brother, this right here is staying exactly as it is. I'm never letting this woman go. Not again.

I lean down and kiss her neck. Once. Twice. I move further down her body. Shoulder, clavicle. Her chest rises and falls rapidly, but she stands and waits to see what I'll do next. She's exquisite.

I reach my hand up and grip one of her breasts, bringing my mouth down on her nipple. I graze my teeth on the bud, and Thea lets out a small squeak of surprise, her hands coming up to my waist. I skim my tongue across her nipple to soothe the sting and feel her nails dig into my sides.

Kneeling down in front of her, I say, "I can't wait to find out how fucking soaked you got for me, baby." I hook my fingers into Thea's panties and slide them down her legs before helping her step out of them. I then run my palms up from her ankles to the tops of her thighs and press my hand between them to feel her center. "Look at you, you're already a mess for me."

My fingers easily slide through her arousal, and I slip two inside her, just wanting to feel her warm pussy around them. The tight squeeze, her musky-sweet scent, the quiet whimper she exhales are all making me feral. I feel my heartbeat in my cock, and I don't think I'll be able to last long when I finally sink inside her.

"Fuuuuuck," I groan out and nuzzle my face into the apex of her thighs.

I can't wait any longer. I need to get inside her one way or another. I lay down on my back in front of her, looking up at her face upside down. If she spreads her legs a little, I'd have the perfect view.

"On your knees, Lemon."

She looks down at me sprawled in front of her and hesitates. She starts to step over as though she'll kneel next to me, but I grab her ankles. "I said... on your knees." Thea pauses for a moment, and then understanding crosses her face at the same time a pretty pink blush blooms on her cheeks.

Thea slowly lowers herself, a knee on either side of my head. As her legs spread to accommodate my face, I get a close up look at her pussy, and I feel my cock leak in my pants.

This fucking woman.

Thea props her hands on my chest while I snake my palms around her hips and pull her down lower as I begin to lap at her pussy. She's dripping, and her cum coats my scruff. I eat at her like a man starved, my hands roaming around her ass, her thighs. She whines and moans above me.

Suddenly she shifts, but instead of grinding down on my face as I expect, her hands travel lower on my body, and she frees my cock from my pants. She lays herself across my body, her breasts grazing my abs, as she starts to pump my dick with her small hand. I groan straight into her clit.

When her hot mouth surrounds the head of my cock, I see stars.

"Yes, baby. Swallow it down. All of it." Like the good, greedy girl she is, she does just that, and the head of my dick hits the back of her throat. The sensation has my hips bucking, causing her to gag.

Goddamn, I love that filthy sound.

She pulls off to catch her breath, and I use my hands to grip her ass and upper thighs to open her up. I plunge my tongue into her as deep as I can get and fuck her with it, using the scruff on my chin to create friction on her clit.

"Fuck, Cary. *That*. Keep... doing that." Thea's thighs tense, and she sucks my cock back into her mouth. We find a rhythm, me eating her cunt like it's my last meal, her mouth bobbing up and down on my dick with just the right pressure.

I'm getting close. My balls are drawing up, and the pressure is building, but I don't want to come just yet. I need to feel her pussy on my cock. I need to feel her clench and pulse and come with me inside her. I want my cum dripping from her.

I feel wild with her tonight.

Unlike a few weeks ago, when we were desperate for each other, and it was more of a reunion, this is a claiming. When Thea wakes up tomorrow, she needs to know she's mine, and I am hers. No more questions, no more doubt.

I pull back and lightly slap Thea's ass. "Up. Move forward." She pulls off me with one last languid lick from root to tip. I close my eyes and breathe, fighting back my orgasm. Her wicked tongue threatens to undo me entirely.

On all fours, she crawls down my body. The sight of her ass has my breath hitching. I sit up pushing onto my knees behind her, shedding my pants. Before she can get too far, I grab her hips and slam into her. Thea yelps in surprise, but is quickly pushing back, fucking herself onto my cock. Her surprise replaced by soft moans and pants.

"God, baby. You take me so well. I want to stay buried inside this sweet cunt all fucking night." My words make her clench around me, and I give her a few hard thrusts, the force reverberating through her skin. I relish the sound of my body slapping against hers.

Burying my hand into her hair, I gently pull, saying, "Sit up." Thea pushes herself up to a kneeling position; my hand moves from her hair to wrap around her throat. I squeeze my fingers a little, her pulse picking up. She clasps one of her hands on my wrist, the other digs into my thigh.

I use my knees to spread hers more, opening her up to me and rendering her immobile. My other arm snakes around her middle, holding her close as I continue to thrust relentlessly. My sweat-soaked chest is plastered to her back, but I still can't get close enough.

Thea turns her head, glassy eyes catch mine, lust-filled and pleading.

"What do you need, baby?" I murmur before plundering her mouth with my tongue. The carnal, primal part of me revels the feeling of filling her so thoroughly. I leisurely move the hand not holding her neck down her body, grazing my fingertips across her belly to the crease of her hip. Her breath hitching, back arching, and her body shivering under my touch ignites something in me. Something feral.

"Tell me," I demand.

"More," she whines.

Fuck. She wants more? I'll give her everything I've got. Nothing but Thea exists right now. All of my senses are wrapped up in her. The sounds she makes are all I hear; her tongue is all I can taste; the hazelnut of her eyes and the flush in her skin are all I can see; her lemony smell mixed with the musk of our sex is the only scent that surrounds me; her smooth skin under the pads of my fingers is all I can feel.

I trail my hand to her pussy, feeling myself plunging in and out of her, her slickness leaking down her thighs. Her needy clit is swollen, waiting for me. I swirl my fingers around the tight bud, and she throws her head back on my shoulder and moans.

"Cary," she groans out. The sound is low and throaty as it reverberates in my chest.

"That's it, Lemon," I say at her temple. "Take it, baby. Your pussy feels so fucking good. You ready to come for me?"

"Yes. Cary," she pants out. "Please. More." Her pleading has my hips picking up their pace. The hand around her throat squeezes a little more, and with the fingers swirling around her clit, I apply more pressure. She clenches, and I know she's on the brink.

It's taking everything in me not to come. I need her to come before me. I need to feel her fall apart in my hands. I want to fill her with my cum as she contracts around my cock.

"Thea. Come. *Now*." And as if my wish is her command, she detonates. Her entire body trembles. The muscles of her thighs constrict with the force of her orgasm. If she's speaking, I can't make it out because I am solely focused on the feel of her cunt squeezing me. My cock unloading inside her, pulsing. My hips relentlessly and mindlessly slamming into her, filling her up.

I've never felt like this during sex. Like I was handing everything I am over to another person. Even with Thea... before.

As I slowly come down from my orgasm, I loosen the grip on Thea's throat. The world around us starts to come back into focus. The fire dying down in the fireplace. The hard floor barely cushioned by the blanket under our knees. My body fully enveloping Thea's small frame. Her pulse thudding under my fingertips.

I let go of her and lower her to the blanketed floor. My softening cock slips free as I lean over her, both of us catching our breath.

I kiss her shoulder, her back, still leaning over her as I hold myself up with my arms.

"I love you, Lemon," I whisper right into her ear.

Slowly. Oh so slowly, Thea turns herself around to lay on her back and looks up at me. My arms are shaky as they bracket her head, and it's taking all of the strength I have left to keep myself from collapsing on top of her.

Her eyes are molten chocolate, eyelids heavy from her orgasm. "I love you, Cary," she says, running her fingers up and down my sides. Her nails rake across my skin. I kiss her softly before dropping down next to her. Thea pulls herself in, her arm circling my middle, head resting on my chest.

I reach around and draw a blanket over us, and we drift off to the soundtrack of the quiet crackling fire.

Epilogue

2 Months Later

"I gotta go, the birthday boy is finally up," I say into the phone, a smile stretching across my face as Cary rolls his eyes with a chuckle at my comment. I'm standing in the kitchen in front of the island, the flour, eggs, and sugar sitting out in front of me. I have Ripley on speaker so I could attempt to make breakfast to surprise my boyfriend, but of course, he woke up before I could finish.

"Alright, babe, call me later," Ripley says, his voice echoing through the room. Cary's face immediately goes stern at the nickname we still use. He hates it with a burning passion.

"She's not your 'babe,' asshole," Cary quips from the living room, his tattooed back on display as he picks up the blanket we tossed to the floor last night. In front of the fireplace has become one of our favorite places this winter. I have to hold in a groan at the sight of his ass in the jeans I love.

"Shit. Forgot I was on speaker. Sorry, Care Bear." I try to hold in my laugh at the use of Cary's nickname from his ex-fiancée. I swear to God, Ripley lives to push his buttons. "I can hear him glaring at me through the phone, so you have fun with that, Thea.

Love you!" He hangs up so quickly I don't even have the chance to say goodbye.

Cary walks toward me, his look of annoyance clearing with each stride. "What's going on in here?" he asks, looking around the kitchen at the mess I've made despite not having anything to show for it yet.

"I..." I follow his gaze. There's a huge mess from my first attempt at pancakes that resulted in me burning them. Flour covers the counters, there's a cracked egg close to the sink, the sugar bag is tipped over, it looks like a baking bomb went off in my kitchen. The sink is even worse with dirty bowls stacked up on one side and a goopy whisk resting on the edge dripping into the basin. A nervous giggle leaves my lips as I find his eyes again. "I was going to make you pancakes but... I've only made a mess so far."

He walks around the breakfast bar, not saying a word. The temperature in the room ticks up from the look in his eyes. His arms wrap around my waist from behind as his chin sits on my shoulder, and a shudder slides down my spine. He turns his head to whisper into my ear as his hands slide down my naked thighs, "You look so fucking hot in this apron, Lem."

My cheeks immediately blush. I'm only wearing his button down shirt with a few of the buttons done up and the apron on top.

"Mhmm, I can say the same for you. Happy birthday, baby," I say as I turn my face to meet his lips. The kiss is short but filled with the love we've poured into our relationship in the last couple months.

It's been a bit of an emotional rollercoaster in the best way possible. After the night he told me he was choosing me and handed me the papers to RED, everything changed. We slipped into a life together. He moved in overnight. I called Rachel and let her know the position had been filled. I felt terrible about it, but Cary coming back permanently and taking the head chef position at RED was a dream come true—one I refused to let slip away.

We still have things to work through, and we are far from perfect, but I can confidently say I am happy. So fucking happy. I, of course, had fears we couldn't work a second time around. I thought maybe it wasn't just Seattle that was the issue.

Thankfully, I'd been wrong. Living with him, being with him, loving him in Indigo Hill felt *right*. It no longer felt like there was a piece missing or like something was wrong on a cellular level. It felt like we were kids again, back when our love was pure and not clouded by adult responsibilities and problems.

"You want help?" he asks into my ear.

I nod my head as I meet his eyes over my shoulder. "Always."

He presses a kiss to my temple, and I spin around in his arms, my flour covered hands coming to the sides of his face, leaving a trail as I press my lips to his. He groans into my mouth, his hands falling to the edges of the counter, caging me in as he presses his hips into mine.

"You keep this up, and we'll be making a baby on this counter, not pancakes." His voice comes out in a rasp telling me that's exactly what he'd rather be doing.

"Hmm, so are you hungry, or should I keep going?" I ask through the laughter bubbling in my chest. We've both been insatiable. It's like we're trying to make up for the eight years lost. It's a wonder we're able to leave the house, honestly.

"Lemon... you know I'm constantly hungry for you."

I thread my fingers through his hair, still untamed from sleep. The long strands streaking white with flour. The sight makes me laugh as I pull back from him to take in the picture in front of me. "Oops, sorry. I got you a little dirty." I try to wipe it away, but it doesn't budge.

Suddenly, Cary lifts me up onto the counter, a surprised yelp leaving my lips. His mouth comes down to my neck instantly, nibbling at the skin then kissing the sting away.

"Hmm, looks like it's my turn to get you a little dirty then," he rasps, the husky tone has arousal pooling between my thighs. His lips slide down my neck, leaving a trail of kisses as he slowly leans me back onto the counter where the flour is scattered. Once his face is at the junction between my breasts, his elbow knocks over the bowl with the remaining flour, spilling it all over the floor. We both break out in laughter, the rumbling of his chest reverberating up through my body. His arms are wrapped around me now, my hands placed firmly on his neck. We're both covered in the white powder, still laughing uncontrollably.

I throw my head back, just barely touching the counter as my leg wraps around his waist. Cary's hand leaves my side and nudges my foot away from his ass. Before I have time to wonder why, he pulls me down from the counter and gets down on one knee.

I've barely had a moment to register what's happening, when he pulls a small box from behind his back.

"Oh—oh my God, Cary!" My hands fly to my mouth, tears spring into my eyes, blurring my vision. He's in front of me, down on one knee, opening the ring box.

"Lemon," he starts, and a sob leaves my throat. "Baby," he laughs, "let me get through this, okay?" I shake my head, not allowing myself to speak. "Years and years ago, I told you I'd put a ring on your finger one day. I vowed to again just two months ago. And I won't lie, it wasn't supposed to happen today. I only have it in my pocket because the jeweler got it back to me yesterday after getting it resized."

Confusion sparks in my eyes, and he must see it because he stops his speech to say, "We're getting there." I just barely nod my head, silently asking him to keep going.

"I had a whole thing planned. But this, Lemon... I want to do this with you every day of my fucking life. I want to wake up and know you'll be my wife, and I get to spend forever with you. So, fuck the plans," he laughs nervously, "we were never good at them anyway."

I blink away the tears still falling down my cheeks.

"I don't want to live another day not knowing if you'll be mine forever. I should have known the second I got the ring back that I'd be itching to put it on your finger. I didn't even make it twenty-four hours." A half-sob, half-laugh breaks through my lips. "You're the one thing I need in this life, Thea. More than my career, more than any accolades I could ever get, more than the air I breathe, *you* are what keeps me going. You are what makes me feel alive. And my greatest accomplishment—if you say yes—will be being your husband. I've known I loved you since I was a kid—and if we're being honest, I knew back then that I wanted to spend forever with you. No one else ever stood a chance. And I know, *I know* we got off track, and we lost so much time. And I know this is quick, I promise, I do. But I don't want to waste any more time. So, Thea Carina Ashford," he pauses to pull the ring from the box, and I swipe the tears from my eyes so I can see it. "Would you make me the happiest, luckiest fucking man in the world, and marry me?"

"How did you—" I start when I realize it's Hazel's ring that Owen proposed to her with, sobbing again at the sight of it.

"Brooks found it among their things. I took a chance by asking about it, and he immediately handed it over but surprisingly pocketed their wedding bands. And he of course had to add a sarcastic remark about me finally getting my shit together."

I reach down to grab his elbows, pulling him up from the floor and crashing my lips into his. He pulls away but only enough so he can speak, "Is that... a yes, then?"

With our foreheads still pressed together, I look down at the ring in front of me, still clasped in his hands. "Yes, of course. The answer was always going to be yes."

He slides the ring on my finger, and I reach around his neck as his hands run down my back until he's cupping my ass and lifting me into his arms. My legs wrap around his waist as my lips find his.

In between kisses, I make sure to tell him, "I love you, Carrington Dillon Grant."

Meanwhile...

Brooks

A Night of Hope Gala

Fuck, fuck, fuck.

I knew Thea would be pissed. I also knew she'd rip me a new fucking asshole, but seeing how disappointed she is really makes me feel like shit.

I hadn't intended to be late for the stupid event or to even go to Hayes asking for a fight. It just... happened. Which is getting old, even to my own ears. What am I supposed to say though? I can't tell her what I was doing. I can't tell anyone. None of them would understand. They'd all just tell me how stupid and irresponsible I'm being. I don't need anyone to remind me, I already know.

But Thea is right, of course she is. It's a fucking domestic violence prevention charity event. I can't walk around looking like I got the shit beat out of me and somehow not cause a scene or raise questions about RED's involvement.

"Fuck!" I yell into the empty space of the distillery as the door shuts behind me. I need to do something to make this better. She'll probably be even more pissed off later, but the least I can do is call Cary and get him here to help.

I pull the phone from my pocket, using my other hand to wipe the running blood from my cheek as I scroll until I find his name in my contacts. I press the call button, knowing he'll answer immediately. I don't exactly call anyone very often, so seeing my name on his screen is sure to raise suspicion.

He answers on the second ring, "Hello?"

"Hey, bro, listen—any chance you can come to RED?" I say as I break the seal on a new bourbon bottle from the most recent batch.

I can already hear the panic building through the phone before his voice breaks through the silence, "Is Thea okay?" There's shuffling in the background like he's rushing to leave.

"Physically? Sure. Mentally and emotionally? To be determined." I take a swig of the bourbon, the smooth taste of it constantly reminding me how fucking good Rip is at what he does.

Cary's panic shifts to impatience. I don't need him to voice it for me to know. "Brooks, what's going on?"

"Travis had some emergency with his daughter. I don't know much, but Josh is stepping in as head chef for this event, and let's just say, he looked green in the face when he found out. Not sure the kid can handle it." It's a shit thing to say about the dude, but it's the truth. I may not be reliable or all that responsible, but at least I know to speak up when I'm in over my head. The kid just stood there as Thea told me he was taking the lead, clear as day on his face that he didn't think he was capable of doing the job.

I hear the car starting up as Cary says, "I'll be there in a minute." He hangs up without so much as a goodbye. I roll my eyes.

Knight in shining fucking armor.

The door towards the back of the distillery shuts as I'm shuffling some old kegs to the back of the line, and pulling up the new ones.

I know it's Cary before he even rounds the corner, and his eyes find me then widen in shock at my appearance. One more person I get to let down today. Fucking great. I was hoping he'd go through the restaurant and avoid the distillery. My eyes fall to the ground as a sigh slips from my mouth, preparing for whatever onslaught I'm about to receive.

"It's nothing. I'm fine," I say in an attempt to push through the conversation without really having to deal with it. I go back to moving the boxes as he walks closer to me.

"You're not *fine*. You're bleeding," he starts, but I cut him off before he can say anything else.

"Save it, okay? Thea already ripped me a new one and exiled me here for the night. I don't need to hear it from you too. Pretty sure I heard her calling a nurse friend to come patch me up." I try to keep the resentment I'm feeling for myself out of my tone, but it's hard knowing I fucked up so bad.

"What happened?" he asks, his voice gentler than before, meaning I was unsuccessful at hiding my own feelings on the matter.

"I fucked up," I pause but bring my gaze up to his for the first time since he walked into the distillery. "She was counting on me today, and I just…" Fuck, this is hard to admit, especially to him. "I needed to blow off some steam, but it got out of control. I don't know why I keep doing this. I feel like I just. Keep. Fucking. Up." I run my hand over my hair as I punctuate each word, letting my anger spew through them.

I see Cary wanting to move in for a hug when the back door creaks open again. A small woman with more hair than body walks in. Her wild dark-chocolate curls frame her face and take my goddamn breath away. She's covered in so many freckles I can see them from across the large space. Her light green eyes pierce through me as they find mine. I don't think a woman has ever stunned me speechless before. But as I study her face, I realize the look she's giving me is pity, and I'm instantly pissed off. I don't need her pity—or anyone else's for that matter.

After they exchange hellos, Cary takes off to find Thea, thankfully without another word. I'm left with the tiny woman standing in front of me, holding a tote bag overflowing with supplies. I'm assuming she's a grown-ass woman—she looks so young that it's hard to tell. I'll feel really fucking gross if she ends up being some teenager. She's so short I'm having to look down so I'm not looking over her head. She's got to be at least a foot shorter than me. She still hasn't introduced herself, but Cary didn't seem concerned.

"I'm Margot, Thea called me. I work at St. Stephen's. She said..." she trails off, wincing as her eyes gaze over my face. "Well, she said she had a friend that needed medical attention. I'm... umm... assuming you're the friend."

Ahh, Lydia's nurse. So, not a teenager then. Thank God. I want to be annoyed with Thea for phoning her damn on-call nurse, but the girl is so fucking pretty I'm finding it hard to be anything but grateful for her presence.

"What gave it away?" I joke, though she doesn't laugh. That's fine, I have other ways of charming the pants off of her.

"I'm going to start with a physical exam. Is there... somewhere you can sit?" she asks, looking around the space.

"Uhh, we can sit at the bar in the tasting room?" I say, more of a question than a statement as I point toward the room off to the side. She looks in the same direction I'm pointing, nods her head, and walks that way. I go to follow behind her but decide my bottle of bourbon deserves to come with me. Chances are I'll need the fucking alcohol to numb whatever pain she's about to cause me.

She's already setting up on the bar, pulling supplies from that Mary Poppins bag of hers, barely paying me any attention. When she sees the bourbon bottle hanging from my fingers, that's the moment she decides to look up and meet my eyes. I can't tell what emotion is shining through them. It shouldn't be a surprise I'm drinking bourbon in a fucking distillery. The moment drags on, and I realize the expression on her face may be disgust, which only pisses me off more.

"What's that look?" I ask, pointing my chin toward her face. She schools her features immediately, as if that will erase whatever contempt she has for me.

"It just… looks like it hurts," she says, shooting her eyes back to the supplies on the bar.

I laugh, shaking my head as I say, "Nah, it's not that bad. I've had way worse."

Once again, she doesn't seem to find me funny. Her eyes widen, and her brows crease as she zones in on the still oozing cut on my cheek.

"You sound proud of that." Her voice comes out more steady than I anticipate, a sliver of judgment lacing through her tone.

"Maybe I am," I state, not allowing her to get under my skin.

"Hmm…" I can tell she doesn't find me the least bit charming which, honestly, annoys the fuck out of me. Chicks love rough guys. I see it constantly at The Pit. Guys come back bloody and bruised, and the girls at the gym go crazy over it. This one must think she's too good.

I don't say anything more. This woman has me questioning just how stupid I've been the last few weeks. Once she's shuffled some things around, she gestures to the chair like she wants me to sit on it. I take a pull of the bourbon, put the bottle on the bartop, and drop myself into one of the high top stools that line the bar. I'm not sure she's thought this through, and I smirk knowing what's coming.

With her little pen-light-thing in hand, she turns back around, pleased to see I did as she asked, but soon enough, the pleased look is replaced by frustration once she notices the height difference. "I can sit on the floor if it'll make it easier, Doc."

The thin-lined lip she gives me almost makes me break out in laughter. *Two can play this game, sweetheart.*

She crosses her arms over her chest, drawing my eyes to her perfect tits. "That won't be necessary. And I'm a nurse, not a doctor," she states plainly. "Oh, and my eyes are up here." She points to her face as she says it.

"Oh, I know exactly where they are," I laugh as the words leave my mouth, and my eyes slide up to hers. I decide getting under her skin may be my new favorite past-time.

She rolls her eyes, not once breaking her stern facade, but her cheeks tinge pink. "I'll need you to remove your shirt."

My smile leaves my face almost instantly. "What? Why?"

That, of all things, makes her release the smallest laugh as she says, "Nervous? I thought you'd make some crude joke about me wanting to undress you."

I don't even touch her quip. "It's just my face."

Her sea-foam-green eyes seem to stare into the depths of my soul as she says, "Then the physical will be over quickly. Now, remove your shirt." After a beat she tacks on, "Please."

I take a deep breath, knowing the moment she sees what's hiding underneath my shirt, nothing about this will be quick. I grab the bottle and take a long swig before setting it back down. I cross my arms and grab the hem of my shirt to pull it up over my head. The moment I start to lift it, I hear a gasp leave her lips. I haven't seen it yet, but I feel all the spots I'm sure are mottled shades of purples and reds. Bruises, old and new. I let my shirt fall to the floor, avoiding her eyes at all costs.

"So, you're a liar."

"What?" I ask in surprise.

"You just lied to me. I would have left here thinking it was just the cut on your cheek, never knowing you had plenty of other injuries that need tending to." She sounds mad. It should piss me off. I should storm out of here and tell her I don't need her to fix me. Instead, I'm intrigued. The idea of her being mad makes my dick twitch.

What the fuck is wrong with me?

"You should see the other guy," I say with a chuckle. "And they're just bruises, Doc. No need to get your panties in a twist."

Her cheeks flush as the word 'panties' leaves my mouth, which only makes me chuckle more.

"Okay, Killer, I'll be the judge of that."

Once Margot has pressed and prodded every single one of my bruises across my chest—with no remorse, I might add—she finally says, "Okay, I'm going to clean the cut on your cheek now."

I roll my eyes, grabbing the bottle once more, taking another long swig. "Fucking great, I'm stoked." The sarcasm rolls off my tongue but doesn't seem to phase her.

She gets up on the chair next to me so we're more at eye level and attempts to scoot it closer to me. I let her struggle for a good five seconds before I reach over and pull the chair toward me, the sound of it scraping the floor echoing through the cavernous, empty room. Her arms land on my biceps as she shoots them out to steady herself and our knees touch. The contact sends a spark through my body that I try to ignore, blaming it on the alcohol in my system instead of this insane attraction to the woman in front of me.

"Thank you," she says once the shock of me pulling her over wears off. It takes a second, but then she notices she's holding my arms and quickly draws her hands back. I grunt in her direction instead of saying you're welcome. "This could sting."

I bite the inside of my cheek as she dabs the antiseptic shit to the cut on my face. It stings, but I've definitely been through worse.

"It's not as deep as it seemed. I can put a butterfly bandage on it, and it should heal fine."

"Just do whatever you gotta do, Doc."

This time, instead of rolling her eyes, I see her lips tick up at the corners like she's fighting a smile. If I were keeping score with her, I'd count that as a win.

"Make sure you ice it at least three times a day for ten minutes so the swelling goes down," she says as she turns back to the supplies on the bar, gathering them up so she can put them back in her bag. "And keep an eye on those bruises on your abdomen, you may need to get x-rays to check for broken ribs."

I wave her off, pushing her chair back to its original spot, making her yelp again. "Sure thing, Doc. I gotta get back to work, but thanks for patching me up." I wink at her with my good eye that isn't almost swollen shut and walk back into the distillery to finish moving the kegs out, bottle in hand.

For the rest of the night, I stay busy making sure the bar is stocked and inventory is accounted for, all the while my mind keeps wandering back to wild dark curls and judgy light green eyes.

Acknowledgements

We have so many people to thank. These are the people who made this book happen. But to anyone we've encountered or interacted with on this journey, know that we appreciate you!

Peter

Thank you for putting up with the endless out of context voice messages you have to overhear, keeping the boys busy while I write, and keeping my wine glass topped off at all times (lovingly). Your male perspective and height (for research purposes ;-)) have been invaluable throughout the process. You might have been more excited about this than I have been at times, and it's really kept me motivated. I hope you get through a full read through of the book one day haha. Thank you for being an inspiration for all of this. I love you!

HANNAHHHHH!!!

You're the OG hype girl. We LITERALLY could not have done this without you. From supporting this wild journey from day one to creating our gorgeous RED logo, you've been our biggest cheerleader! You were the first to read this very rough draft, first to give us feedback, and the first to love these two characters as much as we do. We CANNOT believe this friendship started through Instagram and evolved into a lifelong bestie. And by the time WICB is published, we'll be a month and a half away from meeting you in person for the first time. I HOPE YOU'RE READY FOR HUGS! We love you endlessly, please never leave us or block us. We do know where you live ;)

Family

To our moms and sisters, thank you for supporting us in this dream, DEMANDING shirts lol, and stealing our proof copies for yourself haha. We love you all. Please don't judge us for the spicy scenes........ And maybe don't read book two... or three... and really not four LOL.

Susan

I'm so glad I got you to step out of your usual genres, glad the spice was to your liking haha. Thank you for the support and endlessly plugging me whenever you get a chance. Can't wait to read this at book club with you and die a little at all of the attention haha.

Grayce Rian

You have been invaluable in giving us insight into author life. Thank you for being a mentor and a friend. You never falter in answering our questions or giving advice when we need it. Thank you for constantly supporting us and loving on these characters. We're so happy that Hannah brought us all together and could not have gotten this far without you! PS—thanks for being the inspiration to change Grace's Café to GRACYE's Café! You deserved a personal callout haha.

Ashlynn

Thank you for being our first preorder on our physical copy even though we planned to send you one lol. You are constantly supporting this dream and telling us we'll be huge despite us not believing you haha. No matter how busy you are, you always answer our questions and never get annoyed. Thank you for all your feedback on this story in the early stages. We can never say how much all of it means to us! You've been such an amazing friend, and we're so happy you were brought into our lives. our questions and never get annoyed. Thank you for all your feedback on this story in the early stages. We can never say how much all of it means to You've been such an amazing friend, and we're so happy you were brought into our lives.

Beta Team

Emma, Kacey, Kayla, Heather, Lynzee, Ana, Sara, Maggie, Colleen, thank you so much for your unhinged and undiluted feedback! We loved how much you all loved Thea and Carrington. We could not have made this story what it is without your support. Thank you for always being our sounding board and being enthusiastic about all of our crazy questions haha. We adore you all and cannot wait for you to read the rest of the series!

Ana

You deserve your own callout! We are so obsessed with all of the art you created for this story. Thank you for constantly being such a huge support and never getting annoyed with us haha. We could not be happier with the way everything turned out. We are in awe of your talent and cannot wait to do the rest of the series art with you!

Mel

We were so concerned we wouldn't be able to find a cover designer who understood our vision, but you NAILED it. You took all of our ideas and created a masterpiece. Thank you so much for being in our corner and being such a pleasure to work with. Can't wait to see the rest of the covers we make together!

ARC Readers

Thank you for taking a chance on our book baby! Going into this, we never expected so many people to want to read it or be excited for it. The amount of you that showed up and applied to read WICB ahead of time is INSANE. We can never thank you enough! We hope you continue the series and everything else we have planned for the future.

You, the Reader

Thank you for picking up our book and hopefully loving it haha. As baby indie authors, you're what keeps us afloat and one of our reasons for doing this. We started out as readers, and we know how much one review can do for an author. We hope you stick around for the next book and all of our other crazy ideas! We promise to always bring angst with a HEA!

Ashley James

You'll probably never read this, and that's totally okay haha. But thank you for providing us with the inspiration for Thea and Carrington through the idea of Conrad and Whit's story. We fell in love with them from the very beginning of ESTR and were so excited to see how their story played out. Their second chance was one of the main reasons we wanted to write a book like When I Come Back.

About the Authors

We're romance co-authors living in South Carolina and Connecticut. Two romance obsessed best friends who decided to write together one day and realized it was the best decision ever. We balance each other out with our similarities and differences but are always the other's biggest cheerleader. In our spare time when we aren't with family, we love to read (obviously), drink coffee, and obsess over Canva edits haha.

Stalk Us

Thank you so much for reading When I Come Back! If you enjoyed Thea and Carrington's story, we would love it if you'd leave a review on Amazon and/or Goodreads.

The second book in the Ripple Effect series will be releasing late 2025. Brooks' and Margot's story will overlap with Carrington's and Thea's. We hope you're ready for their angsty slow burn! Both can be read as standalones, but we'd love if you'd read them all! We have intentionally put Easter eggs for every book throughout the entire series, but you'll only catch them if you read them in order!

If you want to stay up to date on everything Alise Monroe and Ripple Effect, please STALK US on all socials haha. For even more updates and in the know information, sign up for our newsletter (on our website), we promise not to spam you!

Instagram: @author.alisemonroe
Threads: @author.alisemonroe
TikTok: @authoralisemonroe

Visit our website for bonus content and any event information
alisemonroe.com